The Oberleutnant's Wife

Rory Diamond

Published by Rory Diamond, 2024.

THE OBERLEUTNANT'S WIFE

First edition. January 13, 2024.

Written by Rory Diamond.

Chapter 1

On a frigid, gray afternoon in early January 1942, *Oberleutnant* Wilhelm Engel alighted from the train at Warsaw's Central Station. He spent the journey wondering what the future held in store for him. Transfers to Poland were viewed with little to no enthusiasm; relations with the women were forbidden, and officers who had committed transgressions but were still useful to the Reich were often stationed there as punishment. Will had heard one positive thing about Warsaw: there were over a dozen food shops and a gourmet grocery chain that catered exclusively to Germans. Being a man who had nothing to look forward to in life except his dinner, he told himself to be grateful for small favors.

Late in December, his superiors at the Hannover garrison finance office where he'd been working for the past year summoned him to a meeting. After lavishing an abundance of praise on the strapping blonde, blue-eyed officer for turning the office into a model of efficiency, they announced his promotion to first lieutenant and notified him of his transfer. As a reward for his hard work, Will would have expected a posting to Paris. There, members of the German military cavorted openly with fashionable women and enjoyed the exclusive restaurants, cabarets, and visits to famous landmarks. If he couldn't indulge in such delights in Warsaw, at least he could eat his fill of quality sausages.

A young, round-faced sergeant in an overcoat buttoned up to his chin and a scarf looped around his neck stood on the platform holding a cardboard sign—*Olt. W. Engel.* Horn-rimmed glasses perched on a down-curved nose gave him the appearance of a baby owl.

"I am Engel," said Will as he approached.

"*Feldwebel* Walther Bach, clerk in the Kommandant's office." His arm shot up. "Heil Hitler!"

"I am pleased to meet you, Feldwebel." Will touched his hand to his cap in the traditional military salute."

"My orders are to take you to the Kommandant's office immediately. Follow me, sir." They walked out of the station to Bach's vehicle, parked at the curb. A gust of wind blew Will's cap off his head. The young man scampered after it, brushed away the snow, and returned it to its owner. "In this weather, it's best to keep it tucked under your arm," he said. He began the short drive into the city center, gesturing at the giant swastika flags hanging from lamp poles, his smooth, hairless face radiating pure pride. "We are honoring our German heritage through the Cultural Days celebration going on currently."

Nazi culture. Will would not be celebrating.

"There are so many exciting events to attend that one will have trouble choosing," Bach gushed. "A person may enjoy an evening of chamber music, another would prefer a poetry reading. I recommend you visit the Theater of Warsaw. I recently attended a performance of the Strauss operetta, *Die Fledermaus.* Exceptional."

"Oh? That is good to know."

He pulled up in front of a building on the city square now called the Adolf-Hitler-Platz, where the Wehrmacht had its military command, its facade adorned by swastika festoons and more flags. He led Will through a large hall with polished floors into a wood-paneled office.

"Oberleutnant Engel, sir," Bach said before leaving.

An older officer, a *Hauptmann* with icy blue eyes and thinning brown hair combed back from a high forehead, returned Will's salute. "I am Captain Hoff, adjutant to *Generalmajor* von Unruh, the Kommandant of Warsaw City. I trust you had a pleasant journey."

"I did, sir." In fact, the trip had been exhausting—he was on tenterhooks for most of it, and the buffet lunch in the dining car was on the lowest rung of good.

"Have a seat. First time in Warsaw?"

"Yes."

"Let me brief you on the current situation," he said, sitting at the desk. "There are several points you should be aware of. Number one. The Warsaw District, like the others in the Generalgouvernement, is under German civil administration. They have taken measures to ensure that this territory, which is of utmost importance for supplies to our troops at the Russian front and for the care of the returning wounded, must not harbor any threat to the health of the soldiers and will remain free of disease. The inhabitants here are hostile and the outlying areas, uncivilized. The peasants are backward and resistant to change. There is to be no fraternization with the Polish; they are the enemy."

"Understood."

"The Wehrmacht's mission here, first and foremost, is to maintain the security of our military installations and warehouses of supplies and replenishments, fuel depots, and the like." The telephone rang. "Excuse me while I take this call."

Will scanned the room. An oversized portrait of grim Hitler took pride of place in the center wall behind the desk, lest anyone forget who was running the show. Red carpet ran throughout, and color-matched velvet curtains with gold tassels hung from tall windows overlooking gardens blanketed with snow. Used to spartan offices, the decor was too garish for his taste.

He wondered if the office had been occupied by a former Polish official and left intact, or had been redecorated by the Wehrmacht with plundered furnishings. Rumors circulated in Germany regard-

ing looting by the military in the occupied territories, which were ve-
hemently denied. *Our military is above reproach!* His eyes fell upon
a cut-glass brandy decanter and a quartet of snifters sitting on an
ornately-carved wooden sideboard. Perhaps Hoff would offer him a
drink. He needed one badly.

Hoff finished his call. "Where was I? Ah, yes. Partisan groups
are attempting to damage our interests by blowing up our railroad
tracks, burning down our grain mills, and committing other acts of
sabotage, but they will be brought under control soon. I warn you
not to wander the streets alone. Keep to the protected German sec-
tions of the city."

"Number two. You are to manage the office supply department,
an important position, not so much in name as in function, given
the state of things. Over time, large shipments of supplies ordered
from and delivered here have disappeared. We believe they have fall-
en into the hands of the resistance and used in their forging operations. The person whose post you now occupy has been, er, reassigned, but these groups seem to have ongoing access to sensitive
information, enabling them to plan their subversive activities, and
there are still problems with the supplies."

The captain paused to let this information sink in. "The intelligence services are responsible for those investigations concerning
the resistance, however you, as supply specialist, are needed to get
to the root of problems before they become serious enough to war-
rant the involvement of other agencies, in other words, to make sure
they don't happen at all. We must be able to control what goes on
in our own departments and uphold the Wehrmacht's reputation. I
want every inkwell, every stamp and stamp pad, every pen and pencil
accounted for."

Another pause. "The Kommandant had me make a request for
a top organizer, and you were highly recommended, so don't disap-

point me. Come up with a plan to tighten the lid and enforce it. I give you free rein. Any ideas at the moment?"

Will was expected to turn the supply office into another model of efficiency, which, given his driven-to-succeed personality he would do anyway, but the unspoken *or else* was disconcerting. He cleared his throat. "I will have to analyze the way the process is currently being handled before making definite recommendations, but to start with, I suggest that every Wehrmacht office be assigned a rating based on the sensitivity of information handled within. All supply requests should be made in advance and in writing, and the storage rooms closely guarded. Direct the typists to save the spools of ribbon when finished—they are carbon copies of correspondence—collect and destroy them instead of throwing them away, as well as any carbon paper used when duplicating letters."

"The waste paper bins should be collected and their contents burned at intervals throughout the day by trusted personnel, rather than once in the evening by outside janitors. Once these changes have been made, records must be kept to confirm the new procedures are being adhered to."

"Excellent suggestions," said Hoff. "You haven't been here five minutes and are already showing your worth. Indeed, let me know what information you need, then put together a written proposal. You will report directly to me on all matters."

"Jawohl, Herr Hauptmann."

"Very good. We will meet again soon. Bach will give you a complete list of your usual responsibilities and daily schedules and take you to your office." He rang for him.

The position didn't seem to involve anything objectionable, but Will wouldn't rest easy until he went over his duties with a fine-tooth comb. The sergeant handed him a large envelope filled with forms, guides, and brochures, then hustled him into the car and started off on a tour of the surrounding areas.

Chapter 2

Bach swung west, then north, and drove past nine-foot brick walls topped with another three feet of barbed wire that enclosed what appeared to be a small city.

"What is this?" Will asked, forgetting his fatigue and sitting straight up.

"This," said Bach, slowing the car and proudly waving his hand as though showing off the finest example of German ingenuity, "is the Warschauer Ghetto. You haven't heard of it?"

"I have not. Why is it so heavily guarded?"

"It's the Jewish Residential Area, formerly the Jewish Quarter. On the orders of Dr. Fischer, the Governor of our District, the Jews have been sequestered here."

"Sequestered? Why?"

"They are carriers of typhus and a public health hazard. They cannot be permitted to roam loose on our city streets and spread their diseases to the general public and to us."

Roam loose? Will shifted in his seat. "What size area is this?"

"A little over a square mile. It was until recently the main tourist attraction for our workers and soldiers passing through and is still the most requested destination of visitors coming in from the Reich, although now special permission is needed to enter."

"Tourist attraction?" Will couldn't believe his ears. "What is there to see? Groups of healthy people were allowed to stroll through in the midst of an epidemic?"

"Not on foot. We came in on buses provided by one of our leisure programs during the summer. With so many Jews in one place, people are naturally curious about them. I must tell you that it was unlike anything I've ever seen and so thrilling to witness firsthand what our Führer has been telling us all along about the plague of the Jews. You should have seen them scurrying along the filthy streets like dark, hairy rats, and stick-like children in rags were selling what looked to be scraps of paper. That's not all. Bony, near-naked tramps were lying on the sidewalk at intervals, asleep or dead. Some of us thought they might have been placed there for entertainment purposes."

"So you got your money's worth then?" Will couldn't resist the dig, which was lost on Bach.

"Oh, we didn't pay. The tour was free for soldiers of the Wehrmacht."

Will wondered if any of the German workers and soldiers who made the *tour* had come away ashamed of their government. "How many people are confined here?"

"All the Jews of Warsaw, sir. That is, those who haven't gone into hiding or gotten away, and there are some from Germany, too. So," he shrugged, "maybe four hundred thousand."

Four hundred thousand! That was just under the present population of Hannover in northwestern Germany, where Will was born and had lived all his life—a city sixty times the size of the ghetto.

"Will those who lived elsewhere be allowed to return to their homes once they are free from disease?"

"I think not, since they are carriers. As I mentioned, they have been ordered to live here. Can you imagine how intolerable it would be to bump into Jews everywhere one goes? They are easier to manage this way."

Easier to manage, the operative words. Will knew about the camps for dissidents in Germany and the thousands of men arrested for being Jewish after *Kristallnacht*—the attack and vandalization of their communities by organized groups of Nazis—but he had never seen or heard of anything like this ghetto. It must be part of the *health measure* Captain Hoff referred to, instituted by Dr. Fischer, and the inhabitants, judging by Bach's callous descriptions, were starving.

"So they are not allowed to leave, correct?"

"They will be shot on sight if they do," Bach said matter-of-factly.

"By the army?"

"Oh no. The special police battalion handles that. Herr Kommandant refuses to let the Wehrmacht shoot the Jews."

For that I can respect him, Will thought. "Are their previous homes standing empty?"

"Reserved for the *Volksdeutsche* the Führer brings in from far and wide. He cares for all his people."

That mendacious bastard Hitler! This is how he planned to further *Lebensraum* and increase the living space after conquering the country: by stripping these poor people of their dignity and property and penning them up to make way for the ethnic Germans living outside the Fatherland's borders. Will had enough of this place and this priggish little sergeant. He had no idea this was just the beginning—the following month, leading Nazi officials would meet at a top-secret conference in a Berlin suburb to draw up plans to rid occupied Europe of the Jews.

"Thank you, Feldwebel. You can drive on now."

Bach drove on, showing off the city, a contrast of bombed-out buildings and tree-lined streets of palaces and mansions. Reconstruction efforts, he said, had begun in some places but were halted after *we* entered Russia to squash Bolshevism, as building supplies were needed there to ensure the continuity of *our* outstanding successes. The tour concluded with a retracing of the parade route used by Hitler in his victory lap the month after the invasion.

The young Nazi bounced up and down in his seat. "It was the most majestic day of my life and an unforgettable sight. On one side, our regiments in full marching order, our officers and soldiers bursting with pride at the victory they had earned, and on the other, the defeated Poles."

Will's tired eyes rolled back. "Impressive, impressive."

Bach prattled on about his upbringing in the Hitler Youth and stated that the people he most admired were his sainted mother in Düsseldorf and his beloved Führer.

"If you don't mind," Will said, rubbing his temples, "I would like to see my quarters now. It has been a long day."

"Certainly. Before I forget, you will have a staff of three: a typist, a clerk, and a guard who will double as a driver when you need him, as a car will be provided for your use. A truck will deposit them at your office and come for them at the end of the day. I might add that few officers of your rank have automobiles," he said in an irritating tone that indicated Will should be indebted to Hoff.

"Then it is a great privilege for me."

They drove to the German residential quarter in Mokotów, a suburb surrounded by barricades twenty-five minutes south of the city center, arriving at a lone, L-shaped white house on a one-way street. A barbed wire fence gave it the air of having been taken prisoner rather than protected. The house had an upper story on the longer leg of the L, consisting of two connecting bedrooms, each with an entrance to the bathroom. Directly below on the ground floor sat a kitchen and laundry. The main living area on the other leg had been turned into an office and was separated from the quarters by an outdoor walkway.

"Nice setup, sir. You are fortunate to have this arrangement."

That tone again. "I am indeed. Did my predecessor occupy this space before he was reassigned?"

"Reassigned? I believe he was arrested."

"I see. Well, thank you for your input, Feldwebel, and your time showing me around. You have been most helpful."

The loquacious sergeant went on his way. Ravenous, Will searched for food and found none. He had forgotten to ask about it, and now it was too late to do anything. The heater didn't work, there was no kindling for the fireplace in his bedroom, and the blankets were as thin as sheets. Tomorrow he would sort things out, but that night, like most Warsovians, Oberleutnant Engel went to bed hungry and cold.

Chapter 3

Will had worked feverishly to become a capable, well-respected officer, though the military had not been his first-choice career. His dream of working the land on his maternal grandfather's beetroot farm was dashed when his father sold it after the old man died. In 1930, the twenty-year-old university graduate joined the *Reichswehr,* the peacetime army, and started his officer training. At that time, the army was limited to 100,000 men by the Versailles Treaty as part of Germany's punishment for its role in the Great War.

His motivation for joining stemmed more from an urge to retaliate against his father for selling the farm without his knowledge and for years of childhood abuse than from a desire to serve his country. Herr Engel was a wealthy banker with a slavish devotion to rules and regulations and detested any deviance from prescriptive norms. A tyrant, he ruled the household with an iron fist and whipped his young son with a cat-o'-nine-tails at every opportunity until Will turned thirteen and was too big to hit. Although he earned excellent grades in school, his father continued to belittle him. Later, his enlistment infuriated Herr Engel, who had lost faith in the military following Germany's crushing wartime defeat and considered soldiering a disgrace to the family name.

Will enjoyed his training regardless of the reasons he signed on. In the early days, his dedication to duties was driven by a newfound patriotism and was characterized by the same perfectionistic striving apparent in every one of his undertakings. A few years later, when Hitler took control and began rearmament in contravention of the treaty, the Reichswehr became the Wehrmacht, and everything changed. Existing members of the military were forced to reswear an oath pledging obedience to the self-styled Führer instead of to people and country.

The organization had become a Nazi tool, and Will's national pride faded like a photograph left too long in the sun. He found Hitler's racial policies and condemnation of the Jews for all of Germany's ills abhorrent, and the way he whipped himself into an orgasmic frenzy during his speeches was repulsive. When his comrades at the military facility in Hannover began voicing their support or opposition to the polarizing leader, he kept silent in order to avoid having a pro- or anti-mark placed on his back. With either he'd be damned, so kept his head down and nose to the grindstone.

After seven arduous years, he received his commission as *leutnant,* second lieutenant, and was given command of training a rifle platoon in the 19th Infantry Division headquartered at the facility. His parents had passed away the year before; his mother went first, and because misery loves company, his father followed shortly. They left him a great deal of money in a Swiss bank account—surprising, he thought, given their lack of affection. Septuagenarian Aunt Helga, his only surviving relative, was living abroad, and there was no one to cheer on the dashing new officer at the ceremony.

Will was used to being alone. His twin brother Gustav suffered from a congenital lung ailment and passed away when they were ten. Frau Engel's attitude toward Will had always been one of silent anger. His robustness at birth, compared to his brother's frailty, was a clear indicator that he had drained Gustav of his strength in the womb and was responsible for his poor health and premature death. Before the funeral, she secluded herself in her room. Herr Engel showed no emotion and closeted himself in the study, making arrangements.

If only Frau Engel would return from her self-imposed exile and see how much Will needed her, perhaps she would kiss his swollen face or run her fingers through his hair. He couldn't remember a time when she had given him a speck of affection or a single expression of love, but there was always hope. The grief-stricken youngster opened her door, took a few steps in, and asked her to hold him. From the depths of the darkened room, she screamed, *"Geh Weg!"* Go away.

He ran downstairs to the study, sidled up to his father, and plucked at his sleeve. Herr Engel moved Will away until he was at arm's length, put his hand on the boy's shoulder, and said sternly, "Men do not cry, Wilhelm. You are weak. Learn to control your emotions."

"But I'm a boy, not a man, and I cannot make my eyes just stop. Why wasn't I allowed to see my brother in the hospital? I never got a chance to say goodbye," he sobbed. "Nobody loves me in this house. I wish I was never born. I'm going to run away, and you will never see me again."

Whap! His father slapped him across the face. "Stop whining, or I will send you to a school for the wayward, and then you will really wish you were never born. You are a disappointment, bawling like a baby. Out, out!"

Desperate for a human touch, Will hung about the kitchen and shadowed Hilde the cook in the hope she would take him in her plump arms, clasp him to her pendulous breasts, and say, "Go ahead and cry," and give him a piece of Linzer torte before dinner. That didn't happen, and he should have known better. Hilde, whose eyes were the cold blue of a Siberian husky and seemingly in the back of her head, became suspicious. "What are you doing behind my skirts? Get out of my kitchen, you bad boy, or I will call your father," she shrieked, and chased him away with a wooden spoon.

Before the family left for the church service and funeral that cold March morning, Herr Engel gave his son a warning. "You are not to weep and embarrass us. You will be sorry if you do." During the ceremony, Will's eyes stayed dry—he couldn't bear to face a whipping.

Then, after his beloved brother had been buried and the family returned home, all Will wanted to do was to run into the woods in the back of the house and cry the tears he'd been afraid to shed, he was forced to sit in the living room with his parents and their guests. Hilde served coffee and *Butterkuchen,* a sweet, fluffy cake topped with sugar and cinnamon. Will licked his lips. *Yes, please!* A big square was just the thing a drained, hungry boy needed to feel better, but she gave him a piece the size of a stick of chewing gum.

His mouth twitched and his cheeks flushed as he stared at the strip of cake on his plate, and then at the cook, who smirked. Hot tears were forming behind his eyes. It appeared that Hilde, too, blamed him for Gustav's death. This mean-spirited treatment would have been his undoing had Granddad not noticed and quickly whispered something to Frau Engel, who said without feeling, "You may eat your cake in the kitchen, then go up to your room, Wilhelm."

Granddad took a fresh plate of cake from the table, and they went into the kitchen. He poured Will a glass of milk and sat with him while he ate. "I am proud of you, Willy. Continue to have courage. I'll see you in the summer," he said, and left to go back to his farm.

Will didn't have a shred of courage. What he had was fear of the *Katze,* the leather strap with nine tails that hung on a hook in a closet in his father's study. Lost without Gustav, he consoled himself by cuddling with the dog, a fair-weather dachshund bitch who allowed it for a few moments if rewarded with a treat. Aunt Helga sent a box of tin soldiers with a note advising him to *soldier on.* He had a loving, imaginary family whom he christened *Die Liebesmacher*—the Lovemakers—and talked to himself aloud as he lay on the bed with his legs in the air, balancing a ball on his feet, and inventing pleasant scenarios in which he was petted and doted upon.

Over the years, Will kept the tears at bay but wasn't as successful with the sadness. He pretended it didn't exist, but it nibbled and gnawed at him like a gribble on wood, biting at the most inopportune times, and he moved through life yearning to love and be loved, finding it only in his fantasies.

Chapter 4

The commission ceremony behind him, Leutnant Engel settled into the tasks of teaching and training the men in his platoon, which he handled with customary aplomb. Unlike his fellow officers who kicked up clouds of dust like wildebeest to get out the door as soon as their leaves were announced, he dragged his heels. There was no one special in his life, no one waiting with open arms.

Will had been with a handful of women and loved none of them. Fortunately, they were the initiators; he never had to go out of his way, but after sex with them, he felt hollow. He sometimes went to bars with his comrades for lack of something better to do on a night off. The women there, older and careworn, were entranced by the virile young soldiers and officers and primed to have sex in an alleyway or under a bush after a few drinks. Will felt sorry for them. They usually had small children and no husbands, and after listening to their sad stories, he slipped a few Reichsmarks into their pockets and either walked them home or sent them in a cab.

He met Karoline at an officer's party in early 1938. Surrounded by a flock of uniformed, rapt admirers, she saw the handsome lieutenant sitting alone and swept over with hawk-like speed to shower him with attention. Serious and quiet around women, Will was uncomfortable making small talk, as his parents hadn't been prime exemplars of skillful repartee. In this case, Karoline the extrovert spared him the discomfort.

Tall and angular with a beakish nose and short, teased brown hair, her piercing green eyes seemed to glow in the dark when she got angry. On the far side of pretty, Karoline was, however, interesting and fun, and they spent Will's time off going to restaurants, clubs, and cinemas and in her apartment having sex. He thought he loved her, though there wasn't the electric attraction and ecstasy described in books and poems. That kind of feeling, he decided, was overrated or didn't exist outside of fiction.

Karoline's job as secretary to an important *Schutzstaffel* officer in the Hannover government offices caused Will concern. The SS was known for its brutality toward anyone suspected of being anti-Nazi, and he didn't want her working for a thug, nor did he want to end up in the man's crosshairs. "You know how I feel about the Nazis," he said, "and you don't agree with their views either. Perhaps you should apply for a position with the Wehrmacht. With your qualifications and years of experience, I'm sure there is suitable employment for you. I will look into it."

"I need to support myself, Willy, and my job pays well. You know the army mostly hires male secretaries, and the pay is low."

"Then I will buy you a house to decorate as you wish, and you won't have to work when we are married," he said, barely three months in.

"Who said anything about marriage?"

"I'm saying it now, and then we can start making babies. I would love to have several," he added, taking her in his arms.

"You won't be around to take care of them," she said snidely, oblivious to the hurt flickering in his eyes.

"I'm an officer doing his duty, and even so, I will be a wonderful father and husband. We can hire a cook and a maid to clean, and you will never want for anything."

The prospect of a house and servants was tempting, but not the pitter-patter of little feet. The thought of losing her trim waistline and looking like a milk cow with hanging teats was utterly unappealing. She hedged. "I don't know. My boss may be moving to SS headquarters in Berlin, and there's been talk of sending me along. I couldn't let him down. Maybe we should keep things light."

Surrounded by men twenty-four hours a day, Will's life at the facility was lonely enough without the love and support of a woman on the outside, and officers were encouraged to marry and start families. He began an aggressive campaign to persuade Karoline to accept his proposal, calling her daily and sending candy and flowers, which, unlike most women, she hated. Fed up with his enticements and the ribbing heaped upon her by coworkers, she agreed to marry him on the condition they wait a year. There was a certain status that came with being engaged to a Wehrmacht lieutenant, and he was also good in bed.

She moved to Berlin to work at the SS headquarters, but Will wasn't discouraged by the distance. On leaves, he traveled over three hundred miles by train from Hannover and back to see her, and she insisted they go out with friends from her office, vigorous Nazi Party supporters he hated socializing with. Karoline soon realized that the SS, a powerful, fanatical organization charged with enforcing Hitler's ideologies, looked down upon the Wehrmacht. There was more prestige and benefit in working for the SS than there would be by marrying an army officer of minor importance, but she didn't want to cut it off with him completely, not yet anyway.

Will's need to be loved and start a family was so great that he ignored the voice in his head that screamed caution and reminded himself Karoline would stop working and return to Hannover before their marriage. Once away from her Hitler-loving cronies and that beast of a boss, she would devote herself to him.

Within a year, Hitler had annexed Austria and occupied Czechoslovakia with little opposition and set his sights on regaining the eastern lands Germany lost under the treaty: the city of

Danzig and the Polish Corridor, the strip dividing the main body of Germany from its province of East Prussia that provided Poland access to the Baltic Sea. The Poles rejected his demands, and he secretly instructed his high command to make preparations for an invasion. By August '39, he was publicly beating the war drums in their direction, leveling claims of persecution of ethnic Germans there. Britain and France had promised to support Poland in the event that Germany made good on its threats to attack, though the Führer didn't believe they would. He told his military leaders to finalize the plans.

Troop movements to assembly points near the Polish border were to be carried out in carefully orchestrated series and camouflaged as regular maneuvers and exercises to avoid arousing the Poles' suspicions. The German navy and Luftwaffe air force were given their directives, and a number of inciting incidents made to show Germany as the victim of aggression were planned to justify their attack.

Will was scheduled to remain at the facility to train the incoming replacement army, which was what he wanted, but his commanding officer changed his mind. "A man of your caliber is needed in the campaign, Engel. Sixty divisions are being sent to attack on three fronts. You are to deploy as part of Army Group South's Tenth Army under *Feldmarschall* von Reichenau, whose division will form the main thrust, strike through southern Poland, then fight north to Warsaw. The battle will be quick. The Poles do not stand a chance against us with their outdated weapons and equipment."

Sixty divisions? Over a million men! If all Hitler wanted were the lost lands, the military would go after those areas and not the entire country. Will contemplated the significance of the invasion. Poland was not going to fall into Hitler's arms overnight like his eager mistresses Austria and Czechoslovakia, and the collateral damage would be staggering. The Poles would give up, the country would fall under Nazi rule, and then what?

The young soldiers in the 19th Infantry, influenced by the Nazi scheme since childhood, would have few pangs of doubt about the prospect of engagement in battle. They were raring to go in service of the good and against the force of evil, the Polish army. For Will, the upcoming operation was an unjustifiable act of wanton aggression. His enmity was towards the Nazi leadership and not the Poles.

The idea of killing men who had done nothing wrong except to have the misfortune of living in a country the megalomaniac-in-chief wanted in order to make more living space for the German people catapulted him into an existential crisis. He thought long and hard. Protecting his men had to be the number one priority, and he would put his personal feelings aside and do what he was trained to, though he would defy any order to kill innocent civilians, come what may.

Will had no way of knowing that Hitler's secret orders to his generals were, "Kill without pity or mercy all men, women, and children of Polish descent or language. This is the way we will obtain the living space." Only the most astute and prescient could foretell the evil plans the suckled-by-wolves *Reichskanzler* and his myrmidons were cooking up behind the scenes.

Chapter 5

The invasion went off with typical German precision at daybreak on Friday, September 1, 1939, but without Leutnant Engel. A few days before deployment, he was sent to supervise a last minute inventory at a weapons depot outside the installation. On the way, his vehicle was struck by a three-ton army cargo truck, whose driver lost control while coming too fast around a bend on the rainslicked highway. Will lay comatose in the garrison hospital, having suffered severe head, chest, and back injuries and a broken kneecap. He awoke from the coma after a week and gradually regained his faculties, though he had no memory of the accident.

Karoline, still living and working in Berlin, visited a couple of times in the early days of his injury. Instead of placing loving hands on him and whispering words of encouragement, she quipped, "Some people will do anything for attention," then proceeded to chat a little too gaily with the young doctor checking charts. Back in Berlin, the letters she wrote him had a distinct businesslike quality.

In his hospital bed, he learned from news reports that western Poland had been annexed into the Greater German Reich. The central area, now known as the Generalgouvernement, was to be administered by German officials for some unclear reason, and the Russians had occupied the eastern part of the country under an agreement with Hitler. Will didn't give a damn about any of it. A languishing, lonely, broken officer surrounded by similar wretches, he had nothing but his fantasies to keep him going and, as always, his dinner.

He endured six months of acute care, then was transferred to a rehabilitation facility, where he would stay for the next half year. Karoline wrote that she was coming to see him, and he set aside his resentment at her earlier lack of attention. On the day of the visit, Will sat in his wheelchair awaiting her arrival with bated breath.

Precisely at three o'clock in the afternoon, preceded by her prominent nose, the heavily lacquered brunette rushed up to the nurse's station, her high heels clacking on the freshly waxed linoleum. "Fräulein Krähe," she said, pulling off her leather gloves finger by finger, "to see Leutnant Engel."

The nurse looked down her nose. "First room on the right."

As the door opened, Will's heart beat in double time. "Karoline, I am so happy to see you."

"Hello, Willy. You're looking much better than last time."

"They tell me I will leave here in a couple of months, as good as new."

"Glad to hear it."

"I have a wonderful nurse. She let me have this room for an hour—an entire hour—so we could have privacy. Can you lock the door and help me to the bed? I am dying to hold you in my arms."

Avoiding his eyes, Karoline opened her handbag to look for something. "I'm sorry, Willy, I can't. I came to return your ring. Here." She put it in his hand. "I'm going to marry *Sturmbannführer* Karl Schulz, my boss," she said, holding her head high.

Bitch! Doubts about her faithfulness he'd had all along, but it was his own fault for not listening to the voice in his head. "You came all the way from Berlin for this? Why didn't you just tell me we were finished in one of your enthralling letters? I don't care about the ring."

"I had to come to Hannover to see my family anyway. I would have told you sooner, but Karl and I thought it best to wait until you were stronger, you know, with your head injury and all your other problems. Again, I'm sorry."

Karl and I? Will's face turned the color his granddad called *Rote-Bete-Rot,* beetroot red. "Get out!" he yelled, then lapsed into a paroxysm of coughing. Never in his life had he shouted at a woman, and if he wasn't so physically and emotionally fractured, he wouldn't have now. When he was young, if he dared raise his voice to his parents or the servants, he would receive a whipping.

The nurse heard the commotion and rushed to the room, nearly colliding with Karoline, who came flying out. "What happened, Herr Engel?"

"She has been carrying on with an SS major all this time," he said, squeezing his temples to stop the throbbing.

"You will find the right woman one day, someone truly deserving."

"By the time that happens, I will be too old to care," he said, his heart sore with wounded pride.

"Love knows no age, sir."

"That remains to be seen, but thank you for going out of your way, Gertruda. You have been so kind."

"Why don't you rest here before dinner? Let me help you to the bed."

"What are we having tonight?"

"Liver and onions, and strudel for dessert."

"Good, good." Something to look forward to. He closed his eyes and slipped into a favorite fantasy. A nubile young woman appeared in his arms. They kissed hungrily.

"I love you, Willy," she murmured, caressing him.

Now that the inevitable had occurred, Karoline Krähe, whose surname literally meant *crow,* took her place in the ranks of women he hadn't loved, and Will would always associate her with the traits those birds are despised for. Glad to be rid of her, he resolved to live with loneliness and vowed never again to beg for love.

His rehabilitation complete, Will went on furlough to Aunt Helga's. Back in Hannover, she had offered him the second bedroom in her small apartment. Her elderly friends came bearing platters of his favorite foods and speaking of granddaughters to set him up with. When he found out they were members of Nazi women's associations, he made excuses not to go out with them. Helga's friends stopped bringing food.

Each morning, Will walked miles to strengthen his muscles, afraid of being discharged from the army due to his injuries. Discharge meant having to join the Nazi Party, assume a leadership role, and wear a uniform with a swastika armband. He would have to force other invalids to join. As long as a man could walk, even if only on one leg, he'd be fair game for recruitment into that dreaded organization. In spite of weakness in his knee and considerable pain in his leg, Will forged ahead.

Near the end of his furlough, he was directed to undergo a medical evaluation to determine his status. "Perhaps I shouldn't have pushed so hard and gotten myself looking so fit," he told Helga, thinking he would be approved for combat, retrained, and put on standby to deal with the vagaries of the schizophrenic Hitler.

"You don't want a discharge, Wilhelm, nor do you want to be declared fit for combat. Is there a middle ground, or perhaps your head wound has affected your powers of reasoning more than you know?" Helga didn't intend to be mean, but she was Herr Engel's sister and had either inherited one of his negative traits, which was making an untimely appearance, or it was due to her advancing age.

"I am hoping for office work, but the army rarely gives a man what he wants."

"Then they had better start hiring drivers who know how to operate their vehicles in the rain. Let your accident be a lesson to them," she said, abruptly changing course and defending him.

Will smiled. "Thank you, Aunt Helga."

After the examination and an interview, the doctor stamped Will's file in red ink, *Kampf Untauglich,* unfit for combat. "You are still lame in one leg due to nerve damage and have suffered a head injury. Although you look well, we must err on the side of caution. I am recommending you for desk work indefinitely," the doctor said in a sorry voice, as if Leutnant Engel would be crushed by the news.

Relief! It was the outcome he hoped for. A notice arrived, ordering him to report to the Hannover garrison, where he'd taken his military training and earned his officer commission. As manager of the finance office, he'd be out of harm's way as long as a British bomb didn't fall on him or another freak accident didn't occur. Now his only concern was if the *Bismarckbrötchen,* pickled herring on a Kaiser roll, was still being served on Fridays in the officers' mess hall.

Chapter 6

Warsaw, 1920. Life was good for Jakub Laska, a bookkeeper at the Commerce Bank. He lived in a large, stately apartment north of the city center, bequeathed to him by his parents and attended by a housekeeper who had worked for the family for years. Jakub didn't mind being a Jew as long as it wasn't apparent he was one, to which end his blonde, blue-eyed Aryan looks were advantageous.

As a young boy, he accompanied his parents to dine, visit friends, and shop for goods in the Jewish Quarter south of their neighborhood. It was the largest community of its kind in Europe and teemed with restaurants, businesses of all kinds, and crowded apartments. The precocious youngster noticed a difference between his folks, a staid older couple who spoke Polish in public and never called attention to the fact they were Jewish, and the haggling, gesticulating Yiddish speakers in the Quarter.

"It's the way they look, they talk, they act. Everything about them screams Jew," he told his parents.

Troubled by their son's insensitivity, they sent him for counseling with the rabbi, with whom he acted contrite. Some years rolled by, and after his bar mitzvah, he told his parents, "I've done my duty—no more Jewish studies. I want to go to a Christian academy," which prompted the Laskas' cry of sacrilege and a taking to sickbeds.

"What is all this nonsense?" his father asked when he rose.

"These days a fellow has to expand his horizons. It will give me an edge in the business world," Jakub said

"Business? What business? You're thirteen!"

"I plan to become an accountant when I'm older, and will need to have a better understanding of the Gentile way of thinking and behaving since they run most of the banks."

"You're a fool. Gentiles hate Jews. They pretend to like us because their financial institutions are infused with our capital, but in their hearts they think we are swine."

"My point exactly. A Jew must avoid making his religious beliefs known when he is outside of his home; he should put on his most neutral face and display noble mannerisms if he wants to be respected."

His father sighed and went to join his wife. "I suppose it could be worse," he whispered, "had he told us he wants to become a priest." Worn down by their son's persistence, the Laskas gave in and enrolled him at the school of his choice.

Jakub picked and chose qualities that would enhance his phenotypic windfall and developed them to excellence. With the help of private tutors, he erased every trace of Yiddish from his speech, and insisted his parents speak Polish at home. He adopted an aristocratic accent, and learned several foreign languages—a skill he considered essential and a hallmark of high intelligence. The Laskas never fully recovered from their sense of failure in raising their son properly and declined in health. Jakub sailed through the Christian preparatory school and went on to earn his accounting degree. He started growing the bushy mustache with sides that grew down and winged out favored by the Polish elite, and entered the business world at the age of twenty-one.

Jakub had avoided the Quarter for years, and the reason he deigned to set foot in the place now was to visit a popular bookstore that carried a selection of hard-to-find French and German novels, and it was there that he met his future wife.

Malka Pustilnik, a petite, blue-eyed blonde who had been working in the bookstore for a couple of years, was well-read, knowledgeable, and always happy to see him. Almost all of Jakub's friends were married, and during gatherings when the wives were present, he felt the odd man out. They provided a stream of available Jewish women, though none appealed to him. One had a strong Yiddish accent and a big nose; the other was as pale and drawn as his mother on her deathbed; and another looked Romani.

"You're too picky." His friends shook their heads and suggested he marry a Gentile.

"What? And sully our children's genes? Never, never," he exclaimed. "I want a Jewish girl who looks and acts like a Gentile."

Malka was the total package. She impressed him with her fashionable style and excellent diction, and best of all, she wasn't religious. In short, she possessed all the qualities he wanted in a wife. Jakub accepted an invitation to meet her parents, Rivka and Gersh Pustilnik, at their apartment in the Quarter and hoped the dinner wouldn't take up too much time. The Pustilniks were transplants from a shtetl in the Ukraine, and what would he talk to them about? Certainly they would speak Yiddish, a language he detested. Well, he would just pretend he didn't understand a word. On the appointed Sunday evening, armed with an engagement ring, boxes of candy, and a bouquet of flowers, he rang the Pustilniks' bell.

"Speak Polish," Malka reminded her parents. "He doesn't know Yiddish."

They were delighted with him, and soon he and Malka set to planning their wedding. He wanted a private civil ceremony with a dinner party afterward, and she hoped for a traditional Jewish one to please her parents. He won. The first couple of years were happy until Jakub suddenly forbade the Pustilniks, who were most comfortable conversing among themselves in their mother tongue, to speak it in his home, falsely claiming it was unfair since he didn't understand it.

Rivka enjoyed irritating him and ignored this new regulation, but when a wooden sign appeared in the living room that read *No Yiddish,* she yelled, *"Kish mein tuchus,"* grabbed her docile husband, and stormed out. This caused a terrific row between the young couple, and Malka packed her bags and moved back home with her parents.

Chapter 7

The Pustilniks had fled their humble home outside of Kiev just before the turn of the century with their teenage nephew, Naftoly Vorobiev, whose parents and siblings had been killed in the anti-Jewish rioting that precipitated their flight. They went west to the Polish lands the Russian Empire claimed when the country was divided under treaty with Austria and Prussia a hundred years earlier. They came first to Wyszków, a town by the Bug River, thirty-five miles northeast of Warsaw. In 1900, soon after Malka's birth, Rivka and Gersh moved to Warsaw without Naftoly, who preferred to stay in Wyszków.

Naftoly had fallen in love with the town: the streets were cobbled, chickens squawked in yards, and flowers and grasses waved in meadows surrounded by pine forests. Big and brawny at sixteen, with a mop of reddish-brown hair and a growing beard, he found work as a woodcutter and rented a room in a boarding house. Of the five thousand residents, just over half were Jews who lived in the center of town. The Poles lived on the outskirts. Despite underlying tensions, the two groups came together on market day, giving the place the flavor of his Ukrainian shtetl.

Over time, he saved enough to buy a small house just outside the town center and met and married Ola, a Catholic peasant who had fled the countryside to escape an arranged marriage and was employed as a maid in a Jewish household. The couple lived happily until World War I broke out. The Germans occupied the Russian-held areas of Poland, took control of raw materials and food supplies to send back to Germany, and brought economic hardship to the people. They established a headquarters in Wyszków and started handing down their rules and regulations.

Their troops went into the surrounding forests through the early spring and summer and savagely slashed at the trees to extract the sap, leaving them to die and Naftoly without a job. Woodcutters were forbidden to cut any tree, dead or alive, or to sell the wood for profit. Ola still had her small maid's salary, and he drove a water cart to make ends meet.

After the war ended in 1918, Poland regained its independence, and life in town was again pleasant, if only temporarily. The fractious relationship between the Poles and Jews worsened when hostilities started between Poland and Soviet Russia, culminating in war in 1919. A Russian military unit, like the Germans before them, had set up a command post in the town and, after their defeat by the Polish army the following year, robbed and looted the Jewish homes on their way out. Bands of Polish roughnecks accused hundreds of Jews of being Bolsheviks and beat them savagely.

The violence reminded Naftoly that it was just as dangerous for Jews in Wyszków as in the Ukraine. He escaped the wrath of the Russophobic and anti-Semitic Poles he worked with at his new job at the sawmill because he was so personable and was seen praying in church with his wife every Sunday.

Ola gave birth to a baby boy that same year, 1920. The Vorobievs named him Andrush, a variation of Andrzej, meaning *manly*. He had his father's topaz-colored eyes, his mother's golden hair, and a smile that never left his face. As he grew, he loved being outside in the fresh air like his father and accompanied him on odd jobs with a toy tool belt strapped around his waist.

"When you're older, I will teach you how to shoot so you can protect yourself should the need arise," Naftoly said.

"I'm a big boy, Papa, and I don't fear anything or anyone."

His father laughed. "Not even Mama? She'll be mighty angry if the chores aren't done. Aunt Rivka, Uncle Gersh, and my cousin Malka are coming today, so let's finish up and get back to the house."

Every summer, the Pustilniks spent a month in Wyszków, though Malka hadn't been back since her marriage and thought a change of scenery would be beneficial. She returned from vacation to her parents' apartment and discovered she was pregnant. Jakub came bearing gifts for everyone, but she refused to come out of the bedroom. "How did he find out we're back? Send him away, Mama. I don't want to see him."

"You shouldn't hide your pregnancy from him. It's his child, and he has a right to know," Rivka said, after Jakub had gone.

"You told him, didn't you? I thought you couldn't stand him; now you're pushing me to go back."

"I don't have to like him, but you have to iron out your difficulties. Let him *think* he's in charge. You can catch more flies with honey than vinegar, then go and spend his money."

"He's so hard to get along with. Even pretending to be nice with him takes too much energy, and he never once told me that he loves me."

"You want words? So ask for them. Papa never tells me he loves me."

"That's different. Maybe I should have married the fellow who owned the fish market. What was his name? Remember how he used to say, 'Look at this sturgeon, ladies, isn't she a beauty? See how her tender flesh quivers?' He was interested in me and wasn't bad looking," Malka said wistfully, twisting her wedding band around her finger.

"Ah, Balborski, the monger. He wasn't good looking either," Rivka recalled. "His ears stuck out like jug handles. Besides, the odor of fish clings to a person who fondles them all day, and it never washes off. Is that how you want your man to smell when he reaches for you in the night?"

Malka sighed. "I guess not."

"Go home and tell your husband the news. It's time."

Jakub was thrilled when he heard the news and was attentive and loving throughout the pregnancy. In July '23, they welcomed a baby girl, whom they named Maritza. The Pustilniks were in their glory and came speaking Polish, even when their son-in-law wasn't home. But soon, Jakub reverted to his old ways. He inserted himself into every aspect of the baby's care, believing himself to be an expert on child-rearing. Malka had it up to her eyeballs.

"For heaven's sake," she cried, "you're a bookkeeper, not an authority on best practices."

"Accountant, Malka, Chief Accountant." Jakub rocked on his heels and puffed out his chest. He had taken a new position at the Bank of Poland.

"Accountant, bookkeeper, beekeeper, barkeeper—who cares? Stop trying to control everyone and everything."

Before realizing the sure-fire way to get him off her back was to drench him in exaggerated flattery, the only method had been to change his focus and replace any current obsession with another. Malka invited Naftoly and his family for a weekend without asking Jakub's permission and waited until the morning of their arrival to inform him of the visit. Ignoring his objections, she told him to leave if he didn't like it. He met the Vorobievs just once when they came for his wedding party, arriving from Wyszków (the provinces, he called it) in an old hay wagon looking the epitome of peasantry. They were coarse, he said, and unworthy of his attention.

From the moment the Vorobievs stepped into the Laskas' Art Nouveau-furnished apartment and four-year-old Andrush laid his eyes on little blonde, blue-eyed Maritza, he was smitten. She had the same effect on him as a new puppy. Fascinated, he touched her hair, eyes, and lips as if she were a doll come to life. When Malka attempted to take her into the bedroom for a nap, Maritza kicked and screamed and stretched her arms out for him. He called her *Mishka*. "Let me take care of Mishka, Cousin Malka. I know what to do." Andrush crooned to her until she fell fast asleep in his capable arms. He was as good as a Norland Nanny.

The Pustilniks came, and the apartment was filled with the women's laughter as they prepared *pierogi*. Pots and utensils clanged, dough was pounded and rolled, onions diced, meat ground, and potatoes sieved. Malka peeked from the kitchen into the living room and saw Gersh talking animatedly with Naftoly, while dour Jakub hid behind his newspaper. Every few seconds, he rattled the pages and cleared his throat, poorly disguised hints that he found their conversation boring.

"May I see you in the bedroom, dear?" asked Malka.

"Yes?"

"Get back out there and act like the high-class gentleman you profess to be," she fizzed, "and treat our guests with respect." Threatened with a stay on all sexual activity, he forced himself to participate in the men's discussion. The weekend was the slowest and most mind-numbing of his life. He couldn't wait for the Vorobievs to leave, and as they were on their way out, he clipped poor Ola's heels in a rush to close the door before she had cleared the threshold.

Chapter 8

Every summer from the time she was two, Andrush took care of little Mishka during the family's month-long visit to Wyszków. When she departed with her mother and grandparents, she cried and he moped. Although he had friends aplenty, he felt halved without her. He couldn't explain the feeling to himself—why a little girl should affect him so much.

The Mishka who came to Wyszków at age seven was a different person. There wasn't anything babyish about her; instead of dolls, she brought books filled with colorful pictures of people, animals, and nature that they spent hours poring over. They were allowed to walk alone in the forest and have picnics in the meadows. Everything they did together was fun. While the adults played cards and lingered over bowls of cut fruit in the evenings, the two children sat outside on the stoop, holding hands and wishing upon stars.

After her visit that summer, Andrush got into fistfights at the slightest provocation, stopped attending to his schoolwork in the fall, and was threatened with expulsion. No one knew the reason for his behavior, and when asked about it, he placed the blame on others.

The adults had their theories. Ola believed he had too much free time, saddled him with extra chores, and insisted he devote more time to prayers. His teachers said he had a nervous disorder, but the doctor found nothing wrong with him. *Boys will be boys.* Naftoly's explanation was almost right: Andrush was angry because he missed the family.

"Maybe we should send him to live in Warsaw with his cousins, where there are better schools and opportunities. He'll only get into trouble here," he told Ola, but she refused to hear of it.

Naftoly went ahead and wrote to Malka, described the problem, and offered to send money each month for his son's room and board and other expenses if she and Jakub agreed. He didn't care for his cousin's husband, a whiny grumbler with an inflated view of his own importance and the opposite of everything a man should be. He had a slender build, hands as dainty and white as a newborn's, and (gasp) manicured nails. The possibility that Andrush might expand his horizons outweighed his sentiments toward Jakub.

Jakub nearly choked on his soup when Malka showed him the letter, then hounded her for an answer as to how anyone in this day and age could be such a poor writer. It boggled his mind how Naftoly, who had been out of the Ukraine for thirty years, had managed to get by with an astonishing lack of skill.

Malka loved her Wyszków relatives dearly. Naftoly might lack knowledge of the mechanics of Polish writing, but he could build a house with his own hands. Ola never learned to read and write—she had no use for those skills, though she was a wonderful storyteller who could hold the attention of the most distracted child and was an accomplished quilter to boot.

Jakub could be inveigled into doing almost anything if showered with praise. This was the most expedient way for Malka to get what she wanted from him. "Well, Naftoly is a lumberman, not a word-meister," she said, forcing herself to keep a civil tongue. "He believes that you would be a great influence on Andrush. You are much brighter than, um, almost anyone, and that's why I married you. Papa brought over some fresh pastries from the bakery. Would you like a plate and a cup of coffee for dessert, darling?"

"Why, yes," Jakub said with a satisfied smile, basking in the light of his wife's compliments. "Such a buttery crust," he said, wiping crumbs from his mustache with a linen napkin and patting his stomach. He sat back in his chair, lit his pipe, and told Malka to plan a weekend trip to Wyszków to bring the boy and inform Vorobiev that he would pay for everything. What a feather in his cap it would be if he could turn the young yokel into an elitist. He imagined the boy fifteen or twenty years later as a successful businessman, doctor, or lawyer, giving a speech in which he expressed deep gratitude to his beloved benefactor, Jakub Laska of Warsaw, for turning him into a Renaissance man.

Maritza did cartwheels across the living room when Malka told her Andrush was coming to live with them.

"Stop that, young lady. Don't let your father see how excited you are."

She didn't need to ask why. If Jakub saw how happy she was, he would impose new limits on her. He controlled most of her activities, and she didn't have a minute for herself. There were piano, art, and dancing lessons to develop her talents, and in addition, he was in the process of teaching her French and German and helping her in mathematics. Taxing and tiring as it was, his tutelage enabled her to outshine everyone in her class.

Two weeks later, Andrush said goodbye to his despondent mother and stoic father and, accompanied by Malka, boarded the train to Warsaw.

Jakub searched for schools for his young charge and decided upon a nonsectarian academy. The evening before classes began, he called the boy into his study. "Now, some fundamentals. Upon entry into your new school, you are to introduce yourself as Andrzej. Always use your proper Polish name."

"My proper name is Andrush. Ahn-droosh, not Ahn-dzray."

Jakub wanted to take a stick to him. "You will call me, sir, and not answer back. Andrush is an old-fashioned country name suited for a swineherd and doesn't command respect. Here, you are to wear this tomorrow to make a good impression on your teachers."

He peered into the bag. "Aw, no!"

"You are to do as I say, or you might be leaving on the next train."

"Yes, sir."

In the morning, Andrush stood scowling in front of the mirror. "I refuse to wear this, Mishka. I will be the laughingstock of the whole school."

"I think you look adorable. If they laugh, laugh with them and say you are in a play after school. Make something up, or go into the lavatory and rip it, then you might be sent home to change. We will get back at Papa for this, don't you worry."

"Yeah, let's do that," he agreed. Mishka was an angel who understood his pain, hadn't laughed at him, and his heart swelled with love. He would do whatever it took to live in the same house with her. So off he went, dressed like Little Lord Fauntleroy in an ill-fitting suit with a red bow tie, cursing her demon of a father under his breath and thinking up ways to get even with him.

Chapter 9

Nearly two years later, Jakub began to see that Andrush was far from the prodigy he hoped for. School reports touched upon below-average grades and excessive daydreaming, and the most inexcusable comment was "the student is quick to anger and aggressive."

"Unacceptable!" he ranted. "I knew I made a mistake taking him on, Malka. He's got dough for brains. Go tell him to pack his bags."

"I will do no such thing. Ease up on him; he's going through puberty."

Jakub stroked his chin. "Puberty, you say? Then we can't risk letting him near Maritza. He leaves tomorrow."

"If anyone is going out of this house, it will be you." Malka stood firm.

Some of the boy's teachers at the academy were clients at the bank, and Jakub worried they might gossip to his colleagues and besmirch the good name of Laska. He thought of a solution to the problem Andrush had created with his substandard school performance. The best place for the pubescent lad would be a vocational school where he would learn the three M's: machinery, mathematics, and mechanics. This turned out to be an excellent choice; Andrush thrived at the new school, and Jakub no longer had to worry about any loss of status in the community.

Maritza entered her teens and blossomed into an elegant, poised young lady with the sharp wit of her mother and grandmother. Andrush was her best friend, confidant, and protector. He took her to school and made mad dashes to his own classes and back in time to escort her home at the end of the day. On weekends, they went alone to the cinema, zoo, parks, and museums. His arm was always around her wherever they went, and when young men dared to glance at her, Andrush made the *I am watching you* hand signal or raised his fist. If he left her side for a minute to bring refreshments at an after-school gathering, heaven help the poor sap who came within a yard of her.

Maritza didn't see his behavior as proprietary; she didn't see it at all. They were in love—an all-consuming adolescent intimacy. Andrush didn't care what people thought of him, couldn't be concerned with niceties, and nothing embarrassed him, although he was on his best behavior in front of Malka, Jakub, and the Pustilniks. Nothing could be worse than being ordered back to Wyszków and separated from Mishka, so he tolerated Jakub's disparaging remarks, which came regardless of his good conduct.

In early July of '38, when Maritza turned fifteen and Andrush was eighteen, he gave her a ring handwoven from silver wire, and they secretly became engaged. "Your father will never give us permission to marry. He can't stand me and will throw me out on my ear if he finds out our intentions. We wait until next year when you finish school. I will have saved enough money to take care of you, and he won't be able to do anything about it. At least we will have the support of your mother and Rivka. *They* love me, but for now we keep our plans to ourselves."

"You know best," she said. She took anything he said as absolute truth.

The grocery bill had tripled, and Jakub saw that the tall, lanky boy-man would soon eat him out of house and home. "Where's it all going, Malka? Are you giving food away to the poor again, or does Vorobiev eat in his sleep? With all the quality nourishment he's getting, you'd think he'd have to pay someone to hold his head up for him."

"Jakub, stop complaining. I can't take much more of it."

A few days later, as they were getting ready for bed, he said, "I don't see why I should continue to support Vorobiev. He's finished with school, and there's no reason for him to be here. Have you seen how he's all over Maritza? He has a perverse obsession with her, and that slimy snake he has coiled up in his pants isn't going to stay quiet for long."

If that oversexed donkey took liberties and got Maritza pregnant, she would have to be sent away to a home in the countryside and give the baby up for adoption. Jakub would have him arrested for rape, and if anyone found out, the Laskas would be lambasted as the worst parents in Warsaw for failing to maintain adequate security. "Fifteen-year-old girls should be attending little parties and dances with suitable boys from fine families, not him. They need to be separated. He's a negative influence."

"Stop being dramatic," Malka said. "Be glad Andrush chaperones her. Would you prefer to do it? You would be tearing out your hair, if you had more of it."

"He's unpredictable. I can see the wheels moving in his head, and I fear one day he might take Maritza and run."

She slammed the dresser drawer shut. "You talk about him as if he's a bad seed. He's a wonderful young man, and I wouldn't be surprised if they married someday. It's not unusual for second cousins—Mama and Papa did. He will be starting work in a few weeks, and machinists are in high demand and make good money. He will be able to provide well for our girl."

"What did you say?"

"You heard me."

"Never! He's a threat to the stability of our lives and must go."

"Don't you dare say a word to him. That will break Maritza's heart, and they just might run off to live with the Vorobievs."

Jakub lay back on the pillow and groaned. "Then I will have him arrested for kidnapping. Bring me a bromide. I'm ill."

The next morning, alone in the kitchen with Andrush, Jakub circled the table with his arms crossed. "The time has come for you to be with your people."

"I am with my people," he replied unfazed, and served himself another hefty portion of scrambled eggs.

"I'm talking about your parents in Wyszków. You know, they must be eager to see the type of man you've become. Go back and show them."

"I will see them in a couple of weeks in the summer, as always."

"Good, then you can remain there or go where you like, but you are no longer welcome here."

Andrush gulped and set his fork down. "Why?"

"Don't look so surprised. Maritza is the reason for your presence here. I know what you're after. I have watched you follow her around with your tongue hanging out. I should have sent you back long ago to the wilds from whence you came, but my wife wouldn't let me. As long as I'm alive, you will never gain intimate access to my daughter."

Andrush's fury flamed. His mouth twisted and his hands curled into fists under the table. He had no interest in the things Jakub was saying about his motives for being in Warsaw. The plans he and Mishka made for their future would come to naught if he wasn't able to save a year's worth of earnings before they married, and jobs in Wyszków didn't pay well.

Jakub checked the wall calendar. "Come August fifteenth, you're out."

Andrush's mind went blank; he couldn't find a solution in the moment, but then he recalled Malka's suggestion for dealing with

Jakub when he became difficult—pretending to agree with him, then outsmarting him. The way she manipulated him was masterful, though grueling. An arsenal of mental tools had to be employed to change Jakub's thinking, but Andrush sensed that no gamesmanship or trickery would work now. He would have to make an appeal from an honest place in his heart, yet having to let this sour pickle of a man who barely came up to his chin see into the depths of his soul, a place accessible only to Mishka, went against his grain.

"Did you hear what I said?"

"Jakub, sir, I was hoping you would let me stay another year so I could save enough money to move out on my own. I have to work for three years in the apprentice program at the munitions factory across the river before I can get my diploma, and I already signed up. It's what I've been training for and what you paid good money for."

"One month."

"Yes, sir. I will do as you say." He put his plate in the sink and ran out the door.

Ah, that went well, Jakub thought, and strutting like a peacock, he went down to hail a cab.

When Malka heard that Andrush was planning to live with Rivka and Gersh in the Quarter, she railed at Jakub, "He stays and you go!"

"You know I can divorce you for this?"

"Go ahead. At least I won't have to put up with your antics."

"You win this round, but your luck won't hold." He shook his fist at her.

"Go and tell him that he can stay."

Andrush was lying on his bed, waiting for Maritza to finish her piano lesson, when Jakub barged in. "You can stay for the year, then I want you the hell out. Meanwhile, I will watch you like a hawk. If you lay one finger on Maritza, I will have you locked up. Furthermore, I am going to open a savings account for you at the bank and deposits are to be made regularly."

"Yes, sir. Thank you."

It would take a good deal of travel time to get to that factory across the Vistula River and back each day, and that meant less time for Vorobiev to spend with Maritza. If he stepped over any line, he would be cleaning toilets in prison or ricking hay in Wyszków for the rest of his life.

Chapter 10

Almost a year later, in the spring of '39, the directors of Jakub's bank held a meeting and told of a partial Polish troop mobilization and reservist call-up in response to tensions with Germany. He didn't share his associates' concerns, believing the threats to be nothing more than bluster. "Hitler is all smoke and no fire," he stated, as if he had insider information.

"You would do well to rethink your stance, Laska," the bank's top brass said. "It is our shared belief that where there is smoke, there is fire."

Jakub's stance remained the same, and thus the directors didn't include him in their emergency plans. In August, Andrush learned from his friends and coworkers at the factory where he'd been working that recruiting bureaus had been set up to train saboteurs to thwart the Germans' expected attack. Civilians would be taught to use weapons and military tactics to carry out raids and ambushes.

A skilled marksman, thanks to the diligent early woodsman training provided by his father, he was an excellent candidate and had been attending meetings. On Tuesday, August 29, he called a family conference and assembled everyone around the dining table.

"What is this about, Andrush?" Jakub asked. "Can it be that you have gathered us to give notice of your departure?"

"Not quite. I have it on good authority that it's almost certain Germany will attack us and there will be war."

"Whose good authority? And there is no such thing as *almost certain*. You are either certain or not. When is soon? Tonight, tomorrow, next month? I paid all that money for your education, and you still can't get it right."

"The signs are there, and it will happen sooner rather than later."

"It's all bombast, I tell you," said Jakub, rolling up his sleeves. "This meeting is a waste of time, and your year is almost up. Malka, is there any cake?"

"Cake now? Get it yourself or wait until later."

"Go on, Andrush," said Gersh.

"I guess we should wait for him." Andrush nodded at Jakub's departing figure and went to stand behind Maritza, who looked back at him adoringly.

Jakub returned, juggling a box from one of the city's premier bakeries, a plate, an overspilling glass of milk, and set them on the table. He lopped off a large piece with his fork and dug in. "Mmm, that frosting. So rich."

"You should choke on it," Rivka muttered in Yiddish. She had long ceased to be afraid of him or his arbitrary rules.

"How do you know there will be war?" Malka asked.

"We've all heard the threats Hitler has been making. The meetings I've been attending are made up of men who want to help defend the homeland but don't want to be under the yoke of the military. There are intelligence officers, men who have been in Germany and have seen the troops and equipment being readied, and others who have analyzed Hitler's speeches. Poles and Jews alike, women, and even young people want to do their part. We have to anticipate and prepare for the worst. The Germans have ten times as many tanks, thousands of planes, and huge guns. We have horses, a couple hundred planes, rifles and sabres. We may be strong in spirit, but that won't mean a thing in the long run," Andrush said.

"What?" Jakub yelped. "You've been attending political meetings while living in this house?"

Gersh moved his chair closer to the table. "What should we do, son?"

"The first consideration is that we will need cash. Jakub, can you withdraw as much money as possible from the bank tomorrow? People will want to keep their money under their mattresses now; you know, have it close at hand."

"Just give my hard-earned money to you? Who the hell do you think you are?"

"I didn't say you should give it to me. I asked if you could take it *out*," Andrush said through clenched teeth. He wasn't going to walk on eggshells around this choleric grouser anymore, not when the Germans were massing an astronomical number of troops along the seventeen hundred mile border they shared with Poland.

"Andrush, will the Germans bomb us or just come into the city?" Maritza asked. "And what will happen if they do? Do you think they are trying to scare us like Papa says?"

"What are you asking him for?" Jakub snapped. "When did he get his prophet's license?"

"Stop insulting him," Malka said. "He's trying to help."

"Now see here. He has no authority in this family."

Andrush ignored him. "They will probably do both. That's what we've been told. Any attack would be made here in the capital first, and if the city falls, we will be under German rule. Maybe Hitler hopes to scare us into giving in to his demands, but we won't, and the whole thing will begin again. They wouldn't have started assembling all those troops near our borders if they didn't mean business."

"There are troops at our borders?" Malka paled. "What should we do?"

"We take the train to Wyszków in a few days," Andrush said. "We will be safer there."

A buzz of surprised voices went around the table. *Wyszków? We just came from there.* Then everyone quieted while trying to come to terms with the interruption to their comfortable lives. Getting out of Warsaw was a must. From the intelligence gathered so far that had been shared with members of his group, thousands of people would die once the Germans attacked. It was too late to flee to another country; the family did not have the proper documents and couldn't get them on such short notice. Russia was out of the question. Any man could be conscripted in a minute, and Andrush hated the Reds almost as much as he did the Germans.

"We can take one bag each. Aunt Rivka, Uncle Gersh, pack your medicines."

"We get to Wyszków, then what?" asked Jakub. "If the Germans attack here, they can attack anywhere. Are we going to caravan from town to town like Gypsies?"

"We can go to my aunt's house in the country. She lives in a little village north of Wyszków, a few hours by wagon. It's not even on the map—the Germans would have a hard time finding it. If we're under attack, we won't have much choice about where to go. There's a large attic and barn. The women can sleep in one place and the men in another. My father and I can make some modifications to accommodate us all. We sacrifice luxury for our lives. At least you won't go hungry. Fresh vegetables, milk right from the cow, home-made cheese, and bread baked daily. Everyone can pitch in and help."

Jakub's jaw dropped, and his eyes looked magnified and lemur-like behind the lenses of his glasses. "Two hours in a wagon? You must be mad," he sputtered, his hands going to the small of his back in anticipation of the pain he would feel from riding in a crude conveyance. "Me, in a barn, sleeping in the filth of animals? You expect me to drink milk straight from the udder with hairs floating around? You need your head examined."

He wouldn't go to Wyszków and certainly not to some babushka's hut under any circumstances, having seen those primitive dwellings when he and his parents drove out into the countryside east of Warsaw to break in their new roadster one summer. Now this provincial idiot was suggesting that he, a person of high standing, toil in fields, hunker down in a barn, and spend weeks, months, or years on top of the foul-smelling Vorobievs and share an outhouse with them. Never.

"It seems you have turned my family into a flock of frightened sheep," Jakub said, "but I'm staying. They will need me at the bank, and I refuse to walk away from everything I've worked so hard for. I will stay and defend my home."

"I can't believe what I'm hearing," Andrush yelled. "You refuse to leave your things and your work, but you'll abandon your family? And what are you going to defend your home with, a fly swatter?"

"Why, you impertinent buffoon! How dare you speak to me that way? Our army will never let the Germans get anywhere near the city, but criminals might loot the homes of those cowardly citizens who ran away in fear. This very building could be targeted, and I will be here to intercept any burglars." Whether he was truly ignorant of the possibility of a German attack or whether his ability to reason was simply constrained by arrogance was anyone's guess.

"I will give you the funds for my family, but you had better use it sparingly. I want an accounting of expenditures, and use your own money first. When you see that this nonsense you've gone on about turns out to be hot air, you are to return my family and funds to this house without delay."

"Yes, sir," Andrush said, and wondered how an educated man could be so stupid. The Germans were waiting like horses in the gates for the *Go*, and this fool was demanding financial records be kept. That was not going to happen.

Chapter 11

Thursday, August 31. "Are you ready, Mishka?" Andrush folded his birth and baptismal certificates into his pack.

"Yes. How do I look?" she asked, adjusting the collar of her floral dress. "I was going to wear white, but I thought I looked too much like a nurse."

"You are ravishing," he said, kissing her. The future was uncertain, and they wanted to marry right away. "You know we won't be able to sleep together when we join the others. We will have to keep our secret until things settle down."

"I'm well aware of that."

"Let's go. We have a lot to do."

Malka and her parents had taken the early train to Wyszków that morning. Andrush told them there were loose ends to be tied, and he and Maritza would follow in a day or so. As soon as Jakub left for work, they went down to find a cab. They wanted to marry in the civil registry office but were told it required a future appointment and parental permission for her. They searched for an obliging priest or a rabbi only to find there were too many religious requirements to be satisfied, and time was running out.

At last, they found a young priest willing to perform the ceremony without a baptismal certificate for Maritza, given the fragile political situation. A man and his wife were brought in off the street to act as witnesses, and after prayers and vows, the beaming couple headed straight home to consummate their marriage. Behind the safety of Andrush's locked door, the two virgins fell upon each other with im-

petuous passion. Nothing, not even an impending war could cloud
the rapture of those moments. Afterward, as they lay in each other's arms, he whispered, "No one will ever love you as much as I do.
You're mine, and we are bound together forever."

These were exhilarating words to the ears of a sixteen-year-old.
"You're the only man I will ever love, and I am yours until the day I
die," she said.

At the break of dawn the following morning, Friday, September
1, the three inside the Laska apartment were awakened by the
sound of air raid sirens. They sprang from their beds and turned on
the radio. "The German army and air force have unexpectedly invaded Polish territory without a declaration of hostilities and have attacked a number of towns all over Poland, and German airmen have
bombed. Casualties have been reported among our civilian population. The bombing continues."

When the *all clear* was announced, Jakub went back to his room
to dress for work, ignoring Andrush's mocking eyes and telling himself the German attack did not mean Armageddon was near. He
stopped at a kiosk for the morning paper before flagging a cab, but
there was nothing about an attack. Except for the distant sounds of
antiaircraft guns firing and a column of smoke rising somewhere to
the north, the city appeared to him the same as it always did. This
was merely an incursion that the illustrious Polish army would put
an end to.

Outside the bank, depositors waited in long lines to enter, while
inside, Jakub was called upon to assist the tellers—a humiliating task.
Having agreed to provide funds for the family, he withdrew a large
amount of savings, though it rankled him to give it to Vorobiev. He
would hold him accountable for every *zloty*.

Later that afternoon, German bombers, unable to effectively hit Warsaw's military facilities due to heavy cloud cover, unleashed their loads on the city, killing dozens of civilians before flying back to base, and on Saturday, the Luftwaffe conducted several raids over Warsaw. The radio instructed citizens to stay indoors and await further news.

Andrush scoffed at reports that the Polish army was beating the enemy. "Once they use up their limited weapons and equipment, they will surrender. We've got to get to Wyszków so I can discuss the next steps with my father. We leave first thing tomorrow."

Sunday morning radio reported that Britain and France had declared war on Germany. "When do you think they will come in and help our army fight the Germans?" asked Maritza.

"Don't expect to see their boots on the ground for a long time," he said. "They'll help us from the air, maybe from the sea, but Germany's a force to be reckoned with. Right now, I'm going out to find someone to drive us."

"Drive us? Who would want to take that risk?" she asked, surprised that anyone would be so foolish.

He pulled a wad of zloty from his pocket. "Money has a way of changing stubborn minds."

She went to the window and saw black smoke in the distance and people rushing about on the street. Jakub shuffled in from his study in his robe and slippers.

"Look at all the smoke, Papa. Please come with us now."

"We are fighting valiantly, and those flying pirates will be stopped."

"Don't hold your breath."

"Vorobiev is poisoning you with his boorishness. You're beginning to sound exactly like him. I am going to follow my plan. We can't risk having looters sweep in to ransack and rob us of our worldly goods."

Soon, Andrush returned and went directly to his room. He emerged with two pistols and handed one to Jakub, who jumped back in horror. "Get that thing away from me!"

"Take it. Don't be a fool."

"You've been storing weapons in my home? Get out of here. You're worse than I thought."

"Come, Mishka. I managed to find a driver." He stuffed one pistol into his waistband and the other into his bag, along with a box of bullets, and took her hand.

"Goodbye, Papa." She turned to look at her father, but he had already closed the door.

Over the course of the next few nights, unbeknownst to Jakub, administrators and officials would remove the bank's gold reserves from its vaults and, in a covert operation, consolidate them with gold from various Polish cities. The tons of reserves would then be transported out of the country for safekeeping by Polish officials and their compatriots.

Chapter 12

"Let's go," Andrush said to the burly driver. A stack of zloty, more than the man might earn in two months, had been needed to persuade him. They set off through the city, east across the bridge over the Vistula River onto the highway that led to Wyszków, and came upon a flight of people in vehicles, carts, and on foot heading in both directions. Their driver wasn't able to advance much behind the snarl. He banged the wheel and cursed until the traffic thinned out.

They arrived in town before noon. The family was beside themselves with worry over the reports of the bombings in Warsaw. Ola ran crying into her son's arms.

"Mama." He hugged her and kissed her forehead. "Where's Papa?"

"The reservists took him to dig ditches by the river, and he hasn't returned."

"I'm going to look for him."

"No!" She clutched his arm. "You mustn't go near there. They are pulling all the young men in to fight with them. If you go, they will take you at gunpoint."

Andrush dropped into a chair, held his head in his hands, and considered her warning. "And that's *our* army, forcing us against our will," he said.

Naftoly returned the next morning. The reservists told him victory was near, but Andrush didn't believe it. Holding off was not the same as achieving victory. Any successes were temporary at best. It had been quiet in town so far, though he thought everyone should go to Ola's sister, Bronislawa, who lived twenty-five miles north.

"What are you thinking?" Ola protested. "Papa can't go. The people will know by his accent that he's not a Pole, and they hate Russians. They might get his pants down and find out he was born a Jew. He hasn't gone there in all the years we've been married."

"Enough of this talk," said Naftoly. He didn't like being the focus of attention.

"Look at the size of him," Andrush laughed. "No one would be crazy enough to lay a hand on him, and he's as much a Pole as any man who loves this country no matter where he was born."

"Won't we be safe here?" asked Gersh. His face had gone from withered to cadaverous in a matter of days, with heavy red pouches beneath his eyes.

"From the way the Germans are bombing the country, Uncle, we won't be for long."

"What about aid from Britain and France now that they are in the war?" asked Malka.

"Operations take time to plan. I wish I had the answers. Right now, we are on our own."

He and his father went outside to talk. "Papa, our army's claims are overblown. They may be putting up a good show of force, but the Germans won't be defeated. They will take over, and we will be living under their rule *if* we survive."

"I don't know what to believe," Naftoly scratched his chin. "The soldiers said we should join up with them because when the Hit-lerites come, they will take all the able-bodied men they find and force them into work details."

"That may be true, but we aren't joining up with them. We have to take the family up north, then you and I will go to Warsaw, find our patriot brothers, and fight against the Huns in our own way."

"I don't want to leave your mother, and with all the extra mouths to feed, your cousin Bogdi will need help."

"That's a good idea, Papa. I just thought—"

"I'm going to grease the axles and get the wagon ready," Naftoly said abruptly. "It needs fixing." In his late fifties, he had no desire to roam through the towns and forests killing Germans, having seen enough violence and death in Russia and two decades prior in Wyszków during the Polish-Russian conflict to last the rest of his life.

Tired and frightened refugees from Warsaw streamed into town, looking for relatives and places to stay. Jakub didn't turn up. Malka knew in her heart he wasn't going to and wiped away a tear. They had been married for almost twenty years, and despite their differences, she loved him. The family listened to more news of their army's victory, but by nightfall, the reserve troops in Wyszków received their orders to retreat south, leaving the town undefended.

Chapter 13

War came to Wyszków on Tuesday, September 5. A group of German Stuka Ju-87 dive bombers, guided by maps showing the perimeters of Polish towns with sizable Jewish populations marked in red ink and *Juden* written alongside, flew overhead in the early morning skies.

Their bombs barreled down with wicked, ear-piercing whistling and exploded in the nearby streets with deafening roars. The earth quaked, fires sprang up, shutters dropped off windows, and whole panes blew out. Inside the Vorobievs' house, glassware and dishes flew from shelves and crashed to the floor. Andrush jumped from the couch to a table and onto the pullout bed to protect Maritza and Malka. Rivka and Gersh clutched each other in bed in another room.

"Don't move," ordered Naftoly, running in from his bedroom in long underwear and boots. Ola followed, ghostly in a billowing white nightgown. "Glass is all over the floor. Don't get up barefoot." He dumped an armload of shoes onto the bed, causing confusion as to whom they belonged.

The assault stopped suddenly, and an ominous silence followed. Everyone froze as if in a tableau and wondered if that was the beginning or end of the bombing. Andrush and Naftoly darted outside to find the sky black with smoke and the air filled with the acrid smell of burning. Pandemonium had broken out. People poured from their houses in nightclothes and ran aimlessly, unsure of where to go.

"Papa, get the horse and wagon now. She will be too hard to control if the bombing starts up. Hurry."

"It's not ready."

"Are the wheels on?"

"Yes, but—"

"Get it. We have to leave."

Naftoly ran to the barns behind the houses. Andrush sped back inside and threw on clothes. He helped everyone gather their belongings, strapped his knapsack on, and slung a rifle over his shoulder. "Take coats," he said. "The forest is cold at night."

Ola grabbed the packages of food, blankets, and her husband's clothes, then herded the group near the door to wait for him. Naftoly drove up, dressed hurriedly, and helped Malka and her parents on. The planes came into view, announcing their presence with drill-like buzzing.

"Get on!" Naftoly shouted. Just as Andrush was about to lift Maritza, the skittish mare reared up. Naftoly pulled the reins back, but she shied and bolted into the road, the wagon careening behind her. Terrified people jumped out of the way to avoid being trampled.

A neighbor holding a cellar door hollered at Andrush and Maritza, "In here, fast." They rushed down rickety stairs into a dank space where a small group of people and children in various states of undress sat packed together. The hatch fell into place, plunging them into darkness.

"Let me out!" a woman screamed. "We'll be trapped here."

"Be quiet and sit down. You're frightening the children. We're safe here," the man said.

A pilot spied a mass of people running toward the bridge over the Bug River and sent his plane into a dive, the wind-driven terror sirens mounted on the undercarriage screeching the way. Straightening out, he released his bombs from six hundred feet. Bang on target—direct hits on the road. Stones and earth and body parts flew up in the air, and the fires from the explosions swallowed everything around in smoke and flame.

In the cellar, the blast shook the walls, dirt fell through the seams in the hatch, and the floor swayed. Maritza buried her face in Andrush's neck. The same woman gave in to hysteria, setting the children off in a wailing chain. "Hear what you've done," someone said.

"How long have we been here?" another asked.

"Not long."

"Can't we open the door a tiny bit to get some air?"

"Not yet," answered the man whose cellar it was.

"Please, I can't breathe."

"Nor can I."

"I said no! There may be more bombs, and it's too risky. We wait a little longer, and I will go out and check."

"Is anyone wearing a watch?"

"It's too dark in here. We can't see the time."

"How about I light a match?"

"No," Andrush said loudly. "Do not. It will suck up the oxygen. There's little enough as it is. Everyone shut up and keep calm."

The air inside the cellar had turned suffocating. The crying and complaints died into murmurs, and as people became woozy, the sounds were of labored breathing, then snoring. *Bam!* A man with burns on his face banged on the door. Everyone jumped. "Come out, they're gone."

The people climbed out, opened their mouths to breathe, and quickly closed them. The sky was heavy with smoke. Ash swirled, covering the ground like apocalyptic snow. Andrush led Maritza into his parents' house to drink from a bucket of water kept at the ready.

"We have to go and find them, Mishka," he said, his voice thick. She nodded. He grabbed undershirts from a drawer and dipped them into the water. They tied them over their mouths and noses and took off down the street in the direction Naftoly had gone. The wood houses near the entrance to the bridge had gone up like tinder. Andrush brought her to a house away from the damage and sat her on the steps. "Stay here while I check." He prayed Naftoly made it to safety.

People with scarves tied over their faces leaving their eyes visible were in the process of covering the dead with sheets and blankets and moving the injured. Breathing in air from the wet shirt, Andrush picked his way around, the heat stinging his eyes and singeing his brows.

He saw the charred remains of his father's wagon and the horse lying on its side, a bone protruding from its foreleg, its coat a patchwork of blackened and raw flesh. Thinking he heard it moan, he fired a shot from his pistol into the animal's neck before realizing the sound had come from his own mouth. The family's bodies lay scattered about, burned, limbs twisted at impossible angles. Ola's arm, blown off in the blast, hung by its bloody sleeve from a branch of a tree that miraculously remained standing.

Andrush fell to his knees, his cries of anguish reaching Maritza. She ran into the road, and seeing him that way, let out a chilling scream.

"They're back," someone shouted. Planes dropped from the clouds. Andrush charged up and threw himself on top of her, driving the air from her lungs. Down swooped the Stukas, one after the other, their machine gunners strafing anything that moved.

Maritza whimpered underneath him as the sounds of shooting, yelling, and dying filled her ears. A searing heat flashed at her side. "I'm hit," she cried.

Andrush rolled off to examine her, sweat dripping from his face. "No, no, you're not hit. The bullets went through the bottom of your coat."

People ran, falling over each other in their haste to reach the bridge and the forest beyond. The Stukas followed the exodus and continued firing, leaving a trail of dead and injured across the bridge. Those who made it to the other side fled into the forest, passing overturned wagons and dodging racing horses. Throngs of people rushed about the trees in a maelstrom of confusion. Desperate parents called for their missing family members, lost children howled. The firing became fiercer, shearing the tops off the conifers and forcing the horde to surge further in. Having wreaked havoc, the planes flew away.

"We have to go now, Mishka, before they come back." Andrush pulled her to her feet. She stood, but her legs gave out. "You've got to walk. Lean on me."

Maritza struggled to make her sluggish legs work. Leaving town, they headed north into another forest. She plodded along, a zombie with vacant eyes, holding tight to Andrush's hand.

Chapter 14

The twice-widowed Bronislawa, or Bronka for short, lived with her nineteen-year-old son and daughter, thirteen, in an unnamed hamlet of forty people and six houses, ringed by forest and accessible by a dirt road just wide enough to accommodate a wagon. The first dwelling one encountered upon entering the village was hers, a lopsided log structure with a thatched roof.

Andrush had been there a few times with his mother in the years before he went to live in Warsaw, and thanks to his keen sense of direction, was able to remember the way. He and Maritza walked for several hours at the edges of unpaved, narrow roads bordered by skinny birches and tall pines. "I can't go on," she said, her feet swollen and her throat burning from thirst.

"There's thicker woods ahead. We can sleep and finish the journey tomorrow." Andrush passed her the last sip of water from a flask, and they walked on until he found a suitable spot. They fell asleep in each other's arms.

Bronka, an ox of a woman who never tired, was in her yard unpinning laundry from a line and admiring the sunset. The sky was streaked with scarlet, and the air filled with the sweet perfume of recently harvested apples nestling in baskets under the nearby tree. Seeing the bedraggled couple coming up the path, she stopped what she was doing and stood with arms akimbo. "Who are you, and what do you want?"

"Auntie, it's Andrush, Ola's son. I've come from Wyszków with my wife."

Bronka gasped at the tall young man, his face and clothing smudged with dirt, and cried, "Andrush, praise the Lord! I never would have known you." She kissed him on both cheeks and glanced at Maritza. "She is your wife?"

"Yes, Mishka, my wife."

"Why, she's just a girl, barely weaned from her mother's breast," Bronka exclaimed. "Hello, dearie."

"Pani," Maritza murmured, not lifting her eyes. Pani was the title for a married woman or widow, and she had to be respectful.

"You look famished. Come inside."

They followed Bronka inside to a neat kitchen. The smell of boiled eggs and cabbage made Maritza nauseous. The room seemed smaller, but everything was just as Andrush remembered: its white-washed log walls decorated with images of the saints, a Russian-style brick stove used for cooking and heating, a narrow bed in the corner, a wood table and chairs beneath the window, the hearth on one wall, and an open closet full of jars and crockery. There was a small bedroom off the kitchen and a ladder that led to an attic loft.

"Krysta, this is your cousin, Andrush, and his wife, Mishka."

The rosy-cheeked girl slicing bread at the table put down the knife and wiped her hands on her apron. "Welcome," she said shyly.

"You're all grown up, Krysta. You were a baby last time I saw you."

She blushed to the roots of her hair.

Bronka peered into Maritza's face. "Is she ill, Andrush? She's as white as the walls."

"She isn't well," he said. "Can we have some water, please?"

Krysta poured water from a jug into cups, and they drank it down.

"How are my dear sister and her husband? It's been too long."

Andrush bowed his head. "We need to talk, Auntie." He steered her into the bedroom.

"Krysta, attend to Mishka," Bronka called over her shoulder.

Her son, Bogdi, came in, his blonde hair lank and face red after evening chores, and stood stock-still. The trembling girl clutching the table with both hands was the most beautiful he'd ever seen, despite her untidy appearance. He looked at his sister.

"Cousin Andrush is here. That's Mishka, his wife," she said. "He's in the bedroom talking to Mama. Something happened."

Bogdi continued to stare at Maritza, who didn't acknowledge him. "Why don't you sit?" he asked, pulling out a chair. He saw her sway and caught her as she passed out.

"Mama!" Krysta yelled.

Andrush and his aunt emerged, their faces stained with tears. He took one look at Mishka in his cousin's arms and said gruffly, "Give her to me."

"Take her into the bedroom," commanded Bronka.

He laid her on the bed and took off her coat and shoes. "Mishka, Mishka," he cried, trying to rouse her, his face creasing with worry.

"Leave her. She's worn out and needs to rest. Krysta and I will take care of her," Bronka said, covering her with a blanket.

They went back into the kitchen. Andrush glanced at his reedy cousin. "You're not a kid anymore."

"That's right."

"Sit and eat, then you can sleep in the attic, Andrush. There are a couple of mattresses and blankets up there." Bronka pushed bread, cheese, and a cup of homemade spirits toward him, then told her son and daughter about the massacre in Wyszków. Krysta sobbed and crossed herself.

"I heard the Germans are in Różan now, and the Jews ran off to Goworowo," said Bogdi.

"Then the Huns will be here in no time." Andrush was so tired that he couldn't comprehend having to run from them so soon.

"There are no Jews here, so the Germans will not come," Bronka said.

"What are you talking about? They'd have to come in order to know that."

"You think they don't already know that? We are not worth their time. They will go in pursuit of the Jews."

Andrush stopped chewing and stared at his aunt. *Nazi bastards.* He downed the rest of the spirits, laid his head over his arms on the table, and dropped into sleep.

"He can't make it up the ladder in his condition," Bronka said. "Let him rest next to his wife tonight. Help me get him into the bedroom, son. Krysta and I will sleep in the attic."

By late afternoon on Friday, September 8, von Reichenau's advance units and tanks were in Warsaw's outer suburbs, southwest of the Laska residence. Jakub saw civilians digging ditches and building barriers, and with the Polish garrison protecting the city, he was confident that Hitler would call his stooges home and end the madness.

He'd eaten all the food Malka left him, and after rooting through the cupboards and finding a couple of packages of raw beans, he began to panic. Now he would have to go out for food. The neighborhood restaurants were closed, and the lines for the grocery stores wound around the blocks. "What are they selling inside?" he asked a woman leaving a store with a bag.

"Potatoes. They'll be out of carrots soon," she said.

"No cake or prepared foods? Fruit?"

"Are you kidding?"

Jakub hurried back to his building, his legs weak from the effort. Thoughts of Rivka's matzoh ball soup with chunks of tender chicken breast, her tangy stuffed cabbage rolls, and even Ola's pierogi made his stomach growl. If he left now, he might make it to Wyszków in time for dinner.

Motivated by hunger, he ran around the apartment, pulling out drawers and unearthing useless objects to take with him: his pipe collection, a miniature marble bust of Chopin, and an English book, *Napoleon at Waterloo.* His gaze rested on the velvet pouch that held his *tallit,* the prayer shawl worn on the occasion of his bar mitzvah. Removing it from the pouch where it had lain untouched for twenty-six years, he pressed it to his lips and tossed it back in. He brought out the rest of the zloty notes withdrawn from the bank, a list of his financial holdings, his shaving things, and threw everything into a suitcase.

Lugging the heavy case down the stairs, its contents jangling inside, he hastened to the street to find a cab. A group of frowning civilians watched in disgust as a company of Polish troops on horseback clopped and clattered by. "You are leaving? Where are you going?" they called out.

"We are regrouping in the east," an officer called back. "The garrison is still holding. You are in good hands."

Jakub blinked. Their revered army was retreating, and his blind faith crashed and burned. Incapable of decisive action under stress, he had misjudged the seriousness of the situation. There were no cabs in sight, and the only streetcars were those the army had overturned to block the Germans' access into the city.

"Why, those spineless fools," said a man standing next to him. "They're leaving us defenseless."

"Are the trains to Wyszków running?" Jakub asked.

"Wyszków? The Germans bombed it days ago."

He trudged back to the apartment. Shaking, he went into his study and collapsed into his chair. Wyszków bombed? Everyone gone? It can't be, he thought. For the first time in his life, tears streamed down his cheeks.

Jakub wanted his family back. Lovely Malka was the envy of all his friends, and his daughter, a perfect specimen of selective breeding. Did he ever tell them how much he loved them? He thought of Rivka, her stockings rolled down around thick ankles and the hideous ties she gave him each year for his birthday, bought in the *last chance* bins on the Quarter's sidewalks. She had always annoyed him to no end, but what a cook she was!

Old Gersh, with his scraggly white beard and Yiddish newspaper tucked under his arm—Jakub had been ashamed to walk with the Pustilniks in the street or dine with them in a restaurant—now he missed them. Even the oafish Vorobiev had *one* redeeming quality, but at the moment, he couldn't remember what it was.

He wondered if everyone made it to the aunt's house. Where was it? With an hour or two of rest, he'd be better able to think of a way to get there. Curling up on the soft mattress, he pulled the downy covers over himself and fell into a deep sleep. He didn't hear the warning sirens; a German bomber roared overhead, and mistaking its target, dropped its load on top of Jakub's building. The massive explosion resulted in an infernal blaze. A fire brigade of citizens with buckets of water attempted to douse the flames in a desperate effort, but soon gave up.

After the fires died down, people buried the human remains under mounds of dirt and topped them with wooden crosses. Later in the month, Jews and Poles ordered by Hitler's minions to clean the rubble from the streets for his upcoming visit and victory parade removed the contents of the makeshift graves and reburied them elsewhere.

Chapter 15

Hitler's various armies continued their blitzkrieg storm through the country. Third Army troops, accompanied by members of the SS death squads, came into Wyszków just before sunset on September 8. Knowing the exact layout, the Germans went straight to the center of town and shot the Jewish men found in the streets, identifiable by their long beards and black coats. They proceeded to the synagogue full of people observing the start of the Sabbath, locked the doors, and set the building on fire.

Afterward, Jews were removed from their homes and concentrated in the market square near the church, where the able-bodied men were taken away for manual labor and the rest shot. Women and children were let go and forced to make their way on foot east to Bialystok, then passed into the Soviet territories, where they later met a similar fate. The Germans, successful in their mission, looted the homes, piled their wagons high with valuables, goods, and linens, and torched the houses.

That same evening, Andrush was waiting for darkness to leave the village. With the Germans tearing through surrounding Jewish towns, it was safest to walk at night. He was eager to return to Wyszków to see what had become of the family's bodies.

"They must have been buried by those good Samaritans who stayed," Bronka said, "and can tell you where. Then you will come back?"

"I have to go to Warsaw to check on Mishka's father and meet up with people who are planning some things, then I will come back."

His desire to help rid Poland of the Nazi evil was an imperative, and he ached to join the fight.

Maritza hardly spoke and still had not shed tears over the tragedy. Bronka said it was a reaction to the most terrible loss a human being can experience: the murder of loved ones. "She's in shock, and the tears will come as she moves through her grief. We will take good care of her. Go and do what you must."

Andrush said his goodbyes and started the journey back to Wyszków. He kept to the wooded areas and did his grieving under the canopy of trees. His father, the kindest, most gentle man ever born, who had never raised his voice or a hand to him and convinced his wife to let their only child go off to Warsaw so he could be among relatives and have better opportunities, was gone forever. Sweet, unselfish Ola. Never again would he feel her kisses on his cheek or see the pride shine in her eyes the way it did when he came home each summer. The image of her arm dangling from the tree limb tormented him.

Malka, his second mother, had been the buffer between him and that overbearing, ill-tempered coward, Jakub. The warm and caring Pustilniks, his great-aunt and uncle, who stuffed him full of delicious food and told stories of his father as a boy in the Ukraine had given him unreserved affection. He could never forget what the Germans did.

September 10. At dawn, the sky was thick with smoke when Andrush arrived at the edge of the forest north of town. He heard rustling in the bushes ahead, saw a figure, and hid behind a tree. Drawing his pistol, he took aim. "Come out with your hands up, or I will blow your head off."

"Don't shoot!" A slender, dark-haired man emerged.

"Basz, you son of a bitch," Andrush said, sticking the gun back into his waistband. "You almost got yourself killed."

"So did you, Vorobiev." Moshe Basz, a childhood friend, opened his jacket to reveal his own pistol. "Are you coming or going?" he asked.

"Coming. I took my wife up north after our family was killed during the bombing. I came back to see about the bodies. I wasn't able to bury them because the bastards shot at us from the air. Why is the town still burning? More bombing?"

"Not after that first day. My mother and I stayed in our cellar until things settled down. Many of the Jews ran away, but some stayed. I helped load the bodies of the dead onto carts, and we buried them in one big grave by the forest." Moshe rubbed his wet, stinging eyes.

"My parents, did you—"

"So many corpses and missing limbs, Andrush. I couldn't look at their faces, and I haven't seen your parents in years. I'm sorry. The Germans came in on Friday at sundown and set the place on fire. Mama insisted I run and save myself. I've been hiding out here, trying to decide where to go."

"They came in?" Andrush's face blanched. "Are they still there?"

"I don't know, and I'm not going back to find out."

"Do you think your mother got away?"

"I'm sure she didn't. She was ill and couldn't walk without assistance. Poor Mama. She devoted her life to me, and I left her to die."

"She wanted you to survive, and you will."

"Maybe you remember her. She owned the bakery and used to give you and your little cousin cookies."

"I do," said Andrush. "She was a nice lady. I married my cousin the day before the invasion. She's sixteen now."

"She was so pretty. What are you going to do? Go back up north?"

"I need to get to Warsaw to check on my father-in-law and make contact with people planning to sabotage the Huns. Are you coming?"

"I'm in."

Andrush gave Moshe a drink from the flask of spirits Bronka had packed and the last crust of bread. They walked through the small villages within a few miles of Wyszków where Jews didn't live and bought food from farmers. The next morning, they met a group of Poles from town. One man had worked in the mill with Naftoly.

"We shot at them, then ran for our lives," he said. "They chased us with dogs, but we got away. Don't go back. There's nothing but char and ash, and the air is foul. The Huns can't breathe it. They're down by the river now."

"Fucking Germans," Moshe spat, his face black with hatred. "That's the air they deserve to breathe."

"Come with us to Warsaw," Andrush said. "We can get our hands on some real weapons and have our revenge."

The men shook their heads. "For now, we're going to find our families. Maybe we will see you in the forests."

Andrush and Moshe arrived a few nights later to find Warsaw under siege. The Poles were holding the Germans on the outskirts, though daily air attacks by the Luftwaffe continued to cause incredible devastation. Fires smoldered everywhere, and dense smoke poisoned the air with a sickening chemical smell. Horses lay dead in the streets, their flesh hacked off by groups of hungry people. It took hours before the young men were able to get near Jakub's street, as mountains of rubble rendered most of them impassable. Climbing through the fallen debris, Andrush looked around, confused. "The building's gone."

No one was around to provide any information until an old man emerged from the shadows. "Who are you looking for, son?"

"Jakub Laska, the banker. Did you know him?"

"No, the remains we found are buried there." He pointed to a long mound of dirt topped with small, wooden crosses at the edge where the building had stood. "Pieces of bodies, you understand." Muttering to himself, the man limped away.

Andrush sat down on a heap of concrete. "Jakub criticized every single thing I did," he told Moshe. "We clashed over everything. I heard him through the wall at night complaining about me to his wife and insulting my parents, yet he paid for my schooling, my clothes, my food. So many times I wished him dead, and now he is. God punished me by taking everyone."

"Open your eyes, man," Moshe said. "There is no God. I know you went to church when you were young, but what good are those teachings now? Your family died through no fault of yours."

The crackling, roar of incoming artillery shells fired from German guns west of the city jerked Andrush out of his preoccupation. "Let's find my people."

The Luftwaffe planes dominated the sky over Warsaw, their bombs blasting huge craters in the streets, destroying building after building. By mid-month, there was no food to buy, and the city established bread lines for more than half the population until those supplies were gone. The Poles fought fiercely, but against overwhelming odds. The Germans launched a relentless artillery and air bombardment that shattered the city. The escalating civilian death toll and lack of food, water, ammunition, and other necessities forced the Poles to surrender. On September 28, the brutal siege was over—Warsaw had fallen.

Chapter 16

L ife in Bronka's settlement revolved around home and small
communal fields where grain and vegetables were grown. Water
had to be drawn from a well, there was no electricity, and rain caused
the paths around the houses to become a quagmire. It was a primitive
place where nothing changed but the seasons, inhabited by women
and very old men—their hands and faces lined and roughened by
years of hard work—and a group of young adults who were born just
before or after their fathers had gone off to fight the Russians twenty
years earlier. Few fathers returned, leaving the village with a lack of
middle-aged men.

There was no school in the village. Bronka had lived in Różan
as a girl and attended school for a few years; she taught the youngsters to read, write, and do simple sums. There had once been a little
church, but it had burned down some years before and wasn't rebuilt.
On Sundays prior to the invasion, the people traveled ten miles by
wagon to church in Różan. They didn't dare go back now for fear the
Germans would take the young men away for forced labor and the
girls into servitude, so they prayed in their homes.

Bronka instructed Bogdi to take charge of Andrush's wife, have
her help him in the field, and show her how to care for the animals:
chickens, geese, a milk cow, a horse, and a couple of pigs, as Krysta
was needed to help preserve food for the coming winter. Maritza
would have liked to help in the kitchen, but unless it was to sweep
or tidy up, she was ordered away. With no cooking experience, her

attempts to prepare meals left much to be desired, and Bronka considered any wasting of food a sin.

Bogdi's attention fell on Mishka like a millstone dropped from on high. She had come unexpectedly, a beautiful white dove, bringing a sense of wonder and excitement to his life. Having her near and breathing her air ennobled him and made him rich. Her voice was a bell, and her smile was a tonic for an ailment he never knew he had. The villagers, though, had other ideas about the newcomer.

Maritza felt their disapproval the moment she was trotted out and introduced around by Bronka. The women recoiled from her, believing she had been sent by evil spirits to bewitch the young men. Bronka, who wielded the most power as head woman, reminded them that Pani Vorobieva was her nephew's wife, the daughter-in-law of dear, departed Ola, and should be treated with respect regardless of her young age.

"Still your wagging tongues and pray away your bitter jealousies," she admonished. Having suffered a tragic loss, the girl needed kindness and affection.

The maidens who had designs on Bogdi, the most attractive of the few eligible bachelors, were angry that he had lost interest in them and were standoffish and cold to Mishka; her perfect posture, compelling beauty, and refined accent were sharp reminders of their lower station in life.

Bogdi didn't want the delicate white hands Mishka stroked him with in his dreams to get dirty in the field. He allowed her to hold open the sack into which *he* harvested and threw the potatoes while the girls and women worked nearby, stooping, digging, and sweating over their own sacks and casting hateful looks at her. He treated her like a rare flower, and when the sun got too hot or the air too cold, he would say, "That's enough for you for today."

"Let me do more," she begged. "I need to keep busy."

On a mild mid-September morning, Bogdi and the men had just taken the girls and women into the forest to pick mushrooms. Bronka was alone in the house baking bread when a German motorcycle came racing up the path while an army truck waited some distance down the unpaved road. The motorcycle, driven by a soldier and carrying an officer in the sidecar, came to a stop outside the house.

Bronka wasn't afraid. If they meant to burn the place down, the Huns would be swarming the village with gasoline cans and flamethrowers. They knocked, and she answered. *"Bitte! Guten Morgen, meine Herren,"* she said pleasantly, speaking the little German she knew. She curtsied and made a motion with her hand that they should come inside. "A drink of cider and some fresh bread?"

"No, thank you," the officer said. "We are in a great hurry. We are looking for Jewish fugitives. Do any Jews live in this village?"

"Not one."

"Have any come through here?"

"No. If any were to come, they'd be driven off with pitchforks." She meant every word.

"Sehr gut." Very good. "I praise your steadfastness."

"Danke, mein Herr." Bronka bowed her head in recognition of the compliment.

The officer clicked his heels, followed by the soldier. They got back aboard the motorcycle and rode off in the direction from which they had come. They had been extremely polite; had taken her at her word, and Bronka saw no need to alarm the others. She felt certain that the Germans wouldn't be back.

Andrush returned late in the month, happy to hear his aunt's report that Mishka had improved. He dreaded having to tell her about the destruction of Wyszków and Jakub's certain death, fearing the news would cause a setback.

"Tell her, then you both must pray," Bronka advised, nodding towards the plaster statue of the Virgin Mary presiding over the room from her perch above the hearth. "Her faith has wavered."

Maritza spent enough time at church in Wyszków with Andrush during the summers to know what to do if Bronka insisted, but she didn't feel like praying. She didn't cry when he told her about Wyszków and her father; she had papered over the hole where her heart used to be. "I'm not surprised," she said. "The Germans went back to finish off the job they started so they could have an official tally to show Headmaster Hitler, and Papa never wanted to listen to reason. He thought he knew everything. We heard the Russians have taken the eastern part of the country, and the dividing line is less than thirty miles away. Do you think they will come here?"

"The Russkis made an agreement with Hitler, and that territory belongs to them now, so they have no reason to. Both sides got what they wanted." He didn't tell her about the persecution that began once the Red Army marched in or the Germans' slaughter of Jews in the nearby towns. "I want you to keep this pistol," he said, removing it from his pack. "You know how to use it—all those summers I made you practice hitting targets on trees. I taught you well."

He wouldn't let her do anything but light women's work, wanting her to be rested for him at night. The time shot by. "You're still too thin," he said before he left. "Promise me that you will eat more. You have to keep up your strength. Do you want to make me a widower at a young age?"

"Stay a little longer, and I will eat until bursting."

Her imploring little face filled him with sadness, but it would be disgraceful to stay cloistered in the village, eating well and enjoying sex every night, while others risked their lives preparing to take up arms against the Nazi invaders, always hungry and living under deplorable conditions. It was a concept so foreign and inconceivable to him that a man should shirk his obligation when physically able. "I have to do this, Mishka. We can't let the bastards get away with what they did and are doing."

"I know you have to do this, but they have already gotten away with it," she said with a petulant droop of lip, "and you can't stop them all. How long can this go on?"

"For however long it takes, and it will take a long time because we are too few."

Andrush pulled the sheet across the line that served as a makeshift door to the attic and kissed her until their passion rose. With Bronka and Krysta in the kitchen below, they had to be quiet, no easy feat for Maritza. Even so, his aunt and cousins got an earful. At night, from his bed in the kitchen, when Bogdi heard a sound of lovemaking coming from the attic, the usually steady young man stuffed wool in his ears and burned with jealous anger, an emotion he had never felt before. He secretly hoped his cousin would be captured and presumed dead, and Mishka would become his wife. These were ungodly thoughts, and he tried to fight them.

Bogdi's future had been decided from the moment of birth. He was expected to marry young and have as many children as God saw fit to grant. Marriage for peasant farmers in the villages was mainly an economic venture. A wife was chosen and valued for the work she could do. When the time came, he would pick the girl he *liked* the best, one who would serve him well, for then he knew nothing of love. Since the advent of Mishka, the thought of marrying any of the girls he had known since childhood was repugnant, and when Bronka reminded him the time was ripe for choosing a wife, he silenced her with a sharp look.

After Andrush left, Bogdi resumed his careful watch over Mishka. Serious and stiff and slow to laugh, his gray eyes always unreadable, she tried to get him to talk by asking questions requiring more than a yes or no answer, hoping for some reaction. Unaccustomed to inhibited men, Maritza wanted a back and forth, some good-natured banter, but Bogdi focused on the task at hand. Working together gave him the chance to be near her, but idle chatter was dangerous. He might slip and give himself away. His love was one-sided, and if she found out, the shame would be unbearable.

Maritza wondered about Bogdi's lack of opinions, given his ability to read and write and the intelligence he displayed in his domain. She wanted to shake him, unaware he was undergoing a radical inner transformation, and not perceiving that once the cork was out of the bottle, the jinni wasn't going back inside.

Chapter 17

The Nazis swept through Poland, rounding up Jews and forcing them into ghettos, killing Poles, expelling them from their villages, or conscripting them for forced labor. Between March and July 1940, they invaded Denmark, Norway, France, Belgium, Luxembourg, and the Netherlands, and their U-boats went on a rampage in the Atlantic, attacking merchant ships.

In secret hideouts that changed often, Andrush, Moshe, and members of their assault group led by a former Polish army officer, were given instruction in attack strategies and went into the countryside to perfect the skills of grenade throwing, preparing explosives, demolition work, and unarmed combat. Their partisan team was one of many that comprised the field units of the Union for Armed Struggle, a resistance movement formed soon after the invasion. Given a break at the beginning of summer, Andrush went to see Mishka, who had just turned seventeen.

"You didn't think I would miss your birthday, did you?" he asked. "Your love keeps me going. I live for the time when we can be together every single day, have a child even. I know you want one."

"Stop trying to placate me, Andrush. Of all the things to say! You've been gone for over eight months. You left in early November, and it's now July. Did you really think I wouldn't be upset? I didn't know if you were dead or alive. If you want to find me in one piece, don't leave me here for so long."

"What would you do if I was away fighting in a regular army?"

"That's irrelevant. I need to know that your words mean something. Who can think of having a child? The life we had is gone. Besides, haven't you done enough?"

"The real work hasn't begun. We've been training all this time," he slipped in.

"Well," she sighed, "I suppose I'm going to be here for quite a while."

"Don't be that way, Mishka. You know how important this is."

"I know. I'm sorry." She understood his need, his motivation; it was just so hard to be away from him. What good would it do to argue? He was with her now. *Don't complain. Make the best of things.*

Andrush returned to Warsaw. Taking advantage of the summer weather, the groups headed into the forests to dig up arms buried by the army in the early days of the invasion, checked on their condition, and waited for deliveries of smuggled weapons. They assisted in the building of underground shelters where the incoming weapons would be stored. These activities were crucial to the success of the partisans' future missions, though he found them unrewarding.

His first kills, made during the seizure of a food warehouse, were underwhelming. Pull the trigger and bang, the man was dead, just like that, not even a whimper. Shooting German soldiers on guard duty was only slightly more gratifying than digging shelters. Andrush wanted to see and hear them suffer—beg for their lives or cry out for their mothers—and he found that thrill on other missions by mutilating his victims in knife attacks and watching them writhe in agony before dying, though this method was only effective against loners. These actions brought a sharp rebuke from his commander.

"Time is of the essence, and we are not savages, Vorobiev. Remember that, and hold yourself to a higher standard."

Andrush understood the commander's point regarding the element of time, so he contented himself with taking pleasure in the pain the families of the men he shot and killed would feel when they received word of their deaths.

Maritza tried to cope with village life. As long as Andrush was with her, she was happy there—being with the person she loved made her surroundings seem quaint, but with him gone for months, the place left her unsettled. The Germans might come; they were long overdue, or the Russians. Bogdi was never far from her side, but she didn't feel as secure with him as she did with Andrush. She could shoot a lone man if he meant to do harm; though the pistol would be useless if a contingent of troops came in.

What if Andrush were captured or killed? How would she know? Years could pass. Bronka might force her to marry Bogdi if he still hadn't chosen a girl or one of the other awkward, ruddy-faced young men, and she would become a rough-hewn farm wife doomed to submit to his advances every night and give birth to a new baby each year.

Andrush was the only antidote for her sadness. She was elated when he returned in late November and announced he would stay until after the new year. He told the family of the conditions in Warsaw. Citizens were taken away in trucks; those who resisted were shot dead in the streets, and their bodies left in pools of blood. Able-bodied teens and men were rounded up and shipped off to work camps in Germany. Jews were required to wear an armband emblazoned with the Star of David and ordered to report to a large ghetto that had been established in the Jewish Quarter.

"There's a high wall around it, so no one can leave. Jewish police and SS guard the inside, and Polish police are outside with orders to shoot anyone who tries to escape."

"Jewish police? Why would they act against their own people?" Maritza asked, careful not to say *our* people. She wasn't much of a

Jew, and Andrush even less, but she was still one by birth and felt a connection to those forced to live in the ghetto.

"Some will do anything to survive," Andrush answered.

"The Germans are using them to keep order, but in the end, they will suffer the same fate as their brethren," Bronka said. Her animus toward the Jews seemed to grow the more she talked about them.

Maritza was tired of hearing about the Germans, and should have asked Andrush about the Jewish police when they were alone. She wanted to enjoy every minute of the time she had with him and looked forward to the upcoming Christmas festivities. Last year, there had been nothing to celebrate, with him away and the murder of their family having happened a few months earlier.

Andrush urged Bronka to hide food in the small, unused cellar beneath the storeroom floor, and she asked him to help Bogdi shore it up. Again bereft of Mishka's attention, the young man went about his work in gloom, and responded to Andrush in monosyllables as they worked. Andrush hadn't noticed this when he helped his cousin with the other chores in the barn or outside, but in the confines of the cellar, it was obvious that something was wrong.

"What the hell is his problem?" he asked her. "He acts like he's mad at the world."

"I don't know. Why don't you ask him?"

"Forget it."

"Bronka has been after him to marry, and the girls love him, but he doesn't want to. Maybe that's the reason."

"Strange," he said. "Wonder why he's holding out. He's no prize."

"He is for them."

As usual, their time together passed quickly. When it came time to leave, Andrush shrugged into his coat. "I will be back when I can."

Maritza wanted to ask when that would be, but didn't. It was better to send him off on a positive note. "Be careful," she said, wrapping his neck in a scarf Krysta had knitted him for Christmas. "Remember, part of being a hero is knowing when not to be one."

"I'm no hero. The real heroes are the ones who are dead, Mishka."

"Oh, please don't talk like that, Andrush. It makes me sad. Just say you'll be careful. It gives me hope."

"I'll be careful. I promise," he said. Driven by revenge, Andrush didn't think about death—his fallen comrades were unlucky, less experienced, or worried too much about dying. His mission was to kill as many Germans as he could to hasten the end of the war and free the country from Nazi oppression.

Hitler invaded the Soviet Union in June 1941, and the Germans needed their supply lines to the east intact. Separate railway sabotage by the partisans and communist resistance throughout Poland caused substantial delays. Teams of SS were sent into the forests to liquidate the groups, and it became unsustainable for them to carry out their sabotage missions. Andrush and Moshe were told to go to Warsaw's Praga District on the east bank of the Vistula to make contact with one of their couriers, a young woman named Zofia, who would set them up in a safe house and give them further instructions when the time came to go back into the field.

Zofia, a comely red-haired Jewess with green eyes and a large rump, delivered written or verbal messages to fellow resistance members throughout Warsaw. Tough-minded and confident, she knew exactly how to handle the German soldiers in the streets. Intrigued by her unusual look, they flirted or waved her on. Andrush had seen her once at a meeting in Warsaw but never spoke with her. She was Moshe's ideal woman, and the two started a friendship.

"We'll bide our time in Zofia's apartment," he told Andrush.

"First, I want to go see Mishka. It's been six months."

"Why don't you bring her? She can stay on when we go back in the field, and you won't have to travel so far to see her each time we get a break. She won't be lonely at Zofia's."

The idea resonated with Andrush, though he wanted assurances Zofia wouldn't involve her in any resistance activity.

"You can discuss it with her yourself when you return," Moshe said.

He left at once to fetch Mishka. Krysta ran in from a neighbor's house, shouting that Andrush was coming into the village. Maritza flew out the door, down the path, and into his arms, nearly knocking him over.

"Oh, Andrush, I knew you would come in time for my birthday."

"Better than that," he whispered between kisses. "I'm taking you with me to Warsaw. We'll leave in a few days, but *ssh*. Let me tell Bronka."

His aunt's reaction was swift and negative. "Warsaw? A poor idea, Andrush, a mistake."

"Praga. East of the river. It's safer there, and I will be able to see her more often."

"What will she do by herself there while you're gone? What will she eat? She can hardly peel a potato. Who will care for her? Leave her with us."

They talked about her as if she wasn't in the room. Maritza almost screamed, *I want to go,* but after all their kindness, saying anything contrary would make her look like an ingrate. What if Bronka talked him out of the plan? Andrush stood with arms crossed, pretending to listen to his aunt's arguments, waiting for the right moment to stop her.

Krysta cried in a corner. Bogdi sat at the table as tense as a rod, pain sawing through his heart. He knew that Mishka would leave when the war ended if Andrush managed to survive, but this announcement was too sudden; he needed time—months—to prepare himself. Before she arrived on his doorstep, he never questioned the quality of his life. Now a vital part of his soul was seeping out and washing away, and without her near, he would never be the same.

He jumped up, his face mottling red. "Mama's right. Mishka shouldn't go. She's safe here with us. You were the one who told us about the crimes and murders happening in Warsaw, and that's where you're taking her? It makes no sense. Why would you do that?"

"Shut up!" Andrush shouted. "Who are you to meddle in our business? Don't you dare question the decisions I make regarding my wife, or has something been going on behind my back?" His hands flew up in fists.

Mortified, Maritza started to cry. She knew Bogdi cared for her, but wasn't aware of the depth of feeling revealed by his outburst. They worked side by side for two years, and he had never acted inappropriately.

"That's enough, Andrush! You forget yourself," cried Bronka.

Bogdi kicked his chair away. "You want to fight? I'm not afraid of you, you selfish pig."

"You will be in a moment. Come on, little boy, I'll snap you like a twig."

"Stop!" Bronka stepped between them and held her son in place with one hand on his chest and the other on her nephew's. Bogdi threw off her hand and stalked away.

Andrush pulled Maritza from the chair and up the ladder into the attic. "I want the truth. Did you do anything with him? Has he touched you?"

"Of course not! He's just concerned, that's all," she said.

"Concerned? He's in love with you. Do you think I'm blind or just stupid? That's why he doesn't want to marry. None of those girls can compare to you."

"That is not my fault!" Maritza exploded. "He's your cousin, and I've done nothing wrong. You should apologize to him and to Bronka."

"I will never apologize to him. He wants my wife, and I'm supposed to say I'm sorry? Are you out of your mind? Who the hell does he think he is, acting like you belong to him? You're mine, and he should know better," he snarled.

"I'm going to talk to him."

"Don't do it, Mishka. You don't know men. Let him be."

"A minute ago you called him a little boy and were ready to fight him. Now you're worried how he will react to me?"

"I'm not worried. I don't want you wasting your time and looking foolish."

Maritza ignored him and went down the ladder into the kitchen. Bronka and Krysta heard everything and kept their heads down over their sewing. She found him in the barn, starting to lead the horse out. "Bogdi, wait."

"There's nothing to discuss," he said in a tight voice. He wouldn't look at her; the shame was too much. "A wife must go where her husband takes her."

Her voice cracked and tears splashed onto her cheeks. "I'm sorry for the things he said."

"He's right. It wasn't my business."

He tried to go around her, but she threw her arms around him. "You mean so much to me. I will never forget you."

He wouldn't reciprocate her hug. "Let me pass, Mishka."

Her arms fell to her sides as he led the horse away. He hates me now, she thought. It was true. She didn't know men.

Back in the attic, she sat on Andrush's lap. He looked into her wet eyes. "Get your things together," he said. "We're leaving now."

They bid farewell to Bronka and Krysta, but broken-hearted Bogdi was nowhere to be seen. He had ridden off somewhere to drown his sorrow in drink.

Chapter 18

"So this is the famous Mishka, all grown up," Moshe said when she arrived in Praga with Andrush. "I met you in Wyszków when you were a little girl. You probably don't remember me."

"I'm sorry, I don't," she said, giving him a big smile.

"That's enough, you two." Andrush didn't like her to be close to any man, and his senses were heightened following the Bogdi incident.

Moshe introduced them to Zofia. "You've quite a reputation, Andrush," she said, pumping his hand. "It's a pleasure to meet you."

"Here's my wife, Mishka." He prodded her forward.

"I know we're going to be good friends," Maritza smiled.

"Sure," Zofia said.

"You look, uh, well fed." Andrush appraised her as one would a fatted calf at market. "You'll take care of my Mishka when we go back? Make sure she eats? I don't want her to wander around alone out there looking for food."

"Oh, that's not a problem. I have connections and can get anything the Germans eat."

They worked out a price that covered her monthly rent and food. With Jakub's money that he had stashed at Bronka's, he paid a year in full, wanting to make sure Zofia wouldn't raise the rates each time he came back. "She will need some clothing, a pair of shoes, and an identity card," he added.

"I can certainly get those."

"Thanks," he said. "I'm glad we can count on you."

This petite, fragile-looking girl holding his hand, who in Zofia's opinion could pass for a child, was not the type she imagined a fearless patriot like Andrush Vorobiev would pick for a wife. Well, to each his own preference. With her small size and innocent appearance, she would be an asset to the courier network, but would first need to provide proof of a backbone. "You'll be helping us out, right, Mishka? We would appreciate your service."

"No, she won't." Andrush pulled Maritza behind him. "I was about to tell you that she is not to be involved in any way. Do I make myself clear?"

"Perfectly."

During the weeks he stayed, Zofia was accommodating and as friendly as could be, allowing them to use the bedroom, while she and Moshe slept on an old couch near the kitchen. She made sure there was food in the apartment, and although she was gone most of the day, the couples spent many pleasant evenings together, playing cards and chatting.

Maritza awoke in low spirits the day Andrush was set to leave. "Must you go so soon?"

"Soon? I've been here for over a month. Look at that long face. Is that how you send your man off? I will be back before you know it. Zofia promised to take care of you." He kissed her and went off with his comrade to continue their fight against the Germans.

Not long after Andrush's departure, Maritza revised her earlier, more favorable opinion of Zofia, having naively based her expectations on the close relationships she had in the past with school friends. When they were together, the redhead was moody and curt. It's nothing I've done, she told herself. She's just that way, and I have to accept it.

Zofia brought food in the evening, and Maritza had to wait until then to eat. Now that she had a forged *Kennkarte,* the identity card the German occupiers required for all civilians, one that showed her as a Catholic Pole, there was no reason to stay in the apartment all day, and she started going out in the neighborhood. Andrush wouldn't like it, but she needed air and exercise, and she was hungry. To her delight, she found she could eat a decent lunch in a Polish restaurant for thirty zloty—an indulgence considering a waitress earned sixty per month. He left her a thick stack, hidden under a loose floorboard in the bedroom closet. Let Zofia keep bringing food for me, she thought, and I can eat double.

There was a park not far from the apartment. There she went and stayed for hours, drawing in a pad of paper. On her first visit, she saw a large, weatherworn sign posted at the entrance: *Jews Forbidden,* written in Polish and German. Her impulse was to run, but she reminded herself that as long as she had her card, there was no need to worry. It had since been decreed that Poles weren't allowed in public parks; some unconscientious officials forgot to amend the sign.

Time passed, and soon it would be winter. "It's been over four months since they left," she said to Zofia. "Aren't you concerned?"

"They'll come when they can. You think only of your feelings for one man, but this is about something larger, the love of country, which you don't seem to understand."

Maritza wanted to pull every last hair out of Zofia's head. "I lost my whole family. Don't talk to me that way," she said, her lips trembling.

"I'm sorry, Mishka. I mean, they're doing important work. I know you miss him. Try not to be sad."

By December, temperatures had dropped to freezing, and snow dusted the ground. There was no fuel for heating; the Germans secured it for themselves. Maritza wore layers of clothing and her coat, but it was so cold in the apartment that she developed chilblains. In

Andrush's unit, nothing could be done in such weather. Supplies and ammunition were nearing depletion, and their commander wanted the men to rest. Andrush and Moshe returned to the apartment late one night before Christmas. She was so glad to see him that her squabbles with Zofia were forgotten.

On *Sylwester,* New Year's Eve, a muted celebration was underway. Moshe poured four shot glasses of vodka. "Let's have a toast," he said.

"None for Mishka," Andrush interjected. "She doesn't drink."

"Oh, don't leave me out. Just a sip, please."

As soon as the glass touched her lips, he took it away. "That's all. I don't want you drunk and dancing on the table."

She eased into his arms, touched his face, and whispered something that made him laugh and kiss her. "All right, you can have the rest."

Later, when they were alone, Moshe said to Zofia, "You see how those two are with each other. I wish you would be that way with me."

"Now is not the time to be sentimental, and there's such a thing as loving too much. It breeds dependence. He treats her like a child, and so she is."

Moshe thought about it. She was right, but he wished she would make him feel more like a man and less like a comrade. Hell, was it too much to ask? Zofia had no problem shaking her fleshy hindquarters at the Germans when she didn't have to cover up in a coat, so why not do it for him? It seemed the only thing that excited her was the cause.

Andrush and Maritza had eight blissful, relaxing weeks, then the men went back to join their unit. She promised herself to keep an optimistic outlook for the future; there were so many people worse off than she was.

Sabotage activities continued to be carried out by the resistance groups, though changes were made soon after the new year. The Union for Armed Struggle was renamed *Armia Krajowa,* the Home Army, which sought to consolidate the various organizations into one movement and took instructions from the Polish government in exile in England.

After blowing up a fuel depot on the outskirts of Warsaw the night before, a dangerous operation that had taken months to plan, Andrush and a group of two dozen exhausted men were resting in a forest northwest of the city.

"Excellent work," the commander said. "We take a break while I wait for permission to start planning the action for fall. The Germans will be looking for the saboteurs, and we should leave here tonight. Our propaganda bureau can pin the destruction of the depot on the Polish communists."

Laughter all around. "That's what they get for not joining us and letting go of their useless ideas."

Andrush leaned back against a tree, excitement burning in his chest at the thought of seeing Mishka. He'd been gone far longer than planned. It had become a habit for him to return for her birthdays—this year her nineteenth. He closed his eyes, remembering the love they made in the apartment, in their private world.

The lookout whistled a warning. Five canvas-covered trucks appeared in the road that ran through the forest, each carrying a dozen SS soldiers in camouflage gear. The partisans scrambled for their weapons. The commander signaled for Andrush and ten men to cross the road and take up positions so the enemy could be hit from both sides. The SS exited the trucks, fanned out into both sides of the forest, moving through slowly, like chameleons. Hiding in a thicket of bushes, Andrush could only see in front of him; there wasn't enough time to get deeper into the forest.

Someone fired a rifle shot, then a volley. The SS answered with their submachine guns. A figure moved in front of the bush. Andrush aimed the Walther P38 pistol taken from a dead German a few weeks earlier and shot the man through the side of the head. One down. Bullets from the partisans' rifles whizzed in and out, along with spray from the Germans' guns. The enemy had the clear advantage. Andrush waited, then peered through the leaves for his next victim. A piercing *whissh* sheared through his back and into his chest, followed by numbness and horrible burning. He lost consciousness and went down.

Five months passed since Maritza last saw Andrush. He didn't come for her birthday, but in keeping with her pledge of optimism, she thought, *any day now.* She tidied the apartment, walked in the neighborhood, and had lunch in the Polish restaurants, where the proprietors gave her free tidbits that she took to the park and ate while she drew. She learned to stay on Zofia's good side, which meant not talking to her, and it wasn't difficult. The redhead swept in at the end of the day with the face of a gargoyle, tossed a small package of food on the table, and went into the bedroom to sleep.

Then, the tragic news. From her contacts, Zofia learned that Andrush, Moshe, and others from their unit had been shot and killed by the SS. No further information was known. Maritza fell screaming to the floor.

"Be quiet! You'll bring the police here." Zofia hauled her to her feet and slapped her. "Get yourself together. Our men gave their lives for Poland. Sacrifices have to be made for the greater good. Life must go on."

Maritza didn't hear the words or feel the blow. She was slipping away to a dark place. The deaths of her family members in Wyszków were, at the time, the most horrible events imaginable, but losing Andrush was infinitely more painful. Without him, she had no reason to go on, fell into depression, and refused to eat. She lay on her cot, staring into space and wanting to die, and awoke each morning surprised to find herself alive. *So not today?* Her heart beat erratically, her vision was blurry, and it hurt to lift her head from the pillow. *Maybe tomorrow.*

Zofia started to worry. If Mishka didn't eat, she would die, and then what to do with her body? Should she wrap it in a sheet and arrange for a funeral cart like the ones used to take corpses out of the ghetto? Ghastly thoughts, but the wife of a freedom fighter deserved better than to be buried in a pit somewhere. Practical considerations had to be taken into account; the police or Gestapo would find out, question the man or men who took the body away, then come around to the apartment and interrogate *her,* the renter. She'd be watched, followed, and have to curtail her activities.

She could wait until the next meeting with her Home Army contact, and ask him what to do, but Mishka's corpse would have to remain in the apartment until then. Oh, this was terrible, terrible. Everything would fall to pieces because the porcelain doll in the next room didn't have the will to live.

Zofia went into the bedroom, where Mishka lay still and white, her eyes open and unblinking. "Sit up, Mishka. I brought some potato soup. You have to eat. It's nice and warm."

"Go away." She turned her head and closed her eyes.

"Please have a few spoonfuls. I can feed it to you if you'll sit up." *No response.* "What would Andrush say if he saw you now?" *Still nothing.* "Don't eat then." She took the cup away.

Maritza's head ached, yet she had a couple of lucid thoughts: if she hung on, there was a chance she might find a caring, honest person to befriend—there had to be someone as lonely and miserable as she was out there, and if Andrush knew she was choosing death, he would be appalled. What he and the rest of their family would have given for another day of life! She felt their hands pulling her up. Barely able to stand, she held onto the walls for support and made it to the kitchen, where Zofia sat, separating zloty notes into piles.

"I will eat now," Maritza said. Her lips, so cracked and dry, bled when she moved them. "You're right. I owe it to Andrush to carry on."

Zofia gathered up the zloty notes, stuffed them into her pocket, and placed the soup cup in front of Mishka. "Sit and eat slowly. Sip, sip, a little at a time. That's a good girl." As soon as the girl was strong enough, she would send her out to work. Andrush's money was dwindling.

Chapter 19

Will had been in Warsaw for six months and was satisfied with his housing arrangement. He bathed, dressed, went downstairs and out through the covered walkway into his office. He couldn't say he enjoyed his work—nothing brought him pleasure, but there was plenty of it to keep him occupied, and his small staff was deferential and pleasant. Though not high-ranking, he was an officer nonetheless, and subordinates were required to show respect. The days passed with familiar regularity. His work environment could be much worse.

During the time between late afternoon and the onset of night, a feeling of longing for something or someone Will had never known but desperately wanted or needed began to lay over him, a reminder that life in Warsaw held no promise of finding a woman to like, let alone love. He would have made do with a dog, but wasn't able to find one. Surely there were dogs somewhere in Warsaw for sale.

He saw a well-dressed woman, probably the wife of a German official in the civil administration, walking a Polish greyhound on the fashionable Nowy Świat Street where he shopped for food. When he stopped to pet it, the damn thing nearly tore his hand off before he could ask the lady how she had acquired it. What a sad existence it was for a man to be unable to at least find a furry companion to give his love to!

Will stayed away from his quarters during the early evening hours by frequenting restaurants and officers' clubs in the hopes of meeting like-minded comrades; however, he soon discovered that going out for food or drink was hazardous to his welfare. The quintessential German officer was one imbued with the Nazi spirit of Aryan superiority, a trait every man was expected to exhibit.

The hardcore Nazis in these places launched into diatribes against the Jews and Poles and goaded regular officers into arguments, and those who gave dissenting views were usually not seen again. Jealousies of others' promotions, nicer offices, and more comfortable assignments abounded and festered. Oftentimes, those greenest with envy would start rumors or try to sabotage the careers of men who had something they coveted. There was no bonhomie to be found in these establishments, and he stopped going.

There were opportunities to socialize with single women in uniform, Wehrmacht helpers, who had come in from the Reich to replace men in communications and clerical areas so they could be deployed to the front lines. Hitler, who had emphasized early on that women had no place in the military, had decreed that the femininity of these women be maintained at all costs in an effort to sway the German public's opinion.

Will hoped to meet an attractive, interesting woman, but was aware that it would be difficult to find someone who shared his negative views on national socialism and had those qualities. He went to an event and left (with his hair standing on end) soon after arriving, convinced that any female who wanted to work for the Wehrmacht had to show proof of teeth filed to razor-sharp points, a high degree of resemblance to a warthog, and the ability to recite *Mein Kampf* in its entirety. The Nazis' ideas of femininity were as ghoulish as their policies.

How did other men deal with the emptiness in their hearts? They drank, traded magazines featuring nude women that left little to the imagination, took mistresses, and frequented brothels. Will drank too, but it didn't make the pain go away.

His usual nighttime fantasies had become monotonous; they needed an infusion of fresh blood. He thought up new ones, cramming in as much sex and derring-do as possible—why not, since true love was going to elude him? Will pictured himself as a swashbuckler with a different voluptuous woman on his arm every night and then in his bed. His strength, stamina, and exploits were legendary, but when the curtains closed on his adventures, he saw himself as an anomaly, a lag of a man, and the only one drowning in loneliness.

Bazar Różyckiego, Warsaw's oldest open-air marketplace in the Praga District, was crowded with people. The Poles sold used household items, miscellaneous objects, and trinkets from long tables and stalls under tattered awnings. Across from the used goods, low-quality fruits and vegetables that the civil administration officials permitted to be brought in from the countryside over the summer were offered for sale. The bazaar also functioned as a black market where a wide variety of goods could be obtained for a steep price or through barter. Some of the policemen assigned to patrol there accepted bribes and looked the other way. Will sometimes came here on Saturdays to escape the tedium of the long, boring weekends, and on this particular day, the summer weather was too splendid to stay inside.

Jozef Kowalski, a former grocer whose shop was destroyed during the invasion, ran a vegetable stall. A squat man in his fifties with a bulbous nose and gray hair, he darkened the lines on his face with ash and walked with a fake limp and a cane to make himself appear weaker and avoid being sent to a labor camp in case of a roundup. Will struck up a conversation one day with him and his wife, Alina, who both spoke a fair amount of German. During subsequent chats, they noticed the oberleutnant had none of the haughtiness of other officers and grew to like him.

When Will discovered Alina needed work, he took out the necessary permits and hired her to cook and clean a few days a week. He paid her the allowable monthly rate, which he augmented generously and didn't report. This arrangement afforded her a level of protection she wouldn't have found elsewhere and gave her husband peace of mind.

The unpleasant vinegary smell of overripe fruit was strong in the air as Will walked through the market. In front of Jozef's stall, a girl wearing a vivid blue headscarf and a faded floral dress stood digging for something in her purse. "Thank you for your patience. I put some in this morning, so they've got to be here," she said, glancing at Jozef, "though I'm beginning to believe my purse eats them." From the corner of her eye, Maritza saw the gray-green uniform and black boots. *Damn German.* She angled away from him and continued searching.

"Allow me," Will said, taking coins from his pocket.

"Oh, no thank you, *Herr Offizier.* That won't be necessary," she said in perfect German, still bent over her purse. "I know they're in here."

"I insist. Why risk getting bitten by whatever is eating your coins?"

She stifled a laugh. *At least this one has a sense of humor.* Swiveling to look at him, she gasped. He was tall, fair, and impossibly handsome.

Will's eyes widened in amazement. The girl's face was one of timeless beauty, reminiscent of a subject from a Vermeer painting: perfectly oval with high cheekbones, full lips, and enormous blue-green, almond-shaped eyes. She took his breath away, and his heart started thumping. The three-second rule of social propriety for looking at the opposite sex had come and gone, but mesmerized, he couldn't take his eyes off her.

Maritza stared back, transfixed. The purse slipped from her hands, causing the contents to spill onto the ground. "Oh, how clumsy I am," she exclaimed.

They crouched down at the same time and gathered the items. "The purse has a hole, see?" He poked his finger through. "The coins must have fallen out."

His face was so close that she could smell the muskiness of his skin and his minty breath. He had beautiful lips for a man, not thin or flabby like the other Germans. Her eyes lingered on them, and she wondered how they would feel against hers. This was madness! Disgusted by her reaction, Maritza stood quickly. "Yes, I remember now. I put them in my pocket. Thank you again," she said to Will without looking at him. She paid Jozef, took her purchase, and hurried away.

Even though the officer seemed almost human and had a face that would make any woman swoon, he was a devil in disguise. These silver-tongued flunkeys in their gray-green livery would never run out of ploys to draw gullible women into their claws, then ram their phalluses between helpless legs. She shuddered at the thought. These men were dangerous, and in the future, she would feign ignorance if any of them spoke to her. Lesson learned.

Crestfallen, Will lingered at the stall, pretending to examine a head of cabbage with large holes in the leaves where insects had eaten through, and asked Jozef if he knew the girl.

"No. I've seen her here once or twice, that's all."

He returned to the market every Saturday for a couple of weeks without seeing her and decided he shouldn't come back for a while. People might suspect him of being a spy if he was observed meandering through the place for hours.

Chapter 20

Soviet fighter planes bombed Warsaw before dawn one morning in late August, targeting German hospitals and military installations. The explosions, heard and felt from miles away, jolted Will from sleep and sent him to shelter under a table. He wasn't hurt, and other than some falling plaster, the damage to his office and quarters was minimal. The bombs must have landed in residential areas as well, he thought, but the Nazis wouldn't care about Polish injuries and deaths.

There was palpable tension throughout the city, and problems sprang up everywhere: machines and equipment malfunctioned, inebriated soldiers fought in bars, traffic accidents occurred on every corner, and speeding SS trucks hit pedestrians. It was one of those bad weeks when nothing went right—as if the earth had tilted too far on its axis and stayed that way.

In Will's office, supplies didn't arrive and had to be located, which meant long hours on the telephone and a stiff neck. The typist broke his finger and was out. His replacement focused on speed instead of accuracy and made so many errors that Will sent him back and did the typing himself. He worked late into the night, and there had been no time to think about the young woman with the angelic face who had taken his breath away in the marketplace.

Will's driver, Hans, was opposed to the Nazi ideology but kept his sentiments hidden from the typist and clerk, who were young and staunch supporters of it. He had the feeling Will shared his views and, in private, told him that the SS had recently deported hundreds of thousands of Jews from the Warsaw Ghetto to a camp in eastern Poland where they were killed in vans or in chambers with a special kind of gas and their bodies dumped into huge pits. There were other such camps and hundreds of other ghettos in the country that fed into them, he said.

Will listened, horrified. He had witnessed a few crimes of violence—including the arrest of elderly people—for what he didn't know, but never any killings. Those, he suspected, were done in the prisons and Gestapo headquarters. It was clear that the speeches Hitler had been making for years prior to the invasion, in which he blamed the Jews for the economic downfall of Germany and all of its problems, had been a prelude to his plan to annihilate them.

Campaigns of genocide happened throughout history; it was one thing to read about them in books and quite another to live where they were taking place. It was the fear of helplessness, of having one's existence snuffed out. Life under the Nazis required permanent vigilance. One wrong move, one misconstrued comment, a denouncement by a jealous officer, and he could be sent away to a camp in Germany like Sachsenhausen or Dachau, or another place of unspeakable horror. If he thought too much about these things, there would be no getting through the day, and no sleep would come at night. Consistently emotionally bankrupt, he attended to his tasks and retreated deeper into his fantasies.

The September days rushed by. October swaggered in and brought chilly weather. The frenzy finally settled down, and Will's workload normalized. On the way back from completing a task in Praga, he and Hans drove past a park just east of the Vistula that beckoned him with its dazzling fall colors.

"Have you been there?" Will asked.

"I haven't," Hans said, "though soldiers go there at night with women they can't otherwise be seen with."

Will had been to Agricola, a park for Germans west of the river. The few times he went, senior officers hogged the tennis courts and target shooting area, making it impossible for anyone below the highest ranks to participate in an activity. The pool had only one slot open the first thing in the morning on a weekday, his busiest time, and the Equestrian Club never had any. He thought about complaining, but dismissed the idea. Those who filed grievances hardly ever received the requested remedy, and their names were put on a list of troublemakers. He decided a stroll in the fresh air might lift his mood.

On Saturday, he drove out to the park and walked around. A group of children playing at the edge ran away as he approached. The place was filled with a great variety of shrubs and trees: beeches, maples, and elms—too many to count. Birds sang sweet songs high up in the trees, oblivious to the pain and suffering going on outside their habitat. As much as Will wanted to commune with nature, he felt more detached from humanity than ever and yearned to enjoy the tranquil setting with a woman in whom he could confide, have meaningful conversations with, and hold in his arms. There was no way out of his dismal existence, not even for an hour.

Chapter 21

Will stopped at the outdoor market after the walk in the park failed to bring about the desired result. No sooner had he walked up to the stall when Jozef motioned for him to look at the people selling their goods across the way. "There's the young lady you were asking about."

He went right over to her. "Hello," he said, his warm smile revealing even white teeth. "I met you here a while back. Do you remember me?"

It was the tall, well-built officer who had offered her coins. Maritza's heart fluttered. "Yes, I do." *Walk away, he's trouble.* She edged past him and continued her search for soap, settling on a small bar that was touted as real but wasn't. It would have to do. She fished a coin from her pocket.

Engel was at her well-worn heels. "May I know your name?"

She stopped and turned. A German officer couldn't be ignored for long. "Marisya," she said.

"Oberleutnant Wilhelm Engel." He bowed slightly.

She looked up at him. The two scars on his forehead didn't detract from his appeal. Sandy blonde hair, neatly combed to one side, faded into a close clip around. His sapphire-blue eyes downturned slightly at the corners and softened his finely chiseled features. She tore her eyes away. "So nice to see you, Oberleutnant, but I must be going."

Will couldn't risk letting her get away again. "Wait, please. There is a park about two miles south of here. I don't get out much and

I wonder if—" He turned red, stuck his hands in his pockets, and looked down, something he always did when self-conscious. "I am not very good at this sort of thing."

"What sort of thing are you referring to?" She wasn't going to make this easy for him and wanted to see him squirm, to dig the knife in part way for what his brethren did to her loved ones, regardless of his good-looks.

"It has been quite a while since I asked a lady to spend time with me. That was almost two years ago when I invited my elderly aunt to see a play," he said.

Afraid to laugh out loud, Maritza held it in while her shoulders shook with mirth.

"I wonder if you would do me the honor of meeting me at the park I was telling you about tomorrow at noon."

"Do you mean the one on Waszyngtona?"

"Yes. I went there this morning, but without someone to talk to, I didn't stay."

He must be lonely, Maritza thought. She never believed a German capable of having any human emotion, and the whole lot of them could go to hell, but the earnestness in his eyes was stripping her defenses away.

"Yes, then?" Will asked.

"Yes."

It was unthinkable that she would accept an invitation from a German and feel anything for him other than revulsion, yet here she was, agreeing to meet him. She would have to be careful, for as kind as he appeared, the one thing she could be certain of was uncertainty. The play-acted respect she showed these men was done to keep them from getting angry and possibly vindictive, and she would continue doing it as long as necessary. A five-foot, barely ninety-pound woman was no match for an aggressive German with a sidearm. At least the park was familiar and so close to the apartment that she could run to it if she felt threatened.

"It's a big park. I go there sometimes to draw. I can meet you near the sculpture of a woman bathing. It's located on the west side of the park."

"Very well."

"Thank you for your invitation."

Will offered his hand. "Until tomorrow."

She glanced around to see if anyone was looking, took his hand briefly, and went on her way.

Jozef, who had observed the interaction from his stall across the way, smiled. One thing the occupation could not stop was the blossoming of love.

Sunday was cool and bright to match Will's mood, and he groomed himself carefully. Cologne? He took a whiff. *Phew.* The Crow had sent it to him for his birthday when he was in the hospital recovering from the accident. What a thoughtless gift. He spilled it out in the sink and threw the bottle away. A touch of aftershave would do nicely.

Maritza was sitting on her coat over a carpet of golden leaves and drawing on a pad when he arrived, the sun creating a halo around her.

"Good morning, Marisya, or should I say, good afternoon?"

"Good morning and afternoon, Herr Oberleutnant. We can hit them both with one shot."

"I am interested in seeing your drawings."

She handed him the pad and he flipped through the pages. The book was full of pastoral scenes done in colored pencils and so finely detailed that at first he thought they were cut and pasted from magazines. Today she had started on the beginning of another masterpiece: a grouping of autumnal trees in a sensational mélange of colors, with a fiery red barn in the forefront.

"These are wonderful! What talent you have. I love farm scenes as well. I spent summers on my grandfather's beetroot farm, but I have always wanted my own land with a variety of animals, maybe two of each, so they could keep each other company."

"How good of you to think of their social welfare," she said. "I always feel sad when I see animals alone. I saw a calf with such mournful eyes standing by itself at a petting zoo when I was young, and I cried for an hour thinking how much it missed its mother."

"Did you miss your mother when you were apart from her?"

"No. I had other family members around."

Maritza asked where he lived and worked, and they continued chatting about art and animals. Oberleutnant Engel was clearly an intellectual. His voice, deep and resonant, drew her in. She hadn't spoken to anyone on this level since her school days. The conversation was stimulating. He was stimulating.

"How did you learn to draw?" he asked.

"I always had a pencil in my hand and found that I could draw, although later I took lessons."

"It seems that nature is your biggest inspiration. What else do you like to draw?"

Maritza hesitated. What inspired her before the Germans came were her family's faces; drawing them now would be too painful.

"People often credit God as inspiration for their art. Do you believe in God?" he asked.

"No, I don't. When I was very young, the wallpaper in my father's study had suns with faces and pointy rays. I thought they were pictures of God. They frightened me, and I avoided going in there."

"I had a similar experience," Will went on. "My parents were devout Catholics. In church at age three or four, I kept hearing about *Gott*, the father of Jesus Christ, and I couldn't find him anywhere in my picture books. I didn't dare ask my parents. My father would have whipped me for not paying attention, but my brother said Gott must be Herr Gott the butcher, the only one we knew by that name. I thought he was a monstrous parent to allow his son to die scantily clad, wearing a crown of thorns, and nailed to a cross. We hid under our beds every time he came to the house to deliver meat."

"Did you think he was going to chop you up?"

He laughed. "That, and I was afraid my mother would hang me on a cross and leave me to die, and crows would come and peck out my eyes."

"What a horrific fear for a little boy to have. Why did you think she would do that?"

"For one thing, she hung a crucifix on the wall behind my pillow, but not my brother's. I was convinced it was a warning of what would happen if I misbehaved."

"I can't imagine parents acting so cruelly to their own flesh and blood."

"My mother wasn't loving to me. She was with my brother, and I was glad. He was sickly and died when we were ten. We were twins."

"How sad to lose a brother, a twin no less."

"It was. My father treated my mother like an object of art, never raising his voice or a hand to her, yet he beat me in front of her, and she never said a word."

It occurred to Will that he had never shared these incidents with anyone before and was delighted to be enjoying this glorious day with this alluring young woman. She was brilliant and captivating, a siren drawing him in with both brains and beauty.

He is stunning, Maritza thought, and so easy to talk to.

"Where did you learn German?" he asked.

"My father taught me German and French, and I learned English in school. He insisted I read entire books with dictionaries by my side and converse with him in one of the languages on certain days of the week. I resented it then, but I've since come to see how important it is to have those skills."

"Wise man, your father. I learned English and French in school in the days when those subjects were taught. Unfortunately, I am not proficient in either. Where are you living, Marisya? Have you been in Warsaw your whole life?"

"Yes. I grew up across the river. Now I'm over there," she said, pointing toward the east. "I wouldn't call it living, though."

"What do you mean?" He had a good idea of what she meant, given the plight of the Poles and the poor condition of the area, but he wanted to hear her explanation.

"It's more like existing—just moving from one moment to the next and waiting for things to happen. There are so many rules, and our choices are few." She told him about the rotten piece of meat she received once a month and the weekly loaves of sawdusty bread given on the ration cards, but said nothing about the food Zofia brought.

"We are getting potatoes now. There isn't enough gas through the day and evening to cook anything, so I usually eat lunch in a restaurant, though all they serve these days is cabbage soup or borscht." She sighed. "By the time there's sufficient flame to cook the potatoes, it's late at night."

Maritza didn't mean to complain, but if they were to be friends, Engel should know what her life was like. There was silence. Will was lost in his own thoughts, his brows and lips drawn. She had rambled on, but what difference would it make to him what her life was like? A Pole should never complain to a German officer about anything; he was liable to have her arrested for being insolent.

"I will do whatever I can to help you." He reached for her hand, so soft and small, it disappeared into his like a child's.

"Oh, no, Herr Oberleutnant. Thank you for your concern, but as you can see, I'm not wasting away." His hand was warm. She wanted to lay her head against his chest, close her eyes, and feel his arms around her. The need for comfort was all-consuming. "I'm fine. Really, I am."

Will didn't believe her, though it seemed best not to argue the point. "Who do you live with over there?"

"A girl."

"And your parents? Where are they?"

"They passed away. I have to go," she said, getting to her feet. Oberleutnant Engel was kind and attractive, but talking to him about the murder of her family by his comrades was not something she was going to do. What if he defended their actions? That didn't seem likely, but in political matters, it seemed safe to assume that what a German says to a Polish woman and what he thinks are two different things. "I've enjoyed the time we spent together."

He took her hand and raised it to his lips. "I have as well. Will you meet me here next Sunday at the same time?"

"I shall try," she said, not wanting to sound too eager. "Goodbye." *It's all right to like him, and I do, very much.*

Chapter 22

Will sat with his feet up, sipping vodka, replaying the events of the day. Marisya was a pleasure to be with. His senses had come roaring to life, simultaneously pleasing and unsettling him. What loomed on his horizon heretofore was an endless stream of meaningless days and deathly quiet nights without any hope of finding a woman.

Through the work week, his feet hardly touched the ground, and his staff noticed a change in his serious demeanor. He laughed and joked and seemed alive. They looked at him with curious smiles. While cleaning out a stack of papers from his desk, Will came across a guide Bach had given him the day he arrived in Warsaw. Had he not met Marisya, it would have gone into the trash, but now he reread it with different eyes. Written by the Kommandant, it outlined protocol for dealing with Poles and cautioned members of the military to avoid fraternizing with them.

To hell with rules and regulations, he thought. People need people. That was a fact of life, but the Germans only had use for Polish women as maids, mistresses, or in their brothels. He wished he could have a regular relationship with Marisya and take her on outings and for a nice meal. Before their next meeting, he bought apples, bread, cheese, cooked sausage, a pot of jam, and a few bars of chocolate for her, then stopped at a bookstore and found a drawing pad, pencils, and a little knife to sharpen them. The ones she had were down to the nub, and her pad was almost full. He wanted to make her happy—she was special.

Sunday brought sparkling weather. Will went to the same spot as before, leaned against a tree and waited. The butterflies in his stomach were unnerving. He waited and waited; noon had come and gone, and there was still no sign of her. Disappointed that he wasn't going to see her and peeved at being stood up, he bent down to retrieve the items and go to the car. There she was, walking fast and waving at him, her coat flapping in the breeze. His pulse quickened.

"Ah, here you are. I was just about to leave."

"I'm sorry. I had to wait until the girl I live with went out. I didn't want to take any chances of her seeing us together." Maritza imagined Zofia's reaction upon seeing her with Engel. She would denounce me as a traitor to her contacts or cast me out into the street, she thought nervously, losing herself in the troubling scenes playing out in her mind.

"Marisya?" The oberleutnant's deep voice yanked her back to the present. "Is everything all right? I don't want to create a problem for you. Does she ever come here?"

"I don't think so. She goes across the river to her, um, work and comes back late. There's no problem at all." Maritza had no idea if Zofia ever met anyone at the park, or where exactly she went every day.

"Let's walk a bit," he said. He wanted to find a more secluded spot. There was a perfect place on the other side of the park where they would be shielded from view should anyone walk by, and he could keep an eye on his car. Tire slashings of Wehrmacht vehicles by Warsaw's youth were not uncommon.

Maritza took a rolled up paper from a pocket, then spread her coat on the ground so they could sit. She slipped the kerchief from her head. A fresh breeze was blowing moist air from the river, and she wanted to feel it through her hair. Out tumbled a riot of glorious yellow-gold curls that fell to her waist, and Will's eyes popped in surprise. Unable to resist the urge to touch it, he reached out his hand at the moment Maritza turned her head to face him. There he was with his arm stretched out in a palsied half-Hitler salute, and not knowing what to do, gave a little wave and grinned. She did the same, and they both laughed.

"These are for you." He handed her the bags.

"All this for me? How thoughtful you are. Thank you," she exclaimed, and leaned over to kiss his cheek. She removed the items and set them out in a line. "Paper and pencils and all this food. I haven't had anything like this in a long time. Can I have some now?"

Although flush with pleasure from her kiss, he kept his composure. "Everything is yours. You don't need permission. I forgot utensils, but I have my pocketknife. May I?"

His gentlemanly behavior pleased her. "Yes, and thank you for these wonderful things."

"You are welcome." Will sliced some bread, cut the sausage into coins, the cheese into wedges, and opened the jam.

"Will you eat?" she asked.

The rich German rye was calling his name, though he resolved not to have any. How silly he would look, smiling away with fat caraway seeds stuck between his teeth. A little white lie was warranted. "No, I ate a large breakfast." He sat back against the tree and watched her.

"Mmm, it's so good," she mumbled through a mouthful of bread and cheese. After eating her fill, she wrapped up everything and wondered where in the apartment she could hide the rest. It would have to go under the floorboard in the closet. Zofia had a nose like a bloodhound, but she wasn't getting a morsel.

"Now, I have something for you." Maritza gave him the scroll tied with string.

Will unrolled it. She had drawn his portrait and captured every feature, every detail of his face so perfectly with those stubs of pencils. Warmth spread through him. "You are a true artist. I am honored you took the time to do this. How did you remember what I looked like?"

"I'm glad you like it. I could never forget your face. It's so pleasing. You didn't remember mine? Did you even think about me?"

"Of course I did."

"What did you think when you thought about me?" she asked with a coquettish grin.

"I thought how lovely you are."

Maritza blushed. "I memorized your face and *voilà*, here you are. I have to admit I felt close to you when I drew it, as if I had taken you apart and put you back together."

Close to him! He wanted to take her in his arms. No one had ever given him such a unique and personal gift.

"You're a lonely man, aren't you, Herr Oberleutnant?"

"What makes you say that?" he bristled. The warmth was now a burning flush that crept up his neck onto his cheeks. He looked down and brushed away a nonexistent piece of lint on his thigh.

His brows were knitted, and his face upset or humiliated, Maritza couldn't tell which, and to lessen the unintended sting of her words, she stroked the side of his face, sending a shiver of excitement through him. "I can tell because I know it when I see it. I'm always lonely except when I'm with you."

What a wonderful person she is, Will thought. Why wasn't I able to admit it? It is true, after all. As much as he wanted to, he could never say those words. None of that mattered now. Lonely was nowhere. He tilted her face up and kissed her on the lips. "You make me happy, Marisya," he whispered,

His kiss gave her a thrill of pleasure, but when he breathed that name so intimately, Maritza remembered her deception and drew back. Prickles of fear darted through her chest. She couldn't let him go on calling her by a false name. How would she explain why she was using one? She felt something real for this man, though it wouldn't mean a thing if he couldn't accept who she was. Germans despise Jews. If she told him the truth, he might spit the taste of her from his mouth, call her horrible names, and hit her.

Marisya had pulled away abruptly, and Will was confused. "I am sorry. I shouldn't have done that."

"I didn't mind."

"You are trembling."

Wait. She didn't have to tell him anything. He could be married for all she knew, though he didn't wear a ring, and their time together wasn't going to last anyway. Why not enjoy him until then? He was the only bright spot in her dreary life, so different from the Germans in the street with their lascivious winks and degrading comments. But I must tell him, she thought, or I will never know what kind of person he is. I can't be with a hateful man.

He didn't know where she lived. She sat on her knees, so if he moved to hit her or pin her down, it would be easier to jump up and run away. "Herr Oberleutnant, I have something to tell you."

"What is that?" he asked, smiling.

"I haven't been honest with you."

"No?" His smile faded.

She took a deep breath. "My name isn't Marisya. I have a false identity card because I'm Jewish," she whispered, rushing through her confession and gripping the edge of her coat. Her heart beat with strange little ticks, and all the moisture fled from her mouth. Engel gave her a look she couldn't read, followed by an excruciating silence. A chill went down her spine. That look could only mean one thing. A sob rose in her constricting chest and burst from her throat.

"I'm s-sorry. I ha-had to tell you. Are you go-going to turn me in?" Her tongue and lips were so dry and woolen that she had trouble forming the words. Panicking, she tried to gauge how long it would take her to grab her coat, but he was sitting on part of it, and she couldn't leave it here. She attempted to pull it out from under him.

"What are you doing?"

"Please let me have my coat, and I will go." Tears rolled down her cheeks. This was her own fault. She should never have gone with a German and think she could trust him. Now she would have to face the consequences.

Will grabbed her hands. "No."

Gripped by wild terror, Maritza tried to wrest her hands from his hold, but he wouldn't let go. She almost shouted for help before realizing that would make things worse. Why didn't I ask about his views first? I'm stupid, stupid, stupid. Oh my God, his pistol! He's going to take it out and shoot me. She let out a doleful wail.

"Please, keep your voice down. I am not going to hurt you."

"Just shoot me and get it over with," she cried.

Fearful that she might start screaming, Will dropped her hands and wrapped crushing arms around her. He held her head in place with one hand until his cheek was against hers and his lips were by her ear. "Stop crying and listen to me. I will not turn you in or hurt you, not now, not ever. I promise." He held her until the tears stopped, and she went limp in his arms. "I have a secret. My pistol has never been fired."

"You didn't know that you had kissed a Jew," she snuffled.

"I kissed you, a woman, and I am going to do it again." He brushed his lips across hers.

A bolt of heat went through her, and she pulled away again. Oberleutnant Engel was saying all the right things, all those she wanted to hear, but being so close to him made her feel disoriented and weak. His scent was so masculine, his arms so strong, and she wanted more than his ephemeral kisses.

"I'm sorry I lied," she said, wiping her face with his proffered handkerchief.

"You were being careful. I thought you were going to tell me something awful—that you were leaving the city and I would never see you again. You are very brave for confiding in me, but you should never tell anyone else. You have an advantage with your fair coloring, and I am relieved you have that card. May I see it?"

Maritza took it from her purse and passed it to him. The name on the card was Marisya Kamińska and gave an address which Will committed to memory. "What is your real name?"

"Maritza Laska." Drained from the multitude of emotions, she needed solitude. "I have to go now, Herr Oberleutnant. Thank you for the presents," she said as he helped her to her feet. She tied the kerchief on, slipped into her coat, and gathered the bags.

Looking stricken, he was at her side in a flash. "Will you come next Sunday?"

"I think so." She drew in a shaky breath. "Yes."

Chapter 23

Will sat on a stone bench in the back of the house posed like Rodin's *The Thinker,* one hand under his chin, the other over his knee. The sun, so brightly beaming an hour or two earlier, had been bullied away by dark clouds. As far as his heart was concerned, it didn't matter that Maritza was Jewish, but the terror in her eyes while waiting for his reaction was something he could not forget. Had it been another officer, disastrous consequences would have followed. Even men who were against the Nazi racial ideas wouldn't be foolish enough to take up with a Jewish woman. She had taken the risk to tell him. Why, he wondered, when she knew so little about him?

You're a lonely man. What an uncomfortable moment that was. Will thought he was doing his utmost to present himself as a paragon of strength and confidence, but he had given himself away at the outset, specifically telling her that he left the park because he had no one to talk to. If that wasn't the definition of lonely, then what was? She told him the truth because she recognized a kindred spirit and thought enough of herself to be selective, even in these desperate times.

What kind of life was this? Every facet of it was controlled by the Nazis. If Will could have a relationship with Maritza, a part of him would be free from the chains that bound him to his insufferable situation. Since that wasn't possible, how would he win her? An effervescent charge had coursed through him the moment he saw her at Jozef's stall, an instant, extreme attraction. He felt something extraordinary when he kissed her: a blend of intense arousal, of being lit by a bright light, and having drunk a strong wine. She was intoxicating and set his insides on fire. The Greeks, he once read, termed this feeling *theia mania,* madness from the gods, for love at first sight.

It was the first time Will had experienced the exquisiteness of full, soft, moist lips. Karoline's were as thin and dry as a line on paper, and her long, rough tongue darted in and out of his mouth like a snake, then whirled as if run on batteries. His hand went to his lips to wipe away the memory.

We cannot go on meeting in a park forever, he thought. They had been lucky so far, but if one do-gooder came along, saw them, and reported his license plate, or a rogue Gestapo man happened by, the penalty for him would be a transfer to the Russian front, even if his file was stamped unfit for combat. Maritza would be sent to a labor camp or straight into a brothel.

There was nowhere else to go. Having her come to his quarters was not an option. Polish women, unless they were maids, were forbidden in officers' living spaces, though some men brought them in and never got caught. Poles were not permitted to ride in officers' vehicles, either. So many obstacles. The one woman he wanted, it seemed he couldn't have.

On Sunday, Will brought more food. "I have utensils this time." He produced a knife and sliced the loaf. It gave him such pleasure to see her eat.

"You think of everything," Maritza cooed.

"I missed you," he said. "I thought about you constantly."

"I thought about you, too."

Her soft fingertips brushed the back of his neck as he leaned in to kiss her, making his skin tingle. He longed to touch her and feel her hands all over his body. It wouldn't do to start kissing her deeply in a park. He wanted to be alone with her in his quarters, but for now the only place for them was beneath a willow tree, hoping they wouldn't be seen. An idea! If Maritza had German identity papers, they would be able to meet in public. He would have to buy her some fresh clothing and shoes. That wasn't a problem, though there was little chance of finding out what documents were needed without arousing suspicion, unless she knew of a way.

"I am curious. How did you get your identity card?"

"My husband arranged it with Zofia, the girl I live with," she said without thinking.

Husband? Will's stomach clenched. He kept his face impassive, as if this bit of information had no effect on him, but he couldn't fool his heart; it knocked against his ribs before deflating, and the air hissed out between his teeth.

He assumed she was single. She had agreed to meet him three times, and he couldn't have prefaced his initial invitation by asking about her marital status. What kind of woman meets a man in a secluded place and kisses him? One whose husband is locked up in a prison or camp or laboring in a German factory. She had kissed him out of loneliness and admitted as much. That in itself was no crime, though he wasn't going to get involved with a married woman whom he shouldn't be interested in to begin with and put himself in a situation that would lead to emotional suffering.

Will was no stranger to loneliness, but he couldn't allow himself to be trifled with. No matter how special Maritza was, he wouldn't see her again. *Good thing I didn't tell her how much I care for her. I would have looked like an idiot,* he thought, his face stony. *She is just amusing herself with me.* A tense silence, then a pointed question from him to satisfy his curiosity before he stood up to leave. "Where is your husband now?"

"Dead. Shot and killed this past year by the SS. He was in the resistance."

Will's waspishness vanished. His rash assumption made him want to shrink into himself. It was wrong to be this preoccupied with his own feelings when Maritza had suffered so much, and he had to be better than his petty thoughts. "I am sorry. You have had the lion's share of heartache."

Maritza pushed Andrush from her mind. "Do you have a wife or girlfriend back in Germany or here?"

"No wife, no girlfriend. I am unattached." Then he scowled, realizing her question was a trap. "I am not the kind of man who would do that." What did she think of him? He wasn't a womanizer in the real world. She must have forgotten his ineptitude when he first asked to spend time with her.

Maritza gave a sudden, short laugh. "You needn't look so insulted, Herr Oberleutnant. It is a fair question. You must be one of the rare birds in this city with intact morals."

Will glanced at her, his feathers ruffled. "I like to think so."

He's one in a million, she thought, savoring the look of him and breathing in the spicy scent his kisses left around her mouth.

Another thought came to him. Perhaps this Zofia could arrange for German identity for Maritza. He would tell her how he felt about her, that he wanted her in his life, and they couldn't continue to meet in the park. The weather was changing, and the leaves of the willows that provided the perfect cover were turning yellow and would soon fall. "I have been thinking," he began.

"I knew I smelled smoke."

There were a few seconds of pause before Will caught on to the joke, then the corners of his eyes crinkled and he burst out laughing. It was deep and hearty, sounded so foreign to his ears, and went on and on until tears formed in his eyes. All his stored-up tensions evaporated.

"I should go," Maritza said, unknowingly disrupting his plans. She wanted to get back and stash the rest of the food.

"Why does time fly when we are together? Next week?"

"Yes, and thank you for everything you brought me."

"I want you to be happy, Maritza."

"I am with you," she said, as he kissed her goodbye.

Before Zofia returned and after having eaten more of the food, she remembered the oberleutnant's kisses. He's a clever one, she thought. He knows how to make a girl want him.

Chapter 24

Will burned to see Maritza again while the days moved with sluggish indifference. Sunday brought gray skies, cold temperatures, and the threat of rain, sending him into a stir. If rain started before or during their meeting, he wouldn't be able to see her, or they would have to go their separate ways and wait another whole week. The weather gods were in a good mood.

After greeting her with a tender kiss, they sat close to each other on her coat. "Why not put it on?" he asked. "Your teeth are chattering."

"I have this sweater, and I don't want you to sit on the damp grass. Your uniform will get dirty," she answered.

"That is the least of my worries. I don't want you to get sick."

She put on the coat, and he noticed the holes. "What happened there?"

"Oh look," Maritza pointed to a bird on a branch of a distant tree. "Isn't that a skylark? I read they fly away around this time of year for warmer countries." She had been euphoric all week waiting to see him, and now he was asking the wrong questions.

"Why do you change the subject?" Will asked, a twinge of annoyance in his voice.

"It's nothing, just a little accident that happened a long time ago, and I don't want to spend our precious time together discussing depressing things."

"Dare I ask about the girl you live with? What does she do?"

"She's a courier for the Home Army." There was no need to withhold this information from him. It couldn't be as significant or dangerous to his existence as locking lips with a Jew. "I don't like her."

"Why do you live with her if she is so unpleasant?"

Maritza didn't want to step into the same muddy waters that would lead back to conversations about the holes in the coat. "I'm waiting for the war to end so I can get to England. That's why I'm living with her." This explanation was downright ridiculous, and she avoided his probing eyes.

"Do you have relatives in England? How are you able to live? You never mentioned work."

"I have no relatives. I just want to go to a free country. It's complicated. My husband left enough for food and rent before he left, but it's almost gone." Maritza looked down at her hands.

"What will you do when the money runs out?"

"I will have to work."

Will thought about that for a moment. He knew what work would entail for her. With her German language skills, she could be employed in an office surrounded by Nazis who would hound her, and one of them might even ship her off to his home in Germany to work as a maid for his family or take her in as a servant here to cater to his every whim. Working in a hotel or restaurant would pay next to nothing and bring her unwanted attention, and the thought of her being pawed at or abused made his blood boil. Even if Zofia could get the German identity papers, the potential for discovery and the risk it brought to both him and Maritza was too high. He eliminated her as a possible source.

"It is worrisome that you live with her. Even though you have nothing to do with her activities, if the Gestapo comes, you will be arrested and taken to Pawiak prison for interrogation. Do you know what goes on in that place?"

"I've heard of it, but—"

"People are tortured and murdered there. I shudder to think of you working. Women are mistreated, and monthly wages are so low that I don't see how Zofia can expect you to meet even a quarter of the cost of living in the apartment, not including food. I wish you would stop coming to this park alone. You think the men on the street are minding their business, but they are unpredictable. Your beautiful hair could attract them to you like a magnet."

Maritza smiled coyly. "And what attracted *you*, Herr Oberleutnant?"

"I am not a predator, though there are plenty of them around. Some miscreant could come upon you when you are engrossed in your drawing, put his hand over your mouth, drag you into the bushes, and have his way with you."

"Are you implying that I cut my hair or not go out? Sooner or later, I will have to work."

"My point is, young lady," Will said sternly, "that you are in harm's way here."

Why was he speaking to her like a cross schoolmaster? She thought any minute now he would take a switch and rap her across the knuckles. "Well, I will just have to move into one of the palaces with round-the-clock guards."

"I am speaking seriously, and you jest? This is the worst part of Warsaw."

"Wasn't this the worst part of Warsaw every time you asked me to meet you here?" Maritza rose, ready for his response, which was sure to be lacking. Men's explanations for their motives were always self-serving. It didn't cross her mind that this principle applied to herself as well as to women in general.

"I didn't realize how unsafe this area is for a young woman alone," he said, standing. "I would like you to come stay with me so I can protect you." Will hadn't planned on saying that and hadn't considered it an option. The words simply flew from his mouth with surprising ease. "I know it is not ideal, and you must stay upstairs in the daytime while I work, but you will be safe. My quarters are separate from the office, and no one will ever know you are there except for my Polish housekeeper, Alina. She is the wife of the vegetable seller at the market and a very caring and loyal person. There is plenty of food to eat and hot water to bathe in. We can't continue to meet outside like this, shivering in the cold. What if it rains and we are not able to see each other for weeks? I would be very sad." He reached for her hands.

"Stay with you?" She snatched her hands away and gave him a withering look. "And then what? You will bring me back here after you tire of me?"

"You have misunderstood my intentions."

"Just what are your intentions, Herr Oberleutnant?"

"I love you," he said, "I want you with me, and will never tire of you." Relieved of its secret, his heart leaped with joy.

Maritza's rosy lips parted as if to let loose a sigh of pleasure or say *I love you too.* She took a step toward him, then stopped. His words, so unexpected, so pure and real, sparked a sudden uncontrollable fear. *Be careful what you wish for,* Rivka used to say, which was never fully understood until now. How she craved to be alone with Engel, but that would lead to heartache and might include falling pregnant. She believed he loved her, and that would last as long as it was convenient. There was no future with a German officer; he was married to the military and should have had the damn sense to consider her feelings before attempting to coax her into a relationship set upon shifting sands.

"Thank you for the offer, but I have managed thus far on my own and don't need your protection or your *love,*" she said, grimacing at the word. "It's best that we not see each other again."

Will's heart plummeted and his face, which a moment ago glowed with optimism, now went slack. Swallowing hard, he shoved his hands into pockets. "If that is your wish. I didn't mean to offend you."

A fire-breathing dragon vaulted from her chest. "You have, you have offended me! How dare you throw me a bone and expect me to jump into your lap like a grateful dog. Go to a brothel if you want a whore." Maritza glowered at him and flounced off.

She had rejected him forcefully without a speck of fear. Now, the impact of her actions triggered alarm bells, and her bravado fell away. Engel admitted men can be unpredictable. That meant *he* was unpredictable. It didn't matter that he promised never to hurt her—that pledge was made before she scorned him, and scorned men in Wehrmacht uniforms would certainly become vengeful. Press one wrong button and their killer instincts could be activated. The typical German sense of entitlement that he had so cleverly concealed might morph into rage, burst forth, and he could attack her from behind or shoot her in the back.

She broke into a run and turned her head once to see if he was closing in, but he was already away in the opposite direction walking towards his car without so much as a backward glance. Of the offenses he committed that afternoon, this was the most egregious.

Chapter 25

Maritza let herself into the apartment and ran to the bedroom in tears, flinging herself on her cot. The wooden frame creaked and rocked, then collapsed onto the floor. Yipping in pain, she clenched her fists and longed for the comfort of Andrush's arms. Why did he have to die and leave her all alone? She sobbed and cursed the Germans for her rotten life; there was no way she could change it for the better. The one man who offered an alternative and his love was a deceitful manipulator and would find a way to punish her for her brash behavior.

Germans want us Polish women meek and at their feet, not to challenge them, she thought frantically. I should have said I wanted to think about his offer, that I had to get home and just never returned to see him. Oh my God, I've gotten myself between the straits! Once the fear got its hooks in, and they were in deep, her intuition and logical thinking put its hands up and surrendered.

Before Engel mentioned the dangers of living with Zofia, Maritza hadn't thought much about it. Zofia never kept anything in the apartment that would arouse suspicion in case of raids by the Gestapo, which they had been fortunate to escape thus far, though they both could be implicated if she or her contacts were caught and buckled under pressure. For days, Maritza sat by the window chewing her nails and looking for the men in leather coats or SS uniforms who were coming any minute to take her and Zofia away to Pawiak. *Two Jewesses—a petite blonde and a red-haired courier.* Engel had seen her address, and it was a matter of time before he turned them in.

Common everyday neighborhood noises, faces of people below in the street, and even clouds took on a sinister aspect. Hissing, devilish voices came through the plumbing pipes, and the thudding of footsteps in the stairwell turned her insides to pulp. Should she warn Zofia? No, that would end in disaster. Admitting that she met with a German officer was tantamount to treason, and her perfidy would not go unpunished.

It was in this state of nervous apprehension that Maritza existed. She tried not to think of Engel, but he hung like a spider in the cobwebs of her mind. In order to drive him from her thoughts, she convinced herself that he was a Janus-faced sexual deviant who roamed the streets looking for girls and women who still had a bit of meat on their bones, and she had stepped right into his trap. He was a liar and tried to use scaremongering tactics to get her into the palm of his hand. Good riddance!

Days passed before Will could bring himself to think about Maritza, before he tried to figure out how it went so wrong. He was certain she cared for him. It was there in her eyes, her touch, the way her face lit up when she saw him. What scared her away? He went over every word of their interactions and, after careful analysis, came to the conclusion that she didn't trust him. Of course, she didn't—he was German, and she was afraid of him.

She deserves a man with whom a future is possible, he thought. A noble sentiment, although entirely unrealistic as long as Poland was under Nazi rule. The days of jollity were gone. There were few decent men around who could provide stability. It was unlikely anyone would know Maritza was a Jew, but a Polish woman was a legitimate target for exploitation, harassment, and abuse.

Will's intentions were never frivolous, nor were they clearly defined. He hadn't considered all possible contingencies. The best he could give her was what he had offered. Their budding relationship was doomed to failure by the preposterous Nazi laws, and there was nothing he could do about it. Someday, he would learn not to trip over his own feet if he ever found someone who stirred him the way Maritza had.

Now that she was no longer in his life and there was nothing to look forward to, the approach of sundown each evening brought a return of the smothering sadness he felt before he met her, and he began to slip back into his old destructive thought patterns. He was unlovable, defective. No one would care if he passed away; no one would mourn him. Not one person would say in five or ten years that he was still missed. Wilhelm Engel was and always would be a blip, an also-ran, a perpetually empty cup.

No matter how hard he tried, Will couldn't stop thinking about her face and the eyes he had drowned in. Despite his best efforts to purge her from his mind, Maritza stayed in his thoughts day and night. The life she was living was as solitary as his, but he had access to things she didn't: real soap, quality foods, medicines, clothing. Why shouldn't two lonely people come together? He loved her. This was not a Karoline type of love where the feeling was only in his head; this was in his heart.

Then he remembered the address from her identity card. He would go there! No, that was out of the question. Going to the outdoor market was one thing—no one dared bother him, but those tenement buildings were filled with unsavory characters and resistance members who wouldn't waste a minute slitting his throat. At meetings, he and fellow officers were told time and again not to go there without specific orders and proper security in place. The Gestapo might also be around, and they had their own agenda. They would ask him what he was doing, and he'd have no satisfactory answer. Once they had you in their sights, those bastards could make life more miserable than it was already.

His only recourse was to go to Maritza's area and perhaps see her in the street, but the image of himself driving round and round like a sly creeper was disturbing. There was something distasteful and intrusive about the idea of searching for her when it was clear he was persona non grata, and he gave up.

In the weeks that followed, Will threw himself into his work with false enthusiasm, though his men noticed there was none of the liveliness in his face and light in his eyes that had been there previously. At the day's end, reluctant to return to his quarters where a malevolent silence awaited, he stayed in the office long after his staff had gone, rearranging systems and making improvements. He kept on, falling prey to *Verschlimmbesserung,* the act of making things worse while trying to make them better. I should have quit while I was ahead, he thought, throwing papers onto his desk. Now I have to put everything back the way it was.

The moment he returned to his room, he sank into the pit of dejection. He needed time off, though all leaves had been canceled until further notice. The last one he had was almost a year ago after Aunt Helga passed away, and he let the lease expire on her apartment. He wouldn't go back to Germany unless it was to celebrate the death of Hitler and freedom from Nazi tyranny, and the chance of that happening was as likely as throwing a seven on a single die.

Chapter 26

In the social hour following an afternoon meeting, as Will was inching towards the door hoping to slip out unnoticed, someone bellowed, "Willy! Willy Engel!"

Oh no. Trotting toward him was Dieter Hahn, an officer he had briefly worked with at the training facility in Hannover and never liked. A compulsive liar and backstabber, Dieter had the ability to compliment and demean in the same breath. His face was chimera-like—a frightening jumble of disparate animal parts guaranteed to bring everlasting trauma to children and probably the reason he never had any.

He had a habit of attaching himself to lower-ranking officers even though he wasn't in charge of them and then making their lives as unpleasant as possible. If a man complained about this, his commanding officer would write a negative comment in his permanent record after consulting with Dieter. *Leutnant X fails to demonstrate proper respect for superiors.* Will stayed out of the bully's way, unwilling to allow *his* perfect record to be ruined.

"Willy, it's been a long time."

"Yes." *Not long enough.* He wanted to kick himself for having chosen that moment to make his exit.

"You are better?"

"Better?"

"You know, the accident. Your head," Hahn said in a loud voice.

"Oh *that.*"

"You must come and meet my family. Dinner this Friday at seven."

"I don't think—"

"I outrank you, so it's an order."

"Very well, Captain. Thank you."

"Why so formal? Call me Dieter." He removed a fountain pen from his pocket and marked his address down on the sheet of paper outlining the meeting's agenda, forming every number and letter slowly, like a child who had recently learned to write. "See you Friday."

The Hahns' house in Mokotów was a couple miles from Will's office, one of the worst pieces of bad luck that could have happened to him. The reluctant guest arrived with a bouquet of winter flowers and a small box of chocolates he had driven around the city in search of—another chore he didn't want to do, but it would be bad form to show up empty-handed.

"Come in, Willy, come in. I see you brought the cold with you," said Dieter. A blast of wintry air howled into the foyer sending a stack of mail flying off the table. Let me take your coat." He introduced his stout, gray-haired wife, Fritzi, and her younger sister, Ludmila.

"It is a pleasure to meet you, Frau Hahn." Will took her hand, touched it to his lips, and presented her with the flowers.

"Thank you, Oberleutnant. How thoughtful."

A buxom blonde clad in a checkered dirndl dress, her hair in a crown of braids, Ludmila resembled an Oktoberfest barmaid, a look Will found cheap and unappealing. She had a sly glint in her eyes as she inspected him.

"Fräulein, a pleasure as well," he said, giving her the chocolates. She tossed the box aside. *What? No Fabergé egg?*

"A drink, Willy?" Dieter asked.

"Yes, please." Familiar aromas of dill and caraway permeated the air and made him very hungry. A small, rectangular table set for dinner had been pushed in front of a crackling fire. Perhaps this evening won't be so bad after all, Will said to himself. He was seated next to Ludmila. Dieter and his wife were at opposite ends. A Polish maid, whose aquamarine eyes reminded him of Maritza's and made him miss her acutely, came in with a large serving dish.

"We are having *Königsberger Klopse,* Willy."

"It smells wonderful. I haven't had this dish in years." The meatballs in a white sauce with boiled potatoes had always been a favorite of his.

"*Fritzi* prepared the food," Dieter told him when the maid left the room, to allay any fears his guest might have that a lowly Pole had mixed the meat with her hands and contaminated it. "We don't eat like this every night, so don't get any ideas that we live like kings, but you were coming, so I thought, why the hell not? I couldn't invite an old comrade over to eat liverwurst, and you looked like you needed a home-cooked meal. The flesh is hanging right off your face—you've gotten as thin as an asparagus spear. I managed to get a little beef, a little pork, through the back channels, if you know what I mean."

"Very kind of you to go to so much trouble."

"Are you married, Herr Engel?" asked Ludmila. She leaned over and pressed her breasts against his arm. "I don't see a ring."

"I am not."

"I find it strange that such an attractive man is single. Is something wrong with you?" She put her hand on his thigh under the table and moved it toward his crotch. He flicked her hand away and crossed his legs.

Dieter's hand zoomed past Will's face, the fork pointed at Ludmila. "Leave him alone."

"Really, Ludmila," objected Frau Hahn.

"You'll have to excuse her, Willy. She doesn't like the officers I usually bring home."

"I like this one," she said.

Unlucky me, Will thought.

The men talked about their time at the Hannover garrison. The maid came to clear away the dinner plates and struggled with the tray. The dishes rattled and slid from side to side.

"Be careful, Marzena!" Frau Hahn warned.

"Entschuldigung, meine Dame." Marzena's lips quivered.

"You should be sorry. Do things correctly the first time."

"I think the tray is too heavy," Will said.

"That's her job." Dieter grabbed his arm. "Sit down."

Ignoring the order, he took the tray and carried it to the kitchen. *"Danke,"* the maid whispered.

"What a gentleman," Ludmila purred when he returned to his seat. She put her hand back on his thigh. He brushed it off again and recrossed his legs.

"Thank you, Herr Engel," said Fritzi. "Those pieces are the last of a dinner service that has been in my family for generations. After Dieter was transferred here last summer, I gave up our Hannover apartment, and Ludmila and I were on our way to Münster to live with our aging mother when her house was destroyed in a bombing raid. She did not survive."

"How dreadful," said Will. "I am sorry."

"Those British swine!" Dieter banged the table. "When our flags fly over their wretched islands, they will wish they never involved themselves in Germany's business. You know, Willy, the presence of our families here in Warsaw is frowned upon for security reasons, but our situation was deemed a special case and an exception was made."

"A most deserving one," Will said. "Again, my condolences."

"The point of my story," she continued, "is that Dieter had a small apartment and ate his meals out, but when we received permission to come, he was assigned this house. It belonged to Jews and came fully stocked. Can you imagine that while waiting for our own things to arrive, we had to eat from the very same dishes that they used? I had no idea at first, and when I found out, I called in a special cleaning service to sanitize everything from top to bottom, which was more affordable than having to buy a whole new set of dishes for the interim."

"Willy, it was the toilets that got to me. I had them changed right away. Imagine parking one's buttocks on the same seat a Jew has sat on, even after it's been disinfected. That's where I drew the line."

"Don't speak of that at the table, dear," his wife said, as if her crude comments didn't stink.

These people are worse than troglodytes, thought Will, the meatballs roiling in his stomach.

"Marzena, bring the cake and coffee!" Dieter yelled.

She walked in slowly, theatrically, her hands firmly gripping the tray with the cake plates and coffee cups, placed it carefully on the table, then ran back into the kitchen and emerged with the coffee pot. A bit of the brew spilled onto the white tablecloth.

"Go away," Frau Engel said impatiently. "I will pour."

"Ja, Madame." Marzena scurried away before her mistress could find more fault with her.

"Real coffee tonight, Willy. I was able to find a small bag."

"Thank you. A treat, indeed."

Right then, a handsome young German shepherd came bouncing in, sniffed Ludmila's leg, latched onto it with its front paws, and began humping. "Get him off me!" she cried. "His nails are ripping my stockings!"

Dieter hopped up and kicked the animal in the ribs with his heavy boots. Will winced. Yelping in pain, the dog limped away. "I told Marzena not to let Bruno in while we are dining. She has as much sense as a Pygmy."

"Have you considered refreshing his training?" Will asked.

"Training? You can see he's untrainable and genetically inferior. He has a white toenail on each of his paws, a definite sign of poor breeding. To use *Reichsführer* Himmler's words, he's a *useless eater* and should be put to sleep."

Will pushed the cake around his plate. "How did you come to have him?" *You don't deserve such a beautiful animal.*

"He turned up one day. Marzena fed him, as if there's food to spare, and he wouldn't leave. She's short on brains."

"It takes brains to learn a second language, and she speaks German well," Will said.

Dieter made a face. "You're defending the Poles? Don't insult our race. She knows the words Fritzi taught her to humble herself. Say, Willy, have you been inside that Jewish ghetto?"

"No." The room suddenly seemed unbearably hot.

"Several German-owned factories that produce armaments and textiles for the Wehrmacht are located there, and I have occasionally accompanied my superiors on business to the establishments where our uniforms and socks are made. Do you know that thousands of Jews work in those plants and are given larger rations than the other ghetto residents?"

"People need energy to work, Dieter. Better-fed workers are more productive, and as a result, profits for the owners of those factories increase. That can't be denied. It is a matter of economics."

"Now you're an expert in economics? The whole thing is an abomination, I tell you. Their greed! It knows no bounds."

"Whose greed?" Will couldn't help himself. He couldn't take any more sanctimonious braying from this jackass.

Dieter's coffee cup halted at his lips. He put it down slowly. "You're joking, aren't you, Willy?"

"Well, I—"

"Of course you are, you funny man. You had me going there for a second. Haha. What I'm saying is that the Jews receive more rations, and some actually receive pay because they themselves demand it. Even in their current state, they are driven by avarice, and it's unbelievable that German businesses run by our brethren are pandering to subhumans! The whole Jewish race is contaminated and must be eradicated, and mark my words, it will be before long."

"What is your opinion, Oberleutnant?" asked Ludmila, taking a dainty bite of her cake.

Will had enough. "That is certainly an important issue," he said, pushing his chair away from the table, "and one that should not follow on the heels of such a delicious dinner. My compliments, Frau Hahn. Dieter, thank you for your hospitality. I must be going."

"You're leaving now? Why so soon?"

"Yes. A mountain of work is waiting to be finished. Good night." He bowed, went to the front door, and grabbed his coat from the hook.

"What a strange man," Ludmila said, followed by laughter.

"He had an accident a few years back. Head wound. I guess that explains it," Dieter added.

Will drove through the dark, silent streets wondering what those so-called superior beings in the house he just left and their fellow *übermenschen* would do when every "subhuman" was gone from the face of the earth and there was no one left to blame and hate. They would start killing each other. If he didn't find something to fill the void in his life, he would go insane. He made a mental note to visit the Wehrmacht kennels to see if they had any dogs available that were slated for execution.

Chapter 27

Trapped inside the apartment once the icy winter settled over Warsaw, Maritza sat on the old couch in her coat and knitted gloves that had unraveled at the fingertips, a blanket wrapped around her. She was hungry and cold and missed her family. All she had left were memories that were too agonizing to recall.

All the emotional turmoil and pain in her life had come from the actions of the filthy Germans. Maritza despised every one of them until she met Engel. He was forbidden fruit—she had a taste and wanted more. Drawing her in with his kisses and seductive voice, tempting her with rich ryes, juicy sausages, and creamy chocolates, he made her fall in love with him. He forced his way back into her mind and stayed there to her dismay, demanding her attention through all her waking hours and on into her dreams, until she had no choice but to think of him through a lens less distorted by fear.

Engel was part of an organization run by Nazis, and she didn't know what he was really like at his core or if he had taken lives. Her heart told her that he was a good man, though the inner workings of the mind of a good German were harder to understand than those of the beasts who ruled her country and killed her family, because to be German was to be bad.

He had caused a dilemma that left Maritza with conflicting, disturbing emotions and without a sense of how to rationally order her feelings for a man who was technically an enemy. Assurances not to hurt her had been given, but uncertainty remained. Doubts washed in and out like the tides. She missed his precise way of speaking, his manliness, and the way he looked at her. The biggest hurdle had been cleared; he didn't care that she was Jewish and had given her a chance to get away from her abysmal existence. They could be together now had she not been so obstinate.

Maritza wondered if he had found another girl. The thought of them kissing or making love caused her to thrum with jealousy. He let her go so easily. Tell a German officer goodbye, and he will walk away, hide his hurt, and pretend the woman he claimed to love never existed. If only he would show up at her door and take her away with him, but Oberleutnant Engel of the warm hands, delicious kisses, and spicy scent was never coming back.

She sat staring out the dirty kitchen window one Friday afternoon. Thirsty, there was nothing to drink. Water had to be boiled first, and there wasn't a drop of tea to be had. She would love a cup right now with a pastry, but the closest she would come to that was a slice of stale bread topped with a piece of smelly, gelatinous cheese.

"Mishka," Zofia began.

"What is it?"

"There's no money left for your portion of the rent and food, so you have to work. I give you a week, two at the most. If you don't find something by then, you'll have to make other arrangements, but first try the Polonia Hotel on Bahnhofstrasse and ask for Izabela. You can apply as a maid, and you get a free meal each day." She neglected to mention that the free meal was a cup of watery soup. "All you need is your identity card."

"I should go and check," Maritza replied with a fake smile.

"Yes. Go now before it gets dark. Andrush would be proud of you."

You uncharitable rag! she raged silently. How dare you bring him up to me and say his name in vain. *Proud?* He would want to choke the life out of you. The memory of him in days gone by chopping wood at Bronka's without a shirt, muscles rippling, golden hair hanging over his eyes, and his sweet smile brought tears to her eyes. He was a hero—vibrant, capable, and strong—and would live that way forever in her heart.

She went into the bedroom. From the back of her sketchbook, she tore a tiny, hand-drawn map of a location nowhere near the hotel, and put on every article of clothing she owned under her coat. Pulling up the floorboard, she stuffed the remaining zloty and the bag of her mother's jewelry into her pockets, slung her fraying purse over her shoulder, and walked out the door.

"Good luck!" Zofia trilled.

That same Friday, a messenger delivered a note to Will from Dieter Hahn inviting him to an evening event and waited for him to write a response. *Dieser Drecksau!* That dirty pig, he wanted to shout. I have to say yes, or he might come here in person. He unscrewed the cap off his pen, wrote *Ja,* and almost threw the note at the messenger.

After a bear of a day spent obsessing over the coming event, Will went to a cinema packed with civil administration officials and only a few Wehrmacht officers. He hadn't read the message carefully enough and damn it, he should have declined.

A gigantic Nazi eagle-on-swastika emblem hung from a screen, and speeches rife with propaganda were given, one segueing into the next. Fantasies of making love to Maritza in a field of swaying grass got him through the haranguing.

Dieter rushed over while an adjustment was being made to the microphone before the final speaker took the stage. "Ah, Willy, glad you could make it. Guess who the special guest is?"

"I give up."

"Why so glum? It's someone important."

"Well, who is it?"

"Dr. Fischer," he whispered, rubbing his hands together gleefully. "Oh! I'm being transferred back to Germany effective next week."

"In that case, would you consider selling the dog to me?"

"Dog? What dog?"

"Bruno. The shepherd with the white toenails."

"Him? Sorry, he ran off and hasn't been since. Let's talk later. It's starting."

You bastard! Will could hardly contain his anger.

Dr. Ludwig Fischer, the Governor of the Warsaw District and one who gave orders for murder, came on stage. A large, heavy man with a youthful face, his heart was made of steel, and apparently he had been absent on the day souls were handed out. According to Feldwebel Bach, Fischer was the person responsible for the creation of the Warsaw Ghetto. Hans said it was he who had ordered mass executions in the city and the deportations of Poles and Jews. Will slept through the speech with his eyes open.

Fischer finished to thunderous applause, put his overcoat over his shoulders, and gave it a dramatic Draculian swirl before marching out between two bodyguards. The evening concluded with the ritual salutes to Hitler, a revolting display that could not be avoided. Will gave a silent curse after each heil, then slipped out before Dieter could catch sight of him. What a sorry lot, he thought, and sped away from the venue.

Chapter 28

Tired and in a foul mood, Will put the key in the door.
"Herr Oberleutnant."

Startled, he wheeled around. Maritza emerged from the shadows, shivering and pulling her threadbare coat around her. "Maritza! What are you doing here?"

"Do you want me to leave?"

"No. I am just so surprised to see you. My God, you are freezing. Come inside." He glanced at the yard, hoping she hadn't been followed, and ushered her in. "How did you get here and find this place?" he asked, gripping her shoulders, then wiping strands of dust from her kerchief.

"You told me where you lived, remember? And I made a little diagram, see?" She dug it out of her pocket. "I took the tram and walked and waited, not sure if you were still here."

"You walked around after curfew, and nobody questioned you? You could have been arrested. How did you get in the gate?"

"I took the long way around the barricades. The gate wasn't locked. I arrived just before curfew and hid in that shed until I saw the lights of the car, and you got out."

Incensed over having to attend the assembly, he had forgotten to lock the gate and was glad Maritza had access to the yard. She had been in that spider-filled shed, though, for hours.

"Is someone here? A lady friend? I don't want to intrude."

He gave a small laugh. "There is no one here."

"Is it possible your offer still stands? Can I stay with you? I know you must hate me for the horrid way I acted."

"I could never hate you, and certainly you can stay. Let me make you some tea and a sandwich, and we can go upstairs to talk." Weeks spent missing her, and here she was in his kitchen. It didn't seem real. "Did you tell Zofia you were coming here?"

"No, I would never tell her anything. She thinks I went to look for work."

"Is she expecting you back?"

"I'm not going back. If you don't mind, I'd like to take a bath, and then I need to sleep," she said, still shivering.

"Have some tea and eat, and I will get it ready."

The congestion left her head as she sank into the soothing hot water. Lathering up with real soap, she scrubbed every inch of herself, letting out the water and refilling the tub. The last bath she took with hot running water was a lifetime ago at home, before the invasion. Will left out a pair of pajamas, socks, and his robe. She put them on and came out flapping her arms like a bird. Everything hung on her.

"I will buy you some new things. Let me help you with your hair so it won't be sopping wet on the pillow."

"I have some money to pay for them," she offered.

"That isn't necessary."

"I insist."

"Ssh," he said.

She gladly gave in to his ministrations as he rubbed her head, blotted her hair, combed it out, and wrapped it in a fresh towel. "Thank you," she said, her eyes closing. He led her to the bed, pulled back the covers, and she was out the moment her head hit the pillow.

Alone in his own bed, Will couldn't sleep. He suspected Maritza had a falling out with Zofia, but whatever the reason, he couldn't be happier that she was there.

Waking early to a gray, snowy morning, Will lit a fire, dressed, and waited for Maritza to get up. To pass the time, he leafed through a book on farming that he'd read to death, put it down after a minute, then paced around the room. I should let her be, he thought. She needs to recover from being out in the cold for so long. Lying on the bed, he tried to arrange the things he wanted to say to her, but couldn't put his emotions into words.

Will wanted to hold and love her the way he did in the simple but beautiful fantasies he created of them together, in which he played himself without needing to swing from vines and beat his chest, though it was much too soon for that.

When the clock struck twelve, he went down to the kitchen and heated some food, brought it up on a tray, and parked himself in a chair by her bed. It was another hour before she opened her eyes. The towel had slipped off, and the mass of curly hair fanned out around her head like a nimbus. "She wakes," he said. "I should sound the trumpets."

She smiled and stretched like a cat. "Good morning."

"Good morning? It is past lunchtime. You slept more than fifteen hours."

"That was the best sleep I've had in years. Mmm, what is that smell?" she asked, sniffing the air.

"Me," he joked.

"Well, you smell good enough to eat."

"I will hold you to that," he laughed. Then he blushed. "Figuratively, I meant."

She giggled. "Of course."

"There are potatoes, onions, and sausage, nothing fancy. My culinary skills go no further than heating and slicing. I am sure it has gone cold by now. Shall I go down and reheat it?"

"I will eat it as is. I'm so hungry."

"Your clothes are in the closet, in case you're wondering."

"I'd like to burn those things. I'm going to stay in your comfortable pajamas and robe, if you don't mind."

"Not at all."

She observed him under her lashes as they ate. He wore plain brown trousers with suspenders that dropped at his sides. The sleeves of his white shirt were rolled up to the elbows and revealed strong arms. His hair fell over his forehead, giving him a boyish look. How strange it is now that we're alone, she thought. I have to make things right with him.

Similar thoughts were weaving through Will's mind. Although Maritza had touched upon it the previous night, neither seemed willing now to broach the subject of the major issue they'd had, the discussion of which would surely be emotionally charged.

"It is snowing," he said.

"Is it?"

"Yes. Were you warm enough last night with your damp hair?"

"I was, thank you."

"Shall I help you comb it?"

Her hands flew to her head. "I must look frightful."

"That is not possible. Would you care for some chocolate?"

"I couldn't eat another bite."

"I found an old Victrola in the attic the other day along with some classical recordings, if you would like to listen to some. They are not in the best condition, but it is something."

"I would," Maritza sparkled. "I haven't listened to music in ages."

Bowing like a French waiter, he opened the door to his room. "After you, Madame."

Will relit the fire while she looked through the records. "I love *Ave Maria*. I used to play it on the piano," she said.

"A woman of many talents. I hope to hear you play one day."

"I hope to play for you one day, if I haven't forgotten how."

They sat on chairs in front of the fire; its light cast that part of the room in a warm glow. When the music stopped, he got up and turned off the player. "Maritza, I apologize for my presumptuous behavior that day. I failed to consider your feelings." His face flushed crimson. "I was remiss in not thinking things through. It was wrong of me to assume you would be interested in having more of a relationship with me."

"Then you regret asking me here?" she asked, crossing her legs away from him.

"I regret distressing you."

"You let me go so easily. Why didn't you come after me?"

"Would going after you have changed anything? You wanted nothing to do with me."

"I didn't mean it."

"You sounded sure of it."

"What I'm sure of is that I love you," she said, coming to stand in front of him. "I was confused and afraid and questioned how I could have such strong feelings for you when we had only seen each other a few times. I wanted to come, not for a quick affair, but to have a real relationship, and how is that even possible in light of the *laws*. That's a lot to ask of a man in these times when he has no firm idea of his future, and it's more likely than not that he will be sent away to another place."

"It was wrong of me to treat you so harshly. I lost everyone and couldn't imagine loving you and then being abandoned. After days and weeks of missing you, I decided I would rather have your love and share your life for whatever time we may have than not to have it at all. That is, if you still want me."

Will's heart flew singing to his throat. "Still want you? I loved you from the first time I saw you at that market. I wished for a real relationship with you but didn't know how to make it happen. Asking you to come here was the only way I could think of, the only way we wouldn't be found out. I missed you so much these past weeks, and I will never forsake you."

"Can I sleep in here with you from now on?"

Overcome with desire, he pulled her close and kissed her. Maritza lost herself in his woodsy scent and the warmth of his mouth. They kissed feverishly. The area between her legs throbbed. She slipped out of the nightclothes, now naked in his arms. All the blood in Will's body flooded into his groin, his heart pulsed, and his breath came in short bursts.

Desperate for him, she unbuttoned his shirt with quick fingers. He tore off his clothes and tossed them away. They lay on the bed and kissed, locked in embrace, their hands roaming over the other's back. "I can't wait," she gasped, "I need you inside me."

Will couldn't wait either. He lifted her hips up and entered her. Pressing together and moving in rhythm, each thrust brought them waves of passion. Uninhibited and vocal, her response to him drove him wild.

When they finished, she stroked his chest and abdomen, her eyes falling on the scars. Captivated by the magic of their lovemaking, with him on top, she hadn't noticed them. "What happened to you?" she asked in a tremulous voice. It never occurred to her to ask if he had participated in the invasion—how else would he have gotten those long scars? As far as she knew, an oberleutnant was an officer who gave orders to his men on the battlefield. Innocent civilians could have died as a result of one he had given, or maybe he killed them himself with a weapon other than his pistol. She was afraid of his answer.

"No. I didn't take part in that," Will said. "I was in an auto accident in Hannover before it took place and almost died. I was in the hospital for a year. I am fine, though." He didn't mention the nerve pain in his leg that bothered him if he lifted something heavy or slept a certain way, at times causing him to limp, and he often suffered severe headaches. She seemed to care deeply about his tribulations, but there was no reason to call her attention to things she hadn't noticed.

"I'm sorry," Maritza burned with shame. How quickly she had judged him.

"That's all right. You didn't know."

At this juncture, love was new, and its future success would depend on much more than physical attraction and rose-colored perceptions of the other person. Will got up and added another log to the fire, sending a shower of sparks up the chimney, while outside the cold wind blew the snow into drifts. They made love again, and afterward he curled behind her, his breath warm against her neck as he dozed. Lying in Oberleutnant Engel's arms, Maritza thought, was pure bliss. With this strong, yet sensitive man who loved her—a good German—she had found a safe haven.

Chapter 29

After a weekend of pleasure in bed with Maritza, Monday morning arrived far too soon for Will. He unwrapped himself from her, forced himself up, and prepared to start the day ahead. "Put the robe on," he said. "Alina will be here in a minute, though stay in bed as long as you like. I am going out when the stores open to buy you some clothing and stop for food. Tell me your sizes."

"You're too good to me," she said, kissing him. "Mmm, I love how you smell. I can't get enough of you."

Aroused now, Will yearned to make love to her again; she had unleashed a fiery lust that he only dreamed possible, but there was no time. The truck bringing his men was idling at the gate. He gave Maritza a quick kiss and went down to let them in.

Alina arrived behind them, and he followed her into the kitchen. "There is a Polish lady upstairs named Maritza, and she is going to be living here from now on. No one can know about this. She will stay upstairs at all times while I am working. I am sure you can understand how important it is that no one discovers she is here. I have already discussed everything with her, and I know I can rely upon your discretion."

"I understand, Herr Engel," she said solemnly and went up to meet her.

Will drove to a German fashion store and ducked in. "Please direct me to the smallest size you have in women's clothing,"

he said to the heavyset sales clerk. "I am in a bit of a rush." This was the first time he had shopped for a woman; had it been in a different time and place he might have enjoyed it, but concerned that he might run into an acquaintance, he wanted to speed things along.

"This way." She lumbered to a rack, then held up a dress large enough to shelter a platoon. Will shook his head. "She is tiny."

"We don't carry anything smaller."

"I will try another shop."

"I'm afraid you won't have much luck, sir. All the shops carry the standard sizes. We German ladies are big and strong, the result of centuries of good breeding."

Too many bread dumplings, he said to himself.

"You might check the teen department at Jablkowski Brothers, or if your lady has a seamstress, I can suggest some things that can be easily altered."

"Yes, thank you."

"I do recommend a garter belt and stockings," she said. "No silk these days, though we do have a few pairs of cotton, nice and thick."

"Very good." He looked at his watch.

"Everything we sell is made in the Reich. Only the finest for our women."

Come off your high horse, Will thought angrily. If Maritza came in speaking German, you would say, *Only the finest for you, Fräulein,* and she would have the last laugh. He took the packages and left.

At the end of the day, he went upstairs. Maritza was still in the robe, though her hair was done up loosely, giving her a regal look. "Alina is going to alter the clothing you bought me, so I stayed like this," she said. "Thank you, Wilhelm, for everything." She cast her eyes down demurely. It was the first time she used his given name.

He laughed. "I prefer Will or Willy."

"Willy, then. I thought you might like this," she said with a provocative smile, let the robe fall, and stood before him in nothing but the garter belt and stockings.

"Oh yes," he murmured, coming to embrace her.

They were too busy making love that evening to eat the dinner Alina had prepared and left out in the kitchen, but it made a fine meal for the resident mouse.

Chapter 30

A tall, thin man wearing dark clothing and a woolen cap made his way through the blustery January night, moving stealthily through neighborhoods of dilapidated apartment houses. His lungs burned from the cold, making it hard to breathe, but the wind at his back propelled him forward.

He came to the building and went up the stairs, his heart hammering with anticipation. The window shades were drawn. Two knocks on the door went unanswered. Patience gone, he picked the lock with the tip of his knife, went in, and switched on the light. The bulb did little to light the shabby room. His gut instinct told him something wasn't right. Slowly, he opened the door to the bedroom and flicked on another dim light. The redhead, alone in the room, was asleep in her bed.

"Get up," he growled, ripping the covers off.

Zofia gave a strangled cry and sat up.

He removed his cap. "Where is she?"

"Andrush?" She rubbed her eyes. "I heard you were dead!"

"Where is Mishka?"

"What happened to you? Where's Moshe? Is he alive?"

"I ask the questions, you give the answers. Where is she?"

His face was so red she could feel the heat coming off it. "I don't know. She went out to look for work and never came back."

"What?" Andrush thought he misheard. "What did you say?"

"One day she went to look for work and didn't return." Zofia didn't dare look into his flashing tiger's eyes.

"Didn't return?" Hit by waves of panic, his heart pounded violently, then shuddered to a stop. "When was this?"

"Maybe two months ago, something like that."

"Something like that? You don't know?" A note of hysteria crept into his voice. He took out a cigarette from a misshapen pack begged from some youths encountered on his journey. It took several tries to light it, his hands shook so. Dragging hard, he forced his thoughts into a semblance of order. Mishka had been gone for months, and the likelihood of finding her declined from the first day she hadn't returned. "Well?"

"I can't think while you're standing over me like that."

"I'm going to do more than just stand over you if you don't come up with better answers." He snuffed out the end of the cigarette with his fingers and put the stub in his pocket. "Why would she need to look for work when I left enough money? What did you do with it all?"

"When we heard you were dead, Mishka didn't want to live and stopped eating. When she was better, it was nearly impossible to find food, and the little I got was so expensive. I told her that she had to work. She agreed and went out and never came back. I searched everywhere here in Praga, asked everyone I knew across the river, and checked with my contacts at the Polonia where she planned to go. She just disappeared. That's all I know."

"The *Polonia*? Where *she* planned to go? She would never think of working in a German hotel. What was she supposed to do there?"

"They were hiring maids."

"You sent my Mishka to seek work as a maid in a Nazi hotel? You promised to keep her safe, bitch!" Gripped by a swirling fury, Andrush raised his hand to hit her, something he had never done to a woman, never imagined he would do.

Zofia covered her head with her hands. "No, don't!"

"Put your hands down," he ordered.

"Don't hit me!"

He lowered his arm. It wasn't going to bring Mishka back.

"I needed help to pay the rent, or we both would have ended up in the street."

"You lived here alone before she came and managed then and now as well, so don't give me any more of your goddamn lies."

"I'm working in the evenings, in the German restaurant on Adolf-Hitler-Platz, and I still can't afford to live here. If I don't find someone to share the expenses soon, I'll have to move."

"Your problem."

"You've been gone a long time, Andrush. What happened? We heard you were shot and killed."

"I got shot by the SS and was incapacitated for all this time. I couldn't get back here. That's what happened. Where are our people?"

"Different people now. What about Moshe? Do you know for a fact he died?"

"The only thing I know for a fact is that my wife is missing because of you."

"Let's not go over it again. I can set up a meeting for you to join a unit."

"Forget it. I need to find her."

"How will you do that?"

"That's not your business. Your concern is a little late. Where are her things?"

"There were some drawings. I threw them out."

"You witch! You never cared about her, did you? First thing tomorrow you're going to find me a place to stay across the river with someone you trust."

"It's safer if you stay here. If you don't have a permit to work for the Germans and they catch you on the streets, you'll be sent to a labor camp."

"I'll take my chances. You said that you searched everywhere here. Now get your fat ass into the other room and make me something to eat."

As soon as the door closed behind her, he pulled up the floorboard in the closet and saw the hiding hole was empty. Mishka was gone, and his eyes welled with tears.

The safe house Zofia found for Andrush, southeast of the city center, was raided by the brutal *Ordnungspolizei,* the Nazi Order Police, responsible for maintaining daily order in the cities. He and hundreds of others captured during similar raids and street roundups that day were beaten, chained, and thrown into trucks, taken to a holding center, and sorted. Some were lined up against a wall and shot. The rest were shoved into cattle cars headed for factories in Germany in need of slave labor.

Sent to work in the Polte ammunition factory in Magdeburg, Andrush was housed in a subcamp of Buchenwald. The conditions were inhumane—filthy, lice-ridden barracks, and starvation rations. He toiled twelve to fourteen hours each day under savage guards who whipped the prisoners if they didn't work fast enough. With every lashing received, and there were many, he vowed to escape and resume his search for Mishka. His participation in the resistance notwithstanding, Andrush's war was just beginning.

Chapter 31

Several months had passed since Maritza had come to live with Will, their time together spent basking in the glow of their love. He bounded up the stairs to see her when his workday was done. Never had he experienced such absolute happiness, such contentment as he found with her.

Their talks had mostly to do with the present. They rarely talked about the past. The future, if it could be counted on, was out of their control, and attaching hopes and dreams to it seemed pointless, much like starving people talking about the succulent food they would eat again when times improved. A person could have total faith in a better tomorrow, but it wouldn't make a whit of difference in the grand scheme of things. As long as Hitler and his sycophants lived, life would continue on its downhill trajectory.

"When the weather turns warm," Will said, "I will buy you a *Badeanzug.* You can wear it while we lie in the sun in the backyard and pretend we are in the French Riviera." That was the extent of their discussions of the future.

He made an arrangement with Jozef and Alina that, in the event something should happen to him, they would take Maritza in or place her with one of their trusted relatives. He loved her so much that it hurt to think of the possibility.

They were sitting in front of the fireplace one night after dinner. "Tell me about your life after university," she said, covering her legs with a blanket and settling in.

He sped through, as if reading key events from a timeline.

"Did you love Karoline?"

"No, I didn't. I was reserving it all for you."

"Oh, Willy, what a horrid woman. If I ever met her, I would scratch her eyes out. She didn't deserve you. You know that, right?" Maritza's delicate face was filled with loving concern.

"It doesn't matter. I was with her for the wrong reasons."

"She did you a huge favor."

"You are an angel, Maritza. You know how to make a man feel special."

"Not *any* man, just you."

"Tell me about your parents and the rest of your family."

"They were killed by the Germans. I already told you that." Her playful mood fizzled.

"You never told me that. You said they had passed away. I thought you meant from old age or illness."

Maritza sighed. "I suppose I should tell you so we won't have to talk about it again." She began with the flight from Warsaw through the time she learned of Andrush's death. There was no crying.

Will listened, sickened by her vivid descriptions of the aftermath of the bombing and the mowing down of screaming people by the Stukas' machine gunners. *"Mein Gott!"* he exclaimed when she finished, his fingers digging into the arms of the chair. "I had no idea. Those bastards."

"No idea? How can that be?"

"I was in Germany at the start of the invasion, in a coma after the accident. I had no clue what had happened and afterward, casualty reports only mentioned numbers."

Before the accident, he thought about the loss of life that would occur during the invasion, but he'd been in such physical pain that the events in Poland were beyond his grasp. Later, the connection came in the form of an awareness of statistics. Will knew nothing of the kind of depravity that continued undeterred for days in the town

Maritza called *Vishkov* and others like it. He couldn't fathom the deaths of such large numbers of people taken from the ghetto and gassed, but hearing details of specific acts of Nazi barbarism from someone he loved affected him as if he witnessed it himself.

"Well, now you know." Her eyes, the color of tropical oceans, filled with tears. "You call the murder of innocent people *casualties*? What your comrades did to my people in Wyszków and to those in all the other places was premeditated murder."

"Yes, it was murder, but the army was not going to call it that. Casualties was their term for it. I am so sorry."

She seemed to be waiting for him to say something more, and not wanting to further distress her, Will remained silent. Whatever response he made would be insufficient and rejected, because when she looked at him through narrowed eyes, he saw resentment there and was unsure of how to reply. "You are so brave and strong to have put this tragedy behind you and moved forward," he finally said.

"Brave and strong?" She stared at him with disbelief, as if he had just fallen in from outer space. "You must be crazy. I will never be able to put this *tragedy* behind me. It lives in my heart as if it happened yesterday, and its weight will never diminish."

Will reached for her hands. "Of course not. I understand that, but you are strong, Maritza, much stronger than you think."

"Stop patronizing me," she cried, jerking her hands away. "You seem oblivious to the fact that we are not equals. I am an *untermensch,* and you wear the same uniform as those who killed my people, yet you act as though you're a breed apart." According to Hitler's twisted racial theory, Poles were a half-step above Jews, though they were both considered subhuman.

"You are no such thing, and I am not like them. Why are we arguing about this? I love you and wish I could take away your pain."

"You're still a servant of the Reich no matter how pure you think you are." She leaped from the chair and balled her hands into fists.

"You found love and lost the ability to feel for anything else, and never once have I heard you denounce your brethren for the inhuman things they've done to people."

"They are not my brethren, and of course I denounce them. I just did. You want to spend our time fighting? I am on your side, and my work *is* different. I have nothing to do whatsoever with inflicting harm upon people, and you should have told me what happened to your family when I first asked about them. I can understand if you were wary of me then, but you don't trust me even now!" Will sprang from his chair, his heart galloping furiously, his face beyond beetroot. An angry cloud hung between them.

"You're an insensitive clod," Maritza sneered, "working like a plough horse to do your part. Go ahead and cling to your misguided belief that you're just an innocent officer doing his job. Take your blinders off, and you will see that you're more like them than you know."

"What the hell are you talking about? Why are you blaming me? I never hurt anyone." The veins stood out on his neck. "My uniform didn't seem to bother you before. I recall that you were concerned it would get dirty when we sat on the ground. Now, all of a sudden, I am like them, but I wasn't when you fell in love with me. What has changed? These are excuses because you are tired of being here and lack the courage to say so."

"Fell in love with you? Ha! Don't flatter yourself, Herr Engel. You want to talk about courage? *You* are the coward. I should never have come here. I hate you, you filthy German!" She slapped him across the face and ran from the room, slamming the door.

Will stood stunned until a wave of nausea sent him staggering to the bathroom to throw up his dinner. Relieved, he splashed his face with cold water. Sagging into his chair, he wondered what he'd done to deserve such treatment. His work was apolitical and concentrated in Warsaw. There was no involvement with activities having anything to do with the various fronts of war.

Yes, Will did his job so well. His superiors had written glowing reports about him: *Essential to office operations. Irreplaceable.* Men who didn't work to the best of their ability received punishments ranging from strict supervision to transfers to places they never came back from. The proposal he put together when he first arrived in Warsaw at the request of Captain Hoff had been fully implemented with excellent results, and after that, they pretty much left him alone.

The resistance still got their hands on sensitive information, but the Kommandant was able to report to the bigwigs in Berlin that he had the records to show everything possible had been done on the Wehrmacht's end to prevent it from coming from their offices.

Maritza called him a *servant of the Reich,* and that was true to an extent. Every man in the German military helped drive the war machine in some way, and Will was no exception. When heiling was called for, his arm went up out of necessity. In doing so, he looked like any other obsequious Hitlerite, but he wasn't one.

There are degrees of involvement, he thought. The cooks who feed the troops on the front lines are enabling them to fight another day and are certainly not as evil as those Nazis who give orders for murder, unless they slaughter animals for no good reason. How could she ever think I am that heartless? She resents me because I wear the uniform of an army that represents evil, but it is not the one I signed on to serve.

Sick of the miserable life he was forced to lead, Will swept everything off the table in one violent motion, sending glasses and bottles crashing to the floor. The door swung open, and Maritza came into the room. "Be careful," he cautioned. "There is glass everywhere. I am sorry if I frightened you."

She walked around the mess and looked up at him. "Are you hurt?"

"No, I am fine, really." He held out his hands and turned them over. "Not even a scratch."

"Too bad," she sniffed, and went out.

Chapter 32

The following evening, Will sat in his room and wondered how long Maritza was going to ignore him. Fate had brought her into his life, and he found joy. Gone were the long, empty nights fraught with deafening silence. She pampered him, made him laugh, and loved him the way he liked. Without ever uttering a complaint, she sat in these rooms with blackout shades drawn, occupying herself day after day.

"People are dying out there, Willy, and you have given me so much. Thank you for loving me."

She thanked him! Without her love, he would have continued to be a hermit, appearing only on demand of duty or perhaps spending more unfulfilling time in the company of shallow officers who had the potential to jeopardize his position, but most likely his heart would have stopped ticking. He wished he could take her for a car ride, to see a play, or on a walk—activities made impossible due to the prohibition of Germans' relations with Poles. Both he and Maritza were in the cages assigned to them by the Reich.

In spite of those limitations, they made their own fun. They played cards and chess, did exercises, went out in the back of the house for some fresh air, and tried to trap that pesky mouse. On the weekends and days when Alina wasn't there, they cooked together, which almost always ended in disaster. Rice bubbled up and blasted the lid off the pot, causing a gastronomic Mount Vesuvius. Eggs, boiling on the stove and forgotten, exploded all over the kitchen. They laughed about these mishaps for days.

Up until the clash, with the exception of the falling out in the park, harsh words had never been spoken. There had been nothing but tender treatment and respect between them, the sublime making of love, and the light they brought to each other's dismal lives. *I hate you, you filthy German.* The words hurt, and Will found it hard to look at himself in the mirror, knowing the woman he loved was disgusted with him.

Maritza was tired of being cooped up; that much was clear, but how did she not realize that she was safest there with him? True, she was able to go out when she lived with Zofia, though beautiful young women didn't last long on Warsaw's streets—there was always the risk of falling victim to a violent crime. It didn't seem possible she would trade their love for a freedom as lacking as the one she left behind.

He moved the curtain aside and looked out the window. The night was moonless and still, and the vague outlines of trees with their spiky, naked branches gave him an unearthly, disconnected feeling. The way to resolve their predicament was to talk about it, but going to her now wasn't a good idea.

After the blow-up, Maritza lay in bed in a lugubrious mood and yearned for Andrush, who, even in death, was the gold standard by which all things concerning love were measured. There was a major issue with Will—one that cast doubt on his otherwise stellar qualities that she hadn't fully explored. If every person working in a clerical capacity in the military, regardless of their beliefs, were removed from service, there would be a breakdown in communications, making it more difficult for Hitler's henchmen to carry out their heinous crimes.

Just being in the military made Will partially responsible for the atrocities that had been committed, and every time he denied it, he trivialized the deaths of her family members and the countless others who lost their lives under the Nazis. *Why doesn't he see that?* Once again, he loomed in her mind as a bad egg, a deceiver to whom she had given her heart and opened her legs. The more she dwelled on this, the more paranoid she became. She had the rest of her father's money; it would be enough to pay someone to take her to Bronka's or to support herself for a while if she went home with Alina.

W ill spent the next workday wishing for time to pass so he could set things right with Maritza, but the hands on the clock didn't seem to move. The truck that came for his men had mechanical trouble, and he had to drive them back to their barracks. Expecting to find her waiting for him when he came upstairs, he was greeted instead by her closed door under which no light was visible.

He ate alone, picking at his food, thinking he had to help Maritza by taking her away from Warsaw and her haunting memories. She couldn't stay mad at him forever—lovers have disagreements, then they make up. If he could get false German identity papers for her, an idea he had briefly entertained but discarded when he was struggling to find a way for them to be together, she would have freedom of movement. The forging of documents was rampant in the Polish resistance, but what did he, an officer who worked behind a desk and had no contact with Poles except for his housekeeper and her husband, know about that process?

His thoughts came fast and furiously. Even if he managed to get papers for Maritza, where would they go? The countries around them were Nazi-occupied; they couldn't just run away. Deserters were a blight on the Reich, and the Gestapo would pursue them relentlessly. There was a long-armed network of agents who would search for him everywhere—men who appeared from the shadows in leather coats with fedoras pulled low over their eyes. They might be disguised as regular fellows who sought to gain his trust, pretending to be anti-Nazi, and out would come the guns.

How many countries had Hitler occupied so far? Eleven, twelve, he'd lost count. News reports had always pointed to the Wehrmacht's successes in Russia, one after the other. Hans said it was true in the beginning, but things had changed. According to the soldiers coming in from the front, the Russians were making mincemeat of the troops, and *Feldmarschall* Paulus had just surrendered his battered armies at Stalingrad in spite of Hitler's order to fight to the last man. Germany couldn't win the war, Will believed, but it would continue, thereby giving him time to formulate a plan to leave Warsaw with Maritza.

Chapter 33

Maritza sat in bed, seething. She had waited two days for Will to come in and ask for forgiveness and own up to his role, but it was too late now. His silence spoke volumes, and she was going to tell him that night she wanted to leave.

Downstairs, Alina was putting food on the two separate dinner trays. Will came to tell her that Jozef was outside.

"Shall I bring these up before I go, Herr Engel?" He looked tired and hadn't smiled in days. Maritza stayed in bed with red eyes. Something had transpired between them—a quarrel perhaps—and she was sorry to see them both so down.

"No, thank you, Alina. I will do it." He walked her out, then put both plates on one tray. It was time to make amends. He would break the standoff. One of them had to in the name of progress. The whole situation—Maritza in one room, he in the other—how idiotic it was for two people who loved each other to keep separated by a wall, wasting precious moments.

He went upstairs, mulling over the words he wanted to say. Setting the tray on the table, he glanced at her. Propped against pillows with the blanket pulled up to her chin, she looked back at him with a blank expression.

"I thought we might talk, then eat our dinner together," he said, coming to sit on the bed. "If you would like, I can light the fire."

"Don't bother," she said coldly. "I can't live with you anymore. I don't love you; maybe I never did. I can go to Alina's or Andrush's aunt, but I just can't be with you."

The blow was so fierce that it knocked his wind out, and for a few seconds, Will couldn't breathe. She had taken his breath away when he first laid eyes upon her and when they first made love, and now she was planning to leave and still robbing him of it. His throat tightened. He got up, shoved his hands into his pockets, unable to stem the tears that dripped from his eyes. *Men don't cry, Wilhelm. You are weak.* His father was right. He was weak, a loser. He'd lived so long in his fantasies that he didn't see the truth.

Maritza saw the redness rushing up the back of his neck, and lashes of pain struck at her chest. Will cleared his throat and walked out of the room. She followed him.

"You have made your decision," he said, his voice rough and low. He poured vodka into a tall glass and drank it like water, welcoming the burn, desperate to feel something other than the unmooring of his heart. "I am going to respect it, so what do you want?"

"I—" She couldn't find the words. It was unbearable to see the tears in his eyes when it was her actions that caused them.

"Since you came in here with nothing to say, then you will open your ears and listen. To be clear, I am not now, nor have I ever been a Nazi. I am ashamed to wear this uniform. When I joined the army years before Hitler came to power, I was proud of it, and when I became an officer, I trained men to defend our country, not conquer others at the whims of a maniac. If I was asked to bring harm to people, I would never do it. You have been traumatized by the murders of your family and your husband, but I am not to blame."

Maritza covered her face with her hands and sobbed.

"I was supposed to lead a rifle platoon into Poland at the start of the invasion, but as the time to deploy drew near, I went through a personal crisis. The idea of going to kill men just so Hitler could have his goddamn lands was unconscionable. At the time, I wasn't aware of what that madman was really planning. Then I had the accident, and my problem was solved. I almost lost my life, and before I met you, I often wished I had."

"Willy please, let me—"

"No, I am not finished. I never meant to minimize your suffering; I didn't know the extent of it! I avoided talking about the Nazis and the war for fear of upsetting you, and you must have mistaken my reticence for apathy. Perhaps years from now, when your hatred has faded and you look back on these days, you will remember how much I loved you. I apologize for my numerous flaws and for not being the man you expected."

Her heart burst into pieces. If only she could turn back time. Biting, vicious, and untrue words had spewn from her lips that showed no regard for his love. He had trusted her with it, and she blamed and sought to punish him for crimes he didn't commit.

"Before you came along, Maritza, I was dying inside, and I thank you for every drop of attention you have given me. Whether it was sincere or not makes no difference now. Without it, I would have withered on the vine." Will left the room, went downstairs, and out to the back of the house.

He stood in the bitter cold and wiped his wet face with his handkerchief. Trapped in a place where people have lost their humanity and an unfathomable number, their lives, he was right back where he started, alone and unloved. I will ask the Kowalskis to take her home with them tomorrow, he planned. The sooner she is gone, the faster I can heal. I gave her all that I was able—what I thought she needed. Let her find a better man, and heaven help him.

Tomorrow, he will erase her from his memory and somehow go on. The Maritza Affair, like the Karoline, would become a thing of the past. Love, he discovered, was a dangerous proposition and turned a man into a starry-eyed fool to be cast aside when a woman had her fill of him. Tomorrow, he will think about the future. Will couldn't sit in his quarters night after night as he'd done before; he needed a new focus, a hobby, something to do that would bring him a reasonable amount of pleasure.

The door opened, and Maritza came up behind him, her footsteps crunching in the snow. "Willy, come in before you catch pneumonia."

"Let me give you some advice. After you tell a man he is no longer or was never loved, don't come around with fake concern. Think how you would feel if I said I didn't love you, then hovered about asking if you were comfortable. You would tell me to drop dead, so have a little respect. Go back inside."

She went in and returned shortly. "I drew you a hot bath. Come in, please." She tugged his arm, and too cold to argue, he followed her upstairs. "Let me help you off with your things," she said, reaching for his buttons.

"Stop. I don't need your help or your sympathy. Go to the other room so I can have privacy. My naked body is no longer available for your viewing. I doubt you would disrobe in front of me if I told you that our relationship was over."

"Take off your clothes and get in before the water gets cold."

"Then turn around."

"You are being ridiculous. Fine, I won't look."

His fingers and toes burned when he stepped in. Maritza sat at the edge of the tub behind him and twined her arms around his neck. "I'm sorry," she sobbed. "Please forgive me."

"You are choking me," he exclaimed, untying her arms. "Is it possible to bathe without an audience? People fall out of love all the time. I am hurt and sad, but I will get over it. That I can promise. I am not one of those men who jumps to his death or shoots himself in the head because a woman is tired of him. Now go back where you chose to be for the last three days and two nights and leave me alone."

She ran from the room. Will saw her pulling things out of his closet. *What the hell is she doing?* He scrambled out of the tub and grabbed a towel. "What are you doing in there, Maritza? What are you looking for?"

"A valise so I can go away like you told me to," she wailed.

"I said you should go into the other room, not *away*. Where do you plan on going? Have you forgotten there is a curfew? Tomorrow I will ask Alina and Jozef to take you home with them, but you are not leaving here tonight."

She wrapped her arms around his waist. "I don't want to go with them. I said hurtful, cruel things to you, and I didn't mean them. You are the dearest, most wonderful person, and I love you with all my heart. This is my fault. When the fears take over, I can't tell what is real or not."

Will picked her up and carried her to the bed. "Come on, ssh, ssh," he said, holding her on his lap and stroking her hair.

"You are my happiness, Willy, and you've done nothing wrong. When I told you what happened to my family, it ignited a chain of memories of those I loved and brought a renewed hatred of the Nazis—not that I ever stopped despising them, but if I had let the hate consume me, I would never have been able to love you."

"You don't know how it is to have a family one minute and the next, they're gone. I wanted to punish you for what the Nazis did, to hurt you so you would know how I feel inside," she cried. "I know you're not like them. I love you so much, and I'm proud of who you are. Say you forgive me."

"You have lived through such disturbing experiences, worse than I ever imagined," he said. "It is I who needs forgiveness. I have been selfish and acting like a hurt child, thinking of my own feelings instead of giving you reassurance. From the beginning, I tried to portray myself as tough, afraid you wouldn't want me if you knew that I am damaged."

She threaded her fingers between his. "We are all damaged, Willy, in one way or another. Whatever you have endured makes you the man I love. Isn't the whole greater than the sum of its parts?"

"You are a blessing. I never considered myself lucky until I met you. We need to trust each other, talk more, and face our fears together. I want to spend my life with you, and it will be far away from here, where we can live in peace. You have given me a reason to go forth everyday while wearing that loathsome uniform. I love you, Maritza."

"I love you, too," she said, her lips seeking his. Now that they had acknowledged their own shortcomings, the words had a deeper meaning than before.

Chapter 34

"I don't believe Germany will win this war," Will said after dinner the following evening, "and at some point the Russians will come west. There is no immediate danger, but I want to plan ahead in order to ensure our future together, or at the very least, secure yours."

She tensed. "At the very least secure mine? What are you saying?"

"Nothing matters to me but you, and I will do everything in my power to make sure that you survive what is yet to come."

"You're not thinking of leaving me alone somewhere?" She clutched the front of his shirt. "Am I to lose *you* now? I won't be separated from you. Please, I can't take any more heartache."

"I don't want to leave you anywhere. I am saying we have to make preparations, have a plan in case the situation deteriorates. Things cannot go on as they have indefinitely, and if some unforeseen event occurs, we will be powerless."

Will was explaining a situation that could become reality in the near future. If he couldn't count on her cooperation, it would be detrimental to them both in the event of an emergency. This man was the very air she breathed, and he needed her now to be his partner and not a child. She had been too much of one the past few days. "I'm listening, Willy."

"We need to secure papers that show you as an Aryan German, who has been living here in Warsaw her whole life. With a German identity, you won't have to hide. The problem is that I can't get them. You mentioned Zofia arranged for your card, and I wonder—"

"No! I want nothing to do with her."

"All right, my love. Never mind. It was just a thought."

"I could ask Alina."

"Alina?" Will said with obvious surprise. "She wouldn't have any knowledge of those activities."

"Well, when I told her about Andrush, she mentioned that resistance members buy firearms through contacts at the bazaar, and that leads me to think she might know how to get the papers."

"Whatever she knows, Jozef knows, and I will ask him. If he can't help, I will have to come up with another plan. This may be premature, but if we were able to get those documents, we could get married. Would you marry me? Say yes."

"Yes!"

When Jozef came to pick up Alina the next evening, Will brought him to the kitchen, where they spoke in cautious whispers.

"He didn't say how, but he can get them," he told Maritza, "and I will provide some of the materials and take your photographs with my camera."

In the middle of April, word spread quickly through Warsaw that the Jews in the ghetto were rebelling against heavily armed SS detachments who entered to enforce a deportation order for the remaining residents. Several hundred young Jewish warriors with limited arms, managed for a month to repel the Germans, who outnumbered them in manpower and weapons. The destruction of the ghetto was complete after all residential blocks were systematically burned to the ground, and the captured sent on to the death camps.

"My grandparents lived in the Quarter," Maritza said. "Mama, Andrush, and I spent so much time there. Had we stayed in Warsaw, we would have been forced to live in the ghetto. Willy, it's all so horrible. I can't stop thinking about all the people we knew."

"Perhaps some of them got away before it was sealed. Andrush was smart, Maritza. He knew he had to get everyone out of the city, and he did the best he could. There was no way he could have known the extent of what was to come, but he was brave. He gave his life for the cause, just like those who made a stand in the ghetto."

"It wasn't enough. The Nazis are too strong."

"They will pay for their crimes," he said.

Jozef brought the documents in late May. Maritza was eager to see her new name. "Maria Lampe. I like it, though I look forward to the day I can use my own."

"That is why we are doing this. Now I will put in a request for leave."

"Where will we go, Willy?"

"I was thinking of Paris."

Hitler was so taken with the city when he visited in June 1940, after the Wehrmacht stormed into France and began its occupation, that each German soldier was promised one visit to Paris. That was, as Will noted, before all hands on deck were needed to support the invasion of the Soviet Union.

"Paris? Really?" Maritza folded her hands over her heart.

"I don't see any alternative."

"Do you think your request will be approved?"

"We can hope. I haven't had any time off since my Aunt Helga passed away, and that was before I met you."

"It will be so hard to come back here after having experienced a bit of freedom in Paris, don't you think?"

"I agree, though we shouldn't worry about that now."

Will applied for leave and waited weeks without receiving an answer. He had given no indication that his request was connected to a plan of marriage, thinking that any mention of the bride-to-be too far in advance would invite deeper scrutiny of her documents.

Bach came into the office one morning at the start of the last week of June. "Hauptmann Hoff wishes to see you, Herr Oberleutnant. You are to come at once."

What the hell was this? "Thank you," he replied, and nodded at Hans to get ready. "I will go directly."

"No, sir. You are to come with me."

"Very well."

The clerk and typist looked up from their work. *What are you staring at? Mind your goddamn business,* Will almost snapped. He pushed away his apprehension, put on his cap, and walked to the door with an air of self-assurance that he didn't feel. The sergeant was subdued on the drive, reinforcing Will's concern that bad news was in store. He must know something and cannot say a word, he thought, or he could be unwell, but Bach would have to be near death for this type of quiet; he would talk to himself if no one was around.

Chapter 35

"Good morning, Oberleutnant. Are you ill? You look positively whey-faced," observed Hoff.

"I am fine, sir."

"Sit down. The insurrection in the Warschauer Ghetto in April and May—terrible business—was mainly an SS and police operation, but several of our brave army engineers were killed while blowing up buildings or capturing dugouts in which the rebels were hiding. We had other casualties, of course. Who would have thought that such motley groups of Jews could hold out for so long?"

"A dreadful operation," Will said. *What does this have to do with me? Get to the point!* Beads of sweat broke out on his upper lip, but he dared not wipe them away.

"Yes it was, for all those charged with eliminating the Jewish pestilence. As a result, we have decided to make some changes in our departments and tighten things up, but first, I have some news about your application for two weeks of leave to visit Paris. It has been denied."

Will's heart dropped out of his chest.

"You look worse than when you came in, Oberleutnant. Relax. That was the bad news. The good news is you are being transferred to Paris. Your excellent management skills are needed in one of the general staff offices, permissions, I believe. Before you report, you will have one month's leave to begin the first of July, and it has been well-earned. At the end of today, all calls to your office will be rerouted to an office in these headquarters. Have everything dismantled and packed up before you leave."

"Excellent news, sir."

"Do you have any questions?"

"Yes, what about my staff?"

"They will take their own home leaves and will be given their new assignments in the regiment upon their return."

"Sir, permit me to speak freely. I was planning to ask you this before I was summoned today, and I hope the coincidence will prove fortuitous. I met a lady here in Warsaw, an Aryan German of course, and I would like to marry her as soon as possible. We are eager to begin producing children for the Reich." If he continued this bowing and scraping much longer, he'd be licking the floor. "Since I am going to Paris, it would be wonderful for her to accompany me there."

"Are her documents in order?" asked Hoff.

"Yes, sir."

"Then Bach will assist you." He rang for him and gave instructions. "Good luck Oberleutnant, and thank you for your dedication and hard work."

"Thank you, sir."

Bach made a phone call, then covered the receiver with his hand. "Would tomorrow be too soon?"

"Tomorrow will be perfect." This was going too well.

The sergeant concluded his conversation and hung up. "The registrar is a dear friend. We went to school together. He will issue the license, and as a special favor, the waiting period will be waived. He will marry you and your beloved immediately following the issuance."

"Very good. Before we head back, while I expect my lodgings will be made known when I report for duty, it seems prudent to alert my superiors in advance that my wife will be with me, in case they plan on housing me in a barracks."

"You are quite right," Bach said, "I will handle those arrangements."

"Oh Willy, I'm so happy," Maritza effused. "Finally, a chance to leave Warsaw! How did it come about?"

"I don't know. I just want to get out of here before whoever made the decision changes his mind."

She grabbed his hand and pulled him onto the bed. "This calls for a celebration. I might even have a drink. A real vacation for a whole month! I can hardly wait."

"Real vacations went down with the Titanic, Maritza." He focused stern eyes upon her. "There will be no celebrations. My transfer is a lateral move, and we don't know what problems await us. We will not go gallivanting around with cameras hanging from our necks as if we haven't a care in the world, not while people are suffering. We are not going there to have fun, and we must keep our heads down and trust no one," he said, already worrying over the unknown variables.

"The Generalgouvernement is a dumping ground for the millions of innocent people the Nazis have deemed unworthy of living. If we went out somewhere here, would you honestly be able to say you had good fun in light of the death and dying taking place?"

"I'm sorry, Willy, I wasn't thinking. I assumed I would have more freedom in Paris than here. There are positives to this move. France is close to England, and that's where we should go when this rotten war ends." The significance of that statement wouldn't be realized for another year.

"There exists an image of Paris as being romantic and seductive with its rich history, food, and beautiful architecture, and rightly so in peacetime, but in the eyes of the oppressed, all Germans are Nazis and hence coprophages," Will continued in a professorial manner.

"We cannot make any plans until we get there and assess the situation, but you will have more freedom. You can come and go as you like, and you speak the language, which is the biggest plus of all."

"I understand that, but what are we going to do for the month before you start work, if not see at least some of the sights?"

"Make love?" He tried to keep a straight face.

"I get to have you to myself all day, everyday for a month?" Maritza's eyes twinkled. "Do restaurants in Paris sell oysters?"

"I believe so. Why?"

"Oysters. You know, for stamina."

"Like I need that?" His brows went up.

"Not now, but we both will need a little help if we're going to be making that much love."

"Then we shall eat oysters galore." They had a good laugh. He told her what Bach had arranged. "I wish I could make it more romantic for you. There is nothing quite like being joined in matrimony in front of a swastika flag."

"Oh Willy, I would marry you anywhere. The important thing is that soon we will be husband and wife."

"I have wanted that all along."

"You were so shy and sweet when I first met you, yet I couldn't imagine there could be anything between me and a German."

"Shy and sweet? No man alive wants to be called that."

"Well, it's true, and I wanted to eat you up. You're no longer shy, but you sure are sweet."

"Feel free to eat me up now," he said, reaching for her.

They awoke the next morning with their stomachs in knots. Before his men arrived, Will explained to Alina that he was being transferred soon but would need her until then. "I will tell Jozef when he comes to take you home this evening."

"Oh, Herr Engel." She dabbed at her eyes. She was so fond of him and Maritza.

"We are going to miss you. Maritza might not have fared as well here without your company. You have been a great help to us both."

Will let his staff in. They had already been told the news of his transfer, sparing him the short speech he had prepared. The men were chatting enthusiastically, looking forward to their home leaves. It would take some work to pack everything up for transfer to the office in the building on the Adolf-Hitler-Platz, where it would be taken by truck at the end of the week. He gave instructions and had the men start, then went up to get Maritza. They slipped down the back stairs, into the car, and out onto the road.

The last automobile she had ridden in was the taxi Andrush hired to take them to Wyszków, and she hadn't been around this part of the city in years. Inundated with memories, she reached for Will's hand.

"I have to shift gears, my love. Try to be calm. You will be asked questions about *Maria's* ancestors, and you need a clear head."

"I know. I was just thinking about my family and how much I would like my real name to appear on the marriage certificate."

"If your name was *mud,* it wouldn't make a difference. You are still you."

Maritza laughed. "How do you come up with these things?"

"That is a secret, but I did lighten your mood.

Chapter 36

They showed their identification to the guards posted outside the building and were directed to a small, windowless room where a young man with prematurely graying hair stood, arranging a stack of papers. Behind him hung the ubiquitous picture of Hitler, and next to it, a swastika flag.

"Heil Hitler." The man raised his arm and gave a flaccid salute.

He must be suffering from hypoxia, Will thought. It is so stuffy here. "Heil Hitler. We are Oberleutnant Wilhelm Engel and Fräulein Maria Lampe for our marriage license and vows. Feldwebel Bach at the *Kommandantur* called you yesterday. Thank you for making time for us."

"Your documents, please." He went through their papers, but did not quiz her on her family tree. *"Alles ist in Ordnung,"* he said, then stamped the certificate declaring her of Aryan blood.

Thank God for that, thought Maritza. I don't think I would have remembered a single name.

After a five-minute ceremony, they were pronounced Herr und Frau Engel, and, as a wedding present from the civil administration of Warsaw, they were given a copy of *Mein Kampf.*

"We did it, my love," Will said in the car. "We pulled the fur over Hitler's ears."

So much for the Nazis' racial theories. A person could buy his or her way into the master race. The newlyweds spent their wedding night like any other, in each other's arms. A piece of paper could never change the depth of their love, but they admitted to feeling a new closeness, and their lovemaking had a more profound quality.

The time flew by. The Engels said goodbye to Alina and Jozef on Thursday evening, the first of July. Maritza presented Alina with a gold chain that had belonged to Malka, and Will gave Jozef his father's gold pocket watch, as well as an envelope containing a six month salary for Alina. He knew the Kowalskis wouldn't wear the jewelry—it would be ripped right from them by thieves, but he wanted them to have it as a reserve.

"Jozef, without you, none of this would have been possible. I am forever grateful," Will said. "You are both wonderful people and will remain in our hearts forever."

"You are a good man, Oberleutnant. I hope we will meet again someday when all the malefactors are out of this country."

Bach arrived to drive them to the station early Friday morning. Will let him into the barren office and introduced his new wife.

"Thank you so much for your assistance, Feldwebel," Maritza said, "in arranging the appointment with the registrar."

Ensorcelled, Bach stared at the fresh-faced beauty and was at a loss for words.

"Maria has that effect on people," Will said, putting his arm around her. "We should go. We don't want to miss the train." Once they were seated in the vehicle, he engaged Bach in conversation before the sergeant had a chance to pepper her with questions.

The Engels took their seats on the train to Berlin. Will handed their documents to a police official. A railway man checked their tickets.

"Whew. Thank goodness that's done," Maritza whispered.

"Ssh," he cautioned.

The trip passed uneventfully. Arriving in Berlin in the late afternoon, they saw the moderate amount of damage caused by the RAF bombing raids, a precursor to the destruction that would occur in the coming months when the Allied attacks intensified. The streets had been cleared, but piles of concrete and brick fragments lined the sides. They took a bus to the stylish Hotel am Steinplatz in the upscale Charlottenburg district.

An air-raid warning sounded as they were getting ready for bed. "Throw on your robe and hurry!" Will grabbed the case containing their valuables and documents. They ran down flights of stairs into the underground shelter. The dim and stuffy tunnel was lined with benches and full of hotel guests. Some read books or newspapers by penlight, others spoke quietly. The musty smells of dampness, cigarette smoke, and an unidentifiable sour odor made Maritza nauseous. Will held her until they were allowed to return to their rooms. There had been no actual bombing—an Allied attack was expected but never materialized.

In the morning, they took a train to Hannover, where Will's family had lived for generations and he had attended university and taken his military training. There were a couple of hours until the afternoon train to Paris, and he wanted to go past his former home.

"You never told me your parents were rich, Willy. This is a mansion, and you were a family of four," she said, shaking her head in wonder.

"Six," he said, with a sheepish grin, "if you count the cook and the maid. While it certainly helps, money is not everything. I would have preferred to live on a farm with loving parents than in that mausoleum."

Will was relieved to see Hannover was still in good shape, having survived a few bombing raids, though the worst was yet to come. The

Engels continued on to the station and boarded the overnight express train that would take them to Paris. Looking at the blackened ruins of towns and cities from the window of the dining car as the train rolled through western Germany, the bile rose in his throat. This is what Hitler wanted, he thought. He doesn't care about Germany or its people.

The consensus of the Germans sitting near the Engels in the dining car was one of extreme anger toward the British for bombing their cities. They made impassioned statements in favor of their great Führer and his armies and vowed revenge on Britain in their name. As if reading Will's thoughts, a senior officer seated next to him murmured, "What a terrible waste of life and property."

"A harrowing sight," said Will, watching his words. The only way not to call attention to yourself was to avoid making statements that alerted others to your political views. While all officers were expected to be aligned with the Nazi outlook, many were not, but one could never be sure who was friend or foe.

Chapter 37

They arrived in Paris at nine the following morning at Gare du Nord, one of the city's busiest stations. Civilians exited the cars quickly and didn't dare make eye contact with the uniformed Germans or loiter by the platforms—the risk of random document checks and arrest by the police or Gestapo was too great.

The officer Will met on the train had his driver take them to the small apartment they had rented for the month. He explained that the city's twenty arrondissements, or neighborhoods, ran clockwise in the shape of a snail, with the first beginning in the center. Their place was in the eighth, the location of Avenue Champs-Elysées and part of the Arc de Triomphe.

"Look Willy," Maritza said, "the sights can see us!"

As in all Nazi occupied territories, swastikas adorned the iconic monuments and hung from all public buildings. There were long queues in front of the food shops as the city was under strict rationing, and a notable absence of young men since large numbers had been sent to work in Germany in the war industry factories or shipped off to camps. A curfew was in effect for Parisians from nine in the evening until five in the morning, during which time the city went dark to prevent Allied planes from using the lights for navigation.

If the French followed all the Germans' rules and were willing to subsist on rations that decreased with each passing year and a dearth of coal for heating, they would be allowed to continue with their hamstrung existence. The military had taken over the luxury hotels, and others were used to house their employees. Few private autos were seen on the streets due to the Germans' appropriation of gasoline; the resourceful citizens rode bicycles everywhere. Instead of taxicabs, men ferried people around in small, open wagons attached to the backs of their bikes. The city was grimy and tired-looking—three years of German occupation had taken their toll.

Contrary to Will's declaration that there would be no sightseeing, the Engels spent time visiting gardens, strolling on the banks of the Seine, browsing in shops, and dining in cafés and restaurants. Soldiers and officers in these establishments twisted their heads to ogle Maritza while their female companions sat by and frowned. Will was proud of her and wouldn't have minded if men glanced discreetly, but their leering was offensive. Maritza saw the effect Will had on those well-dressed, flirtatious French women who had no compunctions about being with a German and would jump at the chance to become his paramour.

"Do you see the way women are looking at you?" she asked with amusement.

"What women?"

"The fancy ones."

"It appears they have a thing for German officers, like you do," he grinned.

She bumped him playfully with her elbow. "Really, Willy, how do they know you're German? You're not in uniform, and they're broadcasting desire with their eyes."

"They must like the type, but I am interested only in you."

"Let's keep it that way," she said, smiling up at him and clinging tighter to his arm.

The novelty of gadding about the city wore off, and they slept late and made a lot of love (aphrodisiacs not needed). Will shared his hopes and dreams for their life together, now that an actual future seemed within reach, and Maritza opened up about her life be-

fore the invasion, telling stories in which Andrush figured promi-
nently. She spoke of him in such reverential terms that Will thought
he should be hailed as a national treasure. From the way she talked
about his strength and agility, it seemed the man could kill a bear
with his hands. What stood out to him was that the whole of her life
had been inextricably tied to Andrush, while he had known her for
one short year.

July zipped by. Will reported for duty at the elegant Hôtel Majestic on Avenue Kléber, the location the German high command
had taken as their headquarters. High-ranking, bemedaled officers
floated through the lobby like ships on parade, while chauffeurs
tended to their luxury automobiles out front in the driveway. Karl
von Stülpnagel, the military commander of occupied France, had his
office there. In other closely guarded offices, the German civil administrators implemented draconian economic policies set forth by the
Reich.

Will was assigned as secretary to an officer who issued permissions for soldiers' leaves. Hugo Schreiber, thirtysomething and slim,
looked as though he had just stepped from the barber's chair—blond
hair perfectly styled and doused in a clove-scented tonic that gave
Will a headache. The man's uniform was superbly tailored and boots
polished to a mirror shine, yet his desk was covered with heaps of paper and files—a very un-German quality, Will thought, for someone
overly concerned with grooming. Schreiber left early, nearly every
day. His wife was in Berlin, so perhaps a French mistress?

The Engels were provided with a modest apartment in the sixteenth arrondissement, in an enclave of Germans who had brought
their wives, part of which was off-limits to those French who lacked
a special pass. In the heart of that neighborhood was Avenue Foch,
a wide, tree-lined boulevard considered one of the most prestigious
addresses in all of Paris.

"See that opulent mansion, number eighty-four, Maritza? It is the equivalent of the Gestapo building on Aleja Szucha in Warsaw," Will said, "and the same acts of torture are inflicted upon prisoners inside."

She shuddered. "Some things never change."

Will was required to wear his uniform at all times, as in Warsaw, once his leave ended. On weekend visits to different parts of the city, they were confronted with the Parisians' animosity. He went into a bakery to buy croissants while Maritza window-shopped a few stores down. A stooped, elderly woman draped in black approached her, hissed *Pute,* whore, and hurried off. A group of youngsters pelted them with pebbles and stones on a side street, then disappeared into a labyrinth of passages. Housewives turned up their noses at her, thinking she was French and a *collaboratrice.*

"I am a liability for you when we are out together," Will said. "From now on, we will do our shopping near the apartment." Hateful looks and mutterings were understandable, but he did not want her to be hurt. For Maritza, the freedom of movement in Paris had come at a price.

Chapter 38

Maritza fell ill in early March with a stomach bug that refused to go away. Will wanted to take her to a doctor, but she insisted that it had to run its course. She didn't improve and called him at work late one afternoon. "I'm dizzy and queasy, and my eyes are dry. I think I'm dying."

Alarmed—those were classic symptoms of dehydration that could cause the blood to thicken and bring on heart failure—he borrowed a car and raced home to take her to the hospital, one of several commandeered by the Germans for their sick and wounded. A thick fog had descended. The vehicle's headlights, equipped with a limiting device, made it difficult for him to see anything ahead. Praying there were no cars or, God forbid, people, he plowed on.

"Here we are," he said, and carried her inside. They were sent to a waiting area to sit on slippery wooden benches. She lay with her head in his lap. A janitor was mopping the floor around them with carbolic soap; its antiseptic smell reminded Will of his stay in the hospital after the accident and made him feel ill. He made a face at the man. *Must you do that now?* They waited and waited. It seemed forever before Maritza's name was called.

"Please return to your seat, Herr Engel," the nurse said, blocking the door with her bulk. "Patients only beyond this point. The doctor will bring you in when he concludes his examination."

Will scowled but did as he was told. He wasn't going to get past that battlewagon anyhow. A young woman with a hacking cough sat down next to him. He slid away from her on the pretext of picking up a newspaper someone left, read the headline: *WEHRMACHT OCCUPIES HUNGARY,* and put it down. Would it ever end? Twenty, thirty minutes passed. What was taking so long? He raked his fingers through his hair.

"A person could get well sitting here," the woman said.

A comedian. He gave an obligatory chuckle. "Very true."

"Herr Engel," the nurse boomed. "You may come in now."

Will followed her into the room. An ancient doctor, dusted off by the Wehrmacht and pressed into service, shuffled toward him. "Sit down, Oberleutnant."

He pulled a chair close to the bed and reached for Maritza's hand. Small, pink circles overlaid her pale cheeks. "Willy, we are going to have a baby! I am pregnant. No wonder I've been feeling this way."

Pregnant? A moment of disbelief, then Will turned red and smiled. *"Das ist wunderbar!"*

"It does appear that way," said the doctor. "A test to confirm will be done along with the usual battery. It is admirable that you are fulfilling your duty to Führer and Fatherland by having children, the first of many I hope," said the doctor.

"Oh yes. An honor." *To hell with the Führer.*

"You will improve with time, Frau Engel. We are going to keep you overnight for observation, perhaps for several days if you are still not well. Congratulations to you both. I will let you know what the tests reveal, if anything significant. Good evening."

Will climbed on the bed and held her. "We are going to be parents, my love. Can you believe it?"

"The doctor said the baby will be born in November. We were careless, Willy."

"Now we can be as careless as we want."

She groaned. That was the furthest thing from her mind.

He turned her onto her side and pressed against her.

"Stop that. They will see."

"See what? I am not going to do anything. I just want to feel you." He slid his hand under the gown and rested it on her belly.

"That feels good. Your hands are so warm."

The nurse returned with a saline drip and medicines. "Herr Engel!" she barked, flustered by the intimate scene before her. "This is a hospital. Your wife is ill and not to be fondled, and your dirty boots have soiled the bed. Ach! I must ask you to leave. You may return tomorrow."

"She must have been a prison matron before she became a nurse. I think she hates men," he whispered to Maritza, then reluctantly bade her goodnight.

As he drove along, Will's elation turned to worry. The baby was due in November. Would the war be over then? He didn't think so. How could they raise a child in this environment? I should have been more careful, he thought—the song of self-reproach sung by men through the ages. Leave it to the Nazis to spoil this blessing. *No.* For years, he dreamed of having his own family, and he wasn't going to allow his child to be indoctrinated into the Hitler cult. He had to find a way out of France before the baby was born.

He toyed with the idea of going to Spain. That wouldn't work. A frail, pregnant woman with a medical condition could not trek through the Pyrénées Mountains that spanned the entire length of the French-Spanish border, a treacherous journey for the fittest female. The serpentine roads that curved through the passes were patrolled by German soldiers, police, bandits, and killers. Even if they made it through, he would be dragged back and executed as a warning to others who had a thought of deserting.

The options here in Paris that he hoped would appear like ripe fruit waiting to be picked were nonexistent. A journey of a thousand miles behind them, and they were still trapped. Wait, and a solution will come, he told himself. There was no other choice.

Maritza was discharged a few days later, having been advised how to manage her condition. Small meals, fresh air, and daily walks were recommended, for which Will set numerous caveats. By the time he finished giving directives, her eyes were going in circles. "We have a long road ahead," she said. "I love that you want the best for me and our baby, but it's a pregnancy, not a deadly illness. I know you're worried because things are up in the air and we don't know what tomorrow will bring, but at least we're here, and it's better than being in Warsaw."

Better than being in Warsaw was too low a bar for him.

Chapter 39

In early May, Will heard that an Allied attack was expected some-
where along the northern coast of France. If it happened and the
Allies were able to breach the Germans' defenses and make inroads,
there was a good chance their fresh armies would be victorious.
America was a vast country with millions more men than the United
Kingdom, even if they were embroiled in war with Japan.

He thought about the Germans who would be taken prisoner
and ultimately interned in Allied camps under the protection of the
Geneva Conventions, and an idea took root in his mind. He, too,
could surrender with Maritza and arrange for her to get to a safe
place. When the war was over, he would be free to go wherever she
and the baby were.

He kept his fingers crossed and ears open for information. The
month wound down without an attack. Disappointed, he brought
home a map and studied the area south of the northern coast. Hitler
believed the invasion would come at the Pas-de-Calais due to its
proximity to England across the Straits of Dover, but on June 6, the
Germans were the first to report "a grand scale amphibious landing"
taking place two hundred miles west, near the Normandy beaches.

"This is the turning point, Maritza," Will said, marveling at such
an enterprise and the planning and teamwork it had taken and praying for its success.

As the days went on, the invasion was the only topic of discussion at the Majestic. In the dining room, the Nazi loyalists echoed
the German news reports that their armies were beating the invaders

back across the English Channel. By late June though, the Allies had taken the town of Carentan and the port of Cherbourg. "They won't get farther than that," said the officials in the dining room, fancying themselves as generals and predicting a complete victory.

Mid-July. Brooding in the Majestic's offices as the general staff struggled to accept reports of Allied troops' southward movements, a situation Will found heartening. The Gestapo were out in full force, zooming through the Paris streets in their black Citroëns and Mercedes, storming apartments and businesses, arresting suspected members of *La Résistance,* and brutalizing citizens. There were fewer Wehrmacht officers in the streets, and the cafés where they once gathered in large numbers were empty or closed. Walking to and from the metro station, Will had to look over his shoulder. Attacks on the military were intensifying.

On the twenty-first, Hitler made a radio announcement: another attempt had been made on his life. He vowed "to call those miserable creatures to account in the way we as National Socialists are used to."

"No ambiguity there," Will told Maritza.

"They went about it all wrong," she said. "A stake should have been driven through his heart. Well, if he had one."

It would later come to light that General von Stülpnagel had been recalled to Berlin, imprisoned, and executed at the end of August for helping to plan the plot.

About a week after Hitler's speech, Will brought Maritza to the couch. "Please hear me out. I don't know how or when, but I want to find a place away from the fighting where I can surrender."

"Surrender?" Her mouth fell open. "What are you talking about?"

"My transfer here was a godsend. It fell into our laps when we had your papers, and we got away easily. We will have no such luck this time if we do nothing. I have no intention of being captured and left unable to ensure your safety."

"My God, it's Warsaw all over again!"

"The situation is coming to a head, my love, and we have to face reality. The Allies will make their way here, and we must have a plan, or I will be captured and you will be treated as the wife of an enemy. If I surrender somewhere away from here and we are together, we can request protection for you because you are Jewish and pregnant and tell the Allies you want to go to England."

"That is the most ridiculous thing I've ever heard in my life. *Tell* them I want to go to England? You are taking a complex problem and making it sound so simple. Just because I want to go doesn't mean I will be sent there. They will laugh and say, 'You want England? You and everybody else, sister, now shut up and get in line for the truck to the camp for displaced persons.' And since when is being Jewish a benefit? The only special treatment Jews receive is a one-way ticket to a concentration camp."

"You think the Allies are not aware of what the Nazis have been doing to the Jews? They must have plans in place for dealing with people who have fled and can't return to their homelands for fear of persecution. Yes, I surrender; we tell them you want to go to England and let them laugh, but it's the squeaky wheel that gets oiled."

"Well, my grandmother used to say, 'The man plans and God laughs.'" She started to cry. "So what do you think of that?"

"I need you to trust me, Maritza. We must do this."

"What if the Germans crush the Allies?"

Will shook his head. "No. They might be able to hold on for another year or so, but the white flag will go up."

"What if Germany surrenders right after you do? Then you will have given yourself up for nothing."

"That is unlikely. Right now, we have to concentrate on what is in front of us."

"Oh, Willy."

He put his arms around her. "It's the only way, my love."

"What will happen to me? Where will I go?" she asked in a small voice.

"I don't know, though it will be someplace safe, and that is what I want for you and our baby. I will be put in a camp and treated decently, and we can find each other when the war ends."

"You say that so cavalierly, but it will be impossible."

"It's not impossible. I will be sent to the States or to England like the Germans and Italians in the Afrika Korps. The Red Cross keeps lists of where prisoners are sent. Please don't cry. We must have faith."

She pushed his arms away. "Faith is for fools, Willy. How will we find each other? Are we going to leave a trail of pebbles, carve messages into tree trunks, or scream each other's name into the wind and expect an answer? I had faith when I waited for Andrush to come back, and he didn't. I could have prayed every minute of every day, and for what? He was killed and couldn't come, so my faith was wasted."

"Any man who fights is at high risk, but separately, you and I thought about our sad, lonely lives and dreamed of finding love, and we did. Now we have a chance to shape our destiny by making conscious decisions in a certain direction as best we can, and faith will see us through."

"That's why I can't lose you. I love you so much."

"You won't lose me. We will find each other. Be strong, for the sake of our baby."

Maritza felt then what she would feel when the day came to be separated from Will and every day until and after—lost and frightened, but he needed to hear that she wouldn't fall apart. Oh, she would, though not in front of him. Malka had been the queen of pretenders, and she was her mother's daughter. "All right. We will live for the lists. I will have faith and do whatever it takes."

He held her tightly. "We will get through this, then start new lives together as a family of three."

She cried alone in the daytime, then washed her face and plastered on a smile the minute he came through the door.

Chapter 40

Major developments occurred over the first two weeks of August. General von Choltitz, the new military governor sent by Hitler to destroy Paris rather than let it fall into Allied hands, arrived on the ninth. Von Choltitz was a portly man with a jutting chin, a small mouth, and large, heavy-lidded eyes, a tough commander known throughout his long military career for strict obedience to orders. He brought an evacuation mandate for non-essential personnel, but they wouldn't be leaving by train; the French railwaymen went on strike the next day.

At work, Will compiled a list of evacuees and typed up documents. On Friday, the eleventh, he heard the most encouraging news: American troops had liberated the city of Le Mans. He rushed home to tell Maritza.

"If I am correct in my thinking, the Americans will go to Orléans next. That is here," he said, showing her the location on his map. Orléans, an ancient and magnificent city where Joan of Arc helped the French troops to victory against the English in the early fifteenth century, was located on the north bank of the Loire River, sixty-five miles south of Paris and eighty from Le Mans. There, the Germans had built a large airport and warehouses full of food and supplies.

"This is the opportunity I've been hoping for. We are bound to meet the Americans if we head in that direction." He had no way of verifying if indeed they would encounter the troops, but if he and Maritza stayed in Paris much longer, they certainly would. "We will need a car."

"Can you get one?"

"I will steal one if I have to."

"What if they decide not to come to Paris and go straight to Germany? What if we leave here and days pass before we see the Americans, or we don't at all?" she asked. "There might be Resistance on the roads, and you could be captured or killed. Willy, your plan is too dangerous."

"We will deal with that possibility later. Let's go to bed." He didn't want to talk anymore; he needed to think. Too many *what-ifs*, and he went over them. It wouldn't make sense for the Americans to bypass Paris, he reasoned, not when they could travel from Le Mans to Orléans in a straight line and swing north to the capital. If confronted by the Resistance and she spoke French, Maritza would be viewed as a collaborator, and he needed to have a credible story ready as to why she was with a German. Nothing he said, though, would convince the hot-blooded French, who had every right to hate him. He tossed and turned.

"What's wrong, Willy?"

"It's the heat, my love. Rest now." His concerns were many; why pile more on her? This wasn't the time for sharing his fears. He fell into a troubled sleep, but was startled awake by thunderclaps that sounded like cannon fire.

Maritza sat up. "What was that?"

"Just thunder, my love." He soothed her to sleep and listened to the steady drumming of the rain on the tile roof until his eyes closed.

The storm had passed by morning, and the sun was struggling to break through the clouds. They went for a walk in the neighborhood to escape the heat of the apartment, but there was no relief. The air was heavy and humid and smelled of rot. The streets were mostly deserted, and fewer cars were parked along the curbs than on any other Sunday.

Monday, August 14. Will walked to work since the trains weren't running. Clerks on the first floor of the Majestic were packing files into boxes. He went up to his office on the floor above. Schreiber stood in front of the open window, picking dead leaves off a potted plant. "It's over for us here," he said without turning around. "We've been ordered by the Führer to return to Germany."

"We?" Will's heart sank.

Schreiber turned to him. "We, the staff. The Allies have broken out of Normandy. They were able to slash through the hedgerows by attaching blades to the front of their tanks and by their relentless bombing. The American General Patton's troops have gotten as far east as Le Mans. It appears we will be overrun. The twenty thousand troops we have in Paris are of dubious quality and certainly not enough to hold the invaders off, but we've still got tens of thousands of men in southern France."

"It seems logical that from Le Mans, the Americans would go to Orléans, then head north to Paris," Will said, trying to find out as much information as possible that would support his theory.

Schreiber shrugged. "Perhaps they will, but why should we care? That is von Choltitz's problem, not ours, and we will be safely away by then. We must leave here tomorrow before the end of the day. I have a driver, and you and your wife can ride with me back to Germany."

Think fast. "That is kind of you, but you see, my wife is pregnant and quite sick. The treatment she underwent in the hospital hasn't helped. She benefits from an herbal preparation made exclusively by a pharmacy in, um, uh, Dourdan," he said, remembering a town north of Orléans from his map. "It is owned by German sympathizers. She is down to the last of the, uh, tonic, and the pharmacist needs two days to prepare it. She must have it, or she will become violently ill on the trip. I wonder if I might borrow a car tomorrow to pick it up."

"I'd be surprised if there are any available. I can try to find an ambulance to transport her to Germany."

"It's the motion that affects her. The preparation works like a charm. She takes it daily."

"You know where our garage is?"

"Yes."

Schreiber took out a form, signed and stamped it. "Take this over there. Maybe they have something, then come back and help me pack up this mess."

Will walked the forty-five minutes to the Wehrmacht garage west of the hotel, sweating profusely under the hot sun. Mechanics were hard at work preparing vehicles seized from the French early in the occupation for officers and officials returning to Germany. A disinterested sergeant took the form and showed him a 1929 Renault coupe devoid of bumpers, wheel fenders, running boards, or headlights. The paint had worn off, and the body was a dull gray. Will didn't care how it looked. "Does it run?"

"It should."

"Well, can you start it up?"

The sergeant glowered. *Can't you see I'm busy?* The car wouldn't start. "Come back tomorrow afternoon."

"We will never get out of Paris at this rate," Will thought while walking back to the hotel.

Tuesday, August 15. In their office, Schreiber was stuffing papers into his briefcase and, as always, freshly shaved, brushed, and smelling of mulled wine. "Good morning, Willy. An abundance of news today. The Allies began an aerial bombardment of the southern coast of France a few hours ago, and their invasion fleet has started discharging troops to shore. They've got those fanatical *Maquisard* guerrillas down there to help them."

"What about our tens of thousands of men?" Will tried to keep the sarcasm out of his voice.

"Word is that our resources are strained, although we do have our 11th Panzer Division. In my opinion, France is a lost cause. She will fall to the Allies, but their armies are in for a shock when they try to make it into Germany. That's when they will be slaughtered. Back to the news here in Paris," Schreiber continued. "Von Choltitz has disarmed the police. They've gone on strike, as have the metro workers, and the communist *résistants* have put up posters urging the citizens to liberate the city before the Americans arrive."

"When will that be?" His whole plan would backfire if he missed his window of opportunity.

"A week, maybe. The Americans are advancing north, south, and east, and their planes have destroyed our vehicles and equipment along the roads. We just received word that one or more of their divisions is heading toward Orléans, so you were right. Our forces there are retreating south of the Loire to reorganize."

There is still time, Will thought, breathing an inaudible sigh of relief. "Has the garrison here been called out?"

"Not as far as I know, but we have our big guns in place," Schreiber said. "Let's finish up, then you had better go and see about the car. They will give you enough gas to get to Dourdan and back, then find a ride and return to Hannover. You'll get your new orders there. You've been a great help," he said, slapping him on the back.

His driver took Will to the garage in an older, well-tended Mercedes, its back seat laden with bags and packages from Parisian shops. Inside the vast space of the garage, officers waited to take possession of their vehicles. When it came his turn, the sergeant pointed at the forlorn Renault. It sat among the other rattletraps that none of those arrogant officers would be caught dead driving. Will got in and turned the key. The engine wheezed and coughed and belched into life. The half tank of gas would be barely enough to get to Orléans, but he knew not to ask for more and drove to the apartment.

"We leave tomorrow, Maritza. I found a car. Take your knapsack with your documents and medicines, but conceal your birth certificate and school card somewhere in your clothing. Pack up some food and water. Bring your coat. I don't know where we will end up. Wear something comfortable and your low-heeled shoes with socks. We might have to do some walking. Bring an umbrella, too. The weather is fickle."

Maritza went about her tasks. Will's instructions were Andrush's words verbatim the night before they left Warsaw back in September '39. Flashbacks of the horrors that followed in Wyszków appeared in rapid succession, paralyzing her with fears that history would repeat itself.

On their last night in Paris, they made love with desperation and clung to each other like limpets. She tried to fight the tears, but they streamed from her eyes as soon as Will fell asleep. What will become of us? she wondered. The only thing left to do was have faith.

Chapter 41

Will rose before dawn and decided not to wear his uniform in case they met the Resistance on the way. He dressed in casual attire: white shirt, brown trousers, a pair of lace-up shoes, and a slouchy jacket. In civilian clothes, he might buy them both a little more time. *I should have bought a beret*, he thought, as if that accessory would make him look more French. He chuckled at the absurdity. They probably weren't made large enough to fit his Teutonic head.

They went down to the car. "This is it?" Maritza asked. "It's a piece of junk, Willy. You didn't tell me—"

"I didn't want you to be discouraged. It was this or nothing."

"Well, as long as it gets us to Orléans," she said.

"That's the spirit." He gave her a grateful look and started it up. The engine made popping noises and juddered. "Don't die on us now," he pleaded, and pumped the gas. He turned on the wiper to clear the windscreen of the night's rain. It whipped back and forth violently, squealing like a rhinoceros. They laughed, temporarily relieving the tension. "Let's hope it doesn't rain," he said. "I won't be able to stand that noise."

They came to the southern outskirts of the city. "There's a checkpoint ahead." He slowed the car and passed her a paper bag.

"What is this for?"

"If they ask questions, act like you are ill."

The soldier, well past his prime, looked at the car and tried not to laugh, then poked his head in. "Identification please."

"Have the rules changed? Do you no longer salute your superiors?" Will thrust their documents at him.

The soldier's attitude changed when he checked Will's papers, and he snapped to attention. "I am sorry, Oberleutnant. I didn't know who you were without your uniform on. We are required to ask what business you have where you are going."

"We are going to a pharmacy in Dourdan to pick up medicine for my wife. An herbal preparation. She is ill."

Maritza placed the bag over her mouth and gagged. The soldier returned their documents quickly and saluted. "How did I do?" she asked as they drove away.

"An award-winning performance, my love. Now close your eyes. This is going to be a very long day."

The sun broke through the curtain of gray clouds, then hid, as if it too couldn't bear to face the day. *If only we could go back to Paris and spend one more night together*, Maritza wished, blinking away tears and glancing at Will. She could tell by the determined set of his jaw that he was thinking the same.

He drove for an hour and a half, and having seen no evidence of Allied troops, he began to doubt the veracity of Schreiber's reports. The gas gauge hovered near the empty mark, and the pit in his stomach grew. He continued on through the countryside, the flat land green and damp from the recent rains. Around ten o'clock, the car started to sputter and chug. *"Scheisse!"* he exclaimed. "Shit! We are out of gas."

"Oh no!" Maritza cried.

Steering the car onto a field, he let it coast to a stop near a stand of trees, and lifted her and their belongings out. They stretched their legs and sat down in the shade.

"What now, Willy?"

"I am going to check and see how far we are from the city." It would take roughly thirty minutes to walk into Orléans proper, but it would be too dangerous. The Resistance would be searching for members of any German squads left behind to pick off the Americans when they entered the city. Will put the map back in his satchel, took out their marriage certificate and her German documents, loosened a small photo of her from one of them, and put it in his pocket. He burned the papers with his lighter, then buried the ashes under a wet patch of grass with his knife.

"Why did you do that?" she asked angrily.

Will pulled her onto his lap and held her. "You don't need them anymore, my love. We don't have to worry about Germans. I told you yesterday that they retreated south."

"But others might come and take you away to fight with them in the south, and that will be the end of us."

This wasn't about the Germans, and they both knew it. It was the Resistance she feared, what they did to women who consorted with the enemy, and what they would do to him.

"I don't feel well, Willy. I'm dizzy, and my belly is tightening up."

Tears stung at his eyes. His decision to come to Orléans was based on logic and information from a reliable source, but there was no guarantee things would turn out the way he wanted. What was he thinking, dragging her on this journey and causing her symptoms to return? He rubbed her belly until she was calmer and able to eat bits of bread and take sips of water.

"I feel better now." She slipped her hand into his. "You always take good care of me. You're wonderful and smart, and I am so proud to be carrying your child."

Will swallowed hard. Maritza never ceased to amaze him. He considered himself at best mediocre, and even in the face of uncertain outcomes, she managed to encourage him. Then he realized what had to be done. If the Americans didn't come, he and Maritza would walk into the city, find the town hall, and simply tell whoever was in charge the truth.

Poles fought the Germans alongside the French in 1940, when the short-lived Battle of France started, and had become active in their resistance groups. Moreover (and here he indulged in fanciful thinking), didn't the French have a reputation for being romantic? His and Maritza's love story was so extraordinary and superior to any tale he could concoct, so perhaps the people he turned himself over to would think that he, this hulking German in civilian clothes, couldn't be all bad.

They might beat him with truncheons before throwing him in jail, though he doubted they would kill him. They would never hurt a beautiful Polish woman in the fifth month of pregnancy, and that was the only thing Will cared about. Having put his thoughts right, he felt less troubled than he had in days.

Shortly after one o'clock, as they began to drift off, a discordant growling, roaring, and buzzing of engines could be heard coming from the west. "Do you hear that?" he asked, pulling Maritza to her feet. In the distance, a group of jeeps led a convoy of tanks and vehicles, behind which, though out of Will's line of vision, were several truckloads of French fighters, holding rifles and light machine guns supplied by the British and U.S. Armies.

His heart raced. "Look Maritza, they are coming! From this moment, speak English."

She followed him and stumbled. Shoving the leather satchel he had slung across his chest to his side, he picked her up, walked into the road, and waited. The jeeps rattled up the highway and ground to a halt. Two dozen American soldiers of the 137th Infantry Regiment's intelligence and reconnaissance platoon jumped out with rifles and pistols drawn.

A soldier shouted, "Put the girl down, and both of you get your hands up!"

Will lowered Maritza and dropped his bag. She slid her knapsack from her shoulders and raised her arms.

"My wife is needing help. She is pregnant and sick," he said, speaking the best English he could muster as the men surrounded them.

A tall soldier searched him and took away his knife and pistol before asking, "Who are you?"

"Oberleutnant Engel, from Paris. I would like to speak to your commanding officer."

"What about?"

"About the safety of my wife."

"Sorry, he's busy. Does your wife have any weapons on her?"

"No."

"Does she speak English?"

"Yes."

He directed a couple of men to go through their bags and another to seat Maritza in the vehicle. "What are you doing near Orléans, Oberleutnant? Where's your unit, and why aren't you in uniform?"

"Reports say you are leaving Le Mans, so I was thinking you would come here next. I wish to surrender, and Paris is too dangerous for my wife. I was a secretary at the military command center. It is better that I don't wear the uniform. It will make me a target of the Resistance. They see it and shoot. I do not want her to be hurt."

"Have you seen any German troops on your way here?"

"No."

He tied Will's hands and placed him behind Maritza in the jeep. "Bring 'em to the rear with the other prisoners and make the lady comfortable. She's in the family way," he said to the soldier who had hopped in next to Will.

The driver shifted into gear, spun around, and sped off toward the cavalcade of vehicles. They were taken to a field along with the dozen Germans captured on the way in from Le Mans. A guard set up a small tent for them, "on account of your condition," he told Maritza.

They lay on the blankets in each other's arms. The plan had been made and followed, but the distress over their impending separation made it hard to get words out over the lumps in their throats. What was there to say, really? They loved each other more than words. Maritza held back her tears. The Americans weren't going to send her back to Poland, and crying would upset Will. She had to be strong.

Chapter 42

The regiment pushed into the city amid the constant sniper fire and shelling from the German artillery positions a few miles across the Loire. During the night, forty-two German prisoners had been taken, and the city of Orléans and the airport were in American hands. In the morning, a jeep pulled up to the field to take Will and Maritza to the former German headquarters in the heart of the city, where the American general in charge of the liberation task force had his temporary office. Having been told about an officer who had just come from Paris and wanted to see him, the general asked his Civil Affairs man to interrogate him.

Their driver passed thousands of jubilant Orléanais parading through the streets, singing *La Marseillaise,* the French national anthem, carrying banners of the flags of the Allied nations, and shouting greetings to their American liberators. The joyous citizens were headed for the main square, surrounded by demolished buildings, where the general was to give a short speech.

Will plunged his bound hands between his knees and stared straight ahead. A rickety, open-bed truck drove past, carrying a group of women who had either collaborated with the Germans or slept with them. Their heads had been shaved by angry citizens. Some wore undergarments; others were naked to the waist, with swastikas painted onto their foreheads or breasts. A tear rolled down Maritza's cheek, and she turned her head away. Maybe some of them had loved a good German, but they would always be known as traitors and ostracized. She might very well have been in that truck.

Captain Knapp, the Civil Affairs officer tasked with restoring normalcy to the city, stood when they entered the room. He had brown hair and eyes and a rectangular, no-nonsense face, and told the soldier to untie Will's hands. "Good morning, Oberleutnant. Your name?"

"Wilhelm Engel, and my wife, Maritza," he said, saluting.

"Ma'am," the captain said, nodding at her, taking in her belly, and gesturing for them to be seated. "I understand you were working in Paris in a clerical capacity at the military command, Oberleutnant. Perhaps you can tell me what you know about the German forces there, and any plans the army has made to defend the city."

Will repeated what he had learned form Schreiber and some things he discovered on his own. "There are about twenty thousand troops of the 325th Division. It is not having the best men," he said. "At La Croix de Berny, a flak battery employing the eighty-eight millimeter gun is guarding the southern entrance to the city. There are about twenty such batteries forming an arc to the west. Most of the general staff have returned to Germany. I was not a member of that staff, just a replacement in a lower office. I know of nothing else to tell."

"Certainly helpful, Oberleutnant."

Will stood. "Captain, my wife is pregnant and ill. She—"

"So I see," Knapp said, with the slightest hint of an edge to his voice. *Rather foolish with a war on.*

"The timing is inconvenient, but a blessing nonetheless," Maritza said quickly, wanting to dispel any notion in the captain's mind that she was a simpleton, and that Will was prone to debauchery. She rose from her chair and leaned on him. He put his arm around her. "What will happen to my husband now?" she asked.

"Your *husband*," he said, now with an unmistakable note of disdain, "has surrendered and is a prisoner of war. He'll be taken to a holding camp where his final destination will be decided."

"Maritza is a Polish Jew," Will said. "Her family was murdered, and she has no home left. She wants to go to England."

Knapp looked at Will and erupted in a rare display of anger. "She wants to go to England! Who do you think you are, making a statement like that? We all want something, and that is for this war to end. Your *Kameraden* started it and deserve the outrage they provoked, and here you are, surpassing the limits of prisoner convention."

"I am nobody, sir," Will said calmly, "and mean no disrespect. Hitler, he starts this war, and I am ashamed. I am only concerning for my wife to be safe."

The captain's face softened. "Tell me how a German officer came to marry a Jewish woman? Isn't that a criminal offense?"

"The Nazis killed her whole family with bombs and shot at her and all the people from the air with machine guns during the invasion. I saw her in a market in Warsaw, and at that moment I fell in love. She speaks German and was alone, so I was hiding her in my house and getting false German papers for her so we could marry and leave Warsaw. I was lucky to transfer to Paris last year."

"Where are these papers?"

"I burn them outside of Orléans in case the résistants come and think she is also German. They will assume we are spies and kill us both."

"Are you spies?"

"Of course not, nor am I a Nazi. I hear reports of the Americans coming and I make a plan to surrender and find safety for her."

Maritza burrowed into Will's arms and began to sob. His face etched with sadness, he gently rubbed her belly and whispered in her ear. The tender way the oberleutnant comforted her and the looks of sadness on both their faces stabbed at Knapp's heart. Their display of intimacy, as if no one else existed, made him look away. He cleared his throat and ruffled some papers on the desk. He now understood the German's concern for the woman he was deeply in love with and regretted having judged him so severely.

"I'm sure we can find a sympathetic family who will board your wife until other arrangements can be made. I assure you she will be quite safe." Knapp turned to Maritza. "Do you have relatives in England?"

"No, but if I can go there, when the war is over, he will know where to look for me. England is so close. I can work hard there, and I have some money to pay for the journey. I won't be a bother to anyone, I promise." She sounded like a child negotiating for a badly wanted privilege and didn't care. Will was her whole world, and she might never see him again, but she wasn't entitled to special treatment because she loved her German husband. He was an enemy of the Allies no matter how wonderful and dear he was to her.

"Given that you have crossed two international borders to get to France and cannot return to Poland due to the persecution of Jews, you might qualify to be evacuated to England. I'll look into it, but can't promise anything."

"Oh, thank you, sir," Maritza wiped her tears away.

"And thank you for the information, Oberleutnant. I sincerely hope you two find each other after the war."

The soldier came inside and started to bind Will's hands. "That won't be necessary," the captain said.

Chapter 43

Back at the field, Will closed the flap of the tent, ignoring the stares of the other prisoners. "Listen carefully, my love. They aren't going to keep us here for long. When the time comes to separate, we will take leave of each other without a show of emotion, or it will be too difficult for us both. I have no idea where I will end up, nor do you at this point, and it will take time for each of us to get wherever they send us. Once you are settled, find someone to help locate me, as we discussed."

"Willy, I will do everything to find you." She buried her face in his neck, wanting to remember his scent.

Knapp came for Maritza in the early afternoon. "I found a place for you to stay for the time being. Say goodbye to your husband. I'll wait outside."

Her heart hung in her chest. *Don't cry. Be strong.* "We've already said our goodbyes." If she so much as looked at Will she would fall apart. It took every ounce of her willpower to keep the tears from spilling. She picked up her knapsack, squared her shoulders, and walked out of the tent.

"You are going to stay with an elderly couple named Ducharme. They are sympathetic to the Poles," the captain said on the way back into the city. "Do you by chance speak French?"

"Yes."

"Good. That will make things easier. I told them you've had a rough time, and they won't be asking you any personal questions."

Within the hour, Maritza was seated in the couple's kitchen, forcing down a stew of root vegetables augmented by bits of corned beef from a tin courtesy of the U.S. Army. The Ducharmes were scrawny and thin-lipped, with narrow, solemn faces, and looked more like brother and sister than husband and wife. Both had white hair—Madame's was pulled into a tight bun at the nape of her neck, and Monsieur's curled around large ears. They stood over her while she ate, then whisked the bowl away.

The apartment was small and once well-appointed, but after four years of hardship under the Germans' stranglehold, many of their items had been sold, bartered, or repurposed. Maritza was glad to see books lining the shelves of an old étagère. *Something to do.*

She was given a tiny bedroom that must have been occupied by the couple's absent daughter when she was young. The room smelled faintly of lavender and had just enough space for the narrow iron bed and a little table. The table held a lamp whose shade bore traces of ribbon and lace, perhaps removed to make a collar. Faded rose *toile de Jouy* covered the walls, peeling near the ceiling where there were visible water stains.

The room was comforting, and it was there that she spent most of the day resting, longing for Will, when not helping Madame clean the apartment and peel vegetables. In the evenings, she sat with the Ducharmes on a worn brocade couch, reading or listening to them sing along to scratched records on a wind-up Victrola that was manufactured two decades before she was born. This was their most prized possession.

Maritza had been wearing the same clothes since she and Will left Paris, but once army engineers repaired the damage to the city's water system that the Germans had sabotaged before they withdrew, she was able to bathe in the tub. On Sunday, the Ducharmes insisted she accompany them to Mass, and it felt good to get out of the apartment. They flanked her, looping their arms through hers in case she decided to run away.

The captain came to the apartment a few days later. "We're moving out. I came to say goodbye."

"Moving out?" Maritza began to tremble. "And my husband?" she whispered. "Is he still in the field?"

"No ma'am. They were taken two days ago to a location up north to await transfer to a permanent camp, but I do have some news that might take your mind off him."

"Oh?" Nothing was going to take her mind off Will.

"I put in a request for your evacuation to England. When it comes through, one of the men in the battalion that is to remain here will come and inform you of the next steps."

"What if it doesn't go through? What will I do then?"

"Let's hope it does," he said, leaving it at that.

"Thank you for everything you've done for me, Captain," Maritza said, putting out her hand.

"It's been a pleasure knowing you, Ma'am." Knapp went to the kitchen to chat briefly with the Ducharmes, and on his way out, he gave her a jaunty salute.

Paris was liberated four days later, on August 25. While waiting for the American advance, Resistance fighters had risen up against the Germans, the French and American troops rolled in, and von Choltitz surrendered without demolishing the city as ordered. General de Gaulle had returned from exile in England and entered the capital. The Ducharmes cried, "Vive la France!" upon hearing the news, uncorked a dusty bottle of wine, and cranked up the record player.

The following week, a stocky lieutenant with dark, close-cropped hair arrived to drive her to a camp for displaced persons near Cherbourg to be examined and processed before setting sail for England.

"Name's Joe De Luca. I have to make a stop in Le Mans. We'll stay the night in the army camp and head up north tomorrow."

Maritza thanked her hosts, kissed them once on each cheek, and said goodbye. They had done their best, in a detached way, to make her stay comfortable.

De Luca spoke with a funny accent, regaled her on the trip with stories of his childhood, and made her laugh. He told her about his wife, a schoolteacher, and said they were planning to make a baby when he returned home. The Americans she met at the camp in Le Mans were just as friendly and easygoing, though it didn't escape her that they were soldiers on a mission. Her heart fluttered with happy anticipation. She was going to England and would find Will through the lists and by any and all means.

Knowing he wouldn't see Maritza again for a long time left a cavity of pain greater than any Will had ever felt, but he was relieved that she was safe in the hands of the Americans and might be eligible for evacuation to England. He kept her little photograph in his breast pocket, close to his heart, and filled the empty hours with memories of their two years together.

On the third day of his captivity, the prisoners were put into trucks and driven three hours north to a makeshift holding camp near Normandy, operated by the British and Canadians. They were herded into a pen to join legions of Germans and foreign Axis fighters captured during the Allied drive.

Will was a deserter; he had disobeyed a superior's orders to return to Germany, actively sought out the enemy, and given himself up. If anyone found out, he could be killed right there in the pen by a zealot who might have squirreled a blade away or a twig sharpened to a point. Sickened by his own foul odor and that of those around him, stiff from sitting on damp ground and nearly out of his mind from the waiting, he wore the expression of an angry gorilla and spoke to no one.

Over the next few days, the prisoners were separated into groups and taken by buses to the port of Le Havre, where they boarded Liberty ships for the journey across the Channel to Southampton. Escorted by military police, they went from there by train to the reception center at Kempton Park in Surrey.

For the better part of a week, Will stood in long lines with belligerent men, first to shower, then while completely naked, given a medical exam, and deloused. He forgot to put the photo of Maritza back in his satchel, and it was lost when his filthy clothing was taken away during the shower. The prisoners were handed brown uniforms with a yellow circle stitched on the back and one on the front leg before being interrogated and finally classified according to their degree of Nazi sympathy. Will received a white armband, an identifier of the lowest level of risk.

He and other officers with white armbands were driven by lorries northeast to Dancers Hill, a small, minimum security camp in South Mimms, Hertfordshire, a village about twenty miles north of London. The perimeter was enclosed by double barbed wire, though there were no guard towers. Fifteen prisoners' huts made of corrugated iron sheets resembling giant tin cans cut in half provided quarters for up to a dozen men each. A bunk with a mattress, albeit a thin one, and the promise of three meals a day prepared by comrade cooks seemed grand compared to the squalid conditions in the holding pen in France.

The men were welcomed by Colonel Jenkins, in charge of the camp. Tall, thin, and ginger-haired, he gave a speech through a prisoner elected to serve as his interpreter. "This is a camp for good Germans and your home for the foreseeable future. Camp rules and regulations are posted in every hut, in German and in English. While your treatment will be in accordance with the terms of the Geneva

Convention, your privileges will be commensurate with your conduct. Any deviation from expected behavior will result in disciplinary measures. Sergeant Jones will take over from here."

Jenkins hurried back to his office. He disliked having to deal directly with prisoners. The Italians who occupied the camp before these Germans were a rebellious bunch and kept him on his toes.

One week after arriving, the men were allowed to send a postcard to their families informing them of their capture and state of health, but Will would have to wait; it was too soon to get any information about Maritza. He was told it was going to take time to locate her since he couldn't say with certainty where she'd been sent.

Chapter 44

Esau Gutman, a German Jewish lawyer, had emigrated to England a few years before Hitler came to power. He changed his name to Goodman, found work in his field of immigration law with a solicitor in London, and bought a house in Hampstead, an affluent neighborhood. The house was three miles north of the London Zoo, and Esau was fond of telling colleagues that on a quiet night he could hear the monkeys howl.

"What you need is a wife, old boy," they said, thumping him on the back, "and it will be you doing the howling."

Having satisfactorily arranged the basics of his life, the slender, dark-haired fellow went in search of one. At a dance for Jewish singles in London, he met Ruth, a bubbly brunette whom he fell for immediately and soon married. Ruth favored flamboyant clothing and had a larger-than-life personality. Esau loved her spunk, eccentricity, and interest in helping the less fortunate.

Chronic asthma exempted him from military service after Britain declared war on Germany, but he soon received a letter from the Aliens Department of the Home Office, the agency responsible for immigration, commanding his services to the government three days per week. He was to assess Germans and Austrians already residing in the United Kingdom and arriving Jews fleeing Nazi persecution for their level of risk to the country. If found to pose a danger to national security, they were interned in special camps. Esau himself was made to submit to such an evaluation after he had started the work, a procedure he decried as being ass- backward.

He devoted six months to his government service and then concentrated his attention on opening his own solicitor's office. He and Ruthie became involved in their temple's fundraising efforts to help British families meet the costs of sponsoring displaced persons. In late August '44, they received a call from an agency seeking their assistance in placing a young, pregnant Polish Jew who was alone in France and had nowhere to go. Unable to have children, the thought of a baby in the house delighted Ruth. She suggested they sponsor the young woman themselves and have her live in their home.

"I'm told she speaks excellent English, so there won't be any communication problems, and she will be able to help me around the house."

Esau, who could never say no to his wife, agreed, and they went about making preparations. Maritza disembarked in Southampton on the sixteenth of September from a hospital ship carrying wounded soldiers and a number of displaced persons going to arranged homes. Depressed and exhausted from her time at the DP camp, she had been ill throughout the six-hour journey across the rough Channel. Not having had a chance to develop her sea legs on board, she wobbled off the ship like a drunken sailor.

A man in a tweed suit and brown fedora and a smiling, red-lipped lady wearing a cap with a large sequin-appliquéd butterfly perched on the side in such a way that it seemed poised to take flight stood waiting, holding up a sign with her name. The man removed his hat, stepped forward, and shook Maritza's hand. "I'm Esau, and this is my wife, Ruth. It's a pleasure to meet you. Let me take your bag."

Ruth took one look at the trembling girl with the protruding belly and blonde hair tied in a long braid, and was overcome with emotion. She flung her arms around Maritza. "Oh, you poor dear," she said. "You look like you've been through the mill. Come on, let's get you home. You'll be right as rain after a few days."

On the train to London, Maritza was shocked to see the devastation wrought by the German bombing campaigns. She wasn't aware how far the evil arm of Nazism stretched until she saw the hollowed, blackened, bombed out buildings and rubble. Posters aimed at motivating public support for the war effort, such as *Give Blood* and *Send Aid to Russia,* were hung in the stations.

My God, she thought. The Russians are Allies, but if I had stayed with Zofia, I can't even imagine what would have happened. The soldiers were said to have brutalized Polish citizens as they pushed toward the Vistula. How lucky I've been because of Will. He was right about everything. Keep safe, my love, wherever you may be. She thought of Andrush's aunt and cousins, Alina and Jozef, too, and hoped they were safe.

The Goodmans were surprised to learn that Maritza had little knowledge of Judaism. Apart from the names of the Jewish foods her grandmother prepared and a smattering of Yiddish words and phrases, she knew nothing. As soon as the German invaders swept into Poland, she knew that Jewish roots must be hidden and never spoken of. Even now in England, away from persecution, she had no need to learn about religion.

"Just come with us to the temple and use the time to pray for your husband and the end of this war," Ruth proposed. "Why sit in the house alone when you could be with people? Then we'll have a little cake and grape juice and come home."

Maritza gave some thought to the idea and decided it was disrespectful to show such little regard for this kind, caring couple. "I will go," she said.

The pilotless V-2 missile attacks on London, launched from sites in Nazi-occupied Europe, began just days after she arrived, killing and injuring thousands. The air-raid sirens terrified her. She thought of Will's strong arms around her in the Berlin hotel shelter, and her soul cried out for him. In order to get through each day, she told herself over and over that at least he was alive—somewhere.

At the Goodmans' suggestion, Maritza volunteered time in the afternoons playing the piano and giving art lessons to the residents of the retirement home affiliated with their temple. It helped to pass the time that would otherwise be spent wondering about Will and wishing for the war to end. When asked about the baby's father, she let it slip that he was a German prisoner of war, then cursed herself. "He's not a Nazi," she said, stating the answer to the question that was surely uppermost on their minds and holding back tears. "He's the most loving, dear man, and it's because of him that I'm here today."

The women rallied around her. "You don't have to explain to us. You alone know what kind of man he is. If you say he's good, he's good. That's all there is to it."

Not everyone at the home was as gracious. Word went around, shocking and angering some of the residents. Men who had endured the horrors of the trenches during the Great War and suffered long-lasting injuries at the hands of the Germans, as well as those who had lost family in the current war, complained to the rabbi of the neighborhood temple when he visited. He advised tolerance and spoke of the harm of making assumptions without knowing facts.

"Reason over emotion," he said. "Switch the placement of the first and third words, and you will see what made it possible for Hitler to rise to power."

The Goodmans did their best to make Maritza feel at home. Ruth called her *Mitzi* and clucked over her like a mother hen. Although food was rationed, Ruth was a gourmet cook and could whip up something superb from nothing. She made nourishing soups and stews from vegetables grown in her backyard garden. The days were busy and bearable, but as soon as darkness fell, so did Maritza's mood. She was fine and laughing one moment, tearful the next, and this pattern went on for weeks. The baby was kicking more and keeping her up at night, and in two months, he or she would be born.

Esau made an inquiry with the Prisoners of War Information Bureau in London for information about Will. "Now we wait," he said.

"What if there is no record of him?"

"Then we will contact the American authorities who can tell us if he is in a camp in the States. We will find him, Maritza. Have faith. One step at a time."

"Of course," she said, her eyes glistening with tears. "Thank you for all you're doing."

"You mustn't get upset," Ruthie opined. "It will affect the baby, and he or she will be born a nervous wreck and develop colic. When my sister was pregnant and her husband was killed in North Africa, she wept nonstop, then gave birth early, and the baby cried constantly. They didn't bond properly."

Esau cleared his throat with a mighty *ahem*, a warning that she should be quiet. Ruthie had no filter; words tumbled from her mouth like rocks down a mountain during an avalanche. Duly chastised, she ended with a weak plea, "Chin up, Mitzi girl."

Chapter 45

L ife in the Dancers Hill camp was tolerable. Will was in with an affable group of officers who had families in Germany they longed to get home to and whose views on the futility of the war and the senseless killing were the same as his own. The food was palatable, there were English classes in the evenings to strengthen conversational skills, and sports activities on Sundays, weather permitting. Will partook of every offer to do or learn something, because he believed *idle hands make fretful minds*. The officers were not required to work, though most did to make time go faster. He signed up for agricultural work and carried out the farmers' assignments, Monday through Saturday, nine to five, earning six shillings a week.

Daughters, wives, or female relatives of the farmers often wandered onto the field to bring refreshments and chat with the prisoners. The women flocked to Will; he was undeniably attractive, but he kept his eyes down, fearful of being accused of impropriety. He longed for Maritza and felt nothing like himself. The only time he truly had was with her. She alone knew how to please, soothe, and make him laugh. Late at night, he began the ritual of recalling their intimate moments. She was there, pressed against him under the blanket, warming him with her heat, and each morning he awoke with a heavy heart to find her gone.

The camp officials were having a hard time locating Maritza, and Will couldn't understand why she hadn't found him yet. If the war ended, where would he go? He had impressed upon her the importance of having faith, but his own was waning.

The men listened to the British radio broadcasts and, into the fall and winter, followed the progress of the battles raging in the Hürtgen and Ardennes Forests as the mostly American troops made slow progress in their push toward Germany. On December 16, the Germans launched a massive attack against them in the Ardennes. Will feared that Schreiber's words about the slaughter that would await the Allied forces if they attempted to enter Germany might come to pass. Every German victory extended the duration of the war, and he had a growing sense that the chances of Maritza finding him were diminishing.

The huts had always been damp and gloomy, and in winter they were so cold that Will's bones ached. The pot-bellied stove in the corner of the room was more of an ornament from the not-so-thrilling days of yesteryear than a functional heater. The space smelled of mildew, sweat, and dirty socks. A few days before Christmas, he returned tired and crabby from work in need of food and a hot drink to find a white envelope on his bunk. Not one piece of mail had come his way, and his expectation of receiving any had shrunk.

Must be for someone else was his first thought, and then, recognizing Maritza's handwriting, he let out a whoop. "Enfield," he read the return address. "Where is that?" he asked the men who were peering over his shoulder. "Does anyone know?"

"Ten to fifteen miles," someone said. "Southeast of here."

That close? Carefully, Will opened the flap and removed the thin white paper, handling it like a priceless artifact. Several photographs were included. The tears trickled down his face at the sight of Maritza smiling into the camera. She looked lovelier than ever, with hair a bit shorter and a slightly rounder face. In another, she presented their infant daughter and had written on the back, *Emily Willow Engel, at five weeks. Looks just like her papa.*

"Ein Mädchen!" he announced, his face red and his eyes shining with tears. "I have a girl! How do you like that? And this is Maritza, my wife."

Günther plucked the photos from his hand.

"Hey," Will tried to snatch them back, "You're wrinkling them. Be careful."

"All right, calm down. Just let us see."

"Sie ist eine Schönheit," they concurred as the picture went around. "She's a beauty. How old is she?"

When they found out Maritza was twenty-one and Will, thirty-four, they made good-natured jokes. "You cradle snatcher. What does she see in you? It must be that big one you have." They laughed and swatted him with their towels.

"Better bigger than those gherkins you fellows have," he wise-cracked. "Now give me my photos back and let me read my letter."

My dearest darling Willy,

Oh, the joy I felt when we finally located you. Look at our precious daughter! She was born on 12 November at noon and weighed six pounds. I named her Emily, as we agreed, and Willow, because that is your favorite tree and the name means "freedom." She is an easy baby and has your eyes and smile. My sponsors, Esau and Ruth Goodman, are the most wonderful people. They have done so much for us. I just moved into a tiny flat in a building they own, where you will come when you're released. I was ecstatic to learn you are so close to where I am living. Every day I've been apart from you has been a struggle. Let this wretched war end soon so we can be together. I live for your delicious kisses and to feel you in my arms. I love you, Willy. I'm allowed to send two letters a month, not more than a page each, but I can send a package. Write soon. M

Will was a new man, ebullient and lighthearted. An enormous weight had been lifted from his shoulders. He lived for Maritza's letters. Ruth Goodman was an avid photographer, and pictures were always included. He followed Emily's development and dreamed of the day he would be reunited with his family.

By the middle of January '45, there was much better news. The Allies had launched a counterattack, slowing and finally halting the German advance. The Soviets were making their way from Poland to within Germany's borders. In mid-April, American, British, and Canadian forces captured the Ruhr, the industrial center of western Germany. Hundreds of thousands of German troops were surrendering. Two weeks later, at the end of the month, a guard rushed into the barracks.

"Your Führer's dream of a thousand-year Reich has gone down the tubes. Old Adolf has committed suicide!"

Approving shouts went up, *Hitler ist tot. Hurra!* Berlin had fallen to the Russians, and on Monday, the seventh of May, as the men were packing up to leave for the day from their respective farms, came the joyous news of V-E Day. After six long years, the bloody war was over.

Colonel Jenkins, besieged with the prisoners' request for information about their release, called an evening assembly on the yard. "There has been no date set, as England still needs workers to plant and harvest the crops and rebuild the infrastructure ruined by the German bombs," he said. "You will be returned to Germany when word comes down, although it could be another year or two." He rushed back to his office to gather his belongings before being driven away in his car by a soldier.

Another year or two? Over the next week, small fights broke out between frustrated prisoners, and some refused to work. A cold dread settled in Will's chest, and he voiced his concerns to the psychologist sent to reassess the men for any Nazi leanings. The war was over, though there was still time to re-educate those who may have had a reversal of rational thought.

"I understand and sympathize with you," the man said, "but I am not in a position to make that decision. My work is limited to the evaluation of the prisoners' links to Nazism. My final determination is that you are anti-Nazi, if that's any consolation."

It wasn't. The only consolation would be the sight of Maritza at the camp gates. Will went to Jenkins, who reluctantly allowed him less than two minutes of his time.

"As I told you before, no one is being released now. You will be repatriated to Germany sometime in the future."

"That's the problem, sir, the repatriation. I want to make you aware that my wife is living in Enfield, and my baby was born here. I can't go to Germany."

"If your family is here, we can examine your case at the appropriate time. Until we hear otherwise, it's business as usual. Now off you go. I'm busy."

He went back to his hut, buoyed by the small ray of hope, but this feeling didn't last long. The men gathered in the assembly tent on movie night with expectations of watching something entertaining. Instead, they were shown a film about the atrocities at the concentration camps discovered by the Allies and Russians as they swept through the Nazi territories.

Will had heard about Auschwitz and Treblinka—the gassing and burning in ovens and the deeds of the Einsatzgruppen—that chilled him to the core, but when he saw the walking skeletons, the bodies of the dead stacked in great piles, he wept. Around him, there were gasps, dropped jaws, and more weeping as the men allowed their individual grief to manifest. The film was gut-wrenching proof of Nazi evil and depravity, and the images could never be unseen. After the viewing, they shuffled back to the huts with bowed heads.

Chapter 46

A guard came into the hut one morning at the end of August before the men left on work detail. "Engel, report up front."

"What for?"

"Get to the office. You can ask your questions there."

The muscles in Will's neck tightened. It was unusual to be called to the office. "I'm being transferred to another camp like those other men a few weeks ago," he said when the guard went out. Why, when Maritza was so close? He could be sent far away, perhaps to work in a Welsh coal mine or to a remote farm near the Scottish border, where he would spend the next few years talking to sheep. The war was over, and he was being shunted around like an itinerant.

"You always think the worst, Willy. They are letting you go because your family is here, you lucky bastard!" His comrades woo-hooed.

"Letting me go? That's right! They're letting me go to another camp, and I will be stuck in the system until after the next war. I would rather stay here with you Neanderthals."

"Listen, you would have to be given advance notice of a transfer. It is stated in the Geneva Convention."

Will had perused the copy posted on the information board in the dining hut months ago and knew this was true, though what constituted advance notice was unspecified. It seemed that those men who were transferred were here one day and gone the next. With each step toward the office he became increasingly nervous, but there the mystery was explained.

Jenkins outlined a program for a small number of model prisoners with excellent character, like Will, in which they are released early under the supervision of a business-owning patron who, for a sum of money paid to the government, guarantees the prisoner will work for him or her for a specific length of time. Not only does the person being sponsored receive valuable training, he will also learn to be a responsible member of British society.

"It's not often that we find immediate families of prisoners of war residing in the United Kingdom, though Mr. Goodman, a London solicitor, has confirmed the presence of yours here. He is prepared to sponsor your release and provide you with employment in his law office. Let's see now," he put on his glasses and shuffled through the papers. "You would be obligated to him for—"

Maritza had written about Goodman in her letters. Will wanted to jump into the air and shout *Yee-Haw,* like the cowboys in the American westerns sometimes shown on film night. He didn't care how long his obligation would be. After a year in the camp, he was going home to his wife and child.

"Am I to assume by the foolish smile on your face that the scheme meets with your approval?"

"Yes, of course! When will I be allowed to leave?"

"Day after tomorrow when the paperwork is complete. Report to the infirmary for an examination."

After completing the exam, the lorry that would have taken Will to the farm had already left, so he offered to help around the camp. He swept the office, emptied trash cans, peeled potatoes—anything to move the time along so he could see his baby and make love to Maritza.

It was a glorious, sunny morning, and time to go at last. He said goodbye to his comrades and made the final walk up to the office where he was introduced to Mr. Goodman, who explained the documents and terms of his release in German. Will was so excited that his own language sounded as foreign to him as Kurdish.

"Best of luck to you." Jenkins shook his hand after the last form had been signed.

Goodman led him outside to his vehicle, a '37 black Vauxhall. "Nice car," Will said.

"I bought it in '39 from a man who was called up for service. Petrol has just come off rationing, though private cars are only permitted four gallons a week. This is a special occasion, so we will drive instead of taking the bus and get there in half the time. Maritza is on glowing coals; she can't wait to see you."

"I sincerely thank you for all you have done. Has she known about this program for long? She never mentioned it in her letters."

"We found out about the sponsor program right after the war ended, and I made an application. It was just approved, so if she had written to you and it hadn't come to fruition, you would have been disappointed."

"Was she able to pay you for your services?"

"Not necessary. Maritza is like a daughter to us, and we are Emily's godparents, but not in a religious sense. Oh, she's a delightful baby."

"How lucky we are that she will grow up with such caring people in her life," said Will.

"As I explained inside, you will be working with me in my law office. I'm swamped with clients, many of them German, and you can help with the paperwork, interviews, etcetera. I will show you what is needed after you get settled."

"I look forward to it."

"Sit back and relax," Esau said. "We will be there in about half an hour."

Will was so tightly wound, he thought he would snap. Goodman was driving at a good clip, but the car seemed to be moving in slow motion. He closed his eyes. In thirty minutes, he would be holding Maritza in his arms.

Esau pulled up in front of a row of two-story brick apartments in Enfield, a town known for its rifle factory as well as the POW camp for high-ranking German officers located three miles to the west, and pointed to one of several red doors. "Go in there and up the stairs to the first flat. Enjoy your reunion. We will talk soon."

Will's heart beat with fury as he opened the door to the flat. Maritza ran into his arms. They clutched each other, trembling and crying, their kisses landing haphazardly. Will kicked the door closed and kissed her hard on the mouth. Fresh from a bath, she was wearing a robe that had fallen open and exposed her body. Her breasts were fuller, but her waist was as tiny as before. Throbbing for her, he slipped it from her shoulders. She wrapped her arms around him and moaned as their kiss deepened. He got his shoes and trousers off and began making love to her on the floor, thrusting in with desperate need and unable to hold back, he buried his face in her neck and gave a guttural cry. It was the most intense release he'd ever experienced.

He could have stayed there, holding Maritza and whispering endearments, but the sound of babbling made him sit up. "My baby! I want to see my daughter." He pulled on his undershorts and followed the sound. Nine-month-old Emily had pulled herself up to a standing position in her crib. A rosy-cheeked cherub with wisps of blonde hair and enormous blue eyes, she reached out her hand for him. At the sight of her, Will's heart filled with love and his eyes with tears. The moment was so emotional that he couldn't speak. He lifted her out, breathed in her powdery scent, and smothered her face and hands with kisses.

"She looks just like you, Willy."

"No, she's beautiful, like her mother."

They oohed and aahed at the miracle their love had created. "I'll feed her and put her down for a nap," Maritza said, taking the baby from him. "We still have a lot of catching up to do." Will went to bathe and came out with a towel wrapped around his middle. He was leaner than before, his muscles harder and more defined. They watched Emily with parental pride as she drifted off to sleep with her thumb in her mouth.

"We made it," he whispered. "We are finally free of the past. Now we can live the life we dreamed of."

They made love again, slowly this time, then Maritza prepared food. They ate and talked until Emily woke up. She curled her tiny fingers around his, leaving her mother's breast to turn her head and smile at him as milk dribbled down her chin. "We are blessed," he said.

Shortly after his return, Will and Maritza were properly married in a civil ceremony with the Goodmans present. He took language classes at night to perfect his English and made the daily, ten-mile commute to work in Esau's London office, preparing paperwork and communicating with clients. Maritza kept house and took care of Emily.

The following year, the Engels moved from Enfield to a larger flat in Muswell Hill, a suburban district seven miles southwest. Built high on a hill, it offered breathtaking views of London. Their place was located on Broadway, one of the shopping districts where the flats were built over rows of stores. Their building had three floors and six flats, and was attached to the one next to it and so forth. With its shops, grassy parks, and proximity to London, Muswell Hill had everything they wanted.

One day in the spring, Will announced he had taken a weekend job on a farm in West Sussex, a trip of up to two hours one way. He would leave early Saturday morning, stay overnight, and return late

Sunday. Maritza was flabbergasted. "Why would you choose to be away from us both days on the weekends? We're doing fine with what you earn, and you work hard enough as it is. We will never see you. Let me get a part-time job."

"Absolutely not. It will only be for a couple of months and the pay is good. It will give us a nest egg for the future."

When his weekend work ended, Will asked Ruth to invite Maritza over for a cooking lesson on a Saturday. Maritza returned late in the day, surprised to see him home.

"Let's sit in here for a while," he said, taking Emily from her arms and guiding her into the living room. There against the wall was a gleaming, in perfect condition used upright piano and on the top, a cardboard folder of sheet music and a vase of beautiful flowers. The card read, *My life began the day I met you.* She burst into tears. The piano was an extravagance, and she never asked for it, but Will knew her heart. It was a testament of his love, just one of the many unselfish, caring things he did for her.

"Can you play *Ave Maria* for me? We listened to it on the phonograph the first time we made love. Remember? The music is in the folder."

"Oh Willy, I don't think I can do it justice. It's been years since I played it." The piece had a special significance for him—it marked the day they consummated their relationship—but she didn't want to be reminded of anything having to do with Warsaw. She viewed her life with Will as having truly begun the day he came home from the POW camp.

"Give it a try."

Maritza went to the piano, arranged the booklet on the stand, ran her hands over the keys, and began to play tentatively, hitting a few wrong notes. She started again and launched into it. At the end, she looked over at Will and saw that his eyes were wet.

Chapter 47

D riven by an incredible will to live, Andrush endured the beatings at the Polte factory. Though he looked for ways to escape,
there were none. In the summer of '44, he and a group of prisoners
were removed from the factory and sent to one in Hannover that
produced batteries used in components of German military vehicles
and weapons. The prisoners were housed in a camp on the factory
grounds and fed once a day: thin soup, as cloudy as dishwater, a small
piece of bread, and no water. They were exposed to hazardous gases
and beaten with heavy hoses. Medical attention was nonexistent.
Men died and were replaced.

A procession of dark and dismal months, a new year—nineteen
forty-five, someone said. Andrush didn't care. More months, then in
April, a miracle—the British liberated the camp and seized the factory. Now a displaced person in the British zone of occupation, he was
taken to a camp in a Hannoverian suburb, which soon swelled with
over two thousand people, mostly Poles and people from the Baltic
States. Malnourished, his lungs inflamed from the factory's fumes,
and his wounds infected from the beatings, it took several months to
regain partial strength.

Andrush didn't find Mishka on any of the DP camp lists, though
his intuition told him that she was alive, but not in Germany or
Poland. He wondered about his aunt and cousins and would have
liked to see them, even Bogdi, whom he didn't have the energy to
hate anymore, but he couldn't go back, not with the Reds there.

As the Soviets swarmed into eastern Poland and drove the Germans west in the summer of '44, their troops passed through Bronka's community en route to Różan, where they planned to build a bridgehead across the Narew River. They rounded up and conscripted the men, raped the women, took the animals, then burned the village to the ground. Andrush never knew what happened, and never saw his aunt and cousins again.

An opportunity arose to go to England through a work program, and he jumped at the chance. Arriving in London in January '46, he checked lists and directories for Maritza Laska/Vorobiev and placed weekly notices in the Polish-language newspaper, which published appeals for information about lost relatives. Time passed, and nothing.

It was possible, he thought, that Mishka had married. He dismissed this, choosing to believe she could never love another man in the same way he could never love another woman. She would remain faithful to his memory, and until he found her, he had to carry on with his life, empty and anemic as it was.

He shared a flat in a building in London's East End that had been spared by the Blitz with several Poles who worked with him in a tool factory. He was comfortable with these fellows; it was important to have allies, especially ones from the homeland. In the beginning, there were English classes in the evenings so the workers could understand the safety rules. When that ended, the men went out to drink beer in pubs. Women there did their darndest to titillate, but Andrush showed no interest. The smells of their stale breath and cheap perfume almost made him retch, but time seemed to move faster in the noisy environment than in the flat, where the minutes passed like hours.

Bored and lonely on the weekends, he sometimes visited London's flea markets to look at collectibles from the war, especially the knives. The knife he favored throughout his days in the resistance was, ironically, a WWI German Nahkampfmesser with a six-inch-long, double-edged steel blade used for fighting in close quarters. When Andrush saw one for sale and held it in his hand, the flashback of slitting Germans' throats was powerful and thrilling, and he bought it on the spot.

On this chilly Sunday morning in early November, he took a bus ride to a market not far from his flat and lit a cigarette outside the entrance before going in. Attired in a brown aviator-style leather jacket and khaki-colored trousers, Andrush dressed for comfort, never having owned or worn a suit in his adult life. He had a look of reckless defiance—the kind of man a woman might fantasize about but whose family would disapprove of. Several women nodded appreciatively at him as they passed by, but he didn't respond.

A bus pulled up a few yards from where he stood, leaning against the wall and smoking. A petite blonde wearing a gray coat and a matching cloche hat with a red bow exited and walked on towards the entrance. There was something familiar about the way she carried herself and the color of her hair. His heart started tapping quick beats. Once, he saw a woman who looked just like Mishka from the back and he almost cried with joy. He pulled her arm and turned her around only to be terribly disappointed. She yelled, "Bugger off!" and walloped him with her handbag.

Andrush threw down his cigarette and followed the blonde inside. As he got closer, the beats ricocheted off his ribs and worked up to a pounding. She stopped to examine a collection of knick-knacks as he pushed through a group of pensioners, jostled them without excusing himself, and shouted, "Mishka!"

Maritza's head jerked up. The color drained from her face. Her legs buckled as he reached her, and she fainted in his arms. Kneeling in the aisle, he held her while people rushed over with offers of help. "No, go away. I've got her," he said. "Give us some space." The shoppers whispered and walked around them. With his arm firmly around her waist, he helped her stand and led her to a bench.

"Andrush," she cried. "Is it really you?"

"My beautiful Mishka, my angel," he said. "It's me, it's me." He planted kisses all over her face, and loving words spilled from his lips.

"Zofia told me you were dead, Andrush."

"I was shot and wounded, then I came for you, but you were gone. I tried to find you and was captured and sent to labor camps in Germany. Not a day has gone by that I haven't thought of you, and my prayers have been answered." He pulled her to him, filled with a sense of peace.

Maritza broke away to look at him. Lines extended across his forehead, and others formed deep parentheses around his mouth. His face was thinner, there were dark rings underneath his eyes. She rested her head on his shoulder and squeezed her eyes shut so she wouldn't cry, but the tears defied her and dripped down her face.

"Don't cry. I'm here now," he whispered, as if expecting they could resume their relationship from the point where it left off.

How was she going to tell him that she had moved on? How would he fit into her life when he hated Germans and she was married to one? She needed time to think about how to prepare him.

"Let me give you my address." She took an old receipt from her bag, ripped it in half, and wrote it out for him. "Now give me your information." He dashed it off, and they exchanged the slips.

"You're shivering," he said. "Let's go somewhere warm where we can talk."

"I can't stay, Andrush. I have to get home."

"You just got here. I saw you come off the bus and ran after you. How can you leave me now?" He tightened his grip on her hand. "No. I'm not letting you go."

"We can spend the evening together tomorrow. Come to my flat at six."

"Why can't you stay a little longer? I want to know what happened to you, where you've been for all this time."

If she didn't leave, she would have to tell him everything, but this wasn't the place. Maritza smoothed a lock of hair away from his eyes, wanting to tell him how much she loved him, though in a different way than before. The walls of her chest closed around her heart. "There will be plenty of time for us to talk tomorrow," she said.

"Please, Mishka."

There was no point going in circles. "I'm married, Andrush, and have a child, a little girl."

A shadow swept over his face. This was a scene from a bad play in which the long-lost husband returns to find his beloved wife married to someone else, and in the moment of discovery, he feels a sense of worthlessness, of having lived in a dream. She was his reason for surviving, his North Star, and all along he stupidly believed that she would always be his.

"Andrush? Will you come to my place tomorrow?"

"Yeah." He couldn't look at her.

"Until then," she said, kissing his cheek and leaving him alone and sullen on the bench.

Will was resting on the bed when Maritza burst in. "You're home so soon. A lot of junk today, I gather. Come give me a kiss. Emily's down for a nap." He sat up. "What's wrong? Your face is so pale."

"Andrush is alive!" The words raced out of her mouth in a breathless holler.

"What? Slow down. Say it again."

"Andrush. I saw him at the flea market."

"What? You're mistaken. It was someone who looked like him, a *doppelgänger*. Supposedly, we all have one."

"We spoke, Willy. It was him."

"How can that be? What did he say?" He stiffened, bracing for more bad news.

"He saw me. I can't remember what he said. It was such a shock."

"And then what happened?"

"I invited him over tomorrow evening at six."

"You invited him *here*? Tomorrow?"

"Yes, tomorrow."

"He knows you're married and have a child? You told him?"

"I did, and Willy, he was in a labor camp in Germany."

Let him go far from here, Will thought, then was promptly ashamed of himself. Maritza was his wife now, and he could afford to be magnanimous. The conditions in the camps were horrendous, and Andrush certainly suffered. He had surfaced in London, and it was important that she hear the facts and have closure. "This has been an ordeal for you," he said, trying his best to be supportive. "I will go out after work so you can have privacy. You've gone through so much, and yet it continues."

"Thank you, Willy. I love you. Can you come back early and meet him?"

"No. I have nothing to say to him. He's always hated Germans, and I'm surprised he would even come here knowing you married one."

She fiddled with a loose thread on her skirt. "I haven't told him that yet."

"Why not?"

"There was no time for particulars."

"That news should go down like a lead balloon." He went into the living room and poured straight gin from a bottle gifted by one of Esau's clients. It seemed implausible that Andrush would simply walk away from Maritza after learning she was secure in her marriage. She once described him as fiercely protective. That kind of man had a propensity for jealousy and instability and might very well try to drill his way back into her life.

Will's stomach knotted, and inquietude mounted within. He knocked back another drink and told himself to steady on, that there was no need to feel threatened. After a *very short* trip down memory lane, Maritza would tell her erstwhile husband how happy she is in her current life and bid him goodbye.

Chapter 48

Yesterday had been surreal, Maritza thought, and it was still hard to fathom that Andrush was alive. So much had happened in the past few years, and the bulk of it involved Will. Their unlikely relationship was fueled by deep love and an intense attraction that was going strong. He was a powerful man in bearing, in principles, and in his devotion to her and little Emily. Over time, sweet thoughts of Andrush remained, but the wrenching sadness diminished; she had let go of her grief once she gave her heart to Will.

Troubled and edgy throughout the day, Maritza was impatient with Emily, then angry at herself for taking her frustrations out on her daughter. Andrush would never understand how she could love a German, marry him, and bear his child. There was a time when she couldn't imagine it either, but she had to try to make him see that Will was different.

She had her arguments neatly lined up. *There were good Germans.* Look at all the plots that were made against Hitler's life. What about that officer, Karl Plagge, who saved hundreds of Jews in Lithuania? And there was that Nazi Party member who helped the Dutch Jews. Oh, nothing she said would matter to him. He might walk out or belittle and insult her; he might call her a *kurwa*, a whore, and spit in her face, in which case *she* would tell him to get out and they would never see each other again.

At the stroke of six, Andrush knocked at the door. She pulled it open so fast that it hit the wall and left a dent. His smile made her heart skip a beat.

"Is anyone here?" he asked.

"My daughter, but she's asleep."

"Where's your husband?"

"He went out so we could talk alone."

"Good."

"Let's go in here." She led him into the living room.

Andrush looked around. "Nice place. A piano too. Your husband does all right for himself."

"Thank you, now come and sit. I want to know everything that happened."

"You are more beautiful than ever, Mishka. Life here has been good to you," he said, reaching for her hands. "It's hard to believe I'm sitting with you after all this time."

"I can't either. I'm so happy to see you."

"How long have you been in London?" he asked.

"Since September of '44."

"You never read the *Polish Daily?* I put a notice with your name in the searching for relatives section every week for months after I came here, almost a year ago."

"No, I never read it. There was no reason to. I wanted to forget the past."

"If only you had, we would've been reunited sooner. So much time wasted. I want to know everything, starting from the time you left Zofia's."

"You first. Tell me what happened from start to finish."

He leaned his head back against the pillows and took a deep breath. "After I left you with Zofia, we had a lot of success with the sabotage, more than anytime in the past because the Nazis had invaded the Soviet Union and were moving so many weapons and supplies from Germany through Warsaw to the east. I didn't mean to stay away so long, but there was much to do and many opportunities. We had just blown up a fuel depot and were told to lie low for a while. I was planning on coming back to you right away."

"Oh, Andrush," Maritza said, squeezing his hand.

"The SS came into the forest by our camp. They had more men, better weapons, and I got shot. I woke up in a barn and had no idea where I was or how I got there until they told me."

"They?"

"The old man and his daughters."

"Who?" she asked.

"After the SS left, some of our men came back, saw I was barely alive, and brought me to a farmer. His three daughters took care of me."

"What kind of daughters?" Maritza's eyes flashed. She pictured a trio of lovely young women nursing him while she sat mourning in that dingy apartment.

"They were strong farm women who did most of the work. I lost so much blood, had a terrible infection, and my ankle was broken. I owe that family my life."

"Then I'm thankful for them too," she said, batting away the childish thoughts.

"I stayed until I was strong enough to make it to Zofia's. Imagine how I felt when I didn't find you there."

"And imagine how I felt when she told me you were dead. It's as if fate conspired to keep us apart. Couldn't you have gotten a message to me?"

"Just because they were willing to nurse a wounded man, I couldn't ask them to bring a message into a place with soldiers and police on every corner."

"But you could have written a letter and told me in different words that you were alive and recuperating."

"A letter?" Andrush laughed. "It wasn't possible." He told her of his capture by the German police. "I went across the river to search for you. They got me during a roundup and sent me to a factory near Magdeburg. They fed us just enough to stay alive and whipped us when we didn't work fast enough. After that I was sent to Hannover to work in a battery factory. Another hell."

"Hannover?" Maritza was about to say, "My husband is from there," but caught herself in time.

"Yeah, you must have heard about the Allied bombings there," Andrush said.

"Yes, of course."

"Let me show you what the bastards did to me." He removed his jacket and shirt. Across his entire back and shoulders was a cross-hatch of raised, thick scars from the floggings that reminded her of cut-up terrain after a battle.

"Oh, Andrush," she murmured, and in a rush of tenderness, she ran her hands over the scars. His arms went around her. She couldn't break free when he tried to kiss her, though she made a half-hearted attempt to move her head, then yielded to his lips. The taste of his mouth and the scent of his skin sent a dart of desire through her breast, and the years melted away. The kiss went on until she felt the bulge of his erection pressing against her. "Mishka," he moaned. "I need you."

She wrenched herself away. "No Andrush. This can never happen again."

Breathing hard, he threw on his shirt and stuffed the bottom back into his trousers. "I'm sorry. It won't."

With a shaky hand, Maritza poured gin into a glass and gave it to him. "I have no ice."

He sniffed it. "Gin. It's fine straight."

"Zofia said that Moshe was also shot and killed. Did you know?"

"Not until she told me. We were like brothers."

"She didn't cry one tear for him, and he was crazy about her. What a heartless person she was. It was awful living with her."

"I really believed she was going to watch over you, but she only cared about the cause. Where did you go, Mishka? Why didn't you return to the apartment?"

"Zofia said the money was gone and told me to look for work as a maid in the German hotel. I was afraid to go around Nazis."

"I know all that, but where have you been these past years?"

"I couldn't stand living with her, so I ran away."

"You ran away? Where to?"

"Yes, well, I met someone in Praga, and then—" Her mouth went dry.

"Where in Praga?" Andrush asked.

"Uh, at the Różycki market."

"I told you never to go there!"

"I only went a couple of times to buy things I needed."

"Well, there's no sense arguing about it now. You met someone there, and then what happened?"

"I met a man, and when I told him that I was Jewish, he hid me in his house."

"You went with a stranger to his house?" Andrush's forehead crinkled. "That's not like you."

"I could tell he was trustworthy. A few months later, we married." She reached for his glass. "Another drink?" She didn't wait for him to answer and poured another.

"You married him for convenience, I assume. I mean, to marry a man you hardly knew, there can be no other reason." He knocked back his drink. "What work did he do?"

She wrung her hands. "He was a first lieutenant in the army, but he worked in an office."

"A former Polish army officer. Nice. I suppose he had to change his identity. What office did he work in?"

"He wasn't in the Polish army."

Andrush's brows rose. "What army, then?"

"The uh, um, the German one."

Rendered speechless by the shock, he froze, then a growl escaped from his throat. "You married a Wehrmacht officer? A Nazi? I cannot believe that you of all people would degrade yourself. You've tarnished the memory of our family. How could you?"

"I fell in love with him. He's a wonderful man, and he wasn't a Nazi. Please don't jump to conclusions about someone you don't know. It makes me sad that you're hurting, and I'm asking you to try to understand that not every German was bad. You just said that life has been good to me, and he is the reason why. I know it's hard for you to hear all this, but it's the truth. If you knew him, you'd see that."

Andrush would never *see that.* He saw his Mishka, whom he had loved since he was four years old, the wife of an oberleutnant in Hitler's army, and naked in bed with him, wrapping her legs around his waist as he pumped her full of his contaminated sperm. Then she gave birth to his child! The image of rough Nazi hands scraping her tender skin and a putrid mouth sucking on her petal-pink nipples disgusted him and brought waves of rage. It was as if the devil himself was having intercourse with her.

For years, he lived with the hope of finding her, kept her alive in his thoughts, and now this. He had been shot, beaten, whipped, and starved, and nothing had broken him, but this was the ultimate betrayal. He wanted to scream obscenities at her and bolt from the room.

Maritza's eyes brimmed with tears. "Will you at least try to understand? I thought you were dead, and I met him. At first, I felt the same way you do now, but once I got to know him, I saw that he hated the Nazis as much as we did."

Something shifted inside him. If he didn't control himself, he would lose her again. "I'm sorry, Mishka," he forced himself to say. "I wasn't expecting to hear this, but you met someone, and he was able to protect you and make you happy. That's what counts." He managed a small, sad smile. "It's getting late. I should go."

It broke her heart to see him this way. He was hurting and alone. They stood by the door with their arms around each other. "I love you," she said, feeling his tears on her cheek as he bent to kiss it. "You were always in my heart, and I want you to be in my life. I will call you soon."

Chapter 49

Will came home and found Maritza standing in front of the bedroom window. "How's my girl? How did it go?" he asked, turning her around.

"Fine," she replied, refusing to meet his gaze.

"Then why are you crying?"

"Willy, the story he told, the things he went through—you can't imagine. He was shot and left to die by the SS, and then taken to a village by some of his people. When he recovered and came for me, I had already left Warsaw with you. He went looking for me and was captured and sent to labor camps. They whipped him so many times, his back looks like railroad tracks."

"How do you know what his back looks like?"

"He showed me. Oh, I feel so sorry for him. He's been searching for me ever since the war ended."

Will put his arms around her. "There, there, my love. It's hard to hear about the trials of someone you care about."

"It wasn't easy for him to learn that you're German. At first he was furious, but he understands now."

"He's taken the news well and is to be commended for setting his rancor aside," Will said, wanting to be done with Andrush. "I don't like to see you upset. Have you eaten? I brought you fish and chips from Chadwick's, crispy, the way you like."

Maritza pushed him away. "I don't want any fish! You think I can eat knowing how he feels? How easy it is for you to dismiss him.

You've never been beaten as a grown man, put into chains, or gone through the things he did."

"I just agreed he's had a dreadful time. I'm trying to be understanding, and now you're comparing us? What does this have to do with me? What is really bothering you?"

"I kissed him, and I don't want to keep it from you. It happened."

Will's stomach lurched.

"A situation has arisen, and we can't pretend his coming back means nothing."

"What does it mean to you, Maritza?"

"I want to spend time with him. He's my former husband, and I love him, not in the way I love you, but as the cousin he is. He's all alone, and needs me right now."

"He's a man for Christ's sake, not a child! Men hurt, they move on, and you're already spoken for. Let him find his own nursemaid."

"You were always bitter where Andrush was concerned, and I'm beginning to see that honesty is not the best policy with you. I don't know why I bothered to tell you. It's impossible to talk with you about this subject," she said, crossing her arms.

He glowered down at her. "Always bitter? I never said anything negative about him. I admired his bravery and told you so several times. You're not thinking clearly. Seeing him has caused an emotional reaction. Your trusting husband went out so you could have time with him, and you let him kiss you? It must have been one hell of a kiss. So what's next? That you sleep with him, then say *it happened*, no big deal, so let's never speak of it again?"

"How dare you! I resent that comment."

"How dare *you* have the audacity to compare me to him and insinuate that he's a better man for having been shot, captured, and whipped? You should be ashamed to speak to me that way."

"You didn't let me finish."

"You have one minute, then I will take my things and go, and you will have a green light to be with your man."

"He's not my man, and you're not going anywhere." Maritza jumped between him and the closet. "Stop acting like a baby. I was about to say I won't let him kiss me again."

"This is riveting, Maritza, riveting." Will raised his eyebrows. "Is there more?"

"You're jealous, and you don't need to be. I assure you that Andrush knows his place."

"Ah, he knows his place. That's why he put his lips on you. He's a cad, plain and simple. What kind of a man tells a married woman he needs her? You don't see the wrong in that?"

"He got carried away."

"I don't understand how and why you gave him the opportunity to get *carried away*. It wouldn't bother you if I had a reunion with someone from my past and came home and said the same thing?"

"There's a difference. You've never been married before."

"In the three years you were married to him before he disappeared, you were together for a total of what—five or six months, and that gives him license to kiss you? You were a girl of sixteen, and knew little of what it takes to make a marriage work. Evidently, you still don't know. It involves people resisting temptations and maintaining their love against the pressures of daily life."

"What are you talking about? I'm not tempted by him. He's been in my life since I was a baby, and you expect me to shut him out?"

"You want to spend time with him? Go right ahead, but no good will come of it, and don't expect me to sit idly by while you two have your little tête-à-têtes. It seems you've forgotten that you have a husband and daughter. You should be concentrating on us and our needs and not on those of that weasel!"

Will sat in the living room with the door closed, fuming and downing a drink, trying to make sense of Maritza's behavior. She had lashed out, shifted blame onto him, and had the gall to tell him she wanted to spend time with Andrush. Maybe I should have put my foot down and forbidden her to see him, he thought. No. The more she feels her freedom is limited, the more she will want to see him and resent me. On the other hand, only a man who's had a lobotomy or one who has a little side action of his own going on would give his wife carte blanche to spend time with a former love.

The thought of Maritza enjoying Andrush's kisses was upsetting, but Will told himself she had given in to some leftover attraction or nostalgia for what they once had rather than passion. She had been truthful, and it hadn't gone further than kissing, yet the more time spent with him, the closer she would come to infidelity. What stung him most was that she had spoken of another man's needs as if they were of paramount importance, thereby relegating her own husband's to second place.

Will realized then that in his relationship with Maritza, he had maintained a certain illusion about love—that their union would always be as happy and rewarding as it had been, even with the realistic expectations of stress brought on by the demands of work and childrearing. Before this point in time, their marriage had been free of conflict and was thus untested. The voice in his head shouted warnings that Andrush Vorobiev was an audacious interloper who was going to destroy the tranquility of their lives, and he suspected they wouldn't be rid of him anytime soon.

Still fuming, Will went to bed, pulled the covers up, and faced the wall. Usually he reached for Maritza right away, but there was no stirring in his loins now. She leaned over and slid her soft hand under the blanket and over his back, as if this evening had passed as calmly and naturally as the hundreds before it when Andrush had been but a memory. "Please don't be angry with me, Willy. I didn't mean to hurt you. I love you," she whispered.

Perhaps he overreacted, expecting her to act with the maturity of someone wise beyond her years rather than the young woman who had experienced the loss of a man she once loved dearly and was now dealing with the complex feelings his return had awakened. Will turned and embraced her. "I'm sorry for losing my temper, my love."

Maritza stroked him between his legs. His vigor returned, and the only thing on his mind was the sweetness of her body. She had a hold on him that was impossible to resist.

Chapter 50

Andrush lay on his bed, smoking, wrapped in thoughts of Mishka and their years together. She had made his life worth living and was the source of his happiness. Her marriage to the German pig was a travesty, but he had to forgive her. She had gone with him out of a desperate effort to survive—there was no way she could love him, not after what his Nazi kin did to their family. This was all Zofia's fault. Sent out into the streets by that red-haired traitor, Mishka latched on to the first person who offered shelter and security. She had run straight into the arms of the enemy!

Andrush knew how German officers in positions of considerable power and with typical self-deceptive superiority treated Polish women. These men, puppeteers with impenetrable hearts, got the women under their thumbs and brainwashed them by setting honey traps and pulling their strings. Mishka's husband was certainly no exception.

Every evening when he returned from his job in the factory, he checked the board by the telephone on his floor to see if there was a message from her. He stopped checking after a month. She's abandoned me, he thought, and grief began anew. Fifteen long miles between his flat and hers, and he had to be closer. A plan took shape in his mind.

During the week, Andrush counted the money saved over time, resigned from the factory, and pocketed his vacation pay. He took buses to the environs of Muswell Hill and responded to an advertisement for part-time mechanic. Having secured employment and a furnished one-room flat a couple of miles from Mishka's, he rode back and spent one last night drinking with his companions. In the morning, he packed his clothing and worldly possessions into a suitcase and headed out to his new life.

One rainy Saturday morning in early December, Will sat by the kitchen window with Emily next to him in her high chair. He combed through the newspaper's classified ads for farm properties, making markings and circles like an eager boy going through a toy catalog. When he reunited with Maritza after the camp, he began to see there were opportunities to be had, despite rationing, conservation, and government appropriation of farm lands. There were many smallholdings for sale, often run down, that could be brought back to life with tender, loving care. They couldn't afford to buy anything now, but one day they would, and each week Will put away money in furtherance of their dream. The defeatist attitudes that plagued him all his life had been replaced with positivity.

The Goodmans were coming to play bridge that evening. Maritza was planning to make a vegetable soup and hoped to find a piece of meat at the market to throw in. While Will had his head buried in the paper and Emily ate her porridge, she went out to the neighborhood stores. The queue at the butcher shop was long, but worth the wait. She scored a piece of beef with the bone attached, then hurried down the street to the greengrocer before they closed and waited for her ration of vegetables. She had just left the counter when Andrush called to her.

"Andrush! What are you doing here?" Her heartbeat sped up, and she scanned the faces of shoppers, expecting Will to be there watching.

"Not even a hello, how are you?" he asked with a broad smile.

"What are you doing here on the Hill?"

"Are you glad to see me?"

"Yes. What a surprise!"

"I live here now. I wanted to be closer to you. We're family."

"Really?" Her face lit up. "I'm glad."

"I got tired of working in the factory and found a job as a mechanic a couple miles north on Cromwell, off Colney Hatch. I waited a month at my old place for you to call, and you didn't. Is that any way to treat me? I thought you were going to include me in your life."

"You worked during the day, and I'm always busy with my family in the evenings. I wanted to call. You were on my mind all the time."

"I feel better hearing that. Now I work in the afternoons, so I'm free all morning."

She opened her purse, pulled out a pencil and a scrap of paper. "Write down your address and telephone number so I can get in touch with you," she said.

"I don't have a phone, but you can call me at work," he said, and jotted down the details. "I miss you, Mishka. Please don't ignore me. I'm just a stone's throw away." He stepped closer and touched her face, gazing at her with the same loving expression she remembered so well.

"I miss you too. I'm busy looking after my family, that's all."

"Let's get out of here," he said, reaching for her shopping bag. "We can take the bus up to my place, and you can tell me about your life after you left Warsaw."

"I'd like to, but not today. I have to get home, or my husband will wonder where I am. I will call you next week, and we can arrange to meet."

"Promise?"

"Cross my heart," she said, and stepped into the street. Andrush, here in her very neighborhood! She could hardly believe it.

At the door of her building, Maritza's excitement disappeared as quickly as a coin in a beggar's hand. Will would not be happy to hear about this—an understatement. *Tell him and get it over with.*

"Willy," Maritza set down her shopping bag and stowed her wet umbrella. "I was in the market, and guess who I saw?"

"The King?"

"No, Andrush."

Will's face spasmed. "What the hell was *he* doing there? What did he say?"

"He has a new job and is living here now." She wasn't going to tell him that Andrush had come to be closer to her.

"Where here?"

"Colney Hatch and Cromwell."

"That's about a mile away! Of all the post-war jobs in London, he had to come to Muswell Hill?" He felt a wave of anxiety, like an animal sensing a storm before it hits. "It's an excuse, Maritza. He moved here to be near you."

"Well, I didn't invite him."

"Don't go back to that same market. Find a different one, and if you see him again, turn and walk in the other direction."

"I'm not going to ignore him, and I have to go to that store. I'm registered there for rationing."

"Re-register someplace else. He had to when he came to our neighborhood."

"I don't appreciate you telling me what I can and cannot do, Will. I'm a grown woman and don't like to be controlled."

He scowled, went into the bathroom, and splashed cold water on his face.

"Your face is red," she observed when he came out.

"I should call the Goodmans and tell them not to come. I'm not in the mood to entertain."

"You're not a ringmaster in the circus. You don't have to enter-tain Esau and Ruth. I happened to see him, and now you can't play bridge? I'm surprised at you, carrying on this way."

"Don't start." Will didn't want to play bridge, didn't want to make smalltalk with the Goodmans. He wanted to sit alone in the living room with a drink and think of ways to dislodge the too-big-for-his-boots Vorobiev from their neighborhood.

"I hope you're not going to be in that sour mood all day." She went to chop vegetables for the soup. There was a knock at the door. Who could that be? "See who it is, Will, would you?"

It was a boy holding several bunches of flowers. "For the lady," he said.

"Who are they from?" asked Will, extracting a coin from his pocket.

"I don't know, sir. I'm just a messenger."

"Who was it?" Maritza poked her head out from the kitchen.

"A messenger with flowers for you. I'm guessing they're from your not-so-secret admirer. He's got some nerve!" Will held the flowers away from his body as if they were poison weeds and started toward the door.

"Where are you going?"

"To the incinerator."

Maritza ran after him. "Don't throw them away. They're so pret-ty." She snatched them from his hand. "It's wrong to destroy them."

"I do not want his flowers on my table," Will said, glaring at her.

"Oh, but they're so colorful and make me happy."

"I see. So, if Hitler were alive and sent you flowers, you would keep them and display them at the table just because they're pretty."

"It's not the same thing, and I'm not going to stand here and ar-gue with you."

"Then keep them. I'm going out."

"Where?"

"For a walk."

"How am I supposed to tell you things if you get so upset?"

Will pulled on his coat, picked up his hat and umbrella, and headed outside. The rain had tapered off, but the sky was full of angry clouds. That damn Vorobiev, he thought, sending flowers to *my* wife. He's wooing her; that's what he's doing. Will walked until he felt better—it wasn't right to blame Maritza, and why let that shark ruin his weekend? He turned around and went home.

After the Goodmans left, while Maritza was putting the leftovers away, he gathered up the garbage and the flowers, went to the incinerator, and dumped it all in.

Chapter 51

Nineteen forty-six was drawing to a close. Although the Goodmans didn't celebrate Christmas, Ruth wanted to make the day special for two-year-old Emily. "You'll come for lunch," she told Maritza. "I have a plump chicken to roast." She was famous for her roasts.

The Goodmans surprised their goddaughter with a load of presents, wrapped in newspaper and adorned with bits of bright fabric and buttons from Ruth's enormous sewing basket. They sat around the crackling fire, drinking the wine Esau had saved for the occasion, and enjoying themselves.

Weeks had passed since Maritza last saw Andrush. Though she was surrounded by people she loved, thinking about him alone on Christmas Day made her sad. Poor Andrush, eating something from a tin, with no one to care about him. She imagined him in the Goodman's living room, mingling and sharing in the festivities, but that was a fantasy. Will would never permit it.

If he had agreed to come home early and meet Andrush the night he came to their flat, the kiss wouldn't have happened, and maybe he would have allowed him to be part of their lives. So, she thought, in a way, it was his fault that Andrush was alone on a holiday. In her zeal to be honest with Will and admit the kiss, she had raised a red flag for him about future encounters with Andrush. In her heart, she knew that Andrush would never come to a gathering where her husband was, but why should she have to give him up because Will was suspicious of his motives? It wasn't fair.

"Should we ask Birdie to watch Emily this Sunday afternoon so we can try that cafeteria-style restaurant on Fortis Green?" asked Will a couple of weeks later. "I read in the paper they will be closing their doors in a few weeks due to withdrawal of government funding." Originally set up to feed those people bombed out of their homes during the German campaigns, these communal restaurants provided tasty meals that didn't require coupons. People paid in cash.

Mrs. Bird, or Birdie, as everyone called her, was a round, middle-aged woman who looked rather like a hen and lived nearby. She took care of Emily while Maritza did the marketing and other errands.

"That's a great idea. I will see if she's available."

On Sunday, the Engels braved the January cold and walked to their destination on Fortis Green, a main thoroughfare. Couples strolled hand in hand, some pushing bundled-up babies in strollers and some stopping to look in store windows.

They ate an economical meal of roast beef, potatoes, and peas, and were lingering over their gooseberry tarts. "Too bad they're going out of business. The food was absolutely delicious," he said, "but let's get home."

"You haven't finished your dessert."

"I'm saving room for you. If Emily is napping, we can, you know."

Maritza laughed. "I'm ready." The thought of his hands and lips on her filled her with desire. They put on their coats and began walking. "Look, Willy, there's Andrush!" On a bench directly across the street, he sat reading the paper.

"Stop pointing. That's him? What an unsightly creature." He had the urge to run across the street, slam his fist into Andrush's mug, and yell, "This is what you get for kissing my wife!"

"That's mean. He's rugged, not unsightly."

"Turn your head and keep walking."

"He isn't looking here."

"How would you know if your head is supposed to be turned?" He took her by the arm and shepherded her down the street.

"Stop pulling me, and why are you walking so fast? You look like you're going into battle."

"This is how I walk. You should know that by now. Imagine him sitting out in this weather, across from the very spot where we were having our lunch. That bastard is spying on us."

"What a thing to say. What reason could he have for spying? He was just sitting and reading. There's a man doing the same thing over there on that bench. I don't see what's so odd about it."

No answer. The day had started like a flower unfolding, and now the whole mood had changed. Maritza didn't want to be at loggerheads with Will on his day off and spend the rest of the afternoon under a cloud, so she tried to bring him back to his earlier cheerfulness. "Are we still going to make love? Are you walking this fast because you can't wait to get me home and naked in bed?" she asked impishly.

He kept his eyes straight ahead. "No, we are not. I'm no longer in the mood. It would take a magician to get me hard."

"How about a magician's assistant?" she asked, grinning.

"You're a barrel of laughs, Maritza."

"What will I do with this burning desire?"

"Read a magazine or clean the windows. We can thank Vorobiev for ruining our Sunday," he smoldered. "He's a bloodstain, seeping into our lives and impossible to get rid of."

"He's done nothing to us. *A bloodstain*. Stop acting like he's some sort of evil being. You're trying to punish me because he moved here."

"I don't want to discuss this anymore," he said.

"That's because your argument lacks substance."

As it turned out, Emily was napping, but the Engels would make no love that afternoon.

The wintry days passed without further incident. Maritza thought about Andrush in the quiet daytime moments, always with a sad yearning for times spent with him in the past. She was smart enough to realize the love she still felt had no place in the present, yet she didn't want to lose him again. As soon as Will came home from work, his presence filled the space and her heart completely, and Andrush went out of her mind. She had just finished tidying up from breakfast one morning, and Emily was resting in her room when she heard a soft knock at the door.

"Andrush!"

"You haven't called. I thought you'd forgotten me."

"I meant to call, but—"

"But you didn't. Can I come in?"

"Oh, no. I'm busy with my daughter." Will would be livid if she let Andrush in, and she couldn't hide it from him.

"Mama come!" Emily called from her room.

"I have to go. My daughter needs me."

Andrush chewed his lip. Mishka was hitting his heart like a punching bag, hurrying him away as if he were a salesman whose wares she had no interest in. "Can you meet me tomorrow? I want to talk to you about something important. Please?"

"Can't you tell me now?"

"Not if you won't let me in."

"Mama!" Emily wailed.

"All right. I'll meet you at three at the Tea Room. It's just past the roundabout. I can't stay long, though."

Maritza went to tend to Emily, a lightness to her step. She was excited to spend an hour with Andrush. The day passed pleasantly until the sound of Will's key in the door reminded her that there was bound to be discord when he learned of her plans.

"I'm meeting Andrush for a quick cup of tea tomorrow at three," she said. Will was sitting at the edge of the tub, watching her bathe Emily.

His face darkened. "Whose idea was this?"

"His. He wants to talk to me about something."

"About what?"

"I don't know. He didn't say."

"Why did you give him our phone number?"

"I never gave him our number. He stopped by here this morning and asked to meet me. I won't be gone long," she said, tired of the grilling. Even in her early teens, she didn't have this much trouble making a plan to leave the house. Then again, Andrush was always with her.

Will's eyes opened so wide that Maritza thought they would spring from their sockets with an audible *boinggg*. "He came *here* when I wasn't home, and you let him in?"

"I did not."

"So he didn't ask to come in? Well, that changes everything. What a fine feathered fellow. I must have misjudged him."

"Stop acting like he's a wolf in sheep's clothing. There's no need for sarcasm. It makes me feel bad."

"Where are you meeting him?"

"At the Tea Room. Come on, my little bumblebee, say goodnight to Papa."

"Bye Papa," Emily said, blowing kisses.

"*Gute Nacht, meine kleine Liebe.*" He kissed her, then turned his attention back to Maritza. "The Tea Room? They know us there."

"So what? I'm allowed to have friends."

"Coming here was the height of disrespect; just when I thought we saw the back of him," he grumbled.

"You're making such a big deal over this." She pushed damp strands of hair from her forehead and left him standing in the bathroom, staring at the floor.

He went into the living room. Feeling a headache coming on, he poured a drink and chugged it, closed his eyes, and tried to relax. *Brringgg.* Startled by the sudden jangle of the telephone, he jumped up and knocked Maritza's purse over, scattering the contents onto the desk. It was Goodman, calling with a work question. After he hung up, Will stuffed the items back in and caught sight of the receipt with Andrush's contact information. He put it in his wallet. Having it helped restore some of the power he felt he had lost when that no-goodnik came to their flat and enjoined Maritza to go out when she should be home tending to Emily. If the man truly loved her, he would leave her the hell alone.

Chapter 52

Andrush was seated at a corner table and stood when Maritza arrived. "You look so pretty," he said. "You always do."

"Thanks. You look nice, too."

The waitress came over. "What will you have?"

"Two regular teas. What else, in a tearoom?" He laughed.

"We do serve other things."

"Madam, would you care for a slice of cream cake or a cucumber sandwich?" Andrush asked Maritza, using an exaggerated, upper-class accent.

"Just the tea, thank you."

The waitress nodded and walked off toward the kitchen.

It seemed to Maritza that everything she loved about Andrush was reflected at that moment in his dear, sweet face, and the memories of their lives before the invasion were so vivid and rich that she was reliving them all at once. "It's so nice being with you like this," she said. "We should meet here for tea once a week. How would that be? What did you want to talk to me about?"

"It's been almost two months since I saw you in the grocery, and you never called. Why did you do that to me, make me wait so long?"

Her chest tightened the instant he started to complain. She wanted to enjoy him and converse about pleasant things. "I told you that I was busy with my family, but we're together now. Let's make the most of our time."

"It's not the same. The only reason you're here is because I came to your flat and begged you to come out. You call meeting once a week for a lousy cup of tea a part of your life? I think you don't really care to have me in it."

"That's not true."

"You know it is."

"It's not that I don't care," she said slowly, looking out the window. The sky had opened up, and rain was pouring down. "I want you in my life more than anything, but my husband is against it. The fact that you and I were married complicates things. It would be different if we were regular cousins."

"Then you do love me, and it's *him*. He doesn't want me in your life."

"Of course I love you. That will never change. I can't blame him, really. He knows how special you are to me, and he's worried about that."

Andrush slid from his seat into the one next to hers and held her. His warm breath on her ear struck a flash of excitement through her, then his lips found hers. Maritza couldn't resist, then fought her way back. "Stop, please." She pushed him away. "That's what my husband is concerned about, and I see he has every right to be. You promised never to do that again. How am I supposed to trust you? Go back to your seat."

"You made a promise, too. Several, in fact."

The waitress brought their tea things on a tray, set it down, and started to pour.

"We can do it, thanks," Andrush said, waving her away.

Rough around the edges, this one, the woman thought. She made a face and went to help another guest.

I should have stayed home, Maritza thought, remorse twanging through her conscience.

"He has no right to keep you from me, Mishka. You talk about him and your daughter as if they're the only ones that matter, but I'm your family, too, and I've known you and loved you for much, much longer."

"He's not keeping me from you. He didn't tell me that I couldn't see you. I have a young child to care for, and I can't be away for extended periods of time. I don't want problems in my marriage."

"Because of me, you mean. Why can't we spend the mornings together a few times a week—do our shopping or take walks? You can bring the kid. If the weather is bad, I can come over to your place, or you could come to mine."

"No. That's not a good idea. I have housework to do and meals to prepare."

Andrush saw how powerful a hold the German had on her and how terrified she must be of crossing him. Desperate now, he had to do something to get through to her—to breach the barrier she had erected to keep him out. "I'll even meet your husband, so he will see that my intentions are honorable. I lost you once, and I can't and won't allow it to happen again."

"Oh, Andrush, it's too late to meet him. I can't imagine that you have any real interest in getting to know him, and I already told him that you kissed me. He will never believe your intentions are honorable, but he does have faith in me and I won't let him down."

"You did what?"

"I didn't want to deceive him."

It's hopeless, Andrush thought. The son of a bitch husband would never allow him to be part of Mishka's life, except for an occasional cup of tea. "Then leave him. I'm here now, and there's nothing to be afraid of. You know we belong together. Come away with me."

She stared at him, incredulous. "Leave him? I would never leave him."

"Be honest with yourself, Mishka. You don't love him. The war is over, and the Kraut has served his purpose. I think you've forgotten this, but you're still my wife. Unless you've had me declared legally dead, your marriage to him isn't valid, and you don't have to stay with him."

"I do love him and don't appreciate you calling him a Kraut. He's a fine man." The accuracy of Andrush's claim didn't matter to Maritza. She was Will's wife. "I love you, too, but in a different way than before. Too much has happened, and things can't be the way they once were. I'm sorry, Andrush. My allegiance is to my husband and daughter."

"You're killing me, Mishka." He threw his napkin down, gave her a scalding look, and got up, pulling coins from his pocket for the bill. "Go back to your Hun." He put his jacket collar up and walked out into the rain.

She sat and cried until the waitress came over. "You all right, baby doll? That's just like a man making such a pretty girl cry. They don't write, they don't call, never there when you need them. Can I bring you something else?"

"No, thank you," she said, wiping her eyes.

Out in the street without an umbrella, Maritza was soaked to the skin. Oh God, I want to get home. She started running, tripped over the curb, and fell, scraping both knees and the palms of her hands. A car sped by, drenching her in a punishment of grimy water. "You idiot!" she yelled as she got to her feet. The wind blew her hat off her head, and it sailed away down the street.

Chapter 53

"My goodness! You poor dear," said Birdie. "I'll stay while you get out of those sodden things and make you a hot cup of tea."

Will came home and saw the bandages on her knees and palms. "What happened?"

"I tripped and fell on the way home."

"It was so necessary to go out in this weather?"

"It wasn't raining when I left," she said, trying hard not to snap at him.

Will kept his anger in check while they ate the dinner she had prepared earlier in the day. He sent her to rest, then put Emily to bed, and cleaned up the kitchen. Maritza was sitting on the bed with both legs stuck out like a doll on a toy store shelf. "Now tell me what was so important that took you away from our daughter in the middle of the day?" he asked, his face dark with suspicion.

Maritza hesitated for a second, which did not go unnoticed. "Uh, he wanted to know why I haven't, uh, kept in touch with him."

"Do you think I'm a fool?" he steamed. "He could have asked you that at the door when he came here uninvited. You're not even upset that he drew you away under false pretense. You fell for his scheme."

"He said it was important," she said in a small voice, "and I gave him the benefit of the doubt."

"You owe him nothing, and you're going to tell me the truth right now. Why did he want to see you?"

"First he asked why I hadn't contacted him, and then he said the war was over and there was no reason for me to stay with you, that you served your purpose and I couldn't love you because you're a Kraut, that I'm still his wife and should go with him where I belong." She started crying.

"Oh, really? But when I asked you before what he said, you only gave me half the story. I guess you thought I would be more interested in the potatoes than the meat."

"I didn't want to upset you. I knew you'd react this way. I told him in no uncertain terms that I love you and would never leave you."

"That was generous of you." He gave her a sidelong glance and crossed his arms. "Thank you for that crumb."

"What do you want from me? How was I supposed to know what he was going to say?"

"What do I want? I want *my* wife to stand in *my* corner with her eyes on *me*. I hear nothing but poor Andrush coming from your mouth. Will he be in your mind when we're making love, and every time I touch you, you're imagining that it's him?"

"You've gone too far. You are going to ruin our marriage."

"Me? When are you going to admit that it's your doing?" Their eyes locked in hostile stares.

"I'm afraid to tell you things because you twist them out of proportion."

Pffff. Will blew out his irritation. "That instigator tried to get you to leave your husband and child and run away with him. He distressed you. That's why you fell and hurt yourself, and you're telling me I twist things? I feel like I'm talking to a wooden post! Are you aware that only a man of emaciated morals would make such a selfish, shameless proposition to a married woman?"

"I understand that a hurt, devastated man would make such a proposition. He needs time to accept the fact that I'm no longer his."

"You're damn right, you're not his, and whether he accepts it or not is none of your concern. Of course, if you want to be his, that can easily be arranged."

"Stop shouting. The whole building can hear you, and stop saying hurtful things that will drive me away."

"I don't care if they hear me in Timbuktu! You want away? Then go. I'm not going to weep like I did in Warsaw when you said you didn't love me. There was a time when I thought I couldn't live without you, but it might surprise you to learn that I'm not the same person now as I was then. I can and will live without you if my alternative is to listen to you championing him."

There were thunderclouds in Will's eyes. He had always been so manageable and accommodating, and she saw he wasn't the same person; he was much more self-assured. Now he was saying he could live without her, something he'd never done before. What was wrong with her? Maritza looked at her magnificent husband, and the thought of losing him was too much. Sobs hiccuped out.

Will couldn't bear to see her cry, but was too angry to feel sorry. "Stop crying and listen to my words carefully, because I'm going to say this once. You know that I would give up my life for you?"

She shook her head *yes,* drew her burning knees up to her chest, and shrank back against the headboard.

"Good. That should leave no doubt how important you are to me, but I will not tolerate lying and deception from you ever!" He banged his fist on the dresser. "If you lie or hide important issues from me again, I will leave you. The woman with whom I share my life, make love, and have children must be faithful and honest; otherwise, I'm not interested. Those are the conditions for this marriage. *Ist das klar?*"

"Yes, very clear," she sobbed.

"Now that your needy little intrigant has shown his true colors, he will stop at nothing to get you back. Granted, no one can take away your memories, but running out to see him only feeds the flames of his desire and gives him hope, and obviously you get some satisfaction from the encounter. He might have been a good person once, but not anymore. A man who claims to love you would do everything in his power to avoid hurting you. It's him or me. Make up your mind, and do it soon. You can't have us both." He grabbed his pillow and stormed off to sleep on the couch. This was the first time since returning from the POW camp that an argument caused him to sleep apart from Maritza.

Chapter 54

I can't let this go, Will said to himself when he woke the following morning. He went into the bedroom. Maritza was sleeping, curled into a ball. She looked so small, and his heart ached. Because of the accursed Vorobiev, he fought with the woman he cherished and spent the night with dark thoughts.

"Hey, you," he said, sitting next to her on the bed. I will be going to work soon. How about a kiss?"

"Oh, Willy," she said, her eyes swollen and red, "I haven't been considerate of your needs and feelings. Is it too late for us? Tell me you still love me," she cried. "Maybe you can live without me, but I can't without you."

"No more tears. I adore you, and I was talking about extremes, Maritza. You're conflicted now, but focus on *us*, our little girl, and our future, and you will see how easy it is to move on from him. I want you now and forever, but whole. I need your heart and mind to be clear. Would you have me any other way?"

"I'm yours, all yours, and no one else's. Last night was awful without you next to me."

"You could have come and seduced me. I'm not able to resist your charms," he said, stroking her arms.

"I was afraid you would tell me to go to hell."

"When have I ever spoken to you like that?"

She sat up to hug him, and her nightgown slipped from one shoulder, exposing a creamy breast and pink nipple. Aroused, Will pulled the nightgown off. Their lover's quarrel was the foreplay; he was erect and ready, and when she opened her legs, he thrust in and moved inside her the way she liked until they reached their climaxes.

"I love you, Willy."

"And I love you. Now try to get some more sleep until Emily wakes up."

The small auto repair shop where Andrush worked was situated in a working-class section of Muswell Hill. The retired owner came in a couple of mornings each week, mainly to check the accounts. Andrush worked alone in the afternoons until early evening. He chose his hours according to the number of vehicles he had to service, and to how hungover he was from the previous night of drinking; some days he didn't go in at all. Today would have been one of those times, but a customer was expecting his car to be ready.

As he put away his equipment, he glanced up to see a man in a dark overcoat and hat standing at the door of the open garage. "I'm about to close. What do you need done?"

"We need to have a little talk."

"Who are you?" Andrush asked, hackles rising.

"The name is Engel. Maritza's husband." Will walked up to Andrush. The two sized each other up in a matter of seconds, both recognizing that the other could become violent under the right conditions, though there wasn't anything extraordinary in the other's expression that gave this trait away. Both men were of equal height—just shy of six feet, but Andrush's thick-soled boots made him taller.

"Well, well, if it isn't the Oberleutnant. What do you want?"

"You upset my wife yesterday and caused her to fall and get hurt."

"I'm sorry to hear that, but I had nothing to do with her falling. Is she all right?"

"She is not. You are responsible for her condition. You came to our flat without permission and lured her away under the guise of an urgent matter," he said through gritted teeth.

"I did not *lure*. I asked, and she agreed. You're angry because she saw me? Maybe you don't trust her?" Andrush raised his eyebrows in mock innocence.

"I don't trust *you*. You're a possessive, opportunistic bloodsucker. How dare you put your hands and lips on her!"

"Who the hell do you think you are, coming here and insulting me?"

"Her husband, that's who. Stay away from Maritza, and don't come to our flat again, or I will have you arrested."

"Oh yeah? Tough guy, are you? *You* come anywhere near here again, and I'll have *you* arrested. This is private property, and you're trespassing. Now that you're here, you might as well hear the truth. Mishka used you to get out of Warsaw. She told me herself that you were nothing more than a ticket out, and now you're a food source. She's just waiting for the right time to leave you."

"You're a liar. You can't accept that she has a new life, and if you bother her again, I will break both your legs,"

"Mishka doesn't love you. That's what you can't accept. Why don't you ask her how she felt when I kissed her?"

Will went to strike him, but Andrush pushed him back. "You're out of shape, you old windbag," he laughed. "You couldn't break the legs off a chair. Now get out of here before I rearrange your face."

"I'm warning you to leave her alone." He threw a dagger look at Andrush and walked out of the garage.

Whatever admirable qualities Andrush once had, Will thought, the Nazis had beaten out of him. Now he was dangerous, delusional, and a pox upon their lives. Maritza would forget him now that he had reminded her of the conditions for their marriage. He never thought he would have to spell them out.

Andrush sat in his room that night, broiling over the altercation with Mishka's husband. The pressure was building, and he was having a grueling time keeping it down. It had taken hours and half a bottle of black market Scotch whisky the previous evening to contain his fury after seeing Mishka and hearing that her husband was trying to keep them apart. The German mentality was always about control. Well, the war was over, and he was not going to let a stinking Kraut order him around.

He put his energy into sharpening his knife on a whetstone. *Wiss swiss, wiss swiss.* Engel wasn't what he expected. He pictured a thin, dark-haired man with dry skin, sunken cheeks, and a hawkish nose who wore his Wehrmacht uniform at home and carried a crop. Engel was film-star handsome. Women would be attracted to him if they didn't know he had toxin in his genes, a point Mishka conveniently overlooked in exchange for the solace and protection he had given her in Warsaw.

Wiss swiss, wiss swiss. Little by little, the sound calmed him. *Wiss swiss, wiss swiss.* Andrush tested the blade by shaving off a small patch of hair on his forearm. Razor sharp. He put it away in its sheath and took a long swallow of his drink.

Chapter 55

Maritza left Emily with the sitter and went to a different market where she re-registered her ration coupons. Will had insisted upon it. About to join the queue, she felt a hand on her shoulder and whirled around to see Andrush. "What are you doing here? Are you following me?" she asked, brushing off his hand.

"Following you?" His face scrunched like a hurt boy's. "Thanks, Mishka. That makes me feel good. I was returning a car to a guy in the building across the street and saw you go in."

She sighed. "I'm sure you have to hurry back to work then, and I want to get the things I need before they're gone."

"Are you in line, Miss?" asked a woman trying to get past her.

"No. You go ahead," Maritza said, moving to the back of the store.

"You act as though I'm a leper, Mishka. "Why are you so cold? It's me, not some stranger."

"You should keep away from me."

"We can't make simple conversation? What's wrong with that?"

She narrowed her eyes. "You know why."

"No, I don't. Tell me."

"You had to let your hatred interfere by making those derogatory remarks about my husband, even though you know nothing about him."

"I was telling the truth. You haven't admitted to yourself that you don't love him, but you will."

"This conversation is going nowhere. If you can't accept who I married, then it's your problem. Seeing you downhearted makes me sad, but I can't live in the past. That was a different life, a different time. I have to live in the present."

"Are you saying it wouldn't matter if you never saw me again?"

"Andrush please, you're making this so hard. If you found a nice girl, you could concentrate on her and be happy." Maritza wanted to make his pain go away, but that was impossible. She could never give him what he needed. He needed her, all of her, forever.

"Happy? I will never be happy without you, Mishka," he said, his eyes falling languidly on hers. "And if you think you can just toss me away like yesterday's newspaper, you're mistaken."

"That's exactly what you wanted me to do with my husband!"

"You're mine, and we will be together. I'm going to give you time to sort out your situation, and until then, I'm putting one foot in front of the other, trying to get through each day." There was no doubt in his mind that he would get her back. It had nothing to do with jealousy. It was a matter of reclaiming what was his.

"Shut your mouth, Andrush. You're living in a fantasy world."

"Shut my mouth?" He laughed. "Is that any way to talk to your real husband? Remember, we are still man and wife, and while we are on that subject, I have to tell you that your temporary one is a thorn in my side."

"What are you talking about? You've been drinking, and it's so early in the day. I can smell it. It's making you crazy, and keep your voice down. People are looking."

"Your Herr Engel came to my work and threatened me."

"Threatened you? When was this?" Maritza didn't know who to be angry with—Will for not telling her or Andrush for blithely using the information as a wedge.

"I can't remember, a couple of weeks ago."

"That's bosh. You can't expect me to believe it. As if you were ever afraid of anyone, and since when do threats bother you? You used to thrive on them."

"I've changed, but your German saviour is a maniac like the rest of his ilk. He came at me swinging punches, but I know you're fond of him, so I held off."

"Do something about your drinking. It's turning your brain to mush. Your parents would be shocked to see how far you've fallen."

"I could say the same thing about yours. Well, I have to go." He bent to kiss her.

She turned away. "Do that again, and I will scream."

"No, you won't," he winked, and was gone before she had a chance to respond.

The meeting with Andrush daunted Maritza. His hurt face and poorly disguised attempts at masking his suffering intruded on her thoughts all through the afternoon and into dinner preparation time. Addled, she burned the sausage links for Will's dinner, over-cooked the potatoes until they dissolved into starch in the boiling water, and spilled Emily's ration of milk. *Damn!* What to make now? Spam sandwiches and carrots—no different than what everyone else was eating.

Maritza dreaded having to tell Will about Andrush. He deserved to know and had warned her about withholding information, but the last thing she wanted was to upset him. The man worked a full day, took a crowded bus from the office to the Underground train, then another bus home, and was hardly ever in a bad mood. She asked him once why that was.

"I could be," he said. "Would you prefer that?"

This was different. The mere mention of Andrush's name would set him off, and unless she roundly agreed with every one of his ex-

coriations of said person, he would scold her. She attacked the carrots, whittling them down to sticks, feeling pulled in two directions
like the wishbone from the chicken she and Will had tugged at on
Christmas. She won then, but there wasn't going to be any victory for
her tonight.

Will came home and gave her a deep kiss that would have led to
a before-dinner trip to the bedroom had Emily been asleep. He gave
his daughter a kiss and a few tickles, eliciting peals of laughter. "How
are my two best girls?"

"Fine. Come and eat. Dinner is ready."

"This is delicious," he said, taking a big bite of his sandwich.

Maritza's heart was full. Darling Willy, she thought. Who can get
excited over salty Spam? As long as she prepared something, he never
complained. "You got a good one, Mitzi," Ruthie was always saying.

She waited until he was almost finished. "I went to the market
this morning."

"Uh, huh, and?" Will asked, crunching on a carrot stick. When
she didn't respond, he glanced at her and pushed his plate away. "He
was there?" His brows rushed together like magnets. "That creep has
crossed the threshold of every market that you happen to be in. Who
would have guessed that a person with a belly so full of hate would
have any appetite. He's no gourmand from the look of him. He has
the glistening eyes of a wild animal."

"How would you know that? You saw him once from afar reading a newspaper, so how would you know what his eyes are like?"

"I've been blessed with x-ray vision, that's how."

"Come on. Why didn't you tell me you went to see him? Why
did I have to learn that from him? You're the one who said you
wouldn't tolerate lying and deception from me. You're being hypo-
critical."

"That's not the deception I was talking about. You're so protective of him, Maritza."

"Willy, enough. Why did you go? He said you threatened him."

"I did. It's a thing a man does when his wife has been disrespect-ed. I needed to make clear that if he continues to pursue you, he will be on the receiving end of this." Will raised his fist. "It's my preroga-tive to do so. Another thing. Why would someone who has killed so many tell you that I threatened him? He's trying to turn you against me. Do you see how underhanded he is?"

"You did the right thing."

"We agree at last. What was his excuse this time for being in the same market? Doesn't it strike you as odd, him showing up at the very place you are?"

"He said he was returning a car to a client and saw me go in."

"Aahh, how convenient." An astringent laugh snaked out of Will's throat. "You believe that rabble? This was no coincidence. It was a ploy, a plot to see you."

Maritza rubbed her temples. "I don't know what to think. He makes me feel sorry for him even though I don't want to, then I'm sad."

"You still feel sorry for him? *Gott im Himmel!* When is this go-ing to end? Because if it doesn't soon, our marriage is headed for the rocks. This is what he wants, to make you feel sorry. He's the wolf, ly-ing in wait to make his move."

"Don't be ridiculous. What kind of move? You think he's going to put a sack on my head and throw me over his shoulder? He would never hurt me."

Will slammed his hand on the table, rattling the plates and Emi-ly, in her high chair, began to cry. "He's hurting you now, and why does he have so much leisure time? He's all over this town like a ra-dioactive cloud!"

"Stop it. You're upsetting her."

"Papa's sorry, *Mein kleiner Engel,* my little angel," he said, picking her up and holding her.

"I refuse to stay hidden in this flat like in Warsaw," Maritza continued. "I thought those days were over."

"As long as that carnivore walks these streets, the past lives on. I can't wait to hear what he said this time." His brows battled for property by his hairline. "Well?"

The conversation was wearing her out. "He just said how he's trying to move on with his life." If she told Will any more, he'd be bedding down on the couch indefinitely.

"I cannot believe we are paying good money for a sitter to watch our child while you, a married woman, stand in a public place talking rubbish with a criminal. You should have walked away before he had a chance to start wagging his forked tongue."

Emily buried her head in the crook of his neck and whimpered. He rubbed her back.

"Calm down, Willy. Let me finish. You have the most annoying habit of interrupting."

"He is the cause of this issue. It's gone far enough and needs to be resolved."

Maritza threw up her hands. "Well, whatever."

This wasn't true apathy on her part, but more of a reluctance to admit that the person she once loved was coming undone before her very eyes. Andrush was displaying the same single-minded purpose in his efforts to attract her attention and win back her love that he had demonstrated in his mission to wipe out every Nazi. She saw how right Will was, yet she continued to challenge him.

"I know this isn't easy for you, Maritza."

"You don't know," she cried. "How could you? You want me to hate him, and I can't. I just can't." The very fabric of her previous life had been woven at Andrush's loom and to cut him out entirely was difficult. It was akin to watching a deteriorating pet suffer, yet hesitating to make the final decision to have it put to sleep.

"It's not about me wanting you to hate him. Understand that he won't let up until he has you in his bed, and you know why? Because somehow he has gotten the idea that it's possible. You've given him hope, either directly or indirectly. He thinks he owns you and will stop at nothing to get you back."

"He's not going to get me back."

"I should pay him another visit, or we should go to the police, tell them he is harassing you, and ask for a stay-away order. I will ask Esau how that is done."

Maritza grabbed his arm as he got up to put Emily to bed. "No, don't go to him, and do not mention this to Esau. This is our private business. He will tell Ruthie, and I will never hear the end of it."

"Who cares what she thinks? You act as though she's the most important person in your life."

"Don't talk about her that way. She's like a mother to me, and—"

"You're ashamed that she should find out because you know you're not doing enough to get rid of him. If she knew about this, don't you think she would ask why you haven't gone to the police? At least she would wonder why you bother talking to him at all."

"Stop trying to psychoanalyze me, Willy. I told him that he should leave me alone."

"Oh boy. You think that limp request is going to scare him away? He needs a firm hand and an ultimatum. This situation is out of control. It's gone on too long, and we are not going to allow ourselves to be influenced by his actions. Those were your own words, and I took them to heart, though it seems you're having trouble following your own advice. So now I am laying down the law. I forbid you to speak to him again. Please give your coupons to Birdie and ask her to do the marketing. Of course we will pay her."

Maritza nodded, resisting the urge to answer Will back. She shouldn't have mentioned a thing about Andrush.

"See to it, and if you persist in going on with him in the same way, I will know where your loyalties lie."

Chapter 56

A few days later, Will came home from work and picked up a flier on the mat outside their door. This was not unusual; stores paid people a nominal amount to go around to the buildings and leave pages for tenants advertising specials, sales, and community events. He glanced at the paper. "Bloody hell," he roared. "Son of a bitch!"

Maritza rushed out of the kitchen. "Willy, what's wrong?" His face was maroon, darker than she'd ever seen it. "What is it?"

"Look at this," he thundered, shoving the paper at her.

Dear Neighbour,

Are you aware that a Nazi is living under your nose? In flat 2A of your very edifice lives one Herr Engel, formerly an officer in Hitler's army. He has a history of violence, especially towards women. Avoid him! Alert friends and family! He rides the 134 bus to Highgate daily. Eyes: blue, Hair: blond, weight ~13 stone/6' tall

And there in the lower right-hand corner, a photo of Will's face.

"My God," she cried. "Where did you find this?"

"Right outside our door," he said, casting a long, searing look at her. "That blasted Vorobiev!"

"Look honey, it says in *flat 2A of this very edifice,* so only the tenants of our building received these papers. We can go and ask them if they saw anyone and explain that someone is trying to hurt you."

"We will do nothing of the sort, and why do you say *someone* when we both know it was him? That sick bastard could have had other papers made up that gave our street and flat numbers and passed them out all over the place. There must be at least sixty flats from here down to the church on this side alone. That means all the residents of Broadway and maybe all of Muswell Hill will know where we live and what I look like."

"Please calm down," Maritza said. "You're going to give yourself an ulcer."

"What's more, in order to know which bus I take, that sneaky, vindictive snake had to be hiding and watching me. I told you he was spying on us. When we're out walking on the weekends with Emily, I put both of you at risk because, as you said, you can't stay hidden in this flat forever. Stones will be thrown at us, just like in Paris."

"You have every right to be angry, Willy, but no one will believe this. Our neighbors know you and like you. The police would never allow a real, violent Nazi to be on the loose. You said that the loyal ones are still being held in the prisoner of war camps."

"I have every right to be angry?" he shouted. "I? You should be too! I'm in this alone?"

"Stop shouting. You'll wake Emily. Of course you're not alone. I'm as upset as you are about this whole thing."

"You could have fooled me." Will went into the living room and poured a gin, downing it in a single gulp. The thought of his neighbors talking about him and believing he was something he wasn't caused rage.

Soon, Maritza came to tell him dinner was on the table. "Stewed steak over rice," she announced with determined cheeriness. "Mmm, doesn't it smell good?"

He was sitting with legs sprawled out, arms crossed, his hair falling every which way, and staring at the fireplace with bleary eyes. "You don't seem to realize the danger your precious Andrush has put us in. We don't know how many papers he distributed, but words are powerful and create fear, and fear causes crazy reactions. People living around here whose loved ones were killed by or died fighting against the Nazis and received one of these will believe it. This is just what someone needs to organize an angry mob to run us out of town." His hands mowed through his hair.

"He's not my precious Andrush, and stop saying things like that. There is something you don't know about him, though. He's always been a terrible writer. Writing and spelling were his worst subjects in school, and those were in Polish, his native language."

"So you admit he's an imbecile?"

"Don't put words in my mouth. People have different strengths. He speaks English well but doesn't have the skills or patience needed to write such a perfect paragraph. I don't think he did this. It's so unlike him."

"Then he enlisted the help of someone. Whose side are you on?"

"Willy, all I'm saying is—"

"Keep defending him, Maritza, and you will find me making a petition in divorce court."

They went into the kitchen and ate in silence, resentments swirling in their minds.

In the morning, Will walked the ten minutes to the police station on Fortis Green to lodge a complaint against Andrush and ask for a stay-away order. "Good morning," he said. "Will Engel. I live on Broadway with my wife and little daughter and have been there for about a year and a half. I am German, and while I understand that some people have animosity toward us, we've had no problems. My wife's former spouse, a Pole, is angry that she married me and has been stalking and harassing her. He sent this flier around the neighborhood." Will showed it to the officer.

"We've already seen it. Several worried residents came in yesterday, and we received a slew of calls."

"You see? He's already incited fear, and I'm concerned my family will get hurt."

"We made inquiries, Mr. Engel, and have no reason to believe that you are dangerous or a Nazi."

"What? Me? You made inquiries about me in less than one day?" Even though it was chilly inside the station, he began to sweat. "You should be investigating *him*, not me. I demand you order him to stay away from my wife and our home. Andrush Vorobiev is his name, and he lives and works at these addresses." He dug the piece of paper out of his wallet and slapped it on the counter."

"Such an order can only be made if there were threats of bodily harm. Has he done that?"

"No, but I suspect he will."

"Return with your wife if the individual threatens harm. She must make the complaint in person." He copied Andrush's information. "I will add this to our files."

"That's all you're going to do?"

"You have no proof that he is responsible for the papers defaming you. We will take action if you can provide evidence. I should add that jilted men often act out. He'll come around and leave your wife alone when he sees he's butting against a stone wall."

"Thank you." *For nothing.* Will scooped up the papers and stuffed them in his pocket. He left the station with a headache, forgot where he was, and jumped on the first available bus. For not paying attention to the designation sign, he was almost two hours late for work.

The fallout from the flier incident was immediate. Several hate notes were sent anonymously to Herr Engel through the post, one in ransom-note lettering: *Prepare to die, Sour-kraut.* "I told you this would happen, Maritza. That agitator has stirred up a hornet's nest." Will shoved the notes into a drawer.

The backlash continued. As he stepped off the bus one evening, a group of juvenile rowdies were waiting for him. "There's the Nazi!" they shouted, and lobbed tomatoes. Will sprang at the ringleader and grabbed him by the arm, but the wiry youth broke free, and the gang ran away laughing. A box containing a rotting pig's head was left at their door. Will brought the mail and the box to the police station.

"What are we supposed to do with this, Mr. Engel, put it in your file?" the sergeant asked, whipping out a handkerchief and holding it to his nose. He motioned to his associate to take the box away.

"If you like. You should know exactly what we are being subjected to. A gang of delinquents threw tomatoes at me the other evening around six-ish when I was coming off the bus—the 134 line that runs from Highgate to Broadway. Mr. Brown, the driver, witnessed the attack. You can ask him."

"I know the line. We will look into the incident, Mr. Engel."

Finally, progress. By the end of January, the furor had died down. The notes stopped coming, no one bothered Will in the street, and nothing had been left at their door. He read in the newspaper that members of the juvenile gang had been caught, given a severe dressing down by a police official and handed over to their parents to face their wrath—more for getting caught, Will thought, than any other reason. Birdie was doing the marketing so Maritza wouldn't have to see Andrush; his name had not been uttered in the Engel household, and life again settled into the comfortable folds of matrimony.

Chapter 57

The weather in February and March was one of the harshest and snowiest in the British Isles. Electricity was cut for hours each day, gas was reduced in the homes, and pipes froze. Vegetables and meat disappeared from shelves, and bathing was done with wet washcloths—a lick and a promise—reminding Maritza of Warsaw and ultimately of Andrush. She hadn't seen him in some time and wondered where and how he was. Best not to think of him, she told herself.

Esau closed the office for two weeks. Will was home and did the shopping, going out in a long black scarf wrapped around his neck and face like a balaclava. If he came across Andrush, he could strangle him with it. No one in his right mind would go out in this weather unless absolutely necessary, he thought, but that was the thing—Vorobiev wasn't of sound mind. There was no way of predicting when and where he would appear.

The snow disappeared in mid-March with the coming of rain. Will wanted Birdie to continue with the shopping, but tired of being housebound, Maritza was eager to get back into her former routine. "We can't ask her to do that indefinitely," she said. "It's too much with all the packages."

"Remember," Will warned, "if you see him, you are not to talk. If he won't go away, call the manager."

"I know, Willy, I know," she sighed. *Stop telling me what to do!* They had gotten along so well the past two months, and he had to ruin the peace by giving orders. Calling a manager over would infuriate

Andrush; she would have to decide in the moment how to treat him despite Will's warnings. There was something stimulating about having the ability to control the situation that made her feel in charge of her life. The expectation that Andrush would show up was present in her mind when she went about her errands. April bloomed, and he was still nowhere to be seen.

During the times when Maritza was completely honest with herself, which usually occurred when she was bathing—*the naked truth*—she wanted to see him. She made a mental list of possible reasons for his disappearance: having given up on her, he left Muswell Hill, found a woman, or a combination of one and two. No. She knew him better than that and felt with every fiber of her being that he was slowly drinking himself to death. She dreamed he was drowning and begging her for a lifeline, but her boat was already sailing away. Curiosity and worry chewed at her. She dithered over what to do and decided to call his work and hang up if he answered. Then she would know that he was okay.

Digging in her purse for his number, Maritza didn't find it and looked up auto repair shops in the telephone directory. A man answered. She asked for Andrush. "He don't work here no more."

A moment of panic, then she remembered his address. What harm could there be in checking on him? They had belonged to each other for most of her life, and that had to count for something. It was wrong to desert him in his hour of need. After picturing him unconscious, the urge to go to him was powerful. If nothing else, she could call for an ambulance and save his life.

Maritza dialed the sitter. "Birdie, I know it's short notice, but there's something I must do. It won't take long. I can bring Emily to you. Excellent. Thank you."

A ten-minute bus ride north, then a short walk looking for the street. Andrush's two-story building, the shabbiest in the neighborhood, was on a dead end. Trash cans overflowed out in front, and young children played unattended. She went up to his flat and knocked repeatedly on the door. She was about to leave when he opened a crack and peered out.

"Mishka?" He was in undershorts, his eyes puffy and bloodshot, a few weeks' growth of a patchy beard, and his hair matted. The room stank of alcohol, the floor was littered with papers, empty bottles, and half-eaten food.

I was right to come. He needs help. As if on cue, a large cockroach crawled up the wall. "Oh my God," she cried, "How can you live like this?"

Andrush sat on the bed, its sheets tangled and the pillow stained yellow from sweat, looking like a rumpled bird that had fallen from the nest. So much of his life had been spent contending with hardship—his younger years under the lash of Jakub's tongue so he could live in the same house with her, through all his trials under the occupation and in the labor camps, to learn he had lost her to Will.

What a cruel hand he'd been dealt, and she was part of it, having turned her back on him. She sat next to him and held him, stroking his head and crying. He cried too, for she had finally come. "You have to get well, Andrush, and make your life worth living," she said, her voice full of pity. "Please stop drinking. Say you will try."

"I will, Mishka. I will clean everything up for you." He wiped his eyes.

"I can help you. Let's start by picking up this garbage." She looked at the papers strewn near her feet and did a double-take. Her mouth fell open. *Dear Neighbour.* "This can't be." A pain slashed through her chest, punishing her for ascribing ulterior motives to Will's warnings and placing unwarranted faith in Andrush's innocence. "It was you. I didn't believe it; I couldn't believe you would do such a thing to my husband."

"Aww, don't be mad. He wasn't letting me see you. You're mine, my wife, and the Hun was keeping you all for hisself, but don't worry.

I'm gonna take you away from here. It'll be you and me, like always. When he finds out you're gone, he's gonna call you a Jew-whore and be glad he's rid of you. He'll keep the kid and go on with his life. You won't be missed. That's how them Krauts are. I've waited so long for you. I knew you'd come, and you did."

The blood froze in her veins. "You are sick in the head! I am not your wife anymore, and you will never, ever have me." She cursed at him, using the most vile words she could think of, and slapped him across the face so hard that his lip split open.

Andrush ran his tongue over the blood. "That wasn't nice, Mishka."

Before she could leap to her feet, he grabbed her and pinned her on the bed, putting all his weight on her and planting his bloody lips over her mouth so she could barely breathe. With one hand, he freed his erection, reached up under her dress and tore her garter belt and underpants down to her ankles. Wrenching one arm loose, she pulled his hair and clawed at his face. Andrush pushed her legs apart with his knees, ramming himself against her, and as he was about to penetrate her, she reached down and dug her nails into his scrotum. Howling in pain, he rolled off and doubled over.

Gasping for breath, Maritza hobbled to the door, flung it open, and stumbled down the stairs, not stopping to pull up her undergarments and adjust her clothing until she was outside in the street. Running and gagging from Andrush's sour smell, she made it to the bus stop and realized that her purse was in his flat. It was as good as gone. Without her bus ticket and money, she had no choice but to walk home. She wiped her mouth on her sleeve and hurried along, shaking, wracking with guilt, and willing Andrush to die.

"You must exercise greater care with your things, my love," Will said when he came home from work. "Perhaps you should buy a purse with a strap that goes across your chest. Have you retraced your steps and checked with the shops? Yes? How much money was inside? Now you'll have to replace your identification. Robbers might have gotten their dirty mitts on it, and knowing our address, could have you in their sights. You must take notice of who is behind you when you go out. I will stop tomorrow at the police station to inquire if someone turned in the purse. If not, the ration books will have to be replaced, and the locks on our door changed as well."

Shut up! Maritza wanted to scream. Will meant well, but she couldn't take his lecturing. She wanted to lie down alone in the bedroom and close her eyes. "You're right, of course," she said. "I will be more careful. Let's not talk about it anymore. Shall we eat?"

Later, in bed, Will reached for her. It was the first time she pretended to enjoy sex with him. Usually they prolonged the process and savored each minute, but now she rushed him along, using every trick she could think of to make him finish. Afterward, the feeling of remorse for having lied to him on so many levels was overwhelming, and she rose from the bed quickly, afraid she would cry.

"You seemed distracted," Will said, putting it mildly. "Is it the loss of your purse?"

"Just tired, that's all."

"You've had a stressful day. I should have realized you were tired. Let me rub your back."

"Really, I'm fine, Willy. Don't worry about me."

A week passed, two. Will *was* worried—there was a marked difference in Maritza's manner—a forced gaiety, nervousness, and evasive eyes. When he slipped his hands inside her house dress, as was his custom when he came home, he encountered layers of resistance: a brassiere, a full slip, and a frightful, girdle-like garment that he'd never seen before, instead of her smooth skin.

"What's all this?" he asked.

She muttered something about trying on clothes, then turned her attention to the stove. At night, she took an extra-long time in the bathroom and came to bed in a long flannel granny nightgown buttoned up to the chin that she wore during the winter snowstorms. It had been so cold then that Emily slept in their bed, nestled in her mother's arms. They waited until she fell asleep, and Will simply lifted the gown and made love to her from behind. Now she wore thick bloomers underneath that came up to her ribcage and down to her knees, another item that he had never seen. When he attempted to remove them, she made excuses.

Maritza had always been an enthusiastic and eager lover, but these days she didn't want to be touched. Will looked at himself critically in the mirror for signs of aging. Ears getting long? Jowls? Extra flesh around his middle? A flat behind? No to all. Gray hairs? He combed through and didn't find many silver strands, or maybe his eyesight was going. The color did seem a bit dull, but nothing too bad. There were deepening lines on his forehead and around his mouth, a slight drooping of eyelids, and a hollowing of his cheeks, all normal for a man of thirty-seven.

He thought about the ebb and flow of desire, and supposed that all couples must experience periods of abstinence. He urged Maritza to have Birdie help her with Emily on a daily basis, if necessary, so she could rest and to see a doctor if her *tiredness* didn't go away.

"I'm perfectly capable of caring for my own child," she said, annoyed. "And I'm not tired anymore. Everything is fine. You're overthinking things. You always do."

Well! It had come on so suddenly, this aversion to him, that he wondered if she had fallen out of love, or maybe she was thinking of Andrush. Hurt and confused, he began to withdraw from her until she saw what was happening between them. The dinner hour had become a time of strained silence; he hid behind the newspaper while she fussed with pots and pans. She had been fully self-absorbed late-ly, had shut him out, driven him away, but was determined to turn things around.

"Any interesting properties, Willy?" she asked brightly as they sat down to eat. He held a fork in one hand and a pencil in the other while he went through the newspaper. "Since the blizzards thrashed the farms, I imagine there are many up for sale or lease."

"I'm looking for flats, not properties," he snapped. "Muswell Hill has lost its charm, and I'm not happy here. Our marriage seems to have lost its spark, and if you have any interest in reviving it, we will need to leave the ghost from the past behind. Surely you've thought of this."

"Yes, I have, and I'm glad you brought it up. Let's get away from here and start fresh somewhere else." Maritza hadn't thought of moving but would do or say anything to show Will how much she loved him—anything except tell the truth.

"Can you ask Birdie to watch Emily on Saturday? We can go see several flats." He reached for her hand and gave her a genuine smile, and that night she put on her sexiest nightgown and made such feral love to him that he thought he'd died and gone to heaven.

Chapter 58

A few days later, Maritza returned from the library with Emily to find a large black swastika painted on the door of their flat and called Will. It was without a doubt the work of Andrush. Conscience-stricken, she stood at the bedroom window and watched her poor husband come flying off the bus, arriving in such a boil that she wondered how the driver ever let him on. He looked at the door and gnashed his teeth, stomped down the stairs, and out the front of the building without a word.

"What have you got, Mr. Engel?" asked the officer at the police desk. "We're closing soon. Has your wife found her purse?"

"She hasn't, but her former husband, Andrush Vorobiev, the same offender I complained about last time, has committed another illegal act. He painted a swastika on the door of our flat. Do you see how he is targeting us? I insist you order him to stay away and cease his reprehensible activities."

"Again, we need evidence. Do you have it?"

"It was him. Why do you refuse to interview him?"

"We cannot go and accuse people on your suspicions alone. It could be anyone. I will take a report about the defacement of your door and send a man around tomorrow morning to take a photograph and question the tenants. Perhaps they saw someone hanging about. The constable who walks the beat in your area will be assigned to pay special attention to your building."

"Thank you," Will said, feeling little encouragement. He once read in the newspaper that constables regularly remained at any given location for five minutes before moving along to the next point on their beats. So maybe ten minutes. Big deal.

The tenants might have seen someone, but it was unlikely that Vorobiev would have entered the building without some sort of disguise, and it was altogether possible that he paid another scoundrel to do the dirty work. Will was hopeful that come the weekend, he and Maritza would find a flat away from Muswell Hill, somewhere in the Greater London area, and start afresh. Instead of going home, he walked back to Broadway and took the bus up to Cromwell Road.

The garage where Andrush worked was closed. Will checked the paper in his wallet for his home address, but couldn't find the street. He asked directions from a boy riding a bicycle.

"Right there," he said, pointing to a run-down building. "Same place where I live. You lookin' for my folks? I wouldn't bother them now. They're havin' a fight."

"No, I'm not looking for your folks."

"Then who?"

"Never mind."

"Say, you got any money? I'd sure like ice cream."

He dug in his pocket for a couple of coins, and the boy pedaled away at full speed.

Will went inside. The couple in the first-floor flat was indeed having an argument. The woman bleated, "I'm sick of you sittin' round here all day. What are we supposed to eat? You think yer somethin' special?"

"Shut up, you fat cow! Look who's talkin'. Yer nothin' to write home about. You get out there and work."

Another disenchanted couple, he thought. The shouting came to an end when he rapped loudly at Andrush's door, which opened faster than he expected.

"Hello Vorobiev." Andrush looked awful; his skin was sallow and scabby, his face bloated, and his eyes tinged with yellow.

"Piss off before I call the police on you for trespassing."

"Me? Trespassing? That's rich. Go ahead, call. I would like to see how that's done without a telephone." Will pushed his way in. He stared at the mess, almost gagging from the smell of decay. "I warned you to stay away from our flat, but you haven't taken heed. I reported you to the police for the fliers you sent around and the swastika you painted on our door."

"I haven't been anywhere near your flat, so stop running your fat Krauty mouth."

"You will also face charges for stalking my wife."

"Stalking?" Andrush laughed. "I don't stalk her. She comes to me." He weaved over to a dresser, and took Maritza's purse out of a drawer. "She left this here; was it last week or the week before? Can't remember. Why don't you ask her how she felt when I fucked her?"

Will smashed his fist into Andrush's face, taking him by surprise and sending him sprawling to the floor. Stunned, he wiped the blood from his nose with the back of his hand. "Nobody gets away with that. Just wait, you stinking Kraut. Just you wait."

Will quickly picked up the purse and went out the door.

"Where have you been, Willy? I was worried."

"At the police station, making a report about the door. They're coming to photograph it in the morning. Be home." Maritza went to hug him, but he marched past her into the bedroom and hung his raincoat in the closet.

"I called the landlord," she said. "Someone will be out to paint it early next week. Dinner's on the table—minced beef cabbage rolls. You love those."

"I'm not hungry. Is Emily asleep?" he asked, loosening his tie.

"Yes. What happened to your hand? It's all red."

"Isn't it strange, Maritza, how a man can be so in love with his wife that he doesn't see her for what she is?"

"What do you mean?" A cold flash whipped through her chest. "What's wrong?"

Will went to the closet, removed her purse from the pocket of his raincoat, and tossed it on the chair. "The purse you claimed to have lost while out shopping turned up in Vorobiev's flat. Imagine that. He said you went there and had sex with him. This is what you do when I'm gone all day, working to provide for you and our child? This is the respect you give me?" Will's voice cracked, but he didn't cry. Gone were the days when he told himself he was worthless. The absence of tears was the biggest indication of his amour propre.

Maritza's heart splintered. "Willy, no, no! It's not true. He's lying. I never had sex with him. I would never do that."

"How did your purse get there? By magic? Ah, a sorceress. Full of surprises, aren't you?" His eyes roamed over her, and his lip went up in a sneer. "The love I gave you wasn't enough, and you needed his too?" He came closer, his eyes full of contempt. "You left our child to go screw that disgusting—you are not a fit mother. *Du bist eine Hure!*"

"No," she cried and shook her head. "It's not what you think. I can explain. I was worried about him. I had a feeling he was dying, and I needed to make sure he wasn't. I don't love him, but he is still my blood. Something told me to check on him, and I think if I hadn't gone, he was on the verge of drinking himself to death. I got there and saw the state he was in, and his place was a mess—filthy and littered with trash."

Will went to the closet and pulled down a suitcase."

No, Willy, wait. Where are you going?"

"Leaving. I'm finished with you and this charade."

She grabbed his arm. "Please, I beg of you. Let me finish. He had copies of the fliers on the floor, and then I knew he was behind them. I confronted him, and he admitted it, and I hit him in the face. He pinned me on the bed and ripped my underwear down. He tried to rape me, but I got away and couldn't go back for my purse. That's the truth, all of it." She hung her head and sobbed.

"Pick up your head and look at me, damn you!" His incredulous eyes bored into hers. "He attacked you, and you hid this from me? A violent madman tried to take you against your will, and you said nothing except to lie about your purse. Look at me, my love, the light of my life, and tell me how you had the temerity to hide his attempt to rape you, and that same night, that very same night, you made love with *me* and pretended to enjoy it. Then after that, you came up with every excuse under the sun to shut me out."

"I'm so sorry, Willy."

"You're sorry? That's all you have to say?" He stood there, his fists clenched, his face burning. "I suppose I got what I deserved by loving you. You knew he sent those fliers, and you hid that as well. How could you?"

"Because I wished it never happened. It was my fault for going there, and I felt so guilty and ashamed that I brought it on and wanted to erase it from my memory. I was afraid you would walk out on me if I told you," she cried, clutching her stomach, "and I couldn't bear to lose you."

"How many times did I tell you that he is deranged? It wasn't your responsibility to conduct a welfare check. You have a commitment of loyalty to *me*. I am your husband, not him! I have to come first. You knew the terms for our marriage, yet you went to him anyway."

Her words gushed out in one forceful stream. "It was a lapse of judgment. Nothing I say will make a difference now. I've ruined our marriage, and that's the cross I have to bear. I was so confused when he came back. I did feel sorry for him, but I hate him now."

"You hate him because, for all his professed love, he betrayed you." Will stared at her, his mouth tight and grim. "You admit this now, but had that reprobate said nothing about it, for as long as you live, you would never have told me the truth. Even if he moved far away, you would have kept that secret to yourself for eternity. You would have lain in that bed with me night after night, pretending to give me all your honest love and taking all of mine."

"There was no reason to hurt you needlessly," she sobbed, heartsick to her core.

"That's always been your excuse for hiding the truth. You're such a child, Maritza. You don't know the meaning of love."

She turned to leave and he pulled her by the arm. "I'm not finished."

"No, I don't want to hear any more!" she shrieked, covering her ears. "You were right about everything. So now you know what kind of person your wife is. You don't have to tell me what a misery I am. I know it and accept the consequences." She was becoming hysterical.

"Stop it, Maritza. You will make yourself sick. Try to breathe and calm yourself." He tightened his hold on her.

"Take your hands off me! You're as bad as he is." She struggled against him like a rabbit caught in a snare. "What do you care now? I know you hate me. I hate myself."

He held her arms until she stopped fighting him. All their problems started when that covetous, grasping blackguard showed up and began a campaign of subterfuge to take Maritza away. Will's anger and hurt was replaced with a surge of protective love for her.

"Don't cry, my love. It breaks my heart," he murmured, drawing her to him. "I see what he's done to you, but you should have told me. How does a man protect his wife when he knows nothing of what went on? We will go to the police, and that animal will be locked up, then sent back to Poland."

He carried her to the bed and curled up next to her. She turned away from him, and despite his entreaties and cradling arms, would not be comforted. Before falling into a broken sleep, Maritza knew tomorrow was going to be worse than today. Will was making an effort to tranquilize her with soothing words, but she convinced herself that when his aim was achieved, he would pack his things and go. She hurt him and let him down. He had shown her in practice what it meant to love, but she hadn't learned from his example. She wasn't worthy of him.

Chapter 59

Will hoped to take Maritza to the police station in the morning, but she'd had a wretched night and was groggy. He planned to leave work early and take her then. Now there was proof Vorobiev was behind the flier incident, and the police could arrest him posthaste for attempted rape.

"Papa!" Emily called out to him before he left. He gave her some milk and crackers and brought her into bed with her mother. "Stay here close to Mama until she wakes up," he said, as she snuggled in.

Unable to concentrate at work, he became overwrought, thinking how close Maritza had come to being violated and how terrifying the moments before she was able to fend that predator off must have been. He called and called, but she wasn't answering the phone.

"What's bothering you? You're pacing like a caged tiger," observed Esau. "Come on, let's eat our lunch in my office. What happened to your hand?"

"I will get to that. Did you know Maritza was briefly married before me to a cousin who was in the resistance?"

"Yes, she mentioned him. He was killed, wasn't he?"

"He survived and is here in London. Please don't mention any of this to Ruthie. Maritza doesn't want her to know. She's afraid it will upset her too much. Well, she ran into him last fall. I let him come to see her at our place, and after that, he became obsessed with her. He moved from the East End to our neighborhood and tried to persuade her to run away with him. Then he started following her and preying on her sympathies."

"Have you tried to reason with him?"

"There is no reasoning with him. The man is crazy—*verrückt im Kopf*—and a drunkard. I did go to warn him to stay away from her. He was hostile, of course, but that's not the half of it. He had these papers printed up and distributed them all around town." Will took it from his pocket. "Look."

Esau whistled. "He has it in for you, man. This is libel."

"I can take care of myself. It's Maritza he's after. His goal is to get her away from me; he knows she still cares for him. That's not all. He painted a huge swastika on our door. I made a police report and asked for a stay-away order. They wouldn't do it without proof, which I didn't have at the time. The worst thing is, he tried to have his way with her. He was unsuccessful, and for the attempt, I went to his flat and hit him in the face, hence my bruised knuckles. She's in no condition to go to the police now, but as soon as she's able, they can arrest him and lock him up for good."

"Why, that disgusting thug." A look of fatherly worry crossed Esau's face. "You want him locked up for good, my friend, but the most he will get if convicted is two years. That's the penalty for attempted rape, and stay-away orders can only be made by the courts."

"Two years?" The police never told him that. A headache clapped at his temples. "Then he will be free to attack her again. What about deportation?"

"I don't know what his status is here, but I doubt he will be deported. I will give you the telephone number of a private detective, an old friend of mine, who should be able to help. He can put the guy under surveillance and guard your flat until an arrest is made. In the meantime, stay away from him and keep Maritza at home."

After lunch, Will continued pacing. I should have confided in Esau at the first hint of trouble, he thought, and then he would have suggested the detective earlier, and that leech wouldn't have been able to ride roughshod over our lives and abuse Maritza.

He went home. The flat was as still as a vault. He started to panic, thinking Vorobiev had come and kidnapped them. No, she wouldn't have opened the door. Where could she be? Could she have gone to the police on her own? Not with Emily. Sometimes Birdie did the sitting at her own flat. He rang her up. No, she hadn't seen the girls. Then he called Ruth. "Do you know where Maritza is? She's not home, and I'm beginning to worry."

"Uh, she's here, Will. She's bathing Emily."

"Why is she doing that at your place?"

"She asked if she could stay with us for a while. What is going on? She's extremely upset and won't tell me a thing. This is worse than when we couldn't find you in the camps. How can I help her if she won't confide in me? You two must have had a doozy of a fight." True to form, Ruthie's mouth ran on.

"I'm coming over. Do not tell her."

"I won't." She told Maritza that he was coming.

"**W**here is she, Ruthie? Sorry about all this."
        "Let me get her."

Maritza came into the room, red-eyed and lachrymose. "What do you want, Will?"

"What do I want? I want to know why you're here. You just take off without a word after all that has happened, and I come home to find you gone. I've been trying to reach you all day."

"Well, I'm here as you can see, so there's no need for you to worry."

"Why aren't you at home waiting for me?"

"I know you're going to leave me, maybe not today or tomorrow, but as time goes on your resentment will grow. When we have an argument you will bring up how I lied and what a bad person I am, and then find someone else. That's how it works, " Maritza said, as if she had enough personal experience with men in similar situations to know what she was talking about. "So I'm saving you the trouble." She folded her shaking hands on her lap.

"That's not how it works for me. I am not leaving, and may I remind you that the only arguments we've had since Warsaw have been because of *him*. Our life here was wonderful until that knave showed up and set out to destroy it. I love you, and everything is fine between us. Now get your things and Emily, and let's go home."

"I'm not coming home. Things are *not fine*. I am not fine."

"This is a bump in the road. We'll get through it and be rid of that schemer. Esau gave me the number of a private detective who can monitor his movements and watch our flat when I'm working until you feel ready to go to the police, but the longer you wait, the more time he has to plot his next move. They won't arrest him on my word alone. You must tell them that he assaulted you. I'm going to call and hire Esau's man."

"Andrush doesn't know I'm here, so what does it matter?"

"It does matter. You can't stay here forever. It's unfair to burden Ruth and Esau with our troubles. We have to deal with this problem and have that drunken lout locked up before it's too late."

She went to stand by the window and sobbed. "I'm not talking to the police. They will blame me for going to him."

"Nobody will blame you," he said softly, putting his hands on her shoulders. "You didn't know how malicious he is."

"Willy, please go away and leave me alone. I can't forget or forgive myself for what I did to you and how thoughtless I've been. You're too good. I'm not worthy of you."

Will turned her around and lifted her chin. "This isn't the end of the world, my love. Problems arise in every marriage. We make mistakes and learn from them. You can't just give up."

She jerked her head away. "You haven't been listening to a word I said."

Will was nearing the breaking point. Any moment now he would raise his voice, tell her *fine, have it your way,* then storm out. This was a side of him—an angry frustration that had emerged when she allowed Andrush to come between them. She wanted him angry, so he would leave, and she could go on hating herself uninterrupted for having taken advantage of his love and trust.

"I heard every word. Now let's go home."

"I'm not going. You're better off without me."

"I'm the judge of what's good for me, Maritza. Stop playing games." Exasperation won out, and his face burned. "Why are you penalizing me? What have I done except love you? Grow up and act like a woman. This behavior is unbecoming."

Maritza raised tearful eyes to Will's and down again. "What do you expect from a child? That's what I am. You said so yourself."

"You're full of excuses for not coming home, and I'm beginning to suspect that your love for me is barely there. Have my daughter ready on Friday afternoon. She will spend the weekend with me. I gave you every drop of love a man can give, and you turned me away. I'm fresh out of patience. This is what Vorobiev wanted all along: to split us up, and he's winning. Three countries and one child later, and you still don't trust me. *So fine, have it your way.* Stay here and feel sorry for yourself."

Chapter 60

Will went home, folded the paper with the name and number of the private detective Esau had given him, and unfolded and folded it again. Since there was no Maritza for Vorobiev to follow, it seemed useless to secure the man's services, and the paper went into the trash.

He had managed without her for a year while at Dancers Hill. Surrendering was something he chose to do, the safest path to take as the showdown between the Germans and the Allies heated up in Paris, giving both him and Maritza the greatest chance of spending the rest of their lives together. Now, he couldn't make it through a day without her. Little Emily was a joy, but the love for one's child isn't the same as the love a man has for his wife.

The sight of her purse in Vorobiev's hand, learning she had been to his flat, and thinking she betrayed him had caused a tsunami of pain and anger. He called her a whore, an unfit mother. How would he atone for that? He was no better than the man in the first-floor flat in Vorobiev's building, saying terrible things to his woman. Now his and Maritza's marriage was in serious trouble; it was falling apart, and there was nothing he could do about it until she came around, *if* she came around.

Ruth answered the door when he went to pick up Emily on Friday afternoon. "Hello there, Will."

He detected a coldness in her voice and hoped he was mistaken. How rude she was not to invite him in, probably under orders not to, though he didn't think Maritza would do that. Then again, there were several things he never thought she'd do.

"Hello Ruthie. Where is Maritza?"

"Resting. She's under the weather."

"She's ill?" he asked, at once concerned. "I would like to see her." He almost pushed past her to go in, but Emily came running to the door and jumped into his arms.

"Well, not ill; it's, uh, you know, women's problems," said Ruth.

"What do you mean?"

"It seems like melancholia to me. She cries and cries and still hasn't told me what's happened between the two of you."

"A misunderstanding," he said. "We will work it out."

"Some misunderstanding," she sniffed.

On Sunday, when Will brought Emily back, Esau answered the door. "Come in. The girls are next door and will be back in a few minutes."

He couldn't believe Maritza was still avoiding him, as if he was responsible for this sorry state of affairs. She didn't have the common courtesy to be around to greet her own child and husband, forcing him to hand over his daughter to Esau. This was all so wrong.

"Come in, have a drink, and stay for dinner. Ruthie made a roast and a Yorkshire pudding."

The smell was divine, making his mouth water. Will was dying to come in and eat, but that would make Maritza uncomfortable. I should stay, but then she might refuse to come to the table, he thought. To further subject himself to that humiliation and the Goodmans to that kind of drama was unthinkable. "No, no, I should be going. Thanks, just the same. See you tomorrow."

Will went home to the empty flat, where the only sound was the sizzle in his head. He made a drink and sat on the living room couch, looking around the room at mementos of their life together: the piano, a Capodimonte figurine they bought at a second-hand sale, a basket of colored shells collected on a visit to the seaside last summer, her framed artwork.

On the mantle was a wooden case showing an old western scene that held an antique revolver given to them by an elderly neighbor before they moved from Enfield. "It seems to be in fine condition," Will said at the time, "but we're not going to shoot it off." He gave it a light oiling anyway, for posterity. Maritza loved the case and wanted to display it, so he put the gun in a shoe box on the top shelf of his closet.

His stomach rumbled, and he regretted not having stayed and eaten roast beef at the Goodmans. He had acted out of pique and put himself at a disadvantage in more ways than one. There was little to eat in the cupboards, and had he stayed, he would be feasting his eyes upon his beautiful wife instead of thinking about her.

Short of a written guarantee, Will had assured Maritza of his love. Perhaps she needed to hear him say it again, needed a little nudge, and then she'd come home. He looked at his watch. Half past seven. She might be busy with Emily or helping Ruth with the dishes. He decided to wait, but the feeling of wanting her was so extreme that he went into the bedroom, took out a see-through nightgown he liked her to wear to bed, and breathed in her scent. A stronger, more visceral pang of yearning cut through his middle and spurred him into action. He picked up the phone and dialed. To his surprise, she answered. "Hello, Maritza."

"Why are you calling, Will?"

"Why am I calling? I am a bother to you? I wanted to tell you how much I love you and how sorry I am for saying those vulgar things. I'm going mad here without you. Please come home."

"I don't want to talk about this."

"I'm not your bloody enemy. Stop freezing me out!" He slammed down the receiver and made himself another drink. A heavy fog of sadness washed over him. He turned on the radio. The thought of Vorobiev putting his filthy hands on Maritza—God, he wanted to kill him, to wring his neck. *Stupid music.* He switched it off. An unbearable silence followed, challenging him to break something. Hurling his glass into the fireplace made him feel no better, and he looked for something else to throw. The Capodimonte figurine went next. Still unable to relax, he cleaned the entire flat until it sparkled, then crawled exhausted into bed.

Somehow, he made it through the week. On Friday afternoon, he went to pick up Emily. Maritza answered the door and greeted him with a glum look. If this is how she wants things, he thought, then this is how she will have them, and glared back at her. Their hands touched as she deposited their daughter in his arms, and his intense need for her resurfaced.

"Your husband needs you home," he whispered. "He's miserable without you." She moved closer, and he thought she might kiss him. Then Emily took his face in her little hands, urging him to hurry, and the moment was lost.

Chapter 61

"Sure you don't want to come play cards with the girls, Mitzi?" Ruth asked late the following afternoon. "It will get you out of the doldrums."

"No thanks, Ruthie." She couldn't imagine spending time with a group of cackling, nosy women who would know something was wrong the minute they looked into her eyes.

"Well, you'll be stuck with Esau all evening."

"Hey, don't bite the hand that feeds you," he joked.

"See you later."

"Maritza, I'd like to talk with you. We haven't had a moment alone." He pulled out a chair for her. "Will told me what happened between you and your first husband, in general terms, so I'm not privy to the particulars, but the fact that you were assaulted upsets and worries me."

There was no escaping this conversation. A flush of shame covered her cheeks, and she bowed her head.

"You must find the courage to go to the authorities before that brute has the chance to hurt you again and in a worse way."

She nodded and wished Esau would finish his speech. At least he wouldn't tell Ruthie about this. She was too emotional and would go on and on.

"Do you love Will?"

"Of course I do," she said, twisting her hands round and round in her lap.

He reached over and placed his hand over hers. "It's not enough to say the words—you have to live them. Your husband needs you, Maritza."

"I've made so many mistakes, Esau, and I'm ashamed of myself," she cried. "He says everything is fine, but I'm afraid he will lord my conduct over my head every time we have a disagreement. I'd rather make a clean break now than be lulled into a false sense of security and then have him walk out."

While Will had pledged his troth and hadn't wavered from it despite his threats, that would change with time. He was so perfectly fitted, as if he had been special-ordered just for her, and she failed him. Real life was throwing her poor behavior in her face like a cream pie flung at a lousy actress on stage. If he had shown a similar regard for a former lover, she would have left him. It was impossible to imagine continuing to live with and actively love a man whose concern for another woman was as strong as hers had been for Andrush.

Sparks of anger appeared in Esau's eyes. "What little faith you have in him. Are you so preoccupied with your own feelings that you can't see how much you mean to him? You're not a little girl anymore. You're an adult, a mother, and above all, a wife."

Why did everything make so much sense coming from Esau? Maritza brightened. "I haven't told him yet, but I'm pregnant."

"Mazel Tov!" He enveloped her in a bear hug. "All the more reason to make your marriage work. You tell Ruth the news, and I'll pretend I didn't know; otherwise, she will skewer me alive. Come, I'll drive you home."

Will finished bathing Emily and tucked her into bed. It had rained on and off for the past two weeks, but the sun made an appearance, and he had taken her to the children's zoo, an ambitious undertaking with an overexcited toddler who wanted to run from one exhibit to the next. A woman stopped to admire her, which made his face swell pink with pride.

"What a beautiful child! Look at those golden curls and eyes as big as saucers. She should be in pictures."

"Thank you. She takes after her mother."

"Working, is she?"

"She wasn't able to come."

Having gotten Emily settled after the long day, Will went to bathe. When he came into the bedroom, his heart began pumping. Maritza was standing by the dresser. "Are you home to stay?" he asked, his voice guarded.

"Yes, I'm home to stay."

He crossed the room and gathered her up in his arms, inhaling the fresh, soapy scent of her skin and hair. "Promise me you won't go away again."

"Oh, Willy, I promise, and I have wonderful news to tell you. We're going to have another baby!"

"My love! You know how much I've wanted another child." This was his dream—to have a brother or sister for Emily and more in the future, if possible, with the woman he loved. "Are you certain?"

"I went to the doctor, and he did a test. I wanted to be sure before I told you."

"When is the baby due?"

"Sometime in December. I'm two months along."

"Would you have come home if you weren't pregnant? Is the baby the only glue that's keeping you with me?" A rent opened in his heart.

"I came home because you are everything to me. Do you really think I could live without you? I felt like a failure and undeserving of your love, and needed time to sort myself out. I thought you were trying to keep me from Andrush out of fear that I might choose him over you. He had gone through so much and had no one. I found love with you, and he had locked that part of himself away. It seemed cruel to ignore him, and I thought it would be possible to have a relationship with him. He became so possessive. Maybe he was always that way, though I didn't mind it when I was younger."

It appeared Maritza had come to a new awareness in the two weeks she'd been gone, and Will ought to acknowledge the significance of this, but his mind whirred with a disturbing thought. She had come so close to being raped, and the new life inside her resulting from their love could have been jeopardized. A vicious animal was out there, waiting to pounce again on his pregnant wife.

"I just wanted a little bit of freedom," she was saying, "to handle him in my own way, but he was uncontrollable. I let him come between us and lost sight of the most important person, you, my one true love. You wanted to protect me, and I made a mess of things."

"You're not safe as long as he is free."

"I won't go out, Willy. I want to rest for the next couple of days, then we can go to the police."

"I can take Monday off and go to the shops in your stead. I don't want you waiting in lines in your condition, and while he's on the loose."

"I'll ask Birdie to go."

Will went to take the detective's phone number out of the wastebasket. Now more than ever, he needed to protect his family. He sat on the couch, thinking of where they should go for the long term. His claim against the Swiss bank holding the money left to him by his father was still pending, and it could be years before he received any. The savings he had now wouldn't last long. How would he support his growing family if he left Esau's employ? He would find something and work day and night.

They would have to go, and soon. No stay-away order, not even an arrest and conviction, would keep that rabid dog from Maritza. Regardless of where they went—it could be as far as New Zealand or

Australia—Vorobiev would hunt them down and hurt her, if it took years.

"Willy? Here you are. I've been waiting for you in bed. What's wrong, my darling? You're the picture of gloom. Aren't you happy about the baby?"

He put his arms around her. She looked so drained and pale. In the first months of her pregnancy with Emily, she'd been ill, and he spent the time before he surrendered preoccupied with getting her to safety. There hadn't been a day free from worry, and here they were in England, still under threat. "Oh, my love, I am happy, and we'll have a proper celebration as soon as Vorobiev is behind bars. Tomorrow I will take care of you and things here, and on Monday you have Birdie, but Tuesday morning without fail we are going to the police."

Chapter 62

The Monday evening traffic on Broadway was at its peak. Vehicles' headlights glowed through the mist left by the earlier rain. Will was later than usual, having stopped to buy flowers for Maritza. His joy over her pregnancy was overshadowed, though, by the specter of Vorobiev and the call he made to the private detective, with whom he would meet the following afternoon after the visit to the police. As twilight fell, he exited the bus, walked to his building, and reached the door.

"Drop the flowers and walk," Andrush hissed from behind, throwing an iron arm around Will's shoulder with one hand and pressing the point of the trench knife through layers of clothing on his back. Will obeyed, his nostrils rebelling at the smells of alcohol and rancid body odor.

"Mr. Engel, wait. You dropped your flowers," a woman called out.

"Ignore her. Don't turn your head." Andrush's eyes gleamed, his breathing heavy with anticipation. This Kraut pig, who stole his Mishka and turned her against him, and whose Nazi brothers murdered their family, was going to die by a knife made in his native land—the icing on the cake. The only thing the Germans were ever good for were their weapons.

The rough rattle of engines, squeaking of brakes, and honks of horns were lost on Will's ears; he heard only the wild pounding of his heart. Passersby hurrying home to their dinner tables paid no mind to these two chaps, one with his arm around the other after too many pints at the pub.

Maritza came out of Emily's room after putting her to bed. Already in her nightgown and robe, she was looking forward to spending the evening in Will's arms. He should have been home by now, she thought. There was a pounding at the door—a sound that would usually be followed by *Aufmachen! Polizei!* Open up. Police. She heard it many times when those goons went around to other apartments in her building in Warsaw. A chill went through her.

It was Mrs. Drake, the lady who lived above them. "Mrs. Engel, the oddest thing happened. I just saw your husband outside. A man pushed him, and he dropped these flowers. I called his name, but he ignored me. Then they walked off."

Icy shanks cut into her chest. "The man, what'd he look like?"

"Tall, goldish hair, sloppy. I didn't see his face."

"Which way, which way did they go?"

"Toward the church. They turned in by the end of the buildings."

"Faster, you fucking tortoise." Andrush pressed the knife further, piercing the skin on Will's lower back. He moved his prey through a narrow passage between two buildings into a small alley. The smells of urine and frying onions hung in the air. A crescent moon sliced through the clouds—a sign of good fortune if one believed in that sort of thing. Will thought only of the seconds he had left to live.

Andrush pushed him against the wall of the building, and waved the knife back and forth, grinning maniacally. "I'm gonna carve you up like a Christmas goose, piece by piece."

"You will hang for that, you heathen!"

"Shut up!" Andrush lunged and slashed Will's cheek. The side of his face went numb. He had to move away from the wall, but he was trapped, cornered. "Herr Oberleutnant isn't so pretty now," Andrush said, positioning his hands.

Crack! A shot rang out. Andrush turned, wild-eyed. The bullet pinged off a garbage can and passed through a wooden fence, becoming lodged in a concrete divider behind it. Maritza stood with legs apart and arms outstretched, holding the smoking revolver with both hands. A dog started barking inside the building—something going on in his territory.

Will whacked the knife out of Andrush's hand and tried to dart away, but his assailant grabbed him by the throat with his left hand, put his right over the cut side of his victim's face and tried to bash his head against the wall. Will jabbed his fingers into Andrush's eye, causing him to stumble backward, but he righted himself, his face contorted with rage, and rushed at Maritza.

She fired a shot into his belly. Sinking to his knees and clutching his middle, he looked up at her, one eye closed. *"Kurwa,"* he rasped. "Fucking whore."

The dog continued barking; its owner wasn't home. A woman in another flat gave a full-throated cry, "Shut your yapper!"

Maritza steadied her hands around the revolver and took aim. "No!" Will yelled, "Put the gun down." She would not listen. This was her decision. He staggered to her side. Before he could stop her, she fired twice, hitting Andrush in the head. Blood trickling down his forehead, he stared at her out of one eye, muttered something, and fell over.

A window opened above them. "What the hell is going on down there?" a man in an undershirt called out.

"Knife attack. I'm injured. Call for the police and an ambulance. Hurry!" The side of his face swelling and bloody, Will took the revolver gently from Maritza's hands and set it down by the knife.

Shaking uncontrollably, Maritza stared at Andrush's crumpled form, her eyes round and glassy. "I killed him. I had to."

"I know," he said, taking her into his arms. "It's over, my brave, brave girl, and everything will be all right. We are finally free of him."

The back door opened, and the man from the window stepped into the alley, the light from the hall ceiling lamp behind him illuminating the grim scene. "You're badly cut, Mister. Help is on the way." He jerked his thumb at Andrush. "And him?"

"Nothing to be done."

Chapter 63

February, 1948. Horsham, West Sussex. The mostly rural district of Horsham sits between London and the seaside resort of Brighton and has a history that stretches back thousands of years. If one heads a couple miles south from the town center, then west for a spell on Coltstaple, hidden behind the most overgrown hedges and bushes on the long, narrow lane is the smallholding the Engels have recently purchased.

It isn't much to look at now in the dim of winter, these dozen acres with a cottage, barn, and an assortment of outbuildings all in need of repair, but Will and Maritza only see the possibilities. Animals will come in the spring: a pair of horses, a miniature pony, a few sheep, and chickens.

They are gathered in front of a roaring fire in the kitchen to celebrate Will's thirty-eighth birthday. The Goodmans are there, and Ruth has baked a *Schokoladenkuchen,* his favorite chocolate cake.

Emily tries to balance on one foot. "When can we sing and have cake and I can hold my bruvver?"

"As soon as Auntie takes the picture. Now come and stand here."

She tries with the other foot.

"Mind your mother, Emily," Will says.

Ruthie gestures with her camera. "Esau, go pose them."

He picks up their goddaughter and rests her in her father's arms. "Get set."

"Wait." Will puts an arm around Maritza who holds their infant son, Alexander Gustav, born in December. "Now we're ready," he says.

"Everyone be still," Ruthie orders. "Big smiles." *Click.*

Maritza takes plates from the cupboard. Will comes up behind her and presses himself close. "I love you. You make me so happy."

"Happy birthday, my darling," she says.

Maritza gave Andrush a proper burial, but she did not mourn. She doesn't think about him often, but when she does, he appears as a tragic figure in a novel—a character who lost his soul as a result of a fatal flaw. True, he was a victim of Nazi trauma, but mainly of his own desires. He had chosen darkness instead of the light and had almost taken Will. The vertical scar on his cheek is a daily reminder of how close she came to losing him. Her focus is on the present; life is fragile and precious, and every moment counts.

About the Author

Rory Diamond is a retired schoolteacher from California and an avid reader. When she isn't working on the sequel to *The Oberleutnant's Wife* or researching her Russian Jewish heritage, she wonders about the intricacies of people's relationships and the contents of their refrigerators. Rory lives in Arizona with her two German shepherds, Stella and Axl.

Printed in Great Britain
by Amazon